samuel r. delany

a, b, c: three short novels

Samuel R. Delany's stories are available in *Aye, and Gomorrah and Other Stories* (science fiction and fantasy) and *Atlantic: Three Tales* (experimental fiction). He has won multiple Hugo and Nebula awards. His novel *Dark Reflections* won the Stonewall Book Award in 2008. He has been inducted into the Science Fiction Hall of Fame and received the Damon Knight Memorial Grand Master of Science Fiction Award. His novels include science-fiction works such as *Nova, Dhalgren, The Fall of the Towers, Babel-17, The Einstein Intersection*; also the four-volume fantasy series Return to Nevèrÿon. Delany is the author of several other novels and works of nonfiction. He lives in New York City and has recently retired after sixteen years of teaching creative writing at Temple University.

also by samuel r. delany

FICTION

The Fall of the Towers
Babel-17
Empire Star
The Einstein Intersection
Nova
Dhalgren
Equinox
Trouble on Triton
Stars in My Pocket Like Grains of Sand
Return to Nevèrÿon:
　　Tales of Nevèrÿon
　　Neveryóna
　　Flight from Nevèrÿon
　　Return to Nevèrÿon
Empire (graphic novel)
The Mad Man
Hogg
Atlantis: Three Tales
Aye, and Gomorrah (collected stories)
Dark Reflections
Phallos
Through the Valley of the Nest of Spiders

NONFICTION

The Jewel-Hinged Jaw
Starboard Wine
The American Shore
Heavenly Breakfast
The Motion of Light in Water
Wagner/Artaud
The Straits of Messina
Silent Interviews
Longer Views
Bread & Wine (graphic novel)
Times Square Red, Times Square Blue
1984: Selected Letters
Shorter Views

a, b, c:

three short novels

with a new foreword and afterword by the author

samuel r. delany

vintage books

a division of penguin random house llc

new york

FIRST VINTAGE BOOKS EDITION, JULY 2015

This is a work of fiction. Names, characters, places, and
incidents either are the products of the author's imagination or
are used fictitiously. Any resemblance to actual persons, living
or dead, events, or locales is entirely coincidental.

The Cataloging-in-Publication Data is available from
the Library of Congress.

Vintage Books Trade Paperback ISBN: 978-1-101-91142-6
eBook ISBN: 978-1-101-91143-3

www.vintagebooks.com

Printed in the United States of America
10 9 8 7 6 5 4 3 2 1

contents

foreword

The Jewels of Aptor . . .
The Ballad of Beta-2 . . .
They Fly at Çiron . . .
Aptor, Beta-2, Çiron . . . A, B, C, and there's my title.
The subtitle tells what follows: *Three Short Novels*.

This book contains my first published novel, a science fantasy, *The Jewels of Aptor*, much as I wrote it in the winter of 1961–62. Officially it was released December 1, 1962. I saw copies late that November.

As I'd conceived and written the book, its audience was my brilliant, talented wife of those years, the poet Marilyn Hacker—nine months younger than I but always at least a year ahead of me in school. Walking up and over the school roof to get to classes, as all the entering students had been instructed to do, so as not to bother the elementary school students with whom we shared the building, we'd met on our first day of high school. Two years later Marilyn went on to NYU as an early admissions student at fifteen and finished her classes in three years. When we married on August 24, 1961, she was eighteen and I was nineteen.

Those interested in the invaluable part she played in discussing the ideas in *Aptor* and getting it published—she wrote some of the poetic spells in the book—can read about it in my autobiography, *The Motion of Light in Water* (1988; exp., 1992). Without her, it wouldn't—it *couldn't* have happened. After our marriage, Marilyn's first job was with the publisher, Ace Books. She took my manuscript in under a pen name. That's how it was submitted. That's how it was read. That's how it was accepted.

Only when contracts were drawn up, did she admit that the

writer was her husband—and the name on the contracts was hastily changed to mine.

Eventually it got a few (generous) reviews; but the thousand-dollar advance I received—$500 on contract signing in April and $500 in December on publication—back then would have covered fifteen months of our $52-a-month rent on our second-floor, four-room tenement apartment—rent for more than a year! (Would that it did so today.) And I could think, "Hey, I'm making my living as a writer!"

And I had a publisher. If I handed in anything that more or less met my editor's genre expectations, I assumed, I could sell it.

For my second book (what today is *They Fly at Çiron*), I took two old fantasy stories and quickly wrote three more. Each section had as a protagonist someone who was a minor character in one of the others. One involved only a name change for a character in one of the already completed tales.* Nor were the landscapes the tales took place in much related to one another. Rapidly reading over passages, I decided on a few more things that might connect them and wrote out bridges from one to the next. But I put into *Çiron* neither the time nor the intensity of thought and imagination I had put into *Aptor*.

A few weeks after I handed it in to Ace Books, Don Wollheim rejected it.

---

* Like thousands on thousands of young writers before and since, I figured the easy way to write a novel was to write a series of interconnected short stories. I'd even thought of it as an experiment—and I still think it could have been an interesting one. But it was an experimental idea that I'd used in place of doing the necessary imaginative work, rather than a formal idea I had brought to life through the work and the thinking that would have opened up and multiplied its resonances and meanings. It was an idea I had thrown away rather than utilized, because I'd hoped it would be interesting in itself, whatever its content. Forty years later I tried it again, with more success—I hope—in a novel called *Dark Reflections*. (It won the Stonewall Book Award in 2008.) But this reflects on something I find myself writing about even today: though the genre can suggest what you might need, it can never do the work for you—whether you are thinking of the text as science fiction, as literary, or as experimental; though, from time to time, all of us (writers and critics both) hope that it will.

Today, I feel that rejection was the most important thing that happened to me in my first years of publishing. I'll try to explain how and why it was *so* useful, *so* instructive, *so* important—though I don't know if, finally, it's possible to describe it in a definitive way.

Understand, I'd had novels rejected before. I'd been writing them since I was thirteen, and from seventeen on I had been submitting them to New York publishers—who'd been declining them. But also I'd been getting a fair amount of attention for them. Two years before, Marie Ponsot, a poet who had been very supportive of both Marilyn and me, spoke to her friend Margaret Marshall, an editor at Harcourt Brace. At Marie's request and on the strength of one of those early manuscripts, Marshall had secured me a work-study scholarship for the Bread Loaf Writers Conference at Middlebury College, Vermont. While attending the novel-writing workshops and lectures on the grassy and sunny Middlebury campus, where, even before the inception of the already legendary conference, novelists as varied as Anthony Hope and Willa Cather had written some of their most critically acclaimed pieces, I'd worked those two July weeks as a waiter in a white-painted dining room with square glass panes in the window doors along one wall. I'd attended the lectures, readings, and novel-writing workshops; I'd talked with writers and editors, new and established, and I'd found two or three who were willing to read my work and were even enthusiastic about it. Both before and since Bread Loaf, I'd submitted my novels. They'd been rejected too. What remains from those rejections, however, are the hours or even days of encouragement preceding them.

Wollheim's rejection, brief and final, I recall, however, with documentary clarity.

Wollheim phoned me at our apartment on East Fifth Street. The phone sat on an end table, discarded by my mother-in-law in the Bronx, and I sat on the armchair's arm. He said, "Hi, Chip. This is Don—Don Wollheim. I read your second manuscript this weekend." Somewhere in an office on Forty-eighth Street in Midtown, he paused. "I don't think they quite make a book, Chip. So I'll pass on them. But I'm certainly interested in seeing the next one you do. Okay?"

I said, "Oh . . . um, yeah. Okay. Yes, I see! Um . . . thanks."

Don said, "You're welcome. So long."

I said, "Good-bye . . . Um, Good-bye," and hung up, surprised and disappointed.

I was twenty. It was still painful when I wrote about it in my autobiography twenty-five years later, so I told it there as quickly as I could. Here's a little more of the tale:

I wanted to talk to Marilyn—badly—but she was out looking for work; so after I hung up I went downstairs and outside for a walk, to think over what had happened. It seemed clear, though.

One reason why I felt it so deeply was because with this particular rejection, the rejection of what would become Çiron, I had been turned down by an editor (and publisher) who had accepted something already.

Walking through the chill spring slums, I thought about the differences between the kind of work I'd done for the book that had been accepted (so enthusiastically, too), and the kind for the book that had been turned down (so summarily). With *Aptor*, before each scene, each writing session at the writing table, or with my notebook, cross-legged on the daybed, I'd worked to picture as many details of that scene and its physicality as I could. Many of those scenes had begun as disturbingly vivid dreams, so that for a number of them—the waterfront, the jungle, the beach, the temple, and the morning light or the evening light that suffused them—already I had complete images in mind, in some cases unsettlingly so.

Others, though, I'd had to visualize from scratch.

Aptor had commanded high imaginative involvement throughout. I had not used all the results or even most of them. But having them when I needed them seemed to loan the work (for me) coherence and authority.

For *Çiron*, however, I'd taken some odd texts, hastily forced them into what I thought might do for a linear narrative, which

I'd realized in the hour since the rejection was nowhere near linear enough. I had read over passages quickly and decided what might connect them to the next and wrote it out; but I'd put into it neither the time nor the intensity of thought and imagination I had put into the earlier book.

For a scene here or there I'd done a bit of the mental work. But the things that I'd felt (that I'd hoped. . .) had made *Aptor* lively, vivid, and given it momentum, were the things I'd failed to do in *Çiron*. Don had read it, felt how thin it was. Now, so did I—and I realized as well what the world's reaction would be, as exemplified by Don and Ace Books.

I'm glad I saw this—with only a sentence from Wollheim to prompt me over the phone, a kindness granted my second book doubtless because he'd published my first, and probably because I *was* twenty. In those days, young writers starting to sell, when and if they found themselves in that position, often didn't understand this.

It didn't need to be another kind of written piece. It needed to be a better quality piece. The book didn't need more sex. It didn't need more violence. It didn't need more action. It needed to be better organized from start to finish. It needed to be more richly imagined, first part to final. That meant I had to do the work, start to finish, I hadn't done. Had I done it, that work would have suggested better organization because I would have seen the material more vividly along with its many incoherent lax spots. The missing or extraneous material would have stood out more clearly and provided me with a clearer view of how to fix it—delete, insert, rewrite, expand, replace, connect to something earlier or farther on, several of them or one, the choice hinging on the clarity and intensity of my apprehension of the whole book.

As I'd read and reread *Aptor*, during its composition, that's how the details had come to me: in further specifics of landscape, characterization, psychology, dialogue, and incidents for the story.

This was the work I hadn't done on *Çiron*.

I thought this, however, not because any of it had been mentioned in the workshops at Bread Loaf or in E. M. Forster's *Aspects of the Novel* or in Lajos Egris's *The Art of Dramatic Writing* or in Orwell's essays or even in Gertrude Stein's *Autobiography of Alice B. Toklas* or *Lectures in America*—books I'd read on writing that already had been, up till then, so helpful. Today I suspect five different writers, each going through some version of this, might go through it in five different ways and arrive at five different conclusions, all of which would accomplish much the same. What seemed most important, however, as I walked through the smells and confusion of our crowded neighborhood was: think about this seriously. Your life hangs on it. (That's another year's rent you don't have now . . . !) You can't fuck around . . . .

It's surprising how far that can take you—about anything.

Returning from my walk, past the East Side tenements, the fish store on Avenue C, turning into the dead end of East Fifth Street where we lived, walking over the broken pavement before the parking garage's gaping door, by the plate-glass window edged in the flaking paint of the bodega next to it, set back, and up three steps, I thought: if I'm a writer and I want my pieces to place, I have to do that work.

This was not a case of writing the kind of pieces that would place. I could decide that pretty easily. I needed to write the quality of pieces that would place. It was neither the acceptance nor the rejection that had been so instructive, but the differences between them and what I knew now I might expect from each, and the information about my future in the world those differences comprised.

I knew what the two kinds of work felt like, behind my face, in my belly, along my arms, in my feet against the floor, my hands moving over the typewriter keys or across the notebook pages as I gripped my ballpoint, now that I could associate each with their different results.

If each had a shape, a shape I could grasp at in the world, even if those shapes were not entirely pensive, spatial, mental, or muscular, descriptions of their form or the content that could arrive to fill them out would always be incomplete—including this one. But now I had a nonverbal sense of what each was.

When Marilyn came home, we talked about what I might do. In my journal I'd already made notes on possible projects. One was the barest sketch for a trilogy of SF novels that would show what war was like in its effects on the country attacking, rather than the country invaded.

After several conversations with Marilyn, a few days later we walked across the Brooklyn Bridge to visit some friends in Brooklyn Heights for brunch. Walking back, we talked about it more. When we got home, I sat down in front of the typewriter, typed out a title page for the entire project, and began the first of the three-volume series I had planned out with her, and began the work I needed to generate the material necessary to construct its first volume, in order to write the best book that, at that very immature age, I could manage.

Basically I'd decided that if I was going to write something of the highest quality I could achieve, it had best be about something I felt was important. And we were a country at war.

It was a lot of work—I've written about it several times. The middle volume was more work than I'd ever imagined it might be. Often, I was afraid the work would defeat me. There are places where I believe it did. But I also knew, by now, that if I didn't do it, not only couldn't I sell it, but I couldn't live with myself either. By now I was afraid to avoid the work or to try for shortcuts.

The three books of *The Fall of the Towers* are not here. But they are still in print.

It's worth repeating: the rejection of *Çiron* gave me the chance to compare two things I had written, not in terms of the differences between the surfaces of the texts, but rather the differences between the mental work I had done writing the accepted text and the mental work I had shirked writing the rejected one.

The writing of *The Ballad of Beta-2* came along to interrupt the trilogy, during the time I'd thought, for a while, the second volume would stop me. I began it in the middle of that stalled second book. I wanted to write a short novel unconnected to the War of Toromon, so that I could give myself the feeling of starting and completing something. Soon I realized I had to stop (or more accurately realized I had already stopped) thinking about selling in order to attain and sustain the level I was reaching for—and always missing and going back in hope of pulling myself closer. Today I suspect even that conflict muddled the causes of the problems I was having.

The Ballad of Beta-2 itself was interrupted when I managed to get back my wind on the trilogy's recalcitrant book two. After the third volume appeared, I finished *Beta-2*. (Yes, I managed to complete the trio; after volume two, work on the third was as surprisingly easy as, for the second book, it had been unexpectedly hard. That meant—to me—it was time to go on to projects which would be harder.) *Beta-2* appeared as the shorter half of another Ace Double at the start of 1965 and then in an Ace volume containing *The Ballad of Beta-2* and another of my short science-fiction novels, *Empire Star*. In 1982 *Beta-2* was again released by Ace, this time in a stand-alone paperback that remained in print till 1987. Altogether the book had a run of twenty-two years in print, as did *The Jewels of Aptor*.

Although *They Fly at Çiron* was, in fact, the third of the three here to be published (which is how it earns its "C"), while I think of it as my second novel, actually it was my nineteenth published. The reason I published it at all is because in 1991, in Amherst, Massachusetts, I took it out and reworked it end to end.

In 1993 *They Fly at Çiron* had two separate hardcover printings, a trade hardcover and a special edition, both from Ron Drummond's incomparable small press, Incunabula. Two years later, a hardcover and a mass-market paperback followed from Tor Books.

The above is all to say, whether the effort was wasted, invisible, or has somehow left its signs either in pleasing or in awkward ways, by the time these three were actual books, I'd worked on them as hard as I could—as did the publishers to see that they were successful in the marketplace—and I hope it says it in a way that conveys three further facts (the second of which I'll return to in my "Afterword"):

First, with each book, moments arrived in the creation process when the text felt as if it required more work than I could possibly do. I gave up. I despaired. Then I came back and tried to do it anyway. In short, it was a process like any other human task. What made it different, however, was that it was primarily internal: the "shape" of its internality made it wholly of itself and only indirectly and incompletely communicable in any rigorous way.

Second, over a very, very long time—tens of thousands to multiple millions and even billions of years, rather than over decades or centuries—a congruence arises between creatures and the conditions that are the landscapes in which they and we dwell.* Along with that congruence arises the illusion of a

---

* Sometimes the uses of evolutionary developments seem obvious. Far more often, though, they are invisible and their uses not necessarily comprehended by the creatures—including humans—who possess them. (This is why the notion that sex is only for reproduction is, itself, an antievolutionary notion.) What are earlobes for? Well, they are blood collectors that help supply the ear with blood and keep the inner ear warm in very cold weather. That's probably why they developed first in northern climates and why smaller earlobes developed nearer the equator. Well, then why don't all northerners have large earlobes and all equatorial people have small ones? Because, over the last four hundred years, quite enough intermixing has occurred in both the north and south to rearrange the genetic distribution, which rearrangements can be considered a natural response to the interbreeding of peoples and the movement that goes along with it and is also a long-ago established evolutionary advantage of genetic reproduction itself, which allows such rearrangements in diploid genetic species for blending-inheritance aspects. (Haploid species—some stages of amoeba and paramecia—can mix genes through a process called syzygy, but that's much rarer and takes even more time to develop anything evolutionary—although it does, some. A science-fiction writer who was most fascinated by that process—and one of the great short fiction writers of the middle of the last century—is Theodore Sturgeon. Read him. He's wonderful.) Two evolutionary ideas to keep in mind: first, by the time anything develops evolutionarily, it always has many uses; and that includes earlobes, large and small. No matter how scientists talk about them, anyone who believes that any evolutionary development has only one use basically misunderstands how evolution works: because the development is slow and gradual, at each stage

guiding intelligence. (There may be a truth behind the illusion. There may not be. But that is metaphysics, however, and not our concern here. The similarly structured illusion of direct animal and human communication through the senses, by the same process imposes the effect/illusion of a metaphysics we arrogantly presume must exist behind our necessarily mediated perceptions to form a reality resonant with our aesthetic wonders and distress, our appetitive pleasures and pain, our political urgencies, disasters, and satisfactions, and their largely unseen structuring forces: another illusion, another effect. The same indirect process that feels so direct to us (and probably to all the animals who utilize it) is what allows wolves to bay out to warn their pack of danger or approaching prey—and humans to tell stories, gossip, and write novels, as well as create cultures: the cultures we form are the only realities we have, however, or can have any

---

the development must be useful enough to give a large-scale statistical survival advantage to a group. Those uses change as the aspect develops but the older uses they met don't necessarily go away. (Humans' external ears are highly erogenous—whether individuals use that aspect or not.) If it isn't useful at all, it breeds out eventually. Carrying around excess still isn't an advantage—though sometimes it only looks excessive to us. Second, any aspect of us that is widespread and has been around for a long time almost certainly has some functional use(s), even if we have never stopped to consider what it might be. Humans had developed a circulatory system with veins, arteries, valves, and a complex heart multiple millions of years before the Egyptians in the sixteenth century BCE and with observations by Romans and Arabs over three thousand years contributed to William Harvey's assembling a viable model of the whole human circulatory system (as well as discussing a few of its uses, but by no means all) in his 1628 publication, *De Motu Cordis*. And we are still discovering aspects of the circulatory system that have been in place since before we branched off the general evolutionary line along with the other great apes, many of which are common to all mammals, birds, amphibians, and fish. In many of their variant forms they do lots of things very well, and a staggering percentage of the greater "us" (almost all of us who aren't plants or worms—and worms are the major planetary population, remember; though we share still other things with them, such as muscles and an alimentary canal) utilize them to interact with the cities, the caves, the rural areas in which they live or have lived, the prairies, the grasses and brambles and ferns, the seas, the seabeds and trenches and shallow reefs, the deserts, the hills, the tundra, the mountains, the jungles, and forests.

access to, and our ignorance of which, when we are aware of it, all too infrequently we take as a mandate for both honesty and humility (the engine of ethics at its best), even as these realities of which we are a part create the curiosities, the yearnings, the passions to know so often perceived to be that arrogance itself. That these multiple realities are parsimoniously plural, however (without having been directly caused by evolution; only the ability to construct them and respond to them is evolutionary, not what is constructed), is the first, but by no means the strongest, evidence for their complex relations,* however functional or problematic their multiplicity.

Third, the work of art—a sculpture we carve or a novel we write—can be and can exhibit a complex structure that appears to mimic some of the world (some of one reality or another; or even some of one that does not exist) because it evolves from the world; it mimics it in much the way certain insects camouflage themselves as the bark or the leaves of the trees they sometimes rest on, in the same way that intelligence can sometimes mimic something greater than itself, both spatially and temporally, even while simpler in its details and less protracted in operation; thus we can camouflage what we have to say as a series of happenings from life. And sometimes something that is not mind but that here and there entails one or millions of minds, at different levels and at different tasks—mind that is as likely to be on the way out (like gigantism in dinosaurs) as it is to be developing into something more useful, the results of which we will not live to see because it (they) will not manifest in any way we might notice or even it itself might notice or comprehend—if ever—for

---

* That multiplicity, thanks to evolution, is always both plural and limited (parsimonious). Their pluralities are the political urgencies, disasters, and satisfactions mentioned above, as they are inchoate to the wonders and distresses, the pains and pleasures, and the symbolic forces that exist only through intellect, from the workings of discourse to the square root of minus one, to the existence of stars, quarks, photons, quasars and pulsars, dark matter, dark energy, galaxies, gravity, and the multiverse they constitute.

another handful of millions of years or more, is only another wrinkle in the bark or the leaf—another fold in the monad, as Leibniz would have it.

The possibility that from time to time such aesthetic work as I have so inadequately described can create anything of interest is another effect: direct causality between work and result is as much an effect here as is any other sort of communication. But because that interest is communicated and therefore indirect, incomplete, constituted of its own inaccuracy and slippage, already there in whatever education from which we can construct our experience of utterances (including what can be spoken about), or of texts (including what can be written about; and they are not necessarily the same). From time to time, locally or briefly, however, something of interest occurs. We suspect it does mostly because, however briefly and locally, we are interested.

April 17, 2014
Philadelphia

a, b, c: three short novels

the jewels of aptor

The waves flung up against the purple glow
of double sleeplessness. Along the piers
the ships return; but sailing I would go
through double rings of fire, double fears.
So therefore let your bright vaults heave the night
about with ropes of wind and points of light
and say, as all the rolling stars go, "I
have stood my feet on rock and seen the sky."

THE OPENING LINES OF THE EPIC
OF THE CONFLICTS BETWEEN LEPTAR AND APTOR,
BY THE ONE-ARMED POET GEO

Afterwards, she was taken down to the sea.

She didn't feel too well, so she sat on a rock and scrunched her toes in the wet sand. She looked across the water, hunched her shoulders a little. "I think it was pretty awful. I think it was terrible. Why did you show it to me? He was only a boy. What reason could they possibly have had for doing that to him?"

"It was just a film. We showed it to you so that you would learn."

"But it was a film of something that really happened!"

"It happened several years ago, several hundred miles away."

"But it *did* happen; you used a tight beam to spy on them, and when the image came in on the vision screen, you made a film of it, and—Why did you show it to me?"

"What have we been teaching you?"

But she couldn't think: only the picture in her mind, vivid movements, scarlets, bright agony. "He was just a child," she said. "He couldn't have been more than eleven or twelve."

"*You* are a child. You aren't sixteen yet."

"What was I supposed to learn?"

"Look around. You should see something."

But it was still too vivid, too red, too bright. . . .

"You should be able to learn it right here on this beach, in the trees back there, in the rocks down here, in the shells around your feet. You do see it; you don't recognize it." His voice brightened. "Actually you're a very fine student. You learn quickly. Do you remember anything from your study of telepathy a month ago?"

" 'By a method similar to radio broadcast and reception,' " she recited, " 'the synapse patterns of conscious thought are read from one cranial cortex and duplicated in another, resulting in a duplication of sensory impressions experienced—' But I can't do it, so it doesn't help *me*!"

"What about history, then? You did extremely well in the examination. Does knowing about all the happenings in the world before and after the Great Fire help you?"

"Well. It's . . . it's interesting."

"The film you saw was, in a way, history. That is, it happened in the past."

"But it was so . . ."—her eyes beat before the flashing waves—"horrible!"

"Does history fascinate you only because it's interesting? Don't you ever want to know the reason behind some of the things those people do in your books?"

"Yes, I want to know the reasons! I want to know the reason they nailed that man to the oaken cross. I want to know why they did that to him."

"A good question . . . Which reminds me: at about the same time they were nailing him to that cross, it was decided in China that the forces of the Universe were to be represented by a circle, half black, half white. To remind themselves, however, that there is no pure force, no single and unique reason, they put a spot of white paint in the black half and a spot of black paint in the white. Interesting?"

She frowned, wondering at the transition. But he was going on:

"And do you remember the goldsmith, the lover, how he

recorded in his autobiography that at age four, he and his father saw the Fabulous Salamander on their hearth by the fire; and his father smacked the boy across the room into a rack of kettles, saying something to the effect that little Cellini was too young to remember the incident unless it was accompanied by pain."

"I remember the story," she said. "And I remember Cellini said he wasn't sure if the smack was the reason he remembered the Salamander—or the Salamander the reason he remembered the smack!"

"Yes, yes!" he cried. "That's it. The reason, the reasons . . ." In his excitement, his hood fell back and she saw his face in the late afternoon's copper light. "Don't you see the pattern?"

Scored forehead, the webbing at his eyes: she traced the pattern of age there, and let her eyes drop. "Only I don't know what a Salamander is."

"It's like the blue lizards that sing outside your window," he explained. "Only it isn't blue and it doesn't sing."

"Then why should anyone want to remember it?" She grinned. But he was not looking at her.

"And the painter," he was saying, "you remember, in Florence. He was painting a picture of La Gioconda. As a matter of fact, he had to take time from the already crumbling picture of the Last Supper of the man who was nailed to the cross of oak to paint her. And he put a smile on her face of which men asked for centuries, 'What is the reason she smiles so strangely?' Yes, the reason, don't you see? Just look around!"

"What about the Great Fire?" she asked. "When they dropped flames from the skies and the harbors boiled; that was reasonless. That was like what they did to that boy."

"Oh, no," he said to her. "Not reasonless. True, when the Great Fire came, people all over the earth screamed, 'Why? Why? How can man do this to man? What is the reason?' But just look around you, right here! On the beach!"

"I guess I can't see it yet," she said. "I can just see what they did to him; and it was awful."

"Well." He pulled together his robe. "Perhaps when you stop

seeing what they did so vividly, you will start seeing why they did it. I think it's time for us to go back now."

She slid off the rock and started walking beside him, barefoot in the sand. "That boy . . . I wasn't sure, he was all tied up; but—he had four arms, didn't he?"

"He did."

She shuddered again. "You know, I can't just go around just saying it was awful. I think I'm going to write a poem. Or make something. Or both. I've got to get it out of my head."

"That wouldn't be a bad idea," he mumbled as they approached the trees in front of the river. "Not bad at all."

And several days later, several hundred miles away . . .

chapter one

Waves flung themselves at the blue evening. Low light burned on the hulks of wet ships that slipped by mossy pilings into the docks as water sloshed at the rotten stone embankments.

Gangplanks, chained to wooden pulleys, scraped into place on concrete blocks; and the crew, after the slow Captain and the tall Mate, loped raffishly along the boards, which sagged with the pounding of bare feet. In bawling groups, pairs, or singly, they howled into the waterfront streets, by the yellow light from inn doors, the purple portals leading to rooms full of smoke and the stench of burnt poppies, laughter, and the sheen on red lips, to the houses of women.

The Captain, with eyes the color of sea under fog, touched his sword hilt with his fist and said quietly, "Well, they've gone. We better start collecting new sailors for the ten we lost at Aptor.

Ten good men, Jordde. I get ill when I think of the bone and broken meat they became."

"Ten for the dead," sneered the Mate, "and twenty for the living we'll never see again. Any sailor that would want to continue this trip with us is crazy. We'll do well if we only lose twenty." He was a wire-bound man, on whom any clothing looked baggy.

"I'll never forgive her for ordering us to that monstrous Island," said the Captain.

"I wouldn't speak too loudly," mumbled the Mate. "Yours isn't to forgive her. Besides, she went with them and was in as much danger as they were. It's only luck she came back."

Suddenly the Captain asked, "Do you believe the stories of magic they tell of her?"

"Why, sir?" asked the Mate. "Do you?"

"No, I don't." The Captain's certainty came too quickly. "Still, with three survivors out of thirteen, that she should be among them, with hardly a robe torn . . ."

"Perhaps they wouldn't touch a woman," suggested Jordde.

"Perhaps," said the Captain.

"And she's been strange ever since then. She walks at night. I've seen her going by the rails, looking from the seafire to the stars and back."

"Ten good men," mused the Captain. "Hacked up, torn in bits. I wouldn't have believed that much barbarity in the world if I hadn't seen that arm, floating on the water. It even chills me now, the way the men ran to the rail, pointed at it. And it just raised itself up, like a sign, then sank in a wash of foam and green water."

"Well," said the Mate, "we have men to get."

"I wonder if she'll come ashore?"

"She'll come if she wants, Captain. Her doing is no concern of yours. Your job is the ship and to do what she asks."

"I have more of a job than that," and he looked back at his still craft.

The Mate touched the Captain's shoulder. "If you're going to speak things like that, speak them softly, and only to me."

"I have more of a job than that," the Captain repeated. Then suddenly he started away; the Mate followed him down the darkening dockside.

The wharf was still a moment. Then a barrel toppled from a pile of barrels, and a figure moved like a bird's shadow between two mounds of cargo.

At the same time two men approached down a street filled with the day's last light. The bigger one threw a great shadow that aped his gesticulating arms on the crowded buildings. His bare feet slapped the cobbles like halved hams. His shins were bound with thongs and pelts. He waved one hand in explanation and rubbed the back of the other on his short mahogany beard. "You're going to ship out, eh, friend? You think they'll take your rhymes and jingles instead of muscles and rope pulling?"

The smaller, in a white tunic looped with a leather belt, laughed in spite of his friend's ranting. "Fifteen minutes ago you thought it was a fine idea, Urson. You said it would make me a man."

"Oh, it's a life to make"—Urson's hand went up—"and it's a life to break men." It fell.

The slighter one pushed black hair back from his forehead, stopped, and looked at the boats. "You still haven't told me why no ship has taken you on in the past three months." Absently he followed the rigging, like black slashes in blue silk. "A year ago I'd never see you in for more than three days at once."

The gesticulating arm suddenly encircled the smaller man's waist and lifted a leather pouch from the belt. "Are you sure, friend Geo," began the giant, "that we couldn't use up some of this silver on wine before we go? If you want to do this right, then right is how it should be done. When you sign up on a ship you're supposed to be broke and tight. It shows you're capable of getting along without the inconvenience of money and can hold your liquor."

"Urson, get your paw off!" Geo pulled the purse away.

"Now, here," countered Urson, reaching for it once more, "you don't have to grab."

"Look, I've kept you drunk five nights now; it's time to sober up. Suppose they don't take us. Who's going—" But Urson, laughing, made another swipe.

Geo leaped back with the purse. "Now, cut that out—" In leaping, his feet struck the fallen barrel. He fell backward to the wet cobbles. The pouch splattered away, jingling.

They scrambled—

Then the bird's shadow darted between the cargo piles; the slight figure bounded forward, swept the purse up with one hand, pushed himself away from the pile of crates with another; and there were two more pumping at his side as he ran.

"What the devil . . ." began Urson, and then: "What the *devil*!"

"Hey, you!" Geo lurched to his feet. "Come back!"

Urson had already loped a couple of steps after the fleeing quadrabrad, now halfway down the dock.

Then, like a wineglass stem snapping, a voice: "Stop, little thief. Stop."

He stopped as though he had hit a wall.

"Come back, now. Come back."

He turned and docilely started back, his movements, so lithe a moment ago, mechanical now.

"It's just a kid," Urson said.

He was a dark-haired boy, naked except for a ragged breech-clout. He was staring fixedly beyond them. And he had four arms.

Now they turned and looked also.

She stood on the ship's gangplank, dark against what sun still washed the horizon. One hand held something close at her throat, and the wind, snagging a veil, held the purple gauze against the red swath at the world's edge, then dropped it.

The boy, automaton, approached her.

"Give it to me, little thief."

He handed her the purse. She took it. Then she dropped her

other hand from her neck. The moment she did so, the boy staggered backward, turned, and ran straight into Urson, who said, "Ooof," and then, "Goddamned spider!"

The boy struggled like a hydra in furious silence. Urson held. "You stick around . . . Owww! . . . to get yourself thrashed . . . there." Urson locked one arm across the boy's chest. With his other hand he caught all four wrists; he lifted up, hard. The thin body shook like wires jerked taut, but the boy was still silent.

Now the woman came across the dock. "This belongs to you, gentlemen?" she asked, extending the purse.

"Thank you, ma'am," grunted Urson, reaching forward.

"I'll take that, ma'am," said Geo, intercepting. Then he recited:

> "Shadows melt in light of sacred laughter.
> Hands and houses shall be one hereafter.

"Thank you," he added.

Beneath the veil her eyebrows raised. "You have been schooled in courtly rites? Are you perhaps a student at the University?"

Geo smiled. "I was, until a short time ago. But funds are low and I have to get through the summer somehow. I'm going to sea."

"Honorable, but perhaps foolish."

"I am a poet, ma'am; they say poets are fools. Besides, my friend here says the sea will make a man of me. To be a good poet, one must be a good man."

"More honorable, less foolish. What sort of man is your friend?"

"My name is Urson." The giant stepped up. "And I've been the best hand on any ship I've sailed on."

"Urson? The Bear? I thought bears did not like water. Except polar bears. It makes them mad. I believe there was an old spell, in antiquity, for taming angry bears."

"Calmly, brother bear," Geo began to recite:

"calm the winter sleep.
Fire shall not harm
water not alarm.
While the current grows,
amber honey flows,
golden salmon leap."

"Hey," said Urson. "I'm not a bear!"

"Your name means bear," Geo said. Then to the lady, "You see, I have been well trained."

"I'm afraid I have not," she replied. "Poetry and rituals were a hobby of a year's passing interest when I was younger. But that was all." Now she looked down at the four-armed boy. "You two look alike. Dark eyes, dark hair." She laughed. "Are there other things in common between poets and thieves?"

"Well," complained Urson with a jerk of his chin, "this one here won't spare a few silvers for a drink of good wine to wet his best friend's throat, and that's a sort of thievery if you ask me."

"I did not ask," said the woman.

Urson huffed.

"Little thief," the woman said. "Little Four Arms. What is your name?"

Silence, and the dark eyes narrowed.

"I can make you tell me," and she raised her hand to her throat again.

Now the eyes opened wide and the boy pushed back against Urson's belly.

Geo reached toward the boy's neck, where a ceramic disk hung from a leather thong. Glazed on the white enamel was a wriggle of black with a small dot of green for an eye at one end. "This will do for a name," Geo said.

"The Snake?" She dropped her threatening hand. "How good a thief are you?" She looked at Urson. "Let him go."

"And miss thrashing his little backside?"

"He will not run away."

Urson released him.

Four hands came down and began massaging one another's wrists. The dark eyes watched her as she repeated: "How good a thief are you?"

Suddenly he reached into his clout and drew out what seemed another thong similar to the one around his neck. He held up the fist, the fingers opened slowly to a cage.

"What is it?" Urson peered over Snake's shoulder.

The woman leaned forward, then suddenly straightened. "You . . ." she began.

Snake's fist closed like a sea polyp.

"You are a fine thief indeed."

"What is it?" Urson asked. "I didn't see anything."

"Show them," she said.

Snake opened his hand. On the dirty palm, in coiled leather, held by a clumsy wire cage was a milky sphere the size of a man's eye.

"A very fine thief," repeated the woman in a voice dulled strangely from its previous brittle clarity. She had pulled her veil aside now. Geo saw, where her hand had again risen to her throat, the tips of her slim fingers held an identical jewel; only this one, in a platinum claw, hung from a wrought gold chain.

Her eyes, unveiled, rose to meet Geo's. A slight smile lifted her lips. "No," she said. "Not quite so clever as I thought. At first I believed he had taken mine. But clever enough. You, schooled in the antiquity of Leptar's rituals, can you tell me what these baubles mean?"

Geo shook his head.

A breath suspired her pale mouth, and though her eyes still fixed his, she seemed to draw away, blown into some past shadow by the sigh. "No," she said. "It has all been lost or destroyed by the old priests and priestesses, the old poets.

> "Freeze the drop in the hand
> and break the earth with singing.
> Hail the height of a man,

also the height of a woman.

The eyes have imprisoned a vision. . . ."

She spoke the lines reverently. "Do you recognize any of this? Can you tell me where they are from?"

"Only one stanza of it," said Geo. "And that in a slightly different form." He recited:

"Burn the grain speck in the hand

and batter the stars with singing.

Hail the height of a man,

also the height of a woman."

"Well." She looked surprised. "You have done better than all the priests and priestesses of Leptar. What about this fragment? Where is it from?"

"It is a stanza of the discarded rituals of the Goddess Argo, the ones banned and destroyed five hundred years ago. The rest of the poem is completely lost," explained Geo. "Your priests and priestesses would not be aware of it, very likely. I discovered that stanza when I peeled away the binding paper of an ancient tome that I found in the Antiquity Collection in the Temple Library at Acedia. Apparently a page from an even older book had been used in the binding of this one. That is the only way it survived. I assume these are fragments of the rituals before Leptar purged her litanies. I know at least my variant stanza belongs to that period. Perhaps you have received a misquoted rendition; I will vouch for the authenticity of mine."

"No," she said regretfully. "*Mine* is the authentic version. So you too are not that clever." She turned back to the boy. "But I have need of a good thief. Will you come with me? And you, Poet. I have need of one who thinks so meticulously and who delves into places where even my priests and priestesses cannot go. Will you come with me also?"

"Where are we going?"

"Aboard that ship." She smiled evasively toward the vessel.

"That's a good boat," said Urson. "I'd be proud to sail on her, Geo."

"The Captain is in my service," she told Geo. "He will take you on. Perhaps you will get a chance to see the world and become the man you wish to be."

Geo saw Urson looking uneasy. "My friend goes on whatever ship I do. This we've promised each other. Besides, he is a good sailor, while I have no knowledge of the sea."

"On our last journey," the woman explained, "we lost men. I do not think your friend will have trouble getting a berth."

"Then we'll be honored to come," said Geo. "Under whose service shall we be, then, for we still don't know who you are?"

The veil fell across her face again. "I am a high priestess of the Goddess Argo. Now, who are you?"

"My name is Geo," Geo told her.

"I welcome you aboard our ship."

Just then, from down the street, came the Captain and Jordde. They walked slowly and heavily from the shadow that angled over the cobbles. The Captain squinted past the ships toward the horizon. Copper light filled the wrinkles and burnished the planes around his gray eyes. The Priestess turned to them. "Captain, I have three men as a token replacement for the ones my folly helped to lose."

Urson, Geo, and Snake frowned at one another and then looked at the Captain.

Jordde shrugged. "You did almost as well as we did, ma'am."

"And the ones we did get . . ." The Captain shook his head. "Not the caliber of sailor I'd want for this sort of journey. Not at all."

"I'm a good sailor for any man's journey," Urson said, "though it be to the earth's end and back."

"You seem strong, a sea-bred man. But this one"—the Captain looked at Snake—"one of the Strange Ones . . ."

"They're bad luck on a ship," said the Mate. "Most ships won't take them at all, ma'am. This one's just a boy and, for all his spindles there, couldn't haul rope or reef sails. He'd be no good to us at all. And we've had too much bad luck already."

"He's not for rope pulling," explained the Priestess. "The little Snake is my guest. The others you can put to ship's work. I know you are short of men. But I have my own plans for this one."

"As you say, ma'am," said the Captain.

"But, Priestess—" began Jordde.

"As you say," repeated the Captain, and the Mate stepped back, quieted. The Captain turned to Geo now. "And who are you?"

"I'm Geo, before and still a poet. But I'll do what work you set me, sir."

"Today, young man, that's all I can ask of any sailor. You will find berths below. There are many vacant."

"And you?" Jordde asked Urson.

"I'm a good sea-son of the waves, can stand triple watch without flagging, and I believe I'm already hired." He looked to the Captain.

"What do they call you?" Jordde asked. "You have a familiar look, like one I've had under me before."

"They call me the handsome sailor, the fastest rope reeler, the quickest line hauler, the speediest reefer—"

"Your name, man, your name!"

"Some call me Urson."

"That's the name I knew you by before! But you had no beard then. Do you think I'd sail with you again when I myself wrote out your banning in black and white and sent it to every captain and mate in the dock? What sort of a crazy hawk would I be to pour poison like you into my forecastle? For three months now you've had no berth, and if you had none for three hundred years it would be too soon." Jordde turned to the Captain now. "He's a troublemaker, sir; he fights. Though he's wild as waves and with the strength of a mizzen spar; spirit in a man is one thing, and a tussle or two the same; but good sailor though he is, I've sworn not to have him on ship with me, sir. He's nearly murdered half a dozen men and probably murdered half a dozen more. No mate who knows the men of this harbor will take him on."

The Priestess of Argo laughed. "Captain, take him." She looked at Geo. "The words for calming the angry bear have been recited before him. Now, Geo, we will see how good a poet you are, and if the spell works." At last she turned to Urson. "Have you ever killed a man?"

Urson was silent a moment. "I have."

"Had you told me that," said the Priestess, "I would have chosen you first. I have need of you also. Captain, you must take him. If he is a good sailor, then we cannot spare him. *I* will channel what special talents he may have. Geo, since you said the spell and are his friend, I charge you with his control. Also, I wish to talk with you, Poet, student of rituals. Come. You all stay on shipboard tonight."

She signaled them to follow, and they mounted the plank onto the deck. At the request to speak with Geo, Urson, Snake, and Jordde had exchanged glances; but now, as they crossed to the hatch, all were silent.

chapter two

An oil lamp leaked yellow light on the wooden walls. A mustiness of stale bedding lay around them as the three entered. Geo wrinkled his nose, then shrugged.

"Well," said Urson, "this is a pleasant enough hole." He climbed one of the tiers of bunked beds and pounded the ticking with the flat of his hand. "Here, I'll take this one. Wriggly-arms, you look like you have a strong stomach; you take the middle. And Geo, sling yourself down in the bottom there." He clumped to the floor. "The lower down you are," he explained, "the better you sleep, because of the rocking. Well, what do you think of your first forecastle?"

The poet was silent. Double pins of light struck yellow dots in his dark eyes, then went out as he turned from the lamp.

"I put you in the bottom because a little rough weather can unseat your belly pretty fast if you're up near the ceiling and not used to it," Urson expounded, dropping his hand heavily on Geo's shoulder. "I told you I'd look out for you, didn't I, friend?"

But Geo turned away and seemed to examine something else.

Urson looked at Snake, who was watching him from against the wall. Urson's glance was questioning. But Snake stayed silent.

"Hey," Urson called to Geo once more. "Let's you and me take a run around this ship and see what's tied down where. A good sailor does that first thing—unless he's too drunk. That lets the Captain and the Mate know he's got an alert eye out, and sometimes he can learn something that will ease some back-bending later on. What do you say?"

"Not now, Urson," interrupted Geo. "You go."

"Would you please tell me why my company suddenly isn't good enough for you? This silence is a bilgy way to treat somebody who's sworn himself to see that you make the best first voyage that a man could have. Why, I think—"

"When did you kill a man?"

Silence rumbled in the cabin, more palpable than the slosh of water outside. Urson stood still; his hands twisted to knots of bone and muscle. Then they opened. "Maybe it was a year ago," he said softly. "And maybe it was a year, two months, and five days, on a Thursday morning at eight o'clock in the brig of a heaving ship. Which would make it one year, two months, five days and ten hours, now."

"You killed a man? How could you go all this time and not tell me about it, then admit it to a stranger just like that. You were my friend; we've slept under the same blanket, drunk from the same wineskin. What sort of a person are you?"

"And what sort of a person are you?" asked the giant. "A nosy bastard that I'd break in seven pieces if . . ." He sucked in a breath. "If I hadn't promised I'd make no trouble. I've never broken a promise to anyone, alive or dead." The fists formed, relaxed again.

"Urson, I didn't mean to judge you. Know that. But tell me about it. We've been like brothers; you can't keep a thing like that from. . . ."

The heavy breathing continued. "You're so quick to tell me what I can or cannot do." Suddenly he raised one hand, flung it away, and spat on the floor. He turned toward the steps.

Then the noise hit. No, it was higher than sound. And it nearly broke their heads. Geo caught his ears and whirled toward Snake. The boy's black eyes darted twin spots of light to Urson, to Geo, and back.

The noise came again, quieter this time, and recognizable as the word *help*. Only it was no sound; rather, the fading hum of a tuning fork rung inside their skulls, immediate yet fuzzy.

You . . . help . . . me . . . together . . . came the words once more, indistinct and blurring into one another.

"Hey," Urson said, "is that you?"

Do . . . not . . . angry . . . came the words.

"We're not angry," Geo said. "What are you doing?"

I . . . thinking . . . The words seemed to generate from the boy.

"What sort of a way to think is that if everyone can hear it?" demanded Urson.

Snake tried to explain: *Not . . . everyone . . . just . . . you . . . you . . . think . . . I . . . hear . . .* came the soundless words. *I . . . think . . . you . . . hear . . .*

"I know we hear," Urson said. "It's just like you were talking."

"That's not what he means," Geo said. "He means he hears what we think just like we hear him. Is that right, Snake?"

When . . . you . . . think . . . loud . . . I . . . hear . . .

"I may just have been doing some pretty loud thinking," Urson said. "And if I thought something I wasn't supposed to— well, I apologize."

Snake didn't seem interested in the apology, but asked again: *You . . . help . . . me . . . together . . .*

"What sort of help do you want?" Geo asked.

"And what sort of trouble are you in that you need help out of it?" added Urson.

You . . . don't . . . have . . . good . . . minds . . . Snake said.

"What's that supposed to mean?" Urson asked. "Our minds are as good as any in Leptar. You heard the way the Priestess talked to my friend the poet, here."

"I think he means we don't hear very well," said Geo.

Snake nodded.

"Oh," Urson said. "Well then, you'll just have to go slow and be patient with us."

Snake shook his head: *Mind . . . hoarse . . . when . . . shout . . . so . . . loud . . .* Suddenly he went over to the bunks. *You . . . hear . . . better . . . see . . . too . . . if . . . sleep . . .*

"Sleep is sort of far from me," Urson said, rubbing his beard with the back of his wrist.

"Me too," Geo admitted. "Can't you tell us something more?"

Sleep . . . Snake said.

"What about talking like an ordinary human being?" suggested Urson, still somewhat perplexed.

Once . . . speak . . . Snake told them.

"You say you could speak once?" asked Geo. "What happened?"

Here the boy opened his mouth and pointed.

Geo stepped forward, held the boy's chin in his hand, examined the face, and peered into the mouth. "By the Goddess!"

"What is it?" Urson asked.

Geo came away now, his face in a sickly frown. "His tongue has been hacked out," he told the giant. "And not too neatly."

"Who on the seven seas and six continents did a thing like that to you, boy?" Urson demanded.

Snake shook his head.

"Now come on, Snake," he urged. "You can't keep secrets like that from friends and expect them to rescue you from I don't know what. Now who was it hacked your voice away!"

What . . . man . . . you . . . kill . . . came the sound.

Urson stopped, and then he laughed. "All right," he said. "I see." His voice rose once more. "But if you can hear thoughts, you know the man already. And you know the reason. And this is what we'd find out from you, if only for help and friendship's sake."

You . . . know . . . the . . . man . . . Snake said.

Geo and Urson exchanged puzzled frowns.

sleep . . . said Snake. *You . . . sleep . . . now . . .*

"Maybe we ought to try," said Geo, "and find out what's going on." He crossed to his bunk and slipped in.

Urson hoisted himself onto the upper berth, dangling his feet against the wooden support. "It's going to be a long time before sleep gets to me tonight," he said. "You, Snake, little Strange One." He laughed. "Where do you people come from?" He glanced down at Geo. "You see them all around the city. Some with three eyes, some with one. You know, at Matra's House they say they keep a woman with eight breasts and two of something else." He laughed again. "You know the rituals, know about magic. Aren't the Strange Ones some sort of magic?"

"The only mention of them in rituals says that they are ashes of the Great Fire. The Great Fire was back before the purges, the ones I spoke to the Priestess about, so I don't know anything more about them."

"Sailors have stories of the Great Fire," Urson said. "They say the sea boiled, great birds spat fire from the sky, and metal breasts rose up from the waves and destroyed the harbors. But what were the purges you mentioned?"

"About five hundred years ago," Geo explained, "all the rituals of the Goddess Argo were destroyed. A new set was introduced into the temple practices. All references to the earlier ones were destroyed, and with them, much of Leptar's history. Stories have it that the rituals and incantations were too powerful. But this is just a guess, and most priests are very uncomfortable about speculating."

"That was after the Great Fire?" Urson asked.

"Nearly a thousand years after," Geo said.

"It must have been a great fire indeed if ashes from it are still falling from the wombs of healthy women." He looked down at Snake. "Is it true that a drop of your blood in vinegar will cure gout? If one of you kisses a female baby, will she have only girl children?" He laughed.

"You know those are only tales," Geo said.

"There used to be a short one with two heads that sat outside the Blue Tavern and spun a top all day. It was an idiot, though. But the dwarfs and the legless ones that wheel about the city and do tricks, they are clever. But strange and quiet, usually."

"You oaf," chided Geo, "you could be one too. How many men do you know who reach your size and strength by normal means?"

"You're a crazy liar," said Urson. Then he scrunched his eyebrows together in thought, and at last shrugged. "Well, anyway, I never heard of one who could hear what you thought. It would make me uncomfortable walking down the street." He dropped his head down and looked at Snake between his legs. "Can you all do that?"

Snake, from the middle bunk, shook his head.

"That makes me feel better," said Urson. "Once we had one on a ship. *Some* captains will take them on. He had a little head, the size of my fist or even smaller. But a great big chest, a huge man in every other way as well. And his eyes and nose and mouth and things weren't on that bald little knob, but on his chest, right here. One day he got into a fight and got his head, if you could call it that, broke right in half with a marlin pin. Bleeding all over himself, he went down to the ship's surgeon, and came up an hour later with the whole thing cut off and a big bandage right where his neck should have been, and his big green eyes blinking out from under his collarbone." Urson stretched out on his back, but then suddenly looked over the edge of the berth toward Geo. "Hey, Geo, what about those little baubles she had. Do you know what they are?"

"No, I don't," Geo said. "But she was concerned over them enough." He looked up over the bunk bottom between himself and Urson. "Snake, will you give me another look at that thing again?"

Snake held out the thong and the jewel.

"Where did you get it?" Urson asked. "Oh, never mind. I guess we learn that when we go to sleep."

Geo reached for it, but Snake's one hand closed and three others sprang around it. "I wasn't going to take it," explained Geo. "I just wanted to see."

Suddenly the door of the forecastle opened, and the tall Mate was silhouetted against the brighter light behind him. "Poet?" he called. "She wants to see you." Then he was gone.

Geo looked at the other two, shrugged, then swung off the berth and made his way up the steps and into the companionway.

On deck it was dark. Stars flecked the heavens, and the only thing to distinguish sea from sky was that the bottom half of the great sphere in which they seemed suspended was light-less. Light fell through a cabin window here and another farther on. Geo paused to look in the first, and then, on distinguishing nothing, went toward the second.

Halfway along, a door before him opened and a blade of illumination sliced the deck. He jumped.

"Come in," summoned the Priestess of Argo. He turned into a windowless cabin and stopped one step beyond the threshold. The walls rippled tapestries, lucent green, scarlet. Golden braziers perched on tapering tripods beneath pale blue smoke that moved into the room, piercing faintly but cleanly into his nostrils like knives. Light lashed the polished wooden newels of a great bed on which silk, damasked satin, and brocade swirled. A huge desk, cornered with wooden eagles, was spread with papers, instruments of cartography, sextants, rules, compasses; great, shabby books were piled on one corner. From the beamed ceiling, hung by thick chains, swayed a branching petrolabra of oil cups, some in the hands of demons or the mouths of monkeys, burning in the bellies of nymphs or between the horns of satyrs' heads, red, clear green, or yellow.

"Come in," repeated the Priestess. "Close the door."

Geo obeyed.

She walked behind her desk, sat down, and folded her hands in front of her veiled face. "Poet," she said, "you have had moments to think. What do you make of this all? What can you tell me of this journey we are about to make that I shall not have to tell you?"

"Only that its importance must be of great concern to Leptar."

"Do you know just how great the concern is?" she asked. "It is great enough to jar every man, woman, and child in Leptar, from the highest priestess to the most deformed Strange One. The world of words and emotions and intellect has been your range till now, Poet. But what do you know of the real world, outside Leptar?"

"That there is much water, some land, and mostly ignorance."

"What tales have you heard from your bear friend, Urson? He is a traveled man and should know some of what there is of the earth."

"The stories of sailors," said Geo, "are menageries of beasts that no one has ever seen, of lands for which no maps exist, and of peoples no man has met."

She smiled. "Since I boarded this ship I have heard many tales from sailors, and I have learned more from them than from all my priests. You, on the docks this evening, have been the only man to give me another scrap of the puzzle except a few drunken seamen misremembering old fantasies." She paused. "What do you know of the jewels you saw tonight?"

"Nothing, ma'am."

"A common thief hiding on the docks has one; I, a priestess

of Argo, possess another; and if you had one, you would probably exchange it for a kiss from some tavern maid. What do you know of the god Hama?"

"I know of no such god."

"You," she said, "who can spout all the rituals and incantations of the White Goddess Argo, you do not even know the name of the Dark God Hama. What do you know of the Island of Aptor?"

"Nothing, ma'am."

"This boat has been to Aptor once and now will return. Ask your ignorant friend the Bear to tell you tales of Aptor; and blind, wise Poet, you will laugh, and probably he will too. But I will tell you: his tales, his legends, and his fantasies are not a tithe of the truth. Perhaps you will be no help after all. I am thinking of dismissing you."

"But, ma'am—"

The Priestess looked up, having been about to fall to some work.

"Ma'am, what can *you* tell me about these things? You have scattered only crumbs. I have extensive knowledge of incantation, poetry, magic, and I know these concern your problem. Give me what information you have, and I will be able to make use of mine in full. I am familiar with many sailors' tales. True, none of Aptor or Hama, but I may be able to collate fragments. I have learned the legends and jargon of thieves through a broad life; this is more than your priests have, I'll wager. I have had teachers who were afraid to touch books I have opened. And I fear no secret you might know. If all of Leptar is in danger, you owe each citizen the right to try to save his brothers. I ask for that right alone."

"No, you are not afraid," admitted the Priestess. "You are honorable and foolish . . . and a poet. I hope the first and last will wipe out the middle one in time. Nevertheless, I will tell you some." She stood up now and drew out a map.

"Here is Leptar." She pointed to one island. Then her finger crossed water to another. "This is Aptor. Now you know as much about it as any ordinary person in Leptar might. It is a barbaric land, uncivilized. Yet they occasionally show some insidious organization. Tell me, what legends of the Great Fire have you heard?"

"I know that beasts are supposed to have come from the sea and destroyed the world's harbors, and that birds spat fire from the air."

"The older sailors," said the Priestess, "will tell you that these were beasts and birds of Aptor. Of course there are fifteen hundred years of retelling and distortion in a tradition never written down, and perhaps Aptor has simply become a synonym for everything evil, but these stories still give you some idea. Chronicles, which only three or four people have had access to, tell me that once, five hundred years ago, the forces of Aptor actually attempted to invade Leptar. The references to the invasion are vague. I do not know how far it went or how successful it was, but its methods were insidious and unlike any invasion you may have read of in history, so unlike that records of it were destroyed and no mention of it is made in the histories given to schoolchildren.

"Only recently have I had chance to learn how strange and inhuman they were. And I have good reason to believe that the forces of Aptor are congealing once more, a sluggish but huge amoeba of horror. Once fully awake, once launched, it will be unstoppable. Tendrils have reached into us for the past few years, have probed, and then have been withdrawn before they were recognized. Sometimes they dealt catastrophic blows to the center of Leptar's government and religion. All this has been assiduously kept from the people. For if it were made known, we would also have to reveal how staggering our ignorance is, and there would be a national paralysis. I have been sent to clear perhaps just one more veil from the unknown. And if you can help me in that, you are welcome more than I could possibly express."

"What of the jewels and of Hama?" inquired Geo. "Is he a

god of Aptor under whom these forces are being marshaled? And are these jewels sacred to him in some way?"

"Both are true, and both are not true enough," replied the Priestess.

"And one more thing. You say the last attempted invasion by Aptor into Leptar was five hundred years ago. It was five hundred years ago that the religion of Argo in Leptar purged all her rituals and instituted new ones. Was there some connection between the invasion and the purge?"

"I am sure of it," declared the Priestess. "But I do not know what it is. However, let me now tell you the story of the jewels. The one I wear at my neck was captured somehow from Aptor during that first invasion. That we captured it may well be the reason that we are still a free nation today. Since then it has been guarded carefully in the Temple of the Goddess Argo, its secrets well protected, along with those few chronicles that mention the invasion—which ended, incidentally, only a month before the purges. Then about a year ago, a small horde of horror reached our shore from Aptor. I cannot describe it. I did not see any of what transpired. But they made their way inland and managed to kidnap Argo herself."

"You mean Argo Incarnate? The highest priestess?"

"Yes. Each generation, as you know, the first daughter of the past generation's highest priestess is chosen as the living incarnation of the White Goddess Argo. She is reared and taught by the wisest priests and priestesses. She is given every luxury, every bit of devotion; and she is made Argo Incarnate until she marries and has daughters. And so it is passed on. At any rate, she was kidnapped. One of the assailants was hacked down: instantly it decayed, rotted on the floor of the convent corridor. But from the putrescent mass of flesh, we salvaged a second jewel from Aptor. And before it died, it was heard to utter the lines I quoted to you before. So I have been sent to find what I can of the enemy, and to rescue or find the fate of our young Argo."

"I will do whatever I can," said Geo, "to help save Leptar and to discover the whereabouts of your sister priestess."

"Not my sister," said the woman softly, "my daughter in blood, as I am the daughter of the last Argo: that is why this task fell to me. And until she is found dead or returned alive"—there she rose from her bench—"I am again the White Goddess Argo Incarnate."

Geo dropped his eyes as Argo lifted her veil. Once more that evening she held forth the jewel. "There are three of these," she said. "Hama's sign is a black disk with three white eyes. Each eye represents a jewel. With the first invasion, they probably carried all three jewels, for the jewels are the center of their power. Without them, they would have been turned back immediately. With them, they thought themselves invincible. But we captured one and very soon unlocked its secrets. I have no guards with me. With this jewel I need none. I am as safe as I would be with an army, and capable of nearly as much destruction.

"When they came to kidnap my daughter a year ago, I am convinced they carried both of their remaining jewels, thinking that we had either lost or did not know the power of the first. Anyway, they reasoned, they had two to our one. But now we have two, and they are left with only one. Through some complete carelessness, your little thief stole one from me as I was about to board when we first departed two months ago. Today he probably recognized me and intended to exact some fee for its return. But now he will be put to a true thief's task. He must steal for me the third and final jewel from Hama. Then we shall have Aptor and be rid of their evil."

"And where is this third jewel?" asked Geo.

"Perhaps," said the woman, "perhaps it is lodged in the forehead of the statue of the Dark God Hama that sits in the guarded palace somewhere in the center of the jungles of Aptor. Do you think your thief will find himself challenged?"

"I think so," answered Geo.

"Somewhere in that same palace is my daughter, or her remains. You are to find them, and if she is alive, bring her back with you."

"And what of the jewels?" asked Geo. "When will you show

us their power so that we may use them to penetrate the palace of Hama?"

"I will show you their power," said Argo, smiling. With one hand she held up the map over which she had spoken. With the other she tapped the white jewel with her pale fingernail. The map suddenly blackened at one edge, flared. Argo walked to a brazier and deposited the flaming paper. Then she turned once more to Geo. "I can fog the brain of a single person, as I did with Snake, or I can bewilder a hundred men. As easily as I can fire a dried, worn map, I can raze a city."

Geo smiled. "With those to help, I think we have a fair chance to reach this Hama and return."

But the smile with which she answered his was strange, and then it was gone. "Do you think," she said, "that I would put such temptation in your hands? You might be captured, and if so, then the jewels would be in the hands of Aptor once more."

"But with them we would be so powerful—"

"They have been captured once; we cannot take the chance that they be captured again. *If* you can reach the palace, *if* you can steal the third jewel, *if* my daughter is alive and *if* you can rescue her, then she will know how to employ its power to manipulate your escape. However, if you and your friends do not accomplish *all* these things, the trip will be useless; and so perhaps death would be better than a return to watch the wrath of Argo in her dying struggle, for you would feel it more horribly than even the most malicious torture of Aptor's evil."

Geo did not speak.

"Why do you look so strange?" asked Argo. "You have your poetry, your spells, your scholarship. Don't you believe in their power? Go back to your berth. Send the thief to me." The last words were a sharp order, and Geo turned from the room into the dark. The sudden chill cleared the inside of his nostrils, and he stopped to look back at the door, then out to sea. A moment later he was hurrying to the forecastle.

chapter three

Geo walked down into the bunk room, still deserted except for Urson and Snake.

"Well?" asked Urson, sitting up on the edge of his berth. "What did she tell you?"

"Why aren't you asleep?" Geo said heavily. He touched Snake on the shoulder. "She wants to see you now."

Snake stood up, started for the door, then turned back.

"What is it?" Geo asked.

Snake dug into his clout again and pulled out the thong with the jewel. He walked over to Geo, hesitated, then placed the thong around the poet's neck.

"You want me to keep it for you?" Geo asked.

But Snake turned and was gone.

"Well," said Urson. "So you have one for yourself now. I wonder what they do. Or did you find out? Come on, Geo, give up what she told you."

"Did Snake say anything to you while I was out?"

"Not a peep," answered Urson. "And I came no nearer sleep than I came to the moon. Now come on, what's this about?"

Geo told him.

When he finished, Urson said, "You're crazy. You and her. You're both crazy."

"I don't think so," Geo said. He concluded his story by recounting Argo's demonstration of the jewel's power.

Urson fingered the stone up from Geo's chest and looked at it. "All that in this little thing. Tell me, do you think you can figure out how it works?"

"I don't know if I want to," Geo said. "It doesn't sound right."

"Damn straight it doesn't sound right," Urson reiterated. "What's the point of sending us in there with no protection to do something that would be crazy with a whole army? What's she got against *us*?"

"I don't think she has anything against us," Geo said. "Urson, what stories do you know about Aptor? She said you might be able to tell me something."

"I know that no one trades with it, everyone curses by it, and the rest is a lot of rubbish not worth saying."

"Such as?"

"Believe me, it's just bilge water," insisted Urson. "Do you think you could figure out that little stone there, if you had long enough, I mean? She said that the priests five hundred years ago could, and she seems to think you're as smart as some of them. I wouldn't doubt you could work it."

"You tell me some stories first," said Geo.

"They talk about cannibals, women who drink blood, things neither man nor animal, and cities inhabited only by death. I'm fairly sure it's not what you'd call a friendly place the way sailors avoid it, save to curse by; still, most of what they say is silly."

"Do you know anything more than that?"

"There's nothing more to know." Urson shrugged. "Every human ill there is at one time or another has been said to come from Aptor, whether it's the monsters that brought the Great Fire, or dandruff. I've never been there and I've never wanted to go. But I'll welcome the chance to see it so that on my next trip I can stop some of the stupid babble that's always springing up about it."

"She said the stories you'd tell would not be one tenth of the truth."

"She must have meant that there wasn't even a tenth part of the truth in them. And I'm sure she's right. You just misunderstood."

"I heard her correctly," Geo assured him.

"Then I just don't believe it. There are half a dozen things that don't match up in all this. First, how that four-armed fellow happened to be at the pier after two months just when she was coming in. And to have the jewel still, not have traded it or sold it already—"

"Maybe," suggested Geo, "he read her mind too when he first stole it, the same way he read ours."

"And if he did, maybe he knows how to work the things. I say let's find out when he comes back. And I wonder who cut his tongue out. Strange One or not, that makes me sick," grunted the big man.

"About that," Geo started. "Don't you remember? He said you knew the man it was."

"I know many men," said Urson, "but which one of the many I know is it?"

"You really don't know?" Geo asked.

"You say that in a strange way," Urson frowned.

"I'll say the same thing he said," Geo went on. "What man did you kill? I just can't understand the reason. . . ."

Urson looked at his hands awhile, stretched his fingers, turned them over in his lap, examining them. Then, without looking up, he said, "It was a long time ago, friend, but the closeness of it shivers in my eyes. I should have told you, yes. But it comes to me sometimes, not like a memory, but like something I can feel, as hard as metal, taste it as sharp as salt, and the wind brings back my voice, his words, so that I shake like a mirror where the figure on the inside pounds his fists on the fists of the man outside, each one trying to break free.

"We were reefing sails in a flesh-blistering rain when it began. His name was Cat. The two of us were the two biggest men aboard, and that we had been put on the reefing team together meant this was an important job to be done right. Water washed our eyes; our hands slipped on wet ropes. It was no wonder my sail suddenly flung from me in a gust, billowing down in the rain, flapping against a half-dozen ropes and breaking two small stays. 'You clumsy bastard,' bawled the Mate from the deck. 'What sort of fish-fingered son of a bitch are you?'

"And through the rain I heard Cat laugh from his own spar.

'That's the way luck goes,' he cried, catching at his own cloth, which threatened to pull loose. I pulled mine in and bound her tight. The competition that should go rightly between two fine sailors drove a seed of fury into my flesh that should have bloomed as a curse or a return gibe, but the rain rained too hard and the wind roared too loud, so I bound my sail in silence.

"I was last down, of course, and as I was coming—there were men on deck—I saw why my sail had come loose. A worn mast-ring had broken and caused a main rope to fly and my canvas to come tumbling. But the ring also had held the nearly split aft mast together, and in the wind, a crack twice the length of my arm pulled open and snapped to, again and again, like a child's noise clapper. There was a rope—a near, inch-thick line—coiled on a spike. Holding myself to a ratline mostly by my toes, I secured it and bound the base of the broken pole. Each time it snapped to, I looped it once around and pulled the wet line tight. They call this whipping a mast, and I whipped it till the collar of rope was three feet long to the top of the cleft and she couldn't snap anymore. Then I hung the broken ring on a peg nearby so I could point it out to the ship's smith and get him to replace the rope with metal bands.

"That evening at mess, with the day's incidents out of my mind and hot soup in my mouth, I was laughing over some sailor's tale about another sailor and another sailor's woman when the Mate strode into the hall. 'Hey, you sea scoundrels,' he bellowed. There was silence. 'Which of you bound up that broken mast aft?'

"I was about to call out, 'Aye, it was me,' when another man beat me by bawling, 'It was the Big Sailor, sir!' That was a name both Cat and me were often hailed by.

"'Well,' snarled the Mate, 'the Captain says that such good thinking in times hard as these should be rewarded.' He took a gold coin from his pocket and tossed it on the table in front of Cat. 'There you go, Big fellow. But I think it's as much as any man should do.' Then he clomped from the mess hall. A cheer went up for Cat as he pocketed the coin; I couldn't see his face.

"The anger in me started now, but without direction. Should it go to the sailor who'd called out the name of the hero? Naw, for he had been down on deck, and through rain and darkness he probably could not have told me from my rival, anyway, at that distance. At Cat? But he was already getting up to leave the table. At the First Mate, the same First Mate of this ship, friend, that we're on now? But Jordde was out stomping somewhere on deck.

"Perhaps it was this that caused my anger to break out the next morning when we were in calmer weather. A careless salt jarred me in a passageway, and suddenly I was all fists and fire. We scuffled, pounded each other; we cursed, we rolled: we rolled right under the feet of the Mate, who was coming down the steps at the time. He sent a boot into us and a lot of curses, and when he recognized me, he sneered, 'Oh, the clumsy one.'

"Now, I'd had a fiery record before. Fights on ship are a breach few captains will allow. This was my third, and one too many. And Jordde, prompted by his own opinion of me, got the Captain to order me flogged.

"So, like meat to be sliced and bid on, I was led out before the assembled sailors at the next sunrise and bound to the mast. I thought my wrath went all toward the First Mate now. But black turned white in my head, hard as something to bite into, when he flung the whip to Cat and cried, 'Here, Cat, you've done your ship one good turn. Now rub sleep off your face and do it another. I want ten stripes on this one's back deep enough to count easily with a finger dipped in salt.'

"They fell, and I didn't breathe the whole time. Ten lashes is a whipping a man can recover from in a week. Most go down to their knees with the first one, if the rope is slack enough. I didn't fall until they finally cut the ropes from my wrists. Nor was it till I heard a second gold coin rattle down on the deck from the First Mate's hand and the words to the crew, 'See how a good sailor gets rich,' that I made a sound. And it was lost in the cheer that sprang from the other men.

"Cat and one other lugged me to the brig. As I fell forward, hands scudding into straw, I heard Cat's voice: 'Well, brother, that's the way luck goes.'

"Then the pain made me faint.

"A day later, when I could pull myself up to the window bars and look out on the back deck, we caught the worst storm I'd ever seen. The slices in my back made it no easier. Pegs threatened to pull from their holes, boards to part themselves; one wave washed four men overboard, and while others ran to save them, another came and swept off six more. The storm had come so suddenly not a sail had been rolled, and now the remaining men were swarming the ratlines.

"From my place at the brig's window I saw the mast start to go and I howled like an animal, tried to pull the bars away. But legs passed my window running, and none stopped. I screamed at them, and I screamed again. The ship's smith had not yet gotten to fix my makeshift repair on the aft mast with metal. Nor had I yet even pointed it out to him as I had intended. It didn't hold ten minutes. When it gave, its breakage was like thunder. Under the tug of half-furled sails, ropes popped like thread. Men were whipped off like drops of water shaken from a wet hand. The mast raked across the sky like a claw then fell against the high mizzen, snapping more ropes and scraping men from their perches as you'd scrape ants from a twig. The crew's number was halved, and when somehow we crawled from under the frayed fabric, one mast fallen and one more ruined, the broken bodies with still some life numbered eleven. A ship's infirmary holds ten, and the overflow goes to the brig. The choice of who became my mate was between the man most likely to live—he might take the harder situation more easily than the others—and the man most likely to die—it would probably make no difference to someone that far gone. The choice was made for the sicker one, and the next morning they carried Cat in and laid him beside me on the straw while I slept. His spine had been crushed at the pelvis and a spar had pierced his side with a hole big enough to put your hand into.

"When he came to, all he did was cry—not with the agonized

howls I had given the day before when I watched the mast topple, but with a little sound that escaped from clenched teeth, like a child who doesn't want to show the pain. It didn't stop. For hours. And such a soft sound, it burned into me deeper than any animal's wail.

"The next dawn stretched copper foil across the window, and red light fell on the straw and the filthy blanket they had laid him in. The crying had been replaced now by gasps, sharp every few seconds, irregular, and . . . so loud. I thought he must be unconscious, but when I kneeled to look, his eyes were opened and he stared into my face. 'You . . .' he rasped at me. 'It hurts. . . . You . . .'

" 'Be still,' I said. 'Here, be still!'

"The next word I thought I heard was 'water,' but there wasn't any in the cell. I should have realized that the ship's supplies had probably gone for the most part overboard. But by now, hungry and thirsty myself, I could see it as nothing less than a stupendous joke when one slice of bread and a tin cup of water were finally brought and with embarrassed silence handed in to us that morning at sunrise.

"Nevertheless, I opened his mouth and tried to pour some of it down his throat. They say a man's lips and tongue turn black from fever and thirst after a while. It's not true. The color is the deep purple of rotten meat. And every taste bud was tipped with that white stuff that gets in your mouth when your bowels stick for a couple of days. He couldn't swallow the water. It just dribbled over the side of his mouth that was scabby with crust.

"He blinked and once more got out, 'You . . . you please . . .' Then he began to cry again.

" 'What is it?' I asked.

"Suddenly he began to struggle and got his hand into the breast of his torn shirt and pulled out a fist. He held it out toward me and said, 'Please . . . please . . .'

"The fingers opened and I saw three gold coins, two of whose histories suddenly returned to my mind like the stories of living men.

"I moved back as if burned, then leaned forward again. 'What do you want?' I asked.

" 'Please . . .' he said, moving his hand toward me. 'Kill . . . kill . . . me,' and then he was crying once more. 'It hurts so. . . . '

"I got up. I walked across to the other side of the cell. I came back. Then I broke his neck with my hands.

"I took up my pay. Later I ate the bread and drank the rest of the water. Then I went to sleep. They took him away without question. And two days later when the next food came, I realized absently that without the bread and water I would have starved to death. They finally let me out because they needed my muscle, what was left of it. And the only thing I sometimes think about, the only thing I let myself think about, is whether or not I earned my pay. I guess two of them were mine anyway. But sometimes I take them out and look at them and wonder where he got the third one from." Urson put his hand in his shirt and brought out three gold coins. "Never been able to spend them, though," he said. He tossed the pile into the air and then whipped them from their arc into his fist again. He laughed. "Never been able to spend them on anything."

"I'm sorry," Geo said after a moment.

Urson looked up. "Why? I guess these are my jewels, yes? Maybe everyone has theirs someplace. You think it was old Cat, sometime when I was in the brig, perhaps, earning that third coin, slicing out that little four-armed bastard's tongue? Somehow I doubt it."

"Look, I said I was sorry, Urson."

"I know," Urson said. "I know. I guess I've met a hell full of people in my wet windy life, but it could be any one of them." He sighed. "Though I wish I knew who. Still, I don't think that's the answer." He lifted his hand to his mouth and gnawed at his little fingernail. "I hope that kid doesn't get as nervous as I do." He laughed. "He'll have such a hell of a lot of nails to bite."

Then their skulls split.

"Hey," said Geo, "that's Snake!"

"And he's in trouble too!" Urson leaped to the floor and started up the passageway. Geo came after him.

"Let me go first!" Geo said, "I know where he is."

They reached the deck, raced beside the cabins.

"Move," ordered Urson. Then he heaved himself against the door: it flew open.

Inside, behind her desk, Argo whirled, her hand on her jewel. "What is the—"

But the moment her concentration turned, Snake, who had been immobile against the opposite wall, vaulted across the bench toward Geo. Geo grabbed the boy to steady him, and immediately one of Snake's hands was at Geo's chest, where the jewel hung.

"You fools!" hissed Argo. "Don't you understand? He's a spy for Aptor!"

There was silence.

Argo said, "Close the door."

Urson closed it. Snake still held Geo and the jewel.

"Well," she said, "it is too late now."

"What do you mean?" asked Geo.

"That had you not come blundering in, one more of Aptor's spies would have yielded up his secrets and then been reduced to ashes." She breathed deeply. "But he has his jewel now and I have mine. Well, little thief, here's a stalemate. The forces are balanced now." She looked at Geo. "How do you think he came so easily by the jewel? How do you think he knew when I would be at the shore? Oh, he's clever indeed, with all the intelligence of Aptor working behind him. He probably even had you planted without your knowing it to interrupt us at just that time."

"No, he—" began Urson.

"We were walking by your door," Geo interrupted, "when we heard a noise and thought there might be trouble."

"Your concern may have cost us all our lives."

"If he's a spy, I gather that means he knows how this thing works," said Geo. "Let Urson and me take him."

"Take him anywhere you wish!" hissed Argo. "Get out!"

Then the door opened. "I heard a sound, Priestess Argo, and I thought you might be in danger." It was Jordde, the First Mate.

The Goddess Incarnate breathed deeply. "I am in no danger," she said evenly. "Will you please leave me alone, all of you?"

"What's the Snake doing here?" Jordde suddenly asked, seeing Geo and the boy.

"I said, leave me!"

Geo turned away from Jordde and stepped past him onto the deck, and Urson followed him. Ten steps farther on, he glanced back, and seeing that Jordde had emerged from the cabin and was walking in the other direction, he set Snake down on his feet. "All right, Little One. March!"

Once in the passage to the forecastle, Urson asked, "Hey, what's going on?"

"Well, for one thing, our little friend here is no spy."

"How do you know?" asked Urson.

"Because she doesn't know he can read minds."

"How do you mean?" Urson asked.

"I was beginning to think something was wrong when I came back from talking to the Priestess. You were too, and it lay in the same vein you were talking about. Why would our task be completely useless unless we accomplished all parts of her mission? Wouldn't there be some value in just returning her daughter, the rightful head of Leptar, to her former position? And I'm sure her daughter may well have collected some useful information that could be used against Aptor, so that would be some value even if we didn't find the jewel. It doesn't sound too maternal to me to forsake the young priestess if there's no jewel in it for mother. And her tone, the way she refers to the jewel as *hers*. There's an old saying, from before the Great Fire even: 'Power corrupts, and absolute power corrupts absolutely.' And I think she has not a little of the un-goddess-like desire for power first, peace afterwards."

"But that doesn't mean this one here isn't a spy for Aptor," said Urson.

"Wait a minute. I'm getting there. You see, I thought he was too. The idea occurred to me first when I was talking to the Priestess and she mentioned that there were spies from Aptor. The coincidence of his appearance, that he had even managed to steal the jewel in the first place, that he would present it to her the way he did: all this hinted at something so strange that 'spy' was the first thing I thought of, and she thought so as well. But she did not know that Snake could read minds and broadcast mentally. Don't you see? Ignorance of his telepathy removes the one other possible explanation of the coincidence. Urson, why did he leave the jewel with us before he went to see her?"

"Because he thought she was going to try and take it away from him."

"Exactly. When she told me to send him to her, I was sure that was the reason she wanted him. But if he was a spy and knew how to work the jewel, then why not take it with him, present himself to Argo with the jewel, showing himself as an equal force, and then come calmly back, leaving her in silence and us still on his side, especially since he would be revealing to her something of which she was nine tenths aware already, and she would watch him no less carefully than if it were unconfirmed."

"All right," said Urson, "why not?"

"Because he was *not* a spy and didn't know how to work the jewel. Yes, he had felt its power once. Perhaps he was going to pretend he had it hidden on his person. But he did not want her to get her hands on it for reasons that were strong but not selfish. Here, Snake," said Geo. "You now know how to work the jewel, don't you? But you just learned how from Argo."

The boy nodded.

"Here, then. Why don't you take it?" Geo lifted the jewel from his neck and held it out to him.

Snake drew back and shook his head violently.

"As I thought."

Urson looked puzzled.

"Snake has seen into human minds, Urson. He's seen things directly that the rest of us learn only from a sort of secondhand observation. He knows that the power of this little bead is more dangerous to the mind of the person who wields it than it is to the cities it may destroy."

"Well," said Urson, "as long as she thinks he's a spy, at least we'll have one of them little beads and someone who knows how to use it. . . . I mean if we have to."

"I don't think she thinks he's a spy anymore, Urson."

"Huh?"

"I give her credit for being able to reason at least as well as I can. Once she found out he had no jewel on him, she knew that he was as innocent as you and I. But her only thought was to get it any way she could. When we came in, just when she was going to put Snake under the jewel's control, guilt made her leap backward to her first and seemingly logical accusation for our benefit. Evil likes to cloak itself as good."

They stepped down into the forecastle. By now a handful of sailors had come into the room. Most were drunk and snoring on berths around the walls. One had wrapped himself completely up in a blanket in the middle berth of the tier that Urson had chosen for Snake. "Well," said Urson, "it looks like you'll have to move."

Snake scrambled to the top bunk.

"Now, look, that one was mine!"

Snake motioned him up.

"Huh? Two of us in one of those?" demanded Urson. "Look, if you want someone to keep warm against, go down and sleep with Geo there. It's more room and you won't get squashed against the wall. I'm a thrasher—and I snore."

Snake didn't move.

"Maybe you better do what he says," Geo said. "I have an idea that—"

"You've got another idea now?" asked Urson. "Damn it. I'm too tired to argue." He stretched out, and Snake's slight body was completely hidden. "Hey, get your elbows out of there," Geo heard Urson mutter before there was only the gentle thundering of his breath. . . .

—*Mist suffused the deck and wet lines glowed phosphorescent silver; the sky was pale as ice, yet pricks of stars still dotted the bowl. The sea, once green, had bleached to blowing white. The door of the windowless cabin opened and white veils flung forward from the form of Argo, who emerged like silver from the ash-colored door. The movement of the scene seemed to happen in the rippling of gauze under breeze. A dark spot, like a burn on a photograph negative, at her throat pulsed like a heart, like a black flame. She walked to the railing, peered over. In the white washing a skeletal hand appeared. It rose up on a beckoning arm and then fell forward in the water. Another arm rose now, a few feet away, beckoning, gesturing. Then three at once; then two more.*

A voice as pale as the vision spoke: I am coming. I am coming. We sail in an hour. The Mate has been ordered to put the ship out before dawn. You must tell me now, creatures of the water. You must tell me.

Two glowing arms rose now, and then a blurred face. Chest high in the water, the figure listed backward and sank.

Are you of Aptor or Leptar? *demanded the apparitional figure of Argo again in the thinned voice.* Are your allegiances to Argo or Hama? I have followed thus far. You must tell me before I follow further.

There was a whirling of sound which seemed to be the wind attempting to say: The sea . . . the sea . . . the sea . . .

But Argo did not hear, for she turned away and walked from the rail, back to her cabin.

Now the scene moved, turned toward the door of the forecastle. It opened, moved through the hall, more like birch and sycamore bark than stained oak, and went on. In the forecastle, the oil lamp seemed rather a flaring of magnesium.

The movement stopped in front of a tier of three berths. On the bottom one lay Geo! But Geo with a starved, pallid face. His mop of hair was bleached white. On his chest was a pulsing darkness, a flame, a heart shimmering with the indistinctness of absolute black. On the top bunk a great form like a bloated corpse lay. Urson! One huge arm hung over the bunk, flabbed, puffy, with no hint of strength.

In the center berth was an anonymous bundle of blankets completely covering the figure inside. On this the scene fixed, drew closer; and the paleness suddenly faded into shadow, into nothing. . . .

Geo sat up and knuckled his eyes.

The dark was relieved by lamp glow. Looking from under the berth above, he saw the gaunt Mate standing across the room. "Hey, you," Jordde was saying to a man in one of the other bunks, "up and out. We're sailing."

The figure roused itself from the tangle of bedding.

The Mate moved to another. "Up, you dogface! Up, you fish fodder! We're sailing." Turning around, he saw Geo watching him. "And what's wrong with you?" he demanded. "We're sailing, didn't you hear? Naw, you go back to sleep. Your turn will come, but we need experienced ones now." He grinned briefly and then went to one more. "Eh, you stink like an old wine cask! Raise yourself out of your fumes! We're sailing!"

chapter four

That dream . . ." Geo said to Urson a moment after the Mate left.

Urson looked down from his bunk.

"You had it too?"

Both turned to Snake. "I guess that was your doing, eh?" Urson said.

Snake scrambled down from the upper berth.

"Did you go wandering around the deck last night and do some spying?" Geo asked.

By now most of the other sailors had risen, and one suddenly stepped between Urson and Geo. "'Scuse me, mate," he said and shook the figure in the second berth. "Hey, Whitey, come on. You can't be that soused from last night. Get up or you'll miss the mess." The young Negro sailor shook the figure again. "Hey, Whitey . . ." The figure in the blankets was unresponsive. The sailor gave him one more good shake, and as the figure rolled over, the blanket fell away from the blond head. The eyes were wide and dull; the mouth hung open. "Hey, Whitey!" the black sailor said again. Then slowly he stepped back.

Mist enveloped the ship three hours out from port. Urson was called for duty right after breakfast, but no one bothered either Snake or Geo that first morning. Snake slipped off somewhere and Geo was left to wander the ship alone. He was walking beneath the dories when the heavy slap of bare feet on the wet deck materialized into Urson.

"Hey." The giant grinned. "What are you doing under here?"

"Nothing much," Geo said.

Urson was carrying a coil of rope about his shoulder. Now he slung it down into his hand, leaned against the support shaft, and looked out into the fog. "It's a bad beginning this trip has had. What few sailors I've talked to don't like it at all."

"Urson," asked Geo, "have you any ideas on what actually happened this morning?"

"Maybe I have and maybe I haven't," Urson said. "What ones have you?"

"Do you remember the dream?"

Urson scrunched his shoulders as if suddenly cold. "I do."

"It was like we were seeing through somebody else's eyes, almost."

"Our little four-armed friend sees things in a strange way, if that's the case."

"Urson, that wasn't Snake's eyes we saw through. I asked him, just before he went off exploring the ship. It was somebody else. All he did was get the pictures and relay them into our minds. And what was the last thing you saw?"

"As a matter of fact," Urson said, turning, "I think he was looking at poor Whitey's bunk."

"And who was supposed to be sleeping in poor Whitey's bunk?"

"Snake?"

"Exactly. Do you think perhaps Whitey was killed instead of Snake?"

"Could be, I guess. But how and why and who?"

"Somebody who wanted Snake killed. Maybe the same person who cut his tongue out a year and a half ago."

"I thought we decided that we didn't know who that was."

"A man you know, Urson," Geo said. "What man on this ship have you sailed with before?"

"Don't you think I've been looking?" Urson asked. "There's not a familiar face on deck, other than maybe one I've seen in a dockside bar, but never one whose name I've known."

"Think, Urson, who on this ship you've sailed with before," Geo repeated, more intently.

"Jordde!" Suddenly Urson turned. "You mean the Mate?"

"That's just who I mean," said Geo.

"And you think he tried to kill Snake? Why didn't Snake tell us?"

"Because he thought if we knew, we'd get in trouble with it. And he may be right."

"How come?" asked Urson.

"Look, we know something is fishy about Argo. The more I think about it, the less I can put my hands on it. But if something is fishy about the Mate too, then perhaps he's in cahoots with her. What about when he came into Argo's cabin last night when we were there?"

"Maybe he was just doing what we said we had been: walking by when he heard a noise. If it was his eyes we were seeing through, then he sees things awfully funny."

"Maybe he's a Strange One too, like Snake, who 'hears' things funny. Not all strangeness shows," Geo reminded him.

"You could be right. You could be right." He stood up from the lifeboat support. "Well, I've got something to do and can't stand here all day. You think some more, friend, and I'll be willing to listen. I'll see you later." He hauled up his rope again and started off in the mist.

Geo looked around him and decided to search for Snake. A ladder led to the upper deck; climbing it, he saw across the boards a tall, fog-shrouded figure. He paused and then started forward. "Hello," he said.

The Captain turned from the railing.

"Good morning, sir," Geo said. "I thought you might be the Mate."

The Captain was silent for a while and then said, "Good morning. What do you want?"

"I didn't mean to disturb you if you were—"

"No disturbance."

"How long will it take us to get to Aptor?"

"Another two weeks and a half. Shorter if this wind keeps up."

"I see," said Geo. "Have you any idea of the geography of Aptor?"

"The Mate is the only one onboard who has ever set foot on Aptor and come off it alive. Except Priestess Argo."

"The Mate, sir? When?"

"On a previous voyage he was wrecked there. But he made a raft and drifted into the open sea, where he had the good fortune to be picked up in a ship."

"Then he will lead whatever party goes to the place?"

"Not him," said the Captain. "He's sworn never to set foot on the place again. Don't even ask him to talk about it. Imagine what sort of a place it must be if probable death on the water is better than struggling on its land. No, he'll pilot us through the bay to the river's estuary, but other than that, he will have nothing to do with the place.

"Two other men we had onboard who'd been there and returned. They went with the Priestess Argo in a boat of thirteen. Ten were dismembered and the pieces of their bodies were thrown in the water. Two survived to row the Priestess back to the boat. One was the sailor called Whitey, who died in the forecastle this morning. Not half an hour ago, I received news that the other one went overboard from the rigging and was lost in the sea. This is not a good trip. Men are not to be lost like coins in a game. Life is too valuable."

"I see," said Geo. "Thank you for your information and time, sir."

"You are welcome," the Captain said. Then he turned away.

Geo descended the ladder and walked slowly along the deck. Something touched him on the shoulder; he whirled.

"Snake, goddamn it, don't do that!"

The boy looked embarrassed.

"I didn't mean to yell," Geo said, putting his hand on the boy's shoulder. "Come on, though. What did you find? I'll trade you what I know for what you do."

You . . . sleep . . . came from Snake.

"I'm sorry, friend," laughed Geo. "But I couldn't take a nap now for money. You're just going to have to 'yell' yourself hoarse and answer some fairly direct questions. And whether knowing the answer is going to get me in trouble or not, you answer right. First of all, whose eyes were we seeing through last night? The Captain's?"

Snake shook his head.

"The Mate's?"

Snake nodded.

"Thought so. Now, did he want to kill . . . wait a minute," said Geo. "Can the Mate read minds too? Is that why you're keeping things from us?"

Snake shrugged.

"Come on now," Geo said. "Do a little yelling and explain."

Don't . . . know . . . Snake thought out loud. *Can . . . see . . . what . . . he . . . sees . . . hear . . . what . . . he . . . hears . . . but . . . no . . . hear . . . thoughts . . .*

"I see. Look, take a chance that he can't read minds and tell me. Did he kill the man in the bed you should have been in?"

Snake paused for a minute. Then nodded.

"Do you think he was trying to kill you?"

Snake nodded again.

"Now, one other thing. Did you know that the man who was killed this morning in your place was one of the two men who came back from Aptor with the Priestess Argo on her last expedition?"

Snake looked surprised.

"And that the other one drowned this morning, fell overboard and was lost?"

Snake jumped.

"What is it?"

Look . . . for . . . him . . . all . . . morning . . . He . . . not . . . dead . . . hear . . . thoughts . . . dim . . . low . . .

"Who's not dead?" Geo asked. "Which one?"

Second . . . man.

"Did you find him?" Geo asked.

Can't . . . find . . . Snake said, *but . . . alive . . . I . . . know . . .*

"One other question." Geo lifted the jewel from against his chest. "How do you work this silly thing?"

Think . . . through . . . it . . . said Snake.

Geo frowned. "What do you mean? Can you tell me how it works?"

You . . . have . . . no . . . words . . . Snake said. *Radio . . . electricity . . . diode . . .*

"Radio, electricity, diode?" repeated Geo, the sounds coming unfamiliarly to his tongue. "What are they?"

Snake shrugged.

Thirty feet in front of them the door to Argo's cabin opened, and the veiled Priestess stepped out. She saw them, and at once her hand rose to her throat. Then it dropped. Snake and Geo were still.

Above, on the deck that topped the cabins, the dim form of the Mate was distinguishable; but Geo could not tell whether Jordde was watching them or had his back to them.

The Priestess paused and then returned to her room.

And the Mate walked away from the rail.

Geo got a chance to report his findings to Urson that evening. The big sailor was puzzled.

"Can't you add anything?" Geo asked.

"All I've had a chance to do is work," grumbled Urson. They were standing by the rail, beyond which the mist steeped thickly, making sky and water indistinguishable and grave. "Hey, Four Arms," Urson asked suddenly, "what are you looking at?"

Snake stared at the water but said nothing.

"Maybe he's listening to something," suggested Geo.

"You'd think there were better things to eavesdrop on than fishes," said Urson. "I guess Argo's given special orders that you two get no work. *Some* people. Let's go eat." As they started toward the convergence of sailors at the entrance of the mess hall, Urson paused. "Oh, guess what." He picked up the jewel from Geo's chest. "All you people are going around with such finery, I took my coins to the smithy and had him put chains on them. Now I'll strut with the best of you." He laughed as they went through the narrow way, crowding with the other sailors into the wide hall.

Night without dreams left them early, and the boat rolled from beneath the fog. Dawn was gray but clear; by breakfast-time a ragged slip of land hemmed the horizon. Halfway through the meal, water was splashing from the brims of pitchers to roll one way, darkening the wooden table; then as the boat heaved, it rolled another.

On the wheel-deck the sailors clustered at the rail. Before them, rocks stuck like broken teeth from the water.

In his new triple necklace, Urson joined Snake and Geo. "Whew! Getting through them is going to be fun."

Suddenly heads turned. The sailors looked back as Argo's dark veils, bloated with the breeze, filled about her as she mounted the steps to the wheel-deck. Slowly she walked among the sailors. They moved away. She stopped, one hand on a stay-rope, to stare across the water at the dark tongue of land.

From the wheel the Captain spoke: "Jordde, disperse the men and take the wheel."

"Aye, sir," said the Mate. "You, you, and you to the tops." He pointed among the men. "You also, and you. Hey, didn't you hear me?"

"Me, sir?" Geo turned.

"Yes, you—up to the top spar there."

"You can't send him up!" Urson called out. "He's never been topside at all before. It's too choppy for any fellow's first time up. He doesn't even know—"

"And who asked you?" demanded the Mate.

"Nobody asked me, sir," said Urson, "but—"

"Then you get below before I brig you for insubordination and fine you your three gold baubles. You think I don't recognize dead man's gold?"

"Now look here!" Urson roared.

Geo looked from Argo to the Captain. The Captain was

puzzled, true; but the bewilderment that flooded the face of the Priestess shocked him.

Jordde suddenly seized up a marlin pin, raised it, and shouted at Urson: "Get down below before I break your skull!"

Urson's fists sprang up.

"Calmly, brother bear—" Geo began.

"In a bitch's ass," snarled Urson and swung his arm forward. Something leaped on Jordde from behind—Snake! The belaying pin veered inches away from Urson's shoulder. The flung fist sank into the Mate's belly and he reeled forward, with Snake still clawing at his back. He reached the rail, bent double over it, and Snake's legs flipped. When Jordde rose, he was free of encumbrance.

Geo rushed to the rail and saw Snake's head emerge in the churning water. Behind him, Urson yelled, "Look out!" Geo dodged aside as Jordde's spike made three inches of splinters in the plank against which he had been leaning.

"Not him!" cried Argo. "No, no! Not him!"

But Jordde seized Geo's shoulder and whirled him back against the rail. Geo saw Urson grab a hanging rope and swing forward. Urson tried to knock Jordde away with his feet. But Argo moved in the way of his flying body and raised her hands to push him aside so that he swung wide and landed on the railing a yard from the struggle.

Then Geo's feet slipped on the wet boards; his body hurled backward into the air. Then his back slapped water.

As he broke surface, Urson called to him. "Hang on, friend Geo, I'm coming!" Urson swung his arms back, then forward; he dove.

Now Geo could see only Argo and Jordde at the rail. But they were struggling!

Urson and Snake were near him in the water. The last thing he saw: Jordde suddenly yanked the chain from Argo's neck and flung it over the sea. She screamed—and her hands reached for jewel, following its arc toward the water.

Then hands were at his body. Geo turned in the water as

Snake disappeared beneath; Urson suddenly cried out. Hands caught Geo's arms as he tried to gulp a breath. And Urson was gone.

Hands were pulling him down.

Roughness of sand beneath one of his sides and the flare of sun on the other. His eyes were hot and his lids orange over them. Then there was a breeze. He opened his eyes and shut them quick, because of the light. He turned over, thought about pillows and stiff new sheets. Reaching out, he grabbed sand.

He opened his eyes and pushed himself up. His hands spread on warm, soft crumblings. Over there were rocks, thick vegetation behind them. He swayed to his knees, the sand grating under his kneecaps. He looked at his arm in the sun, flecked with grains. Then he touched his chest.

His hand came to one bead, moved on, and came to another! He looked down. Both the chain with the platinum claw and the thong with the wire cage hung around his neck. Bewildered, he heaved to his feet. And sat down again as the beach went red with the wash of blood behind his eyeballs. He got up again slowly. The sand was only warm, which meant the clouds that had hung so thickly at dawn couldn't have been gone for long.

Carefully Geo started down the beach, looking toward the land. When he turned to look at the water, he stopped.

At the horizon, beyond the rocks, was the boat, sails lowered. So they hadn't left yet. He swung his eyes back to the beach: fifty feet away was a man lying in the sun.

He ran forward now, the sand splashing around his feet, sinking under his toes, so that it was like the slow-motion running of dreams. Ten feet from the figure he stopped.

It was a young Negro, with skin the color of richly humused soil. The long skull was shaved. Like Geo, he was almost naked. There was a clot of seaweed at his wrist, and the soles of his feet and one upturned palm were grayish and shriveled; Geo thought about what happened when he sat in the bath too long.

He frowned and stood for a full minute. He looked up and down the beach once more. There was no one else. Just then the man's arm shifted across the sand like a sleeper's.

Immediately Geo fell to his knees beside the figure, rolled him over, and lifted his head. The eyes opened, squinted in the light, and the man whispered, "Who are you?"

"My name is Geo."

The man sat up and caught himself from falling forward by jamming his hands into the sand. He shook his head, then looked up again. "Yes," he said. "I remember you. What happened? Did we founder? Did the ship go down?"

"Remember me from where?" Geo asked.

"From the ship. You were on the ship, weren't you?"

"I was on the ship," Geo said. "And I got thrown overboard by that damned First Mate in a fight. But nothing's happened to the ship. It's still out there; you can see it." Suddenly Geo stopped. Then he said, "You're the guy who discovered Whitey's body that morning!"

"That's right." He shook his head again. "My name is Iimmi." Now he looked out at the horizon. "I see them," he said. "There's the ship. But where are we?"

"On the beach at Aptor."

Iimmi screwed his face up into a mask of dark horror. "No . . ." he said softly. "We couldn't be. We were days away from . . ."

"How did you fall in?"

"It was blowing up a little," Iimmi explained. "I was in the rig when suddenly something struck me from behind and I went toppling. I thought a spar had come loose and knocked me over. In all the mist, I was sure they wouldn't see me, and the current was too strong for me, and . . ." He stopped, looked around.

"You've been on this beach once before, haven't you?" Geo asked.

"Once," said Iimmi. "Yes, once."

"Do you realize how long you've been in the water?" Geo asked.

Iimmi looked up.

"Over two weeks!" Geo said. "Come on; see if you can walk. I've got a lot of things to explain, if I can, and we've got some hunting to do."

"Is there any water on this place?" Iimmi asked. "I feel like I could dry up and blow away." He got to his feet, swayed, straightened.

"Find water," said Geo. "A good idea. Maybe even a large river. And once we find it, I want to stay as close to it as possible as long as I'm on this place, because we've got some friends around here."

Iimmi steadied himself, and they started up the beach.

"What are you looking around for?" Iimmi asked.

"Friends," Geo said.

Two hundred feet up, rocks and thick vegetation cut off the beach. Scrambling over boulders and through vines, they emerged on a rock embankment that dropped fifteen feet into the wide estuary. A river wound back into the jungle. Twenty feet farther, the bank dropped to the water's surface. They fell flat on wet rock and sucked in cool liquid, watching the blue stones and white and red pebbles shiver.

There was a sound. They sprang from the water and crouched on the rock.

"Hey," Urson said through the leaves, "I was wondering if I'd find you." Light through branches lay more gold on the gold hung against his hairy chest. "Have you seen Snake?"

"I was hoping he was with you," said Geo. "Urson, this is Iimmi, the other sailor who died two weeks ago!"

Both Iimmi and Urson looked puzzled. "Have a drink of water," Geo said, "and I'll explain as best I can."

"Don't mind if I do," said Urson.

While the bear man lay down to drink, Geo began the story of Aptor and Leptar for Iimmi. When he finished, Iimmi asked, "You mean those fish things in the water carried us here? Whose side are they on?"

"Apparently Argo isn't sure either," Geo said. "Perhaps they're neutral."

"And the Mate?" asked Iimmi. "You think he pushed me overboard after he killed Whitey?"

"I thought you said he was trying to kill Snake," said Urson, who had finished drinking.

"He was," explained Geo. "He wanted to get rid of all three. Probably Snake first, and then Whitey and Iimmi. He wasn't counting on our fishy friends, though. I think it was just luck that he got Whitey rather than Snake. If he can't read minds, which I'm pretty sure he can't, he probably overheard you assigning the bunks for us to sleep in, Urson. When he found out he had killed Whitey instead, it just urged him to get Iimmi out of the way more quickly."

"Somebody tried to do me in," Iimmi agreed. "But I still don't see why."

"If there is a spy from Aptor on the ship, then Jordde is it," said Geo. "The Captain told me he had been to Aptor once before. It must have been then that he was recruited into their forces. Iimmi, both you and Whitey had also been on Aptor's shore, if only for a few hours. There must be something that Jordde learned from the Island that he was afraid you might learn, something you might see. Something dangerous, dangerous for Aptor; something you might see just from being on the beach. Probably it was something you wouldn't even recognize; possibly you wouldn't see the significance of it until much later. But it probably was something very obvious."

Now Urson asked, "What did happen when you were on Aptor? How were those ten men killed?"

In the sun, Iimmi shivered. He waited a moment, then began: "We took a skiff out from the ship and managed to get through the rocks. It was evening when we started. The moon, I remember, had risen just above the horizon, though the sky was still blue. 'The light of the full moon is propitious to the White Goddess Argo,' she said from her place at the bow of the skiff. By the time we landed, the sky was black behind her, and the beach was all silvered, up and down. Whitey and I stayed to guard the skiff. As we sat on the gunwale, rubbing our arms against the slight chill, we watched the others go up the beach, five and five, with Argo behind them.

"Suddenly there was a scream. They came like vultures. The moon was overhead now, and a cloud of them darkened the white disk with their wings. They scurried after the fleeing men, over the sand. All we could really make out was a dark struggle on the silver sand. Swords raised in the white light, screams, and howls that sent us staggering back into the ocean . . . Argo and a handful of the men who were left began to run toward the boat. The beasts followed them down to the edge of the water, loping behind them, half flying, half running, hacking one after another down. I saw one man fall forward and his head roll from his body while blood shot ten feet along the sand, black under the moon. One actually caught at Argo's veils, but she screamed and slipped away into the water; she climbed back into the boat, panting. You would think a woman would collapse, but no. She stood in the bow while we rowed our arms off. They would not come over the water. Somehow we managed to get the skiff back to the ship without foundering against the rocks."

"Our aquatic friends may have had something to do with that," said Geo. "Iimmi, you say her veils were pulled off. Tell me, do you remember if she was wearing any jewelry?"

"She wasn't," Iimmi said. "She stood there in only her dark robe, her throat bare as ivory."

"She wasn't going to bring the jewel to Aptor where those monsters could get their hands on it again," said Urson. "But, Geo, if Jordde's the spy, why did he throw the jewel in the sea?"

"Whatever reason he had," said Geo, "our friends have given them both to me now."

"You said Argo didn't know whose side these sea creatures were on, Leptar's or Aptor's," said Iimmi. "But perhaps Jordde knew, and that's why he threw it to them." He paused for a moment. "Friend, I think you have made an error; you tell me you are a poet, and it is a poet's error. The hinge in your argument that Snake is no spy is that Argo must have dubious motives to send you on such an impossible task without protection, saying that it would be meaningful only if all its goals were accomplished. You reasoned, how could an honest woman place the life of her daughter below the value of a jewel—"

"Not just her daughter," interrupted Geo, "but *the* Goddess Argo Incarnate."

"Listen," said Iimmi. "Only if she wished to make permanent her temporary return to power, you thought, could she set such an impossible task. There may be some truth in what you say. But she herself would not bring the jewel to the shores of Aptor, though it was for her own protection. Now all three jewels are in Aptor, and if any part of her story is true, Leptar right now is in more danger than it has been in five hundred years. You have the jewels, two of them, and you cannot use them. Where is your friend Snake, who can? Both Snake and Jordde could easily be spies and the enmity between them feigned, so that while you were on guard against one, you could be misled by the other. You say he can project words and images into men's minds? Perhaps he clouded yours."

They sat silent for the lapsing of a minute.

"Argo may be torn by many things," continued Iimmi. "But you, in watching some, may have been deluded by others."

Light from the river quivered on the undersides of the leaves.

Urson spoke now. "I think his story is better than yours, Geo."

"Then what shall we do now?" asked Geo softly.

"Do what the Goddess requests as best we can," said Iimmi. "Find the Temple of Hama, secure the third stone, rescue the young Goddess, and die before we let the jewels fall into the hands of Aptor."

"From the way you describe this place," muttered Urson, "that may not be far off."

"Still," Geo mused, "there are things that don't mesh. Why were you saved too, Iimmi? Why were we brought here at all? And why did Jordde want to kill you and the other sailor?"

"Perhaps," said Iimmi, "the God Hama has a strange sense of humor and we shall be allowed to carry the jewels up to the tem-

ple door before we are slaughtered, dropping them at his feet."
He smiled. "Then again, perhaps your story is the correct one,
Geo, and I am the spy, sent to sway your reason."

Urson and Geo glanced at each other.

"There are an infinite number of theories for every set of
facts," Geo said at last. "Rule number one: assume the simplest
theory that includes all the known conditions to be true until
more conditions arise for which the simplest no longer holds.
Rule number two: then, and not until, assume another."

"Then we go into the jungle," Iimmi said.

"I guess we do," said Urson.

Geo stood up. "So far," he said, "the water creatures have
saved us from death. Is there an objection to following the river
inland? It's as good a path as any, and it may mean more safety
to us."

"No objection here," said Iimmi.

"What about the jewels?" asked Urson. "Perhaps we ought
to bury them someplace where no one could ever find them. Perhaps if they were just completely out of the way . . ."

"It may be another 'poet's error,'" said Geo, "but I'd keep
them with us. Even though we can't use them, we might be able
to bluff our way with them."

"I'm for keeping them too," said Iimmi.

"Though I'm beginning to wonder how good any of my
guesses are," Geo added.

"Now don't be like that," cajoled Urson. "Since we've got
this job, we've got to trust ourselves to do it right. Let's see if we
can put one more of those things around your neck before we're
through." He pointed to the two jewels hanging at Geo's chest.
Then he laughed. "One more and you'll have as many as me."
He rattled his own triple necklace.

chapter five

Light lowered in the sky as they walked beside the river, keeping to the rocky bank and brushing away vines that strung into the water from hanging limbs. Urson broke down a branch thick as his wrist and tall as himself and playfully smote the water. "This should put a bruise on anyone who wants to bother us." He raised the stick and drops ran the bark, sparks at the tips of dark lines.

"We'll have to go into the woods for food soon," said Geo, "unless we wait for animals to come down to drink."

Urson tugged at another branch, and it twisted loose from fibrous white. "Here." He handed it to Geo. "I'll have one for you in a moment, Iimmi."

"And maybe we could explore a little before it gets dark," Iimmi suggested.

Urson handed him the third staff. "There's not much here I want to see," he muttered.

"Well, we can't sleep on the bank. We've got to find a place hidden in the trees."

"Can you see what's over there?" Geo asked.

"Where?" asked Iimmi. "Huh." Through the growth was a high shadow. "A rock or a cliff?"

"Maybe," mused Urson, "but it's awfully regular."

Geo started off into the underbrush; they followed. The goal was farther and larger than it had looked from the bank. Once they crossed an area where large stones fit side by side, like paving. Small trees had pushed up between some of them, but for thirty feet, before the flags sank in the soft jungle, it was easier going. Then the forest thinned again and they reached a relatively clear area. Before them a ruined building loomed. Six girders cleared the highest wall. The original height must have been eight or ten stories. One wall had completely sheared away and fragments of it chunked the ground. Broken rooms and severed halls suggested an injured granite hive. They approached slowly.

To one side a great metal cylinder lay askew a heap of rubbish. A flat blade of metal transversed it, one side twisting into the ground where skeletal girders showed beneath ripped plating. Windows like dark eyes lined the body, and a door gaped in an idiot oval halfway along its length.

Fascinated, they turned toward the injured wreck. As they neared, a sound came from inside the door. They stopped, and their staves leaped a protective inch from the ground. In the shadow of the door, ten feet above the ground, another shadow moved, resolving into an animal's muzzle—gray, long. They could see the forelegs. Like a dog, it was carrying a smaller beast, obviously dead, in its mouth. It saw them, watched them, was still.

"Dinner," Urson said softly. "Come on." They moved forward again. Then they stopped.

The beast sprang from the doorway. Shadow and distance had made them completely underestimate its size. Along the sprung arc flowed a canine body nearly five feet long. Urson struck it from its flight with his stick. As it fell, Iimmi and Geo were upon it with theirs, clubbing its chest and head. For six blows it staggered and could not gain its feet. Then, as it threatened to heave to standing, Urson rushed forward and jabbed his stave straight down on the chest: bones snapped, tore through the brown pelt, their blue sheen covered a moment later by blood. It howled, kicked its hind feet at the stake with which Urson held it to the ground; then it extended its limbs and quivered. The front legs stretched and stretched while the torso pulled in on itself, shrinking in the death agonies. The long mouth, which had dropped its prey, gaped as the head flopped from side to side, the pink tongue lolling, shrinking.

"My God!" breathed Geo.

The sharp muzzle had blunted now and the claws in the

padded paw stretched, opened into fingers and a thumb. The hairlessness of the underbelly had spread to the entire carcass. Hind legs lengthened and bare knees bent as now human feet dragged through the brown leaves and a human thigh gave a final contraction, stilled, and one leg fell out straight again. The shaggy, black-haired man lay on the ground, his chest caved in and bloody. In one last spasm, he flung his hands up and grasped the stake to pull it from his chest; too weak, his fingers slipped back down as his lips snarled open over his perfectly white, blunt teeth.

Urson stepped back, then back again. The stave fell, pulled loose with a sucking explosion from the ruined mess of lung. The wolf man had raised his hand to his own chest and touched his triple gold token. "In the name of the Goddess!" he finally whispered.

Geo walked forward now, picked up the carcass of the smaller animal that had been dropped, and turned away. "Well," he said, "I guess dinner isn't going to be as big as we thought."

"I guess not," Iimmi said.

They walked back to the ruined building, away from the corpse.

"Hey, Urson," Geo said at last. The big man was still holding his coins. "Snap out of it. What's the matter?"

"The only man I've ever seen whose body was broken in that way," he said slowly, "was one whose side was struck in by a ship's spar."

They decided to settle that evening at the corner of one of the building's ruined walls. They made fire with a rock against a section of rusted girder. After much sawing on a jagged metal blade protruding from a pile of rubble, they managed to quarter the animal and rip most of the pelt from its red body. With thin branches to hold the meat, they did a passable job of roasting. Although it was partially burned, partially raw, and without seasoning, they ate it, and hunger abated. As they sat at the fire by the wall, ripping red juicy fibers from the bones, night swelled through the jungle, imprisoning them in the shell of orange flicker.

"Shall we leave it going?" asked Urson. "Fire keeps animals away."

"If there are animals," reminded Geo, "and they do want anything to eat . . . well, they've got that thing back there."

On leaves raked together they stretched out by the wall. There was quiet—no insect hum, no unnameable chitterings—except for the comforting river rush beyond the trees.

Geo woke first, eyes filled with silver. He was dreaming again the strange happenings he had dreamed before. . . . No. He sat up: the entire clearing had flooded with white light from the amazingly huge disk of the moon sitting on the rim of the trees. The orange of the fire had bleached before it. Iimmi and Urson looked uncomfortably corpse-like. He was about to reach over and touch Iimmi's outstretched arm when there was a noise behind him. Beaten cloth? He jerked his head around and stared at the gray wall. He looked up the concrete that tore off raggedly against the night. There was nothing but stone and jagged darkness. Fatigue had snarled into something unpleasant and hard in his belly that had little to do with tiredness. He stretched his arm in the leaves once more and put his cheek down on the cool flesh of his shoulder.

The beating came again, continued for a few seconds. He rolled his face up and stared at the sky. Something crossed on the moon. The beating sounded once more. His eyes rose farther. Something . . . no, several things were perched on the broken ledge of the wall. A shadow shifted there; something waddled along a few feet. Wings spread, drew in again.

The flesh on his neck, his back, his chest, grew cold, then began to tickle. He reached out, his arm making thunder in the leaves, and grabbed Iimmi's black shoulder. Iimmi grunted, started, rolled over on his back, opened his eyes—Geo saw the black chest drop with expelled breath. A few seconds later the chest rose again. Iimmi turned his face to Geo, who raised his finger to his lips. Then he turned his face back up to the night. Three more times the flapping sounded behind them, behind the wall, Geo realized. Once he glanced down again and saw that Iimmi had raised his arm and put it over his eyes.

They spent a few years that way.

A flock suddenly leaped from the wall, fell toward them, only to catch air in a billow of wings across the moon. They circled, returned to the wall, and then, after a pause, took off again. Some of them fell twenty feet before the sails of their wings filled and they began to rise again. They circled wider this time, and before they returned, another flock dropped down on the night.

Then Geo grabbed Iimmi's arm and pulled it down from his eyes. The shapes dropped like foundering kites: sixty feet above them, forty feet, thirty. There was a piercing shriek. Geo was up on his feet, and Iimmi beside him, their staffs in hand. The shadows fell, shrieking; wings began to flap violently, and they rose again, moving out from the wall. Now they turned back.

"Here it comes," whispered Geo. He kicked at Urson, but the big sailor was already on his knees, then feet. The wings, insistent and dark, beat before them, flew toward them, then at the terrifying distance of five feet, reversed. "I don't think they can get in at the wall," Geo mouthed.

"I hope the hell they can't," Urson said.

Twenty feet away they hit the ground, black wings crumpling in the moonlight. In the growing horde of shadow, light snagged on a metal blade.

Two of the creatures detached themselves from the others and hurled themselves forward, swords swinging above their heads in silver light.

Urson grabbed Geo's staff and swung it as hard as he could, catching both beasts on the chest. They fell backward in an explosion of rubbery wings, as though they had stumbled into sheets of dark canvas.

Three more leaped the fallen ones, shrieking. As they came down, Urson looked up and jammed his staff into the belly of a fourth about to fall on them above. One got past Iimmi's whistling staff and Geo grabbed a furry arm. He pulled it to the side, overbalancing the sailed creature. It dropped its sword as it lay for a moment, struggling on its back. Geo snatched the blade and brought it up from the ground into the gut of another, who spread its wings and staggered back. He yanked the blade free and turned it down into the body of the fallen one; it made a sound like a suddenly crushed sponge. The blade came out and he hacked into a shadow on his left. And a voice suddenly, but inside his head . . .

The . . . jewels . . .

"Snake!" bawled Geo. "Where the hell are you?" He still held his staff; now he flung it forward, spear-like, into the face of an advancing beast. Struck, it opened up like a black silk parachute, knocking back three of its companions before it fell.

His view cleared for an instant; Geo saw the boy, white under the moonlight, dart from the jungle edge. Geo ripped the jewels from his neck and flung the handful of chain and leather over the heads of the shrieking beasts. At the top of their arc the beads made a double eye in the light before they fell on the leaves beyond the assailants. Snake ran for the jewels, picked them up, and held them above his head.

Fire leaped from the boy's hands in a double bolt that converged among the dark bodies. Red light cast a jagged wing in silhouette. A high shriek, a stench of burnt fur. Another bolt of fire fell in the dark horde. A wing flamed, waved flame about it. The beast tried to fly, but fell, splashing fire. Sparks sharp on a brown face chiseled it with shadow, caught the terrified red bead of an eye, and laid light along a pair of fangs.

Wings afire withered on the ground; dead leaves sparked now, and whips of flame ran in the clearing. The beasts retreated, and the three men stood against the wall, panting. Two last shadows suddenly dropped from the air toward Snake, who still stood with raised arms out in the clearing.

"Watch out!" Iimmi called to him.

Snake looked up as wings fell at him, tented him, hid him momentarily. Red flared beneath, and suddenly they fell away, sweeping the leaves—moved by wind or life, Geo couldn't tell. Wings rose on the moon, circled farther away, were gone.

"Let's get out of here!" Urson said. They ran forward toward Snake.

Geo said, "Am I ever glad to see you!"

Urson looked up after the disappearing figures and repeated: "Let's get out of here."

Glancing back, they saw the fire had blown back against the wall and was dying. They walked quickly toward the forest. "Snake," said Geo when they stopped, "this is Iimmi. Iimmi . . . we told you about him."

Iimmi extended his hand. "Pleased to meet you."

"Look," said Geo, "he can read your mind, so if you still think he's a spy . . ."

Iimmi grinned. "Remember your general rule? If he is a spy, it's going to get much too complicated trying to figure why he saved us."

Urson scratched his head. "If it's a choice between Snake and nothing, we better take Snake. Hey, Four Arms, I owe you a thrashing." He paused, then laughed. "I hope someday I get a chance to give it to you. Sometimes you seem more trouble than you're worth."

"Where have you been, anyway?" Geo asked. He put his hand on the boy's shoulder. "You're wet."

"Our water friends again?" suggested Urson.

"Probably," said Geo.

Snake now held one hand toward Geo.

"What's that? Oh, you don't want to keep them?"

Snake shook his head.

"All right," said Geo. He took the jewels and put them around his neck again.

"So that's what our treasure can do," said Iimmi.

"And much more than that," Geo told him. "Why don't you take one, Iimmi? Maybe we better not keep them all together."

Iimmi shrugged. "I suppose it's a lot of weight for one person. I'll carry one of them."

Geo took the chain with the platinum claw from his neck and hung it around Iimmi's. As they moved through the moon dapples, the jewel blinked like an eye in his black chest. Snake beckoned them to follow him. They stopped only to pick up swords from among the shriveled darkness. As they passed around the corner of the broken building, Geo looked for the corpse they had left there, but it was gone.

"Where are we going?" asked Urson.

Snake only motioned them on. They neared the broken cylinder and Snake scrambled up the rubble under the dark hole through which the man-wolf had leaped earlier that evening. They followed cautiously.

At the door, Snake lifted the jewel from Geo's neck and held it aloft. It glowed now; blue-green light seeped into the corners and crevices of the ruined entrance. Entering, they stood in a corridor lined with the metal frames of double seats from which ticking and upholstery had either rotted or been carried off by animals for nests. Shreds of cloth hung at the windows, most of which were broken. Twigs and rubbish littered the metal floor. They walked between the seats toward a door at the far end. Effaced signs still hung on the walls. Geo could distinguish only a few letters on one white-enameled but chipped and badly rusted plaque:

n . . sm . k . . g

"Do you know what language that is?" asked Iimmi.

"I can't make it out," said Geo.

The door at the end was ajar, and Snake opened it all the way. Something scuttered through a cracked window. The jewel's light showed two seats broken from their fixtures. Vines covered the front window, in which only a few splinters of glass hung on the rim. Draped in rotten fabric, metal rings about wrists and ankles, two skeletons with silver helmets had fallen from the seats . . . perhaps five hundred years before. Snake pointed to a row of smashed glass disks in front of the broken seats.

Radio . . . they heard in their minds.

Now he reached down into the mess on the floor and dislodged a chunk of rusted metal. *Gun* . . . he said, showing it to Geo.

The three men examined it. "What's it for?" asked Urson.

Snake shrugged.

"Are there any electricities or diodes around?" asked Geo, remembering the words from before.

Snake shrugged again.

"Why did you want to show us all this?" Geo asked.

The boy only started back toward the door. When they reached the oval entrance, about to climb down, Iimmi pointed to the ruins of the building ahead of them. "Do you know what that building was called?"

Barracks . . . Snake said.

"I know that word," said Geo.

"So do I," said Iimmi. "It means a place where they used to keep soldiers together. It's from one of the old languages."

"That's right," said Geo. "From when they had armies."

"Is this where the armies of Aptor are hidden?" Urson asked. "Those horrors we just got through?"

"In there?" asked Geo. The broken edges were grayed now, blunted under the failing moon. "Perhaps. It sounded like they came from in there at first."

"Where to now?" Urson asked Snake.

The boy only started back toward the door. They followed him into the denser wood, where pearls of light scattered the tree trunks. They emerged at the broad ribbon of silver, the river, broken by rocks.

"We were right the first time," Geo said. "We should have stayed here."

Ripple and slosh and the hiss of leaves along the forest edge—

these accompanied them as they lay down on the dried moss behind the larger rocks. Boughs hung with moss and vines shaded moonlight from them. The weight of relief on them, they dropped, like stones down a well, into the bright pool of sleep—

—*bright pool of silver growing and spreading and wrinkling into the shapes of mast, the deck rail, the powder-white sea beyond the ship. Down the deck another figure—gaunt, skeletal—approached. The features, distorted by whiteness and pulled to grotesquerie, were those of the Captain.*

Oh, Mate, *the Captain said.*

Silence while Jordde gave an answer they couldn't hear.

Yes, *answered the Captain.* I wonder what she wants too. *His voice was hollow, etoliated as a flower grown in darkness. The Captain knocked now on Argo's cabin door. It opened, and they stepped in.*

The hand that opened the door was thin as winter twigs. The walls were draped in spider webs, hanging insubstantial as layered dust. The papers on top of the desk were tissue thin, threatening to scatter and crumble with a breath. The chandelier gave more languishing white smoke than light, and the arms, branches, and carved oil cups looked for all the world like a convocation of spiders.

Argo's pale voice sounded like thin webs tearing.

So, *she said.* We will stay at least another seven days.

But why? *asked the Captain.*

I have received a sign from the sea.

I do not wish to question your authority, Priestess . . . *began the Captain.*

Then do not, *interrupted Argo.*

My Mate has raised the objection that—

Your Mate has raised his hand to me once, *stated the Priestess.* It is only my benevolence—*here she paused, and her voice became unsure*—that I do not . . . destroy him where he stands. *Beneath her veil, her face might have been a skull's.*

But—*began the Captain.*

We wait here by the Island of Aptor another seven days, com-manded Argo. She looked away from the Captain now, straight into the eyes of the Mate. From behind the veil, hate welled from the black sockets.

They turned to go. On deck, they stopped to watch the sea. Waves like gray smoke swirled away; beyond that, at the horizon, a sharp tongue of land licked dark mountains. The cliffs were chalky on one side, streaked with red and blue clays on the other. There was a reddish glow beyond one peak, like a simmering volcano. Dark as most of it was, the black was backed with purple, or broken by the warm, differing grays of individual rocks. Even through the night, at this distance, beyond the silver crescent of the beach, the jungle looked rich, green even in the darkness, redolent, full, and quiveringly heavy with life—

Then the thin screams—

chapter six

Geo rolled over and out of sleep, stones and moss nibbling his shoulder. He grabbed his sword and was on his feet. Iimmi was also standing with raised blade. Dawn was white and gray through the trees. The air was chill, and the river slapped coldly behind them.

The thin scream came again, like a hot wire drawn down the gelid morning. Snake and Urson were also up now. The sounds came from the direction of the ruined barracks. Geo started forward cautiously, curiosity pulling him toward the sound, fear pushing him from the relatively unprotected bank and into the woods. The others followed.

Abruptly they reached the forest's rim, beyond which was the clear space before the broken building. They crouched now behind the trees to watch, fascinated.

Between ape and man, it hovered in the shadow of the wall. It was Snake's height, but Urson's build. An animal pelt wrapped its middle and went over its shoulder, clothing it more fully than any of the four humans observing. Thick-footed, great-handed, it loped four steps across the clearing, uttered its piercing shriek, and fell on one of the beasts that had dropped from the sky last night, rolling its head back and forth as it tore at the corpse. Once, it raised its head and a sliver of flesh shook from its teeth before it fell again to devour.

Suddenly another rushed from the forest. Halfway across the clearing, it stopped over a piece of fallen carnage ten feet from Geo's hiding place. As it crouched before them, they watched the huge fingers upon broad flat palms, tipped with bronze claws, convulse again and again in the fibrous meat. The tusked mouth ripped.

A third entered from the woods now, slowly. It was smaller than the others. Suddenly it sighted a slain body from the night's encounter. It paused, stooped, then fell on the throat with bared teeth. Whether it was a breeze or a final reflex, Geo couldn't tell: one of the membranous sails rose darkly and beat about the oblivious thing that fed.

"Come on," Urson whispered. "Let's go."

A thin scream sounded, and they started.

The first figure crouched apishly before them, head to the side, with deep, puzzled eyes blinking below the ridged brow. The clawed fingers opened and closed like breathing, and the shaggy head was knotted with dirt and twigs. The breath hissed from the faintly shifting, full lips.

Urson reached for his sword, but Geo saw him and whispered, "No, don't . . ." Geo extended his hand and moved slowly forward.

The hulking form took a step back and mewed.

Iimmi suddenly caught the idea. Coming up beside Geo, he made a quick series of snaps with his fingers and said in a coaxing, baby voice: "Come, come, come . . ."

Geo laughed softly to Urson back over his shoulder. "It won't hurt us."

"If we don't hurt it," added Iimmi. "It's some sort of necrophage."

"A what?" asked Urson.

"It only eats dead things," Geo explained. "They're mentioned in some of the old legends. Apparently, after the Great Fire, so the story goes, there were more of these things around than anything else. In Leptar, though, they became extinct."

"Come here, cutie," said Iimmi. "Nice little, sweet little, pretty little thing."

It mewed again, bowed its head, came over and rubbed against Iimmi's hip. "Smells like hell," the black sailor observed, scratching behind its ear. "Watch out there, big boy!" The beast gave a particularly affectionate rub that almost upset Iimmi's balance.

"Leave your pet alone," said Urson, "and let's get going."

Geo patted the simian skull. "So long, beautiful." They turned toward the river again.

As they emerged on the rocky bank, Geo said, "At least we know we have seven days to get to the Temple of Hama and back again."

"Huh?" asked Iimmi.

"Don't you remember the dream, back on the ship?"

"You had the same dream too?"

Geo put his arm around Snake's shoulder. "Our friend here can relay other people's thoughts to you while you sleep."

"Who was thinking that?" asked Iimmi.

"Jordde, the First Mate."

"He makes everybody look dead. I thought I was having a nightmare. I could hardly recognize the Captain."

"You see one reason for believing Jordde's a spy?"

"Because of the way he sees things?" Again Iimmi smiled. "A poet's reason, I'm afraid. But I see."

The thin shriek sounded behind them, and they turned to see the hulking form crouched on the rocks above them.

"Uh-oh," said Urson, "there's your friend again."

"I hope we haven't picked up a tagalong for the rest of the trip," said Geo.

It loped down over the rocks and stopped before them.

"What's it got?" Iimmi asked.

"I can't tell," said Geo.

Reaching into the bib of its pelt, it brought out a gray hunk of meat and held it toward them.

Iimmi laughed. "Breakfast," he said.

"That?" demanded Urson.

"Can you suggest anything better?" Geo asked. He took the meat from the beast's claws. "Thanks."

It turned, looked back, and bounded up the bank and into the forest again.

Geo turned the meat in his hands, examining it. "There's no blood in it at all," he said, puzzled. "It's completely drained."

"That just means it'll take longer to spoil," said Iimmi.

"I'm not eating any of that," Urson stated.

"Do you think it's all right to eat, Snake?" Geo asked.

Snake shrugged and then nodded.

"Are you eating any?"

Snake rubbed his belly and nodded again.

"That's enough for me," said Geo.

With fire from the jewels and wooden spits from the forest, they soon had the meat crackling and brown. Grease bubbled down its sides and hissed onto the hot stones they had used to rim the flame. Urson sat apart, sniffed, and then moved closer, and finally plowed big fingers across his hairy belly and grunted, "Damn it, I'm hungry!" They made room for him at the fire.

Sun struck the tops of the trees for the first time that morning, and a moment later, light splashed concentric curves on the water, the gold stain spreading farther and farther.

"I guess time's getting on," said Urson, tearing a greasy handful of meat. He ducked his head to lick the juice running down his wrist.

"Well," said Geo, "now we know we have two friends."

"Who?" asked Urson.

"Up there." Geo pointed back to where the ape-beast had disappeared in the forest. "And down there." He pointed to the river.

"I guess we do," said Urson.

"Which reminds me," Geo continued, turning to Snake. "Where the hell were you before you got here last night? Come on, now, a little mind yelling."

Beach . . . said Snake.

"And our fishy friends got you up here by way of the river after us?"

Snake nodded.

"How come we didn't find you on the beach before when Urson and Iimmi and me got together?"

Not . . . yet . . . get . . . there . . . Snake said.

"Then where were you?"

Ship . . .

"You were back on the ship?"

Not . . . on . . . ship . . . Snake said. Then he shook his head. *Too . . . complicated . . . to . . . explain . . .*

"It can't be that complicated," said Geo. "Besides, even with all the help you've been, you're under some pretty heavy suspicion."

Suddenly Snake stood up and motioned them to follow. They rose and followed him, Urson still chewing a mouthful of meat. As they scrambled up the bank again, back into the woods, Urson asked, "Where are we going now?"

Snake merely beckoned them on, accompanied by a gesture to be silent. In a minute they were back in the clearing by the barracks. There was not a bone or body left. As they went, Geo glimpsed Urson's fallen stave, dark with blood on one end. It lay alone in the leaves. Snake led them to the base of the ruined barracks. The sun was high enough to put yellow edges on the grass blades blowing against the wall. Snake paused once more, lifted the jewel from Iimmi's neck, and made a light with it. A second time he cautioned silence and then stepped over the broken threshold of the first empty cubicle.

They crossed the cracked cement floor to the black rectangle of another doorway. Snake stepped through. They followed. Just beyond the edge of the sunlight, in the artificial illumination from the jewel, huge rumpled black sacks hung close together along naked pipes of the exposed plumbing along the ceiling. They walked forward until they found one single sack more or less alone. Snake brought the light close to its bottom and waved it there.

"Is he trying to tell us they can't see?" whispered Urson.

They whirled on the big sailor, fingers against their lips. At the same time there was a rustling like wet paper from the sack as one wing defined itself, and in the uncovered upside-down face, a blind red eye blinked . . . then closed. The wing folded, and they tiptoed back across the chamber and into the sunlight. No one spoke until they could see the river again.

"What were you—" began Geo; his voice sounded annoyingly loud. More softly he said, "What were you trying to tell us?"

Snake pointed to Urson.

"What he said? That they can't see, just hear."

Snake nodded.

"Gee, thanks," said Geo. "I figured *that* out last night."

Snake shrugged.

"That still doesn't answer his questions," said Iimmi.

"And another one," said Geo. "Why are you showing us all these things? You seem to know your way around awfully well. Have you ever been on Aptor before?"

Snake paused for a moment. Then he nodded.

They were all silent.

Finally Iimmi asked, "What made you ask that?"

"Something in that first theory," Geo said. "I've been thinking it for some time. And I guess Snake here knew I was thinking
it too. Jordde wanted to get rid of Iimmi, Whitey, and Snake,
and it was just an accident that he caught Whitey first instead
of Snake. He wanted to get rid of Whitey and Iimmi because of
something they had seen or might have seen when they were on
Aptor with Argo. I just thought perhaps he wanted to get rid of
Snake for the same reason. Which meant he might have been on
Aptor before."

"Jordde was on Aptor before too," said Urson. "You said
that's when he became a spy for them."

They all looked at Snake again.

"I don't think we ought to ask him any more questions," said
Geo. "The answers aren't going to do us any good, and no matter what we find out, we've got a job to do, and seven—no . . .
six and a half days to do it in."

"I think you're right," said Iimmi.

"You *are* more trouble than you're worth," Urson addressed
the boy. "Get going."

Then Snake handed the metal chain with the pendant jewel
back to Iimmi. The black youth hung it on his chest once more.
They started up the river.

By twelve, the sun had parched the sky. They stopped
to swim and cool themselves. Chill water gave before reaching
arms and lowered faces. They even dove for their aquatic help-
ers, but grubbed the pebbly bottom of the river with their fingers, coming up with dripping twigs and wet stones. Soon they
were in a splashing match, of which it is fair to say, Snake won—
hands down.

Later they lay on the mossy rocks to dry, slapping at small
bugs, the sun like gold coins warm on their eyelids. "I'm hungry," said Urson, rolling over.

"We just ate," Iimmi said, sitting up. "But I'm hungry too."

"We ate five hours ago," Geo said. The sun curved loops of

liquid metal in the ripples. "And we can't lie around here all day. Do you think we can find one of those things we got from the . . . wolf, yesterday?"

"Or some nice friendly necrophage?" suggested Iimmi.

"Ugh." Urson shivered.

"Hey," Iimmi asked Geo, "does not asking Snake questions mean not asking him where the Temple is?"

Geo shrugged. "We'll either get there or we won't. If we were going wrong and he knew about it, he'd have told us by now if he wanted us to know."

"Goddamn all this running around in circles," Urson exclaimed. "Hey, you little four-armed bastard, have you ever seen where we're going?"

Snake shook his head.

"Do you know how to get there?"

Snake shook his head.

"Fine!" Urson snapped his fingers. "Forward, friends, we're off for the unknown once more." He grinned, doubled his pace, and they started once more behind him.

A mile on, hunger again thrust its sharp finger into their abdomens. "Maybe we should have saved some of that stuff from breakfast," muttered Urson. "With no blood in it, you said it wouldn't have spoiled."

Geo suddenly broke away from the bank toward the forest. "Come on," he said. "Let's get some food."

The vines were even thicker here, and they had to hack through with swords. Where the dead vines had stiffened in the sun, it was easier going. The air had been hot at the river; here it was cool, damp, and wet leaves brushed their arms and shoulders. The ground gave spongily under them.

The building they came upon: tongues of moss licked twenty and fifty feet up the loosely mortared stones. A hundred yards from the water, the jungle came right to its base. The edifice had sunk a bit to one side in the boggy soil. It was a far more stolid and primitive structure than the barracks. They scraped and hacked to the entrance, where two columns of stone, six feet at the base, rose fifty feet to support an arch. The stones were rough and unfinished.

"It's a temple!" Geo said suddenly.

The steps were strewn with rubbish, and what spots of light spilled from the twisted jungle stopped at the total shadow below the great arch. A line of blackness up one side of the basalt door showed that it was ajar. Now they climbed the steps, moving aside a fallen branch. Leaves chattered at them. They kicked small stones from the cracks in the rock. Geo, Iimmi, then Snake, and at last Urson squeezed through the door.

Ceiling blocks had fallen from the high vault so that shafts of sun struck through the slow shift of dust to the littered floor.

"Do you think it's Hama's Temple?" Urson asked. His voice boomed in the stone room, magnified and hollow.

"I doubt it," whispered Geo. "At least not the one we're supposed to find."

"Maybe it's an abandoned one," said Iimmi, "and we can find out something useful from it."

Something large and dark flapped through a far shaft of sun. With raised swords they stepped back. After a moment of silence, Geo handed his jewel to Snake. "Make some light in here. Now!"

The blue-green glow flowed from the upraised jewel in Snake's hand. Columns supported the broken ceiling along the sides of the temple. As the light flared, then flared brighter, they saw that the flapping had come from a bird perched harmlessly on an architrave between two columns. It ducked its head at them, cawed harshly, then flew out one of the apertures in the ceiling. The sound of its wings still thrummed seconds after it had gone.

They could not see the altar, but there were doors between the columns, and as their eyes grew sensitive, they saw that one section of wall had not withstood time's sledge. A great rent was nearly blocked with vines. A green shimmer broke here and there through the foliage.

They started forward now, chips and pebbles rolling before their toes, down the great chapel toward the altar.

Behind a twisted railing, and raised on steps of stone, sat the ruins of a huge statue. Carved from black rock, a man sat cross-legged on a dais. One arm and shoulder had broken off and lay in pieces on the altar steps. The hand, fingers as thick as Urson's thigh, lay just behind the altar rail. The idol's head was missing. Both the hand still connected and the one on the steps looked as though they had once held something, but whatever it was had been removed.

Geo walked along the rail to where a set of stone boxes were placed like footstones along the side of the altar. "Here, Snake," he called. "Bring a light over here." Snake obeyed, and with Iimmi's and Urson's help, he loosened one of the lids.

"What's in there?" Urson asked.

"Books," said Geo, lifting out one dusty volume. Iimmi reached over his shoulder and with dark fingers turned the pages. "Old rituals," Geo said. "Look here." He stopped Iimmi's hand. "You can still read them."

"Let me see," Iimmi said. "I studied with Eadnu at the University of Olcse Ohlwn."

Geo looked up and laughed. "I thought some of your ideas sounded familiar. I was a pupil of Welis. Our teachers would never speak to each other! This is a surprise. So you were at Olcse Ohlwn too?"

"Uh-huh," said Iimmi, turning pages again. "I signed aboard this ship as a summer job. If I'd known where we'd end up, I don't think I'd have gone, though."

Stomach pangs were forgotten momentarily as the two looked at the rituals of Hama.

"They're not at all like those of the Goddess," Iimmi observed.

"Apparently not," agreed Geo. "Wait!" Iimmi had been turning pages at random. "Look there!" Geo pointed.

"What is it?" Iimmi asked.

"The lines," Geo said. "The ones Argo recited . . ."

He read out loud:

> "Forked in the heart of the dark oak
> the circlet of his sash

rimmed where the eye of Hama broke
with fire, smoke, and ash.

Freeze the drop in the hand,
break the earth with singing.
Hail the height of a man,
also the height of a woman.

Take from the tip of the sea
salt and sea kelp and gold,
fixed with a shaft in the brain
as the terror of time is old.

Salt on the walls of the heart.
Salt in each rut of the brain.
Sea kelp ground in the earth,
Returning with gold again.

The eyes have imprisoned a vision.
The ash tree dribbles with blood.
Thrust from the gates of the prison
smear the yew tree with mud.

"It's the other version of the poem I found in the pre-purge rituals of Argo. I wonder if there were any more poems in the old rituals of Leptar that parallel those of Aptor and Hama?"

"Probably," Iimmi said. "Especially if the first invasion from Aptor took place just before, and probably caused, the purges."

"What about food?" Urson suddenly asked. He was sitting on the altar steps. "You two scholars have the rest of time to argue. But we may starve before you come to some conclusion."

"He's right," said Iimmi. "Besides, we have to get going."

"Would you two consider it an imposition to set your minds to procuring us some food?" Urson asked.

"Wait a minute," Geo said. "Here's a section on the burial of the dead. Yes, I thought so." He read out loud now:

"Sink the bright dead with misgiving
from the half-light of the living . . ."

"What does that mean?" asked Urson.

"It means that the dead are buried with all the accoutrements of the living. I was pretty sure of it, but I wanted to check. That means that they put food in the graves."

"First, where are we going to find any graves; and second, I've had enough dead and half-dead food." Urson stood up.

"Over here!" cried Geo. With Snake following, they came to the row of sealed doors behind the columns along the wall. Geo looked at the inscription. "Tombs," he reported. He tried to turn the handles, a double set of rings that twisted in opposite directions. "In an old, uncared-for temple like this, the lock mechanisms must have rusted by now if they're at all like the ancient tombs of Leptar."

"Have you studied the ancient tombs?" asked Iimmi excitedly. "Professor Eadnu always considered them a waste of time."

"That's all Welis ever talked about," laughed Geo. "Here, Urson, you set your back to this a moment."

Grumbling, Urson came forward, took the rings, and twisted. One snapped off in his hand. The other gave with a crumbling sound inside the door.

"I think that does it," Geo said.

They all helped pull now, and suddenly the door gave an inch, and then, on the next tug, swung free.

Snake preceded them into the stone cell.

On a rock table, lying on its side, was a bald, shriveled body. Tendons ridged the brown skin, along the arms, along the calves; bits of cloth still stuck here and there. On the floor stood sealed jars, heaps of parchment, piles of ornaments.

Geo moved among the jars. "This one has grain," he said.

"Give me a hand."

Iimmi helped him lug the big pottery vessel to the door.

Then a thin shriek scarred the dusty air, and both students stumbled. The jar hit the ground, split, and grain heaped over the floor. The shriek came again.

Geo saw, there on the broken wall across the temple, five of the apelike figures crouched before the shingled leaves, silhouetted on the dappled green. One leaped down and ran, wailing, across the littered floor, straight for the tomb door. Two others followed, then two more. And more had mounted the broken ridge.

The loping forms burst into the cell, one, and then its two companions. Claws and teeth closed on the shriveled skin. Others screamed around the entrance. The body rolled beneath hands and mouths. One arm swept into the air above the lowered heads and humped backs. It fell on the edge of the rock table, broke at midforearm, and the skeletal hand fell to the floor, shattering.

They backed to the temple door, eyes fixed on the desecration. Then they turned and ran down the temple steps. Not till they reached the river and the sunlight on the broad rocks touched them did they slow or breathe deeply. They walked quietly. Hunger returned, and occasionally one would look aside into the faces of the others in an attempt to identify the vanishing horror that still pulsed behind their eyes.

chapter seven

A small animal crossed their path, and in a blink, one of Snake's hands scooped up a sharp rock, flung it and sunk it into the beast's head. They quartered it on Iimmi's blade and had almost enough to fill them from the roast made with fire from the jewels. Following their own shadows into the afternoon, they continued silently up the river.

It was Urson who first pointed it out. "Look at the far bank," he said.

The river had become slower, broader here. Across from them, even with the added width, they could make out a man-made embankment.

A few hundred meters farther on, Iimmi sighted spires above the trees, still across the river. They could figure no explanations till the trees ceased on the opposite bank and the buildings and towers of the great city broke the sky. Many of the towers were ruined or cracked. Nets of girders were silhouetted against the yellow clouds, where the skin of buildings had stripped away. Elevated highways looped tower after tower, many of them broken also, their ends dangling colossally to the streets. The docks of the city across the water were deserted.

It was Geo who suggested: "Perhaps Hama's Temple is in there. After all, Argo's largest temple is in Leptar's biggest city."

"And what city in Leptar is *that* big?" asked Urson in an awe-filled voice.

"How do we get across?" asked Iimmi.

But Snake had already started down to the water.

"I guess we follow him," Geo said, climbing down the rocks.

Snake dove into the water. Iimmi, Geo, and Urson followed. Before he had taken two strokes, Geo felt familiar hands grasp his body from below. This time he did not fight; there was a sudden sense of speed, of sinking through consciousness.

Then he was bobbing up in chill water. The stone embankment rose to one side and the broad river spread to the other. He shook dark hair from his eyes and sculled toward the stones. Snake and Urson bobbed at his right, and a second later, Iimmi at his left. He switched from sculling into a crawl, wondering how to scale the stones; then he saw the rusted metal ladder leading into the water. He caught hold of the sides and pulled himself up.

The first rung broke with his full weight, dropping him half

into the water again, and his hands scraped painfully along the
rust. But he pulled himself up once more, planting his instep
on the nub of the broken rung; it held. Reaching the top, he
turned back to call instructions: "Keep your feet to the side."
Snake came up now, then Urson. Another rung gave under the
big man's bare foot when he was halfway up. As he sagged backward, then caught himself, the rivets of the ladder tugged another
inch out from the stone. But they held. Iimmi joined them on the
broad ridge of concrete that walled the river. Together now on
the wharf, they turned to the city.

Ruin stretched before them. The buildings on the waterfront
looked as though they had been flung from the sky and broken
on the street, rather than built there. Girders twisted through
plaster, needling to rusted points.

They stepped down into the street and walked a narrow avenue between piles of debris from two taller buildings. After a few
blocks, the building walls were canyon height. "How are you
going to go about looking for the Temple?" Urson asked.

"Maybe we can climb up and take a look from the top of one
of these buildings," Geo suggested. They raised their eyes and
saw that the sky was thick with yellow clouds. Where it broke,
twilight seeped.

They turned toward a random building. A slab of metal had
torn away from the wall. They stepped through into a high,
hollow room. Dim light came from white tubes about the wall.
Only a quarter of them were lit; one was flickering. In the center
of the room hung a metal sign:

NEW EDISON ELECTRIC COMPANY

Beneath it, in smaller letters:

"LIGHT DOWN THE AGES"

Great cylinders, four or five times the height of a man, humped
over the floor under pipes, wires, and catwalks. The four made

their way along one walk toward a spiral staircase that wound up to the next floor.

"Listen!" Urson suddenly said.

"What is it?" Geo asked.

One of the huge cylinders was buzzing.

"That one." Urson pointed. They listened, then continued. As they mounted the staircase, the great room turned about them, sinking. At last they stepped up into a dark corridor. A red light glowed at the end:

EXIT

Doors outlined themselves along the hall in the red haze. Geo picked one and opened it. Natural light fell on them. They entered a room in which the outer wall had been torn away. The floor broke off irregularly over thrusting girders.

"What happened here?" Urson asked.

"See," Iimmi explained. "That highway must have crashed into the wall and knocked it away."

A twenty-foot ribbon of road veered into the room at an insane angle. The railing was twisted but the stalks of streetlights were still intact along the edge.

"Do you think we could climb that?" asked Geo. "It doesn't look too steep."

"For what?" Urson wanted to know.

"To get someplace high enough to see if there's anything around that looks like a temple."

"Oh," said Urson in a reconciled voice.

As they started across the floor toward the highway, Geo suddenly called, "Run!" As they leaped onto the slanted sheet of concrete, a crack opened in the flooring over which they had just walked. Cement and tile broke away and crashed to the street, three stories down. The section of road on which they perched now wavered up and down a good three feet. As it came to rest, Geo breathed again and glanced down to the street. A cloud of plaster settled.

"That way is up," Urson reminded him, and they started. In general the walk was in good shape. Occasional sections of railing had twisted away, but the road itself mounted surely between the buildings on either side of them through advancing sunset.

It branched before them and they went left. It branched again, and again they avoided the right-hand road. A sign half the length of a three-masted ship hung lopsidedly above them on a building to one side:

WMTH

THE HUB OF

WORLD NEWS,

COMMUNICATION,

& ENTERTAINMENT

As they rounded the corner of the building, Snake suddenly stopped and put his hand to his head.

"What is it?" asked Geo.

Snake took a step backward. Then he pointed to WMTH.

It . . . hurts . . .

"What hurts?" asked Geo.

Snake pointed to the building again.

"Is there someone in there thinking too loud?"

Thinking . . . machine . . . Snake said. *Radio . . .*

"A radio is a thinking machine, and there's one in there that's hurting your head?" interpreted Geo tentatively, and with a question mark.

Snake nodded.

"Yes what?" asked Urson.

"Yes, there's a radio in there and it's hurting him," said Geo.

"How come the one he showed us before didn't hurt him?" Urson wanted to know.

Iimmi looked up at the imposing housing of WMTH. "Maybe this one's a lot bigger."

"Look," Geo said to Snake. "You stay here, and if we see anything, we'll come back and report, all right?"

"Maybe he can get through it," Urson said.

Snake looked up at WMTH, bit his lip, and suddenly started forward, resolutely. After ten steps he put his hands to his head and staggered backward. Geo and Iimmi ran forward to help him. When they got back beyond the effects of WMTH, Snake's face looked drained and pale.

"You stay here," Geo said. "We'll be back. Don't worry."

"Maybe it stops later on," Urson said, "and if he ran forward, he could get out the other side. It may just stop after a hundred feet or so."

"Why so anxious?" asked Geo.

"The jewels," said Urson. "Who's going to get us out of trouble if we should meet up with anything else?"

They were silent then. Their shadows over the pavement faded as the yellow tinge of the sky fell before blue. "I guess it's up to Snake," Geo said. "Do you think you can make it?"

Snake paused, then shook his head.

Geo said to the others: "Come on."

A click—and lights flickered all along the edges of the road. Almost a third of the lights still worked and now flared along both sides of the rising ramp, closing with the distance through the twilight.

"Come on," Geo said again.

The lights wheeled double and triple shadows about them on the road as they reached the next turnoff that led to a still higher ramp. Geo looked back. Snake, miniature and dimmed by distance, sat on the railing, his feet on the lower rung, one pair of arms folded, one pair of elbows on his knees above a puddle of shadow.

"I hope someone is keeping track of where we're going," Geo said a few hundred yards on.

"I can get us back to New Edison," said Iimmi. "If it'll do any good," he added.

"Just keep track of the turns," said Geo.

"I'm keeping," Iimmi assured him.

"By the time we get to the top of whatever we're trying to get to the top of," rumbled Urson, "we won't be able to see anything. It'll be too dark."

"Then let's hurry," Geo admonished.

Sunset smeared one side of the towers with copper while blue shadows slipped down the other. Smaller walkways led to the buildings around them. By way of a plastic-hooded stair, they mounted another eighty feet to a broader highway where, stepping out, they could look down on the necklace of light they had just left. New Edison and WMTH still towered behind them. There was an even taller building before them. They had cleared the lower roofs.

On this road fewer lights were working. There were often five or six dark in a row, so that they moved with only the glow of a neighboring roadway twenty yards to the side to light them. They were just about to enter another of these dark sections when a figure appeared in silhouette at the other end.

They stopped.

The figure was gone.

Deciding it was only their imagination, they started again, peering through the incomplete darkness on either side. A little farther, Geo suddenly halted. "There . . ."

Two hundred feet ahead of them, what may have been a naked woman rose from the ground and began to walk backward until she disappeared into the next length of dark road.

"Do you think she was running away from us?" Iimmi asked.

Urson touched the jewel on Iimmi's chest. "I wish we had some more light around here."

"Yeah," Iimmi agreed. They continued.

The skeleton lay at the beginning of the next stretch of functioning lights. The rib cage marked sharp shadows on the pavement. The hands lay above its head, and one leg twisted over the other in an impossible angle.

"What the hell is that?" Urson asked. "And how did it get there?"

"It looks like it's been there a little while," said Iimmi.

"Do we turn back now?" Urson asked.

"A skeleton can't hurt you," Geo said.

"But what about the live one we saw?" countered Urson.

"And here she comes now," Geo whispered.

In fact, two figures approached them. As Urson, Geo, and Iimmi moved closer, they stopped, one a few steps before the other. Then they dropped. Geo couldn't tell if they fell or lay down quickly on the roadway.

"Go on?" asked Urson.

"Go on."

Pause.

"Go on," Geo repeated.

Two skeletons lay on the road where the figures had disappeared a minute before. "They don't seem dangerous," Geo said. "But what do they do? Die every time they see us?"

"Hey," Iimmi said. "What's that? Listen."

It was a sickly, liquid sound, like mud dropping into itself. Something was falling from the sky. No, not from the sky, but from the roadway that crossed theirs fifty feet overhead. Looking down again, they saw that a blob of something was growing on the pavement ten feet from them.

"Come on," Geo said, and they skirted the mess dripping from the road above and continued up the road. They passed four more skeletons. The plopping behind them became a sloshing.

As they turned, it emerged under the white and flaring lamps. Translucent insides bubble-pocked and quivering, it slipped forward across the road toward the skeletons. Impaling itself on the bones, it flowed around them, covered them, molded to them. A final surge, and its shapelessness contracted into arms, a head, legs. The naked man-thing pushed itself to its knees and then stood, its flesh now opaque. Eye sockets caved into the face. A mouth ripped low on the skull, and the chest began to move. A wet, steamy sound came from the mouth hole in irregular gasps.

It began to walk toward them, raising its hands from its sides. Then, behind it in the darkness, they saw the others.

"*Damn,*" said Urson. "What do they . . ."

"One or both of two things," Geo answered, backing away. "More meat or more bones."

"Whoops!" Iimmi said. "Back there—!"

Behind them seven more stood, while the ones in front advanced. Urson slipped his sword from his belt. The gleam of the streetlight ran down the blade. Suddenly he lunged at the leading figure, hacked at an upraised arm, sprang back. Severed at the elbow, the wound dribbled down the figure's side.

The arm splashed on the macadam. Quivering, the gelatinous mud contracted from the bone. As Urson danced back, one of the figures behind the injured one stepped squarely on the blob, which attached itself to its ankle and was absorbed.

A covered flight of stairs had its entrance here, leading to the next level of highway. They ducked into it and fled up the steps. Geo glanced back once: one of the forms had reached the entrance and had started to climb. They were high enough to get some idea of the city. Outside the transparent covering of the steps, the city spread in a web of lights, rising, looping, descending like roller-coaster tracks. Two glows caught him: beyond the river, a pale red haze flickered behind the jungle and was reflected on the water. The other was within the city, a pale orange nested among the buildings.

He took all this in during a glance as he ran up the steps. A gurgling became a roar behind them as they reached the top. Geo was only clear of the entrance when he yelled, "Run!"

They slipped from the doorway and staggered back. A mass of jelly the size of a two-story house flopped against the entrance. They edged by its pulsing sides. The lamplight pierced its translucent sides, where a skull caught in the jelly swirled to the surface, then sank.

"By Argo . . ." swore Urson.

"Don't try to cut it again, Urson!" Geo said. "It'll drown us!"

It sucked from the entrance and shivered ponderously. Something was happening at the front. A half-dozen figures were detaching themselves from the parent and preceding it.

Geo: "They can't go very fast—"

"Let's get the *hell* out of here!" Urson said.

They ran up the road, plunging suddenly into a darkened section. There was a glow in front of them. Suddenly Urson yelled, "Watch it!"

Abruptly the road sheared away. They halted and approached the edge slowly. The surface of the road tore away and the girders, unsupported, sagged toward the ruined stump of the building from which rose the orange glow. One wall of the building still stood, topped by a few girders that spiked the darkness. The glow came from the ruin's heart.

"What do you think that is?" asked Geo.

"I don't know," Iimmi said.

It sloshed along the road behind them. They looked. In the shadow, numberless figures marched toward them. Suddenly the figures fell to the ground, and without a halt in the sound, flesh rolled from bone, congealed, and rose, quivering, into the light.

"Get going!" Geo ordered.

Iimmi started out first on the twisted beams that descended to the glowing pit.

"You're crazy," Urson said. It flopped another meter. "Hurry up," he added. With Urson in the middle, they started along the twenty-inch width of girder. Lit from beneath, most of their bodies were in the shadow of the beam. Only their arms, outstretched for balance, burned with pale orange.

Before them, legible on the broken wall,

ATOMIC ENERGY FOR THE BETTERMENT OF MAN

was flanked by purple trefoils. The beams twisted sideways and then dropped to join others. Iimmi made the turn, dropped to his knees and hands, and then started to let himself down the four feet to the next small section of concrete. Once he saw something, let out a low whistle, but continued to lower himself to the straightened girder. Urson made the turn next. When he saw what Iimmi had seen, his hand shot to Geo's chest and grabbed the jewel.

Geo took his wrist. "That won't help us now," he said. "What is it?"

Urson expelled a breath and then continued down slowly, without speaking. Quickly Geo turned to drop—

The beam structure over which they had just come was coated with trembling thicknesses of the stuff. Globs hung pendulously from the steel shafts, glowing in the light from below, quivering, smoking, dropping off into the darkness. Here and there something half human rose to look around, to pull the collective mass farther on; but then it would fall back, dissolve. Sagging between the girders, noisome, thick, it bulged forward, burning in the pale light, smoking now, bits shriveling, falling away. Geo was about to go on. Then he called, "Wait a minute."

It wasn't making progress. It rolled to a certain point in the sherbet-colored light, sagged, smoked, and dropped away. And smoked. And dropped.

"It can't get any farther?" Urson asked.

"It doesn't look it," said Geo.

A skeleton stood, flesh running in the orange light. It tottered, steaming, and fell with a sucking noise into hundreds of feet of shadow. Geo was holding tightly to the girder in front of him.

The orange light fell cleanly over his hand, wrist, shadow starting at his elbow.

What happened made him squeeze until sweat came: the gargantuan mass, which had only extended tentacles till now, pulsed to the jagged edge and flung itself on the metal beams. It careened toward them. They jerked back.

Then it stopped.

It boiled, it burned, it writhed. And it sank, smoking, through the naked girder work. It tried to crawl back. Human figures leaped toward the road edge, missed, and plummeted like smoking bullets. It hurled a great pseudopod back toward the safety of the road; it fell short, flopped downward, and the whole mass shook. It slipped free of the beams, tentacles sliding across steel, whipping into air. Then it dropped, breaking into a dozen pieces before they lost sight of it.

Geo released the girder. "My arm hurts," he said.

They climbed back to the road. "What happened?" asked Iimmi.

"Whatever it was, I'm glad it did," said Urson.

Something clattered before them in the darkness.

"What was that?" asked Urson, stopping.

"My foot hit something," Geo said.

"What was it?" asked Urson.

"Never mind," said Geo. "Come on."

Fifteen minutes brought them to the stairway to the lower highway. Iimmi's memory proved good, and for an hour they went quickly, Iimmi making no hesitation at turnings.

"God," Geo said, rubbing his forearm. "I must have pulled hell out of my arm back there. It hurts like the devil."

Urson looked at his hands and rubbed them together.

"My hands feel sort of funny," Iimmi said. "Like they've been windburned."

"Windburned, nothing," said Geo. "This hurts."

Twenty minutes later, Iimmi said, "Well, this should be about it."

"Hey," said Urson. "There's Snake!" They ran forward as the boy jumped off the rail. Snake grabbed their shoulders and grinned. Then he began to tug them forward.

"Lucky little so-and-so," said Urson. "I wish you'd been with us."

"He probably was in spirit, if not in body." Geo laughed.

Snake nodded.

"What are you pulling for?" Urson asked. "Say, if you're going to get migraines at times like that, you'd better teach us what to do with those beads there." He pointed to the jewel at Iimmi's and Geo's necks.

But Snake just tugged them on.

"He wants us to hurry," Geo said. "We better get going."

The fallen floor had made descent through New Edison impossible. But the roadway still continued down, so they followed it along. Twice it cracked widely and they had to clamber along the rail. All the streetlights were out here, but they could see the river, struck with moonlight, through the buildings. Finally the road tore completely away, and four feet below them, over the twisted rail, was the mouth of the street that led to the waterfront. Snake, Iimmi, and then Urson vaulted over. Urson shook his hands painfully when he landed.

"Give me a hand, will you?" Geo asked. "My arm is really shot." Urson helped his friend over.

And almost as though it had been in wait, thick liquid gurgled behind them. A wounded thing, it emerged from behind the broken highway, bulging up into the light, which shone on the wrinkles in its shriveled membrane.

"Run it!" bawled Urson. They took off down the street. In the moonlight, the ruined piers spread along the waterfront to either side.

They saw it bloat the entrance of the street, fill it, then pour across the broken flags, slipping across the rubble of the smashed buildings.

On the edge of the wharf they looked back. Now the thing wavered, spreading tentacles left and right. From one of these a man formed. Standing at the head of the flowing mess, he raised a hand and beckoned to them in the moonlight.

Geo hit water and was aware of two things immediately as the hands caught him. First, the thong was yanked from around his neck. Second, pain seared his arm as if the nerves and ligaments were suddenly laced by white-hot strands of steel. Every vein and capillary had become part of a web of fire.

It was a long time before consciousness. Once he was lifted and he opened his mouth, expecting water. But there was only cool air. And when he opened his eyes, the white moon was moving fast above him toward the dark shapes of leaves, then was gone behind them. Was he being carried? And his arm . . . There was more drowsy half consciousness, and once a great deal of

pain. When he opened his mouth to scream, however, darkness
flowed in, swathed his tongue, and he swallowed the darkness
down into his body and into his head, and called it sleep—

*—a spool of copper wire unrolled over the black tile.
Scoop it up quick. Damn, let me get out of here. Run past the
black columns, glimpsing the cavernous room and the black
statue at the other end, huge, rising into shadows. Men in dark
robes walking around. Just don't feel up to praying this afternoon. I am before the door; above it, a black disk with three
white eyes on it. Through the door, now up the black stone steps.
Wonder if anyone will be up there. Just my luck I'll find the Old
Man himself. Another door with a black circle above it. Push it
open slowly, cool on my hands. A man is standing inside, looking into a large screen. Figures moving on it. Can't make them
out; he's in the way. Oh, there's another one. Jeepers . . .*

I don't know whether to call it success or failure, *one says.*

The jewels are . . . safe or lost?

What do you call it? *the first one asks.* I don't know anymore.
He sighs. I don't think I've taken my eyes off this thing for more
than two hours since they got to the beach. Every mile they've
come has made my blood run colder.

What do we report to Hama Incarnate?

It would be silly to say anything now. We don't know.

Well, *says the other*, at least we can do something with the
City of New Hope, since they got rid of that superamoeba.

Are you sure they really got it?

After the burning it received over that naked atom pile? It was
all it could do to get to the waterfront. It's just about fried up
and blown away already.

And how safe would you call them? *the other asks.*

Right now? I wouldn't call them anything.

*Something glitters on the table by the door. Yes, there it is. In
the pile of junked equipment is a U-shaped scrap of metal. Just
what I need. Hot damn, adhesive tape too! Quick, there, before*

they see. Fine. Now, let the door close, reeeeeal slow. Oops. It clicked. Now come on; look innocent, in case they come out. I hope the Old Man isn't watching. Guess they're not coming. And down the stairs again, the black stone walls moving past. Out another door into the garden: dark flowers, purple, deep red, some with blue in them, and big stone urns. Oh, priests coming down the path. Oops again, there's Dunderhead. He'll want me inside praying. Duck down behind that urn. Here we go. What'll I do if he catches me? Really, sir, I have nothing under my choir robe. Peek out.

Very, very small sigh of relief. Can't afford to be too loud around here. They're gone. Let's examine the loot. The black stone urn has one handle above. It's about eight feet tall. One, two, three: jump, and . . . hold . . . on . . . and . . . pull. And try to get to the top. . . . There we go. Cold stone between my toes. And over the edge, where it's filled with dirt. Pant, pant, pant.

Should be just over here, if I remember right. Dig, dig, dig. Damp earth feels good in your hands. Ow! my finger. There it is: a brown paper bag under the black earth. Lift it out. Is it all there? Open it up; peer in. At the bottom in the folds of paper: tiny scraps of copper, a few long pieces of iron, a piece of board, some brads. To this my grubby little hand adds the spool of copper wire and the U-shaped scrap of metal. Now slip it into my robe and . . . once you get up here, how the hell do you get down? I always forget. Turn around, climb over the edge, like this, and let yourself . . . Damn, my robe's caught on the handle.

And drop.

Skinned my shin again. Someday I'll learn. Uh-oh, Dunderhead is going to blow a condenser when he sees my robe torn. Oh, well, sic vita est.

Now let's see if we can figure this thing out. Gotta crouch down and get to work. Here we go. Open the bag and turn the contents out in the lap of my robe, grubby hands poking.

The U-shaped metal, the copper wire, fine. Hold the end of the wire to the metal and maneuver the spool around the end of the rod. Around and around and around. Here we go round the mulberry bush, the mulberry bush, the mulberry bush. Here we go round the mulberry bush; I'll have me a coil by the morning.

A harsh voice: And what do you think you're doing?

Dunderhead rides again. Nothing, sir, *as metal and scraps and wires fly frantically into the paper bag.*

The voice: All novices under twenty must report to afternoon services without fail!

Yes, sir. Coming right along, sir. *Paper bag jammed equally frantically into the folds of my robe. Not a moment's peace. Not a moment's! Through the garden with lowered eyes, past dour priest with small paunch. There are mirrors along the vestibule, reflecting the blue and yellow from the colored panes. In the mirror I see pass: a dour priest, preceded by a smaller figure with short red hair and a spray of freckles over a flattish nose. As we pass into prayer, there is the maddening, not quite inaudible jingle of metal, muffled by the dark robe—*

Geo woke up, and almost everything was white.

chapter eight

The pale woman with the tiny eyes rose from over him. Her hair slipped like white silk threads over her shoulders. "You are awake?" she asked. "Do you understand me?"

"Am I at Hama's Temple?" he asked, the remnants of the dream still blowing in at the edges of his mind, like shredding cloth. "My friends . . . where are they?"

The woman laughed. "Your friends are all right. You came

out the worst." Another laugh. "You ask if this is Hama's Temple? But you can see. You have eyes. Don't you recognize the color of the White Goddess Argo?"

Geo looked around the room. It was white marble, and there was no direct source of light. The walls simply glowed.

"My friends . . ." Geo said again.

"They are fine. We were able to completely restore their flesh to health. They must have exposed their hands to the direct beams of the radiation only a few seconds. But the whole first half of your arm must have lain in the rays for some minutes. You were not as lucky as they."

Another thought rushed Geo's mind now. *The jewels . . .* he wanted to say, but instead of sounding the words, he reached to his throat with both hands. One fell on his naked chest. And there was something very wrong with the other. He sat up in the bed quickly and looked down. "My arm . . ." he said.

Swathed in white bandages, the limb ended some foot and a half short of where it should have.

"My arm—?" he asked again, with a child's bewilderment. "What happened to my arm?"

"I tried to tell you," the woman said softly. "We had to amputate your forearm and most of your biceps. If we had not, you would have died."

"My arm . . ." Geo said again. He lay back on the bed.

"It is difficult," the woman said. "It is only a little consolation, I know, but we are blind here. What burned your arm away took our sight from us when it was much stronger, generations ago. We learned how to battle many of its effects, and had we not rescued you from the river, all of you would have died. You are men who know the religion of Argo and adhere to it. Be thankful then that you have come under the wing of the Mother Goddess again. This is hostile country." She paused. "Do you wish to talk?"

Geo shook his head.

"I hear the sheets rustle," the woman said, smiling, "which means you either shook or nodded your head. I know from my study of the old customs that one means yes and the other no. But you must have patience with us who cannot see. We are not used to your people. Do you wish to talk?" she repeated.

"Oh," said Geo. "No. No, I don't."

"Very well." She rose, still smiling. "I will return later." She walked to a wall. A door slipped open, and then it closed behind her.

He lay still for a long time. Then he turned over on his stomach. Once he brought the stump under his chest and held the clean bandages in his other hand. Very quickly he let go and stretched the limb sideways, as far as possible away from him. That didn't work either, so he moved it back down to his side and let it lay by him under the white sheet.

After a long while, he got up, sat on the edge of the bed, and looked around the room. It was completely bare, with neither windows nor visible doors. He went to the spot through which she had exited, but could find no seam or crack. His tunic, he saw, had been washed, pressed, and laid at the foot of the bed. He slipped it over his head, fumbling with only one arm. Getting the belt together started out a problem, but he hooked the buckle around one finger and maneuvered the strap through with the others. He adjusted his leather purse, now empty, at his side.

His sword was gone.

An unreal feeling, white like the walls of the room, filled him like a pale mixture of milk and water. He walked around the edge of the room once more, looking for some break.

There was a sound behind him and the tiny-eyed woman in her white robe stood in a triangular doorway. "You're dressed." She smiled. "Good. Are you too tired to come with me? You will eat and see your friends if you feel well enough. Or I can have the food brought—"

"I'll come," Geo said.

He followed her into a hall of the same luminous substance. Her heels touched the back of her white robe with each step. His own bare feet on the cool stones seemed louder than those of the blind woman before him. Suddenly he was in a larger room, with benches. It was a chapel of Argo. But the altar at the far end, its detail was strange. Everything was arranged with the simplicity one would expect of a people to whom visual adornment meant nothing. He sat down on a bench.

"Wait here." She disappeared down another hall.

She returned, followed by Snake. Geo and the four-armed boy looked at each other silently as the woman disappeared again. A wish, like a living thing, suddenly writhed into a knot in Geo's stomach, that the boy would say something. He himself could not.

Again she returned, this time with Urson. The big sailor stepped into the chapel, saw Geo, and exclaimed, "Friend . . . what . . ." He came to Geo quickly and placed his warm hands on Geo's shoulders. "How . . ." he began, and shook his head.

Geo grinned suddenly and patted his stump with his good hand. "I guess Jelly-belly got something from me, after all."

Urson took up Geo's good hand and examined it. It seemed pale. Urson held his own forearm next to Geo's and compared them. The paleness was in both. "I guess none of us got out completely all right. I woke up once while they were taking the scabs off. It was pretty bad, and I went to sleep again fast."

Iimmi came in now. "Well, I was wondering . . ." He stopped and let out a low whistle. "I guess it really got you, brother." His own arms looked as though they had been dipped in bleach up to the mid-forearms, leaving them pinkish until they turned their normal purple-brown at the elbows.

"How did this happen?" Urson asked.

"When we were back doing our tightrope act on those damn girders," explained Iimmi, "our bodies were in the shadow of the girders and the rays only got to our arms. It's apparently a highly directional form of radiation, stopped by anything like steel, but—"

"A highly who of what?" Urson asked.

"I've been getting quite a course." Iimmi grinned. "And I've got something you'll be interested in too, Geo."

"Just tell me where the hell we are," Urson said.

"We're in a convent sacred to Argo," Iimmi told him. "It's across the river from the City of New Hope, which is where we were."

"That name sounds familiar; in the—" began Urson. Snake gave him a quick glance; and Urson stopped and then frowned.

"We knew of your presence in the City of New Hope," explained the blind Priestess, "and we found you by the riverside after you managed to swim across. We thought you would die, but apparently you have a stronger constitution than the inhabitants of Aptor do. After crossing the river, you managed to cling to life long enough for us to get you back to the convent and apply what art we could to soothe the burns from the deadly fire."

There was no jewel around Iimmi's neck either. Geo could feel the hands ripping it from his neck in the water again. Iimmi must have just made the same discovery when he looked at Geo, because his pale hand rose to his own chest.

"If you gentlemen will come with me," said the blind Priestess of Argo. "None of you have had more than intravenous feeding for the past two days. You may eat now." She turned down another hall; again they followed.

They arrived at an even larger room, this one set with white marble benches and long white tables. "This is the main dining room of the convent," their guide explained. "One table has been set up for you. You will not eat with the other priestesses, of course."

"Why not?" asked Iimmi.

Surprise flowed across the blind face. "You are men," she told them matter-of-factly. Then she led them to a table with wine, meat, and bowls piled with strange fruit. As they sat, she disappeared once more.

Geo reached for a knife. For a moment there was silence as the nub of his arm jutted over the table. "I guess I just have to learn," he said after the pause. He picked up the knife with the other hand.

Halfway through the meal, Urson asked, "What about the jewels? Did the Priestess take them from you?"

"They came off in the water," said Iimmi.

Geo nodded corroboration.

"Well, now we really have a problem," said Urson. "Here we are, at a Temple of Argo, where we could return the jewels and maybe even get back to the Priestess on the ship and out of the silly mess; but the jewels are gone."

"That also means our river friends are working for Hama," said Geo.

"And we are just being used to carry the jewels back to Hama's Temple," added Urson. "Probably, when they found we were almost dead after that thing in the city, they just took the jewels from us and abandoned us on the shore."

"I guess so," said Iimmi.

"Well," Geo said, "Hama's got his jewels then, and we're out of the way. Perhaps he delivered us into Argo's hands as a reward for bringing them this far."

"Since we would have died anyway," said Iimmi, "I guess he was doing us a favor."

"And you know what that means," Geo said, looking at Snake now.

"Huh?" asked Urson. Then he said, "Oh, let the boy speak for himself. All right, Four Arms, are you or are you not a spy for Hama?"

Geo could not read the expression that came over Snake's face. The boy shook his head not in denial but bewilderment. Suddenly he got up from the table and ran from the room. Urson looked at the others. "Now don't tell me I hurt his feelings by asking."

"You didn't," said Geo, "but I may have. I keep on forgetting that he can read minds."

"What do you mean?" Urson asked.

"Just when you asked him that, a lot of things came together in my mind that would be pretty vicious for him if any of them were true."

"Huh?" asked Urson.

"I think I know what you mean," said Iimmi.

"I still—"

"It means that he is a spy," exclaimed Geo, "and among other things, he was probably lying about the radio back at the city. And that cost me my arm."

"Why, the . . ." began Urson, and then looked down the hall where Snake had disappeared.

They didn't eat much more. When they got up, Urson felt sleepy and was shown back to his room.

"May I show my friend what you showed me?" Iimmi asked the Priestess when she returned. "He is also a student of rituals."

"Of course you may." The Priestess smiled. "However, as students of the rituals of Argo you show surprising ignorance."

"As I tried to explain," said Iimmi, "we come from a land where the rituals have changed a great deal with time."

"Surely not that much," said the Priestess, smiling. "But you make such a fuss. These are only our commonest prayers. They do not even touch the subjects of magic." She led them down the hall. "And your amazement quite amazes me. Yours must be a young and enthusiastic people."

A door opened and they entered another room similar to the one in which Geo had awakened. As she was about to leave, Iimmi said, "Wait. Can you tell us how to leave the room ourselves?"

"Why would you want to leave?" she asked.

"For exercise," offered Geo, "and to observe the working of the convent. Believe us; we are true students of Argo's religion."

"Simply press the wall with your hand, level at your waist, and the door will open. But you must not wander about the convent. Rites that are not for your eyes are being carried out. . . . Not for your eyes," she repeated. "Strange, this phrase has never left our language. Suddenly, confronted by people who can see, it makes me feel somehow . . ." She paused. "Well, that is how to leave the room."

She stepped out. The door closed.

"Here," said Iimmi, "this is what I wanted to show you." On his bed was a pile of books, old but legible. Geo flipped through a few pages. Suddenly he looked up at Iimmi.

"Hey, what are they doing with *printed* books?"

"Question number one," said Iimmi. "Now, for question number two. Look here." He reached over Geo's shoulder and hastened him to one page.

"Why, it's the . . ." began Geo.

"You're damn right it is," said Iimmi.

"*Hymn to the Goddess Argo,*" Geo read aloud. And then:

> "Forked in the eye of the bright ash
> there the heart of Argo broke
> and the hand of the goddess would dash
> through the head of flame and smoke.
>
> Burn the grain speck in the hand
> and batter the stars with singing.
> Hail the height of a man,
> also the height of a woman.
>
> Take from the tip of the sea
> salt and sea kelp and gold.
> Vision, a shaft through the brain,
> and the terror of time is old.
>
> Salt to scour the tongue,
> salt on the temple floor,
> sea kelp to bind up my hair
> and set forth for gold once more.
>
> The eyes have imprisoned a vision,
> the ash tree dribbles with blood.
> Thrust from the gates of the prison,
> smear the yew tree with mud.

"That must be the full version of the poem I found the missing stanza to back in the library at Leptar."

"As I was saying," said Iimmi. "Question number two: what is the relation between the rituals of Hama and the old rituals of Argo? Apparently this particular branch of the religion of the Goddess underwent no purge."

"If the librarian at Olcse Ohlwn could see these," breathed Geo, "he'd probably pick them up with long tongs, put his hand over his eyes, and carry them to the nearest fire."

Iimmi looked puzzled. "Why?"

"Don't you remember? These are forbidden. One of the reasons they were destroyed was because nobody was supposed to know about them."

"I wonder why?" Iimmi asked.

"That's question number three. How did you get hold of them?"

"Well," said Iimmi, "I sort of suspected they might be here. So I just asked for them."

"And I think I've got some answers to those questions."

"Fine. Go ahead."

"We'll start from three, go back to one, and then on to two. Nice and orderly. Why wasn't anybody supposed to know about the rituals? Simply because they *were* so similar to the rituals of Hama. You remember some of the others we found in the abandoned temple? If you don't, you can refresh your memory right here. The two sets of rituals run almost parallel, except for a name changed here, a color switched from black to white, a variation in the vegetative symbolism. I guess what happened was that when Hama's forces invaded Leptar five hundred years ago, it didn't take Leptar long to discover the similarity. From the looks of the City of New Hope, I think it's safe to assume that at one time or another—say, five hundred years ago—Aptor's civilization was far higher than Leptar's, and probably wouldn't have had too hard a time beating her in an invasion. So when Leptar captured the first jewel and somehow did manage to repel

Aptor, the priests of Leptar assumed that the safest way to avoid infiltration by Hama and Aptor again would be to make the rituals of Argo as different as possible from the ones of their enemy, Hama. There may have been a small following of Hama in Leptar before the invasion, but all traces of it were destroyed with the rituals."

"Why do you say that?"

"Well, there's apparently a small peaceful following of Argo here in Aptor. There may have even been trade between the two, which is why the stories of Aptor survive among sailors. The ghouls, the flying things, they parallel the stories the sailors tell too closely to be accidents. How many men do you think have been shipwrecked on Aptor and gotten far enough into the place to see what we've seen, and then gotten off again to tell about it?"

"I can think of two," said Iimmi.

"Huh?"

"Snake and Jordde," answered Iimmi. "Remember that Argo said there had been spies from Aptor before. Jordde is definitely one, and I guess so is Snake."

"That fits with rule number one." He got up from the bed. "Come on. Let's take a walk. I want to see some sunlight." They went to the wall. Geo pressed it and the triangular panel slipped back.

When they had rounded four or five turns of hallway, Geo said, "I hope you can remember where we've been."

"I've got a more or less eidetic memory for directions," Iimmi said.

Suddenly the passage opened onto steps, and they were looking out upon a huge white concourse. Down a set of thirty marble steps priestesses filed below, their heads fixed blindly forward. Each woman's hand rested on the shoulder of the one ahead of her. There were over a hundred, but the lines never collided. One row would merely pause for another to pass, and then begin to glide forward again. The silence and the whiteness were dreamlike.

At the far end was a raised dais with a mammoth statue of a kneeling woman, sculptured of the same effulgent, argic stone. "Where do these women come from?" whispered Iimmi. "And where do they keep the men?"

Geo shrugged.

A priestess came across the temple floor now, alone. She reached the bottom steps, and as she began to ascend, Geo recognized her as the one in charge. She climbed directly toward them, stopped in front of them, and said almost inaudibly, "Gentlemen, you are disturbing the hour of meditation. I asked you not to wander indiscriminately about the convent. Please return with me."

As she glided past, Geo and Iimmi frowned at each other. After they had rounded a few corners, Geo said, "Excuse me, ma'am, we didn't mean to be disrespectful, but we are used to natural day and night. We need fresh air, green things. This underground whiteness is oppressive and makes us restless. Could you show us a way into the open?"

"No," returned the blind Priestess quietly. "Besides, night is coming on and you are not creatures who relish darkness."

"The night air and the quiet of evening are refreshing to us," countered Iimmi.

"What do you know of the night?" answered the Priestess with faint cynicism in her low voice. Now they reached the chapel where the friends had first met after their rescue.

"Perhaps," suggested Geo, "you could talk to us awhile, then. There are many things we would like to know."

The Priestess turned, sighed softly, and said, "Very well. What would you like to talk about?"

"For instance," said Geo, "what can you tell us about the Dark God Hama?"

The blind Priestess shrugged, and sat on one of the benches. "There is little to say. Today he is a fiction; he does not exist. There is only Argo, the One White Goddess."

"But we've heard—"

"You were at his abandoned temple," said the Priestess. "You saw yourselves. That is all that is left of Hama. Ghouls prey on the dust of his dead saints."

Iimmi and Geo looked at each other again, puzzled. "Are you sure?" Geo asked.

"Perhaps," mused the Priestess, "somewhere behind the burning mountain a few of his disciples are left. But Hama is dead in Aptor. You have seen the remains of his city, the City of New Hope. You have also been the first ones to enter it and return in nearly five hundred years."

"Is that how long the city has been in ruin?" asked Geo.

"It is."

"What can you tell us about the city?"

The Priestess sighed again. "There was a time," she began, "generations ago, when Hama was a high god in Aptor. He had many temples, monasteries, and convents devoted to him. We had few. Except for these religious sanctuaries, the land was barbaric, wild, uninhabitable for the most part. There had once been cities in Aptor, but these had been destroyed even earlier by the Great Fire. All that we had was a fantastic record of an unbelievable time before the rain of flame, of tremendous power, vast science, and a towering, though degenerate, civilization. These records were extensive and almost entirely housed within the monasteries. Outside, there was only chaos; half the children were born dead and the other half deformed. Because of the monstrous races that sprang up over the Island now as a reminder to us, we decided the magic contained in these chronicles was evil, and must never be released to the world again. But the priests of Hama did not come to the same decision. They decided to use the information in these chronicles, spread it to the people; they were sure they would not commit the same mistakes that had brought the Great Fire. They opened the books, and a dream materialized from their pages, and that dream was the City of New Hope, which sits in ruin now on the far shore. They made giant machines that flew. They constructed immense boats that could sink into the sea and emerge hundreds of miles away in another harbor in another land. They even harnessed for beneficial use the fire metal, uranium, which had brought such terror to the world before, and had brought down the flames."

"But they made the same mistake as the people before the Great Fire made?" suggested Iimmi.

"Not exactly," said the Priestess. "That is, they were not so stupid as to misuse the fire metal that ravaged the world so harshly before. History is cyclic, not repetitive. A new power was discovered that dwarfed the significance of the fire metal. It could do all that the fire metal could do, and more efficiently—destroy cities or warm chill huts in winter—but it could also work on men's minds. They say that before the Great Fire, men wandered the streets of the cities terrified that flames might descend on them any moment and destroy them. They panicked, brought flimsy, useless contraptions to guard themselves from the fire.

"Geo, Iimmi, have you any idea how terrifying it would be to know that while you are walking the streets, at any moment, your mind might be snatched from you, raped, violated, and left broken in your own skull? Only three of these instruments were constructed. But the moment their existence was made known by a few fantastic demonstrations, the City of New Hope began the swerve down the arc of self-destruction. It lasted for a year and ended with the wreck you escaped from. During that year invasions were launched on the backward nations across the sea with whom, months before, there had been friendly trade. Civil wars broke out and internal struggles caused the invasions to fall back to the homeland. The instruments were lost, but not before the bird machines had even destroyed the City of New Hope itself. The house of the fire metal was broken open to release its death once more. For a hundred years after the end, say our records, the city flamed with light from the destroyed power-house. And mechanically, to this day, our instruments tell us, the lights along its elevated highways flare at sunset, as if dead hands were there to operate them. During the first hundred years more and more of our number were born blind because of the sinking fire in the city. At last we moved underground, but it was too late." She rose from her seat. "And so you see, Hama destroyed himself. Today, loyal to Argo, are all the beasts of the air, of the land . . ."

"And of the waters," concluded Iimmi.

She smiled again. "Again, not exactly. We have had some trouble with a certain race of aquatic creatures, as well as the ignorant ghouls. Right after the Great Fire, evolutionary processes were tremendously turned awry, and we believe this is how these creatures developed. For some reason we cannot control them. Perhaps their intelligence is too elemental even to respond to pain. But all the rest are loyal," she said. "All."

"What about the . . . the three instruments?" Geo asked. "What happened to them?"

The blind Priestess turned to him. "Your guess," she said, smiling, "is as good as mine." She turned and glided from the room.

When she left, Geo said, "Something is fishy."

"But what is it?" asked Iimmi.

"For one thing," said Geo, "we know there is a Temple of Hama. From the dream I would say that it's just about the size and organization of this place."

"Just how big is this place anyway?"

"Want to do some more exploring?"

"Sure. Do you think she does know about Hama but was just pretending?"

"Could be," said Geo. They started off down another corridor. "That bit about going into men's minds with the jewels . . ."

"It gives me the creeps."

"It's a creepy thing to watch," said Geo. "Argo used it on Snake the first time we saw her. It just turns you into an automaton."

"Then it really is our jewels she was talking about."

Stairs cut a white tunnel in the wall before them, and they mounted, coming finally to another corridor. For the first time they saw doors in the wall. "Hey," said Geo, "maybe one of these goes outside."

"Fine," said Iimmi. "This place is beginning to get to me." He pushed open a door and stepped in. Except for the flowing white walls, it duplicated in miniature the basement of the New Edison building. Twin dynamos whirred and the walls were laced with pipes.

"Nothing in here," said Iimmi.

They tried a door across the hall. In this room sat a white porcelain table and floor-to-ceiling cases of glittering instruments. "I bet this is the room your arm came off in," Iimmi said.

"Probably."

The next room was different. The glow was dimmer, and there was dust on the walls. Geo ran his finger over it and looked at the gray crescent left on the bleached flesh. "This looks a little more homey."

"This is what you call homey?" Iimmi gestured toward the opposite wall. Two screens leaned from the face of a metal machine. A few dials and meters were set beneath each rounded rectangle of opaque glass. In front was a stand that held something like a set of binoculars and what looked like a pair of earmuffs.

"I bet this place hasn't been used since before these girls went blind."

"It looks it," Iimmi said.

Geo stepped up to one of the screens, the one with the fewer dials on it, and turned a switch.

"What did you do that for?"

"Why not?" Suddenly a flickering of colored lights ran over the screen: swellings of blue, green, scarlets. They blinked. "That's the first color I've seen since I've been here."

The colors grayed, dimmed, congealed into forms, and in a moment they were looking at a bare white room in which stood two barefoot young men. One was a dark Negro with pale hands. The other had an unruly shock of black hair and one arm.

Iimmi gestured: the figure on the screen gestured too. "That's us!" Geo walked forward and the corresponding figure advanced on the screen. He flicked a dial and the figures exploded into colors and then focused again into complete whiteness. "What's that?" asked Iimmi.

"We must be looking at a room with no people in it." Geo flicked the dial again. When the screen focused, they were looking at the dining room. Now a hundred or more women sat at the long tables, each bending and raising her blind face over bowls of red soup. In one corner, empty, was the table at which they had eaten. "I bet we could look into every room in the place." He switched the dial again. "Maybe we can find Urson and Snake." Two more rooms, then the great temple hall formed on the screen, empty save for the statue of Argo kneeling. As the next room passed, Geo called out, "Wait a minute!"

"What is it?"

In this room stood three of the blind women. On one wall was a smaller screen similar to the one in their own room. The women, of course, were oblivious to the picture, but the face on the screen had stopped Geo.

One of the women had on an earmuff apparatus and was talking into a small metal rod that she carried with her as she paced.

But the face! "Don't you recognize him?" demanded Geo.

"It's Jordde!" exclaimed Iimmi.

"They must have gotten in contact with our ship and are arranging to send us back."

"I wish I could hear what they're saying," said Iimmi.

Geo looked around and then picked up the metal earmuffs from the stand in front of the screen. "That's what she seems to be listening through," Geo said, referring to the Priestess in the picture. He fit them over his ears.

"Hear anything?" Iimmi asked.

Geo listened.

"Yes, of course," the Priestess was saying.

"She is set upon staying in the harbor for three more days, to wait out the week," reported Jordde. "I am sure she will not stay any longer. She is still bewildered by me, and the men have become uneasy and may well mutiny if she stays longer."

"We will dispose of the prisoners this evening. There is no chance of their returning," stated the Priestess.

"Detain them for three days, and I do not care what you do with them," said Jordde. "She does not have the jewels; she does not know my . . . our power; she will be sure to leave at the end of the week."

"It's a pity we have no jewels for all our trouble," said the Priestess. "But at least all three are back in Aptor and potentially within our grasp."

Jordde laughed. "And Hama never seems to be able to keep hold of them for more than ten minutes before they slip from him again."

"Yours is not to judge either Hama or Argo," stated the Priestess. "You are kept on by us only to do your job. Do it, report, and do not trouble either us or yourself with opinions. They are not appreciated."

"Yes, Mistress," returned Jordde.

"Then farewell until next report." She flipped a switch and the picture on the little screen went gray.

Geo turned from the big screen and was just about to remove the hearing apparatus when he heard the Priestess say, "Go; prepare the prisoners for the sacrifice of the rising moon. They have seen too much." The woman left the room, Geo removed the phones, and Iimmi looked at him.

"What's the matter?"

Geo turned the switch that darkened the screen.

"When are they coming to get us?" Iimmi asked excitedly.

"Right now, probably," Geo said. Then, as best he could, he repeated the conversation he had overheard to Iimmi, whose expression grew more and more bewildered as Geo went on.

At the end the bewilderment suddenly flared into frayed indignation. "Why?" demanded Iimmi. "Why should we be sacrificed? What is it we've seen, what is it we know? This is the second time it's come close to getting me killed, and I wish to hell I knew what I was supposed to know!"

"We've got to find Urson and get out of here!"

"Hey, what's wrong?"

Indignation had turned into something else. Geo stood with his eyes shut tight and his face screwed up. Suddenly he relaxed. "I just thought out a message as loud as I could for Snake to get up here and to bring Urson if he's anywhere around."

"But Snake's a spy for—"

"—for Hama," said Geo. "And you know something? I don't care." He closed his eyes again. After a few moments, he opened them. "Well, if he's coming, he's coming. Let's get going."

"But why?" began Iimmi, following Geo out the door.

"Because I have a poet's feeling his mind reading may come in handy."

They hurried down the hall, found the stairs, ducked down, and ran along the lower hall. Rounding a second corner, they emerged into the little chapel simultaneously with Urson and Snake.

"I guess I got through," said Geo. "Which way do we go?"

"Gentlemen, gentlemen," came a voice behind them.

Snake took off down one of the passages; they followed, Urson looking particularly bewildered.

The Priestess glided behind, calling softly, "Please, my friends, come back. Return with me."

"Find out from her how the hell to get out of this place!" Geo bawled to Snake. The four-armed boy darted up a sudden flight of stairs, turned, and ran up another. They came out in a hall, behind Snake.

The boy's four hands flew at the door handle, turning it carefully this way and back.

Two, three seconds.

Geo glanced back and saw the Priestess mount the head of the stairs and start toward them. Her white robes floated from her, brushing the walls.

The door came open; they broke through leaves and were momentarily in a huge field surrounded by woods. The sky was pale with moonlight.

A hundred fifty yards across the field was a white statue of Argo. As they ran through the silver grass, doors opened in the base and a group of priestesses emerged and began to hurry toward them. Geo turned to look behind him. The blind Priestess had slowed, her face turned to the moon. Her hands went to her throat, she unclasped her robe, and the first layer fell behind her. As she continued forward, the second layer began to unfold, wet, leprously white, spreading from her arms, articulating along the white spines; then, with a horribly familiar shriek, she leaped from the ground and soared upward, white wings hammering the air.

They fled.

Dark forms shadowed the moon. The priestesses across the field joined her aloft in the moon-bleached night. She overtook the running figures, turned above them, and swooped down. The moon lanced white on bared teeth. The breeze touched pale furry breasts, filled the bellying wings. Only the tiny, darting, blind eyes were red, rubies in a whirl of white.

Snake changed direction and fled toward the trees.

With only one arm, Geo found himself off balance. He nearly fell twice before he crashed into the bushes where the winged things could not follow. Branches raked his face as he followed the sound the others made. Once he thought he had lost them, but a second later he bumped against Iimmi, who had stopped behind Snake and Urson. Above the trees was a sound like beaten cloth, diminishing, growing, but constant as once more they began to tread through the tangled darkness.

"Damn . . ." sighed Iimmi after a minute of walking.

"It's beginning to make sense," Geo said, his hand on Iimmi's shoulder. "Remember that man-wolf we met, and that thing in the city? The only thing we've met on this place that hasn't changed shape is the ghouls. I think most creatures on this Island undergo some sort of metamorphosis."

"What about those first flying things we met?" whispered Urson. "They don't change into anything."

"Probably we have just been guests of the female of the species," said Geo. "I think that's what Snake was warning us about when he took us to see them in the barracks. He was trying to tell us that we might meet them again."

"You mean those others could have changed into men too, if they wanted?" Urson asked.

"If they'd wanted," answered Geo. "But it was more convenient to stay outside the convent. They come together only for mating, more than likely."

"Which just might be what this ceremony of the rising moon is about," Iimmi observed. "The ones flying against the moon were the other kind, the men. You know there are sections over in Leptar where the female worshipers of Argo completely avoid the male members."

"That's what I was thinking of," said Geo. "It first dawned on me when they wouldn't let us eat with the women."

In front of them now appeared shiftings of silver light. Five minutes later, they were crouching at the edge of the trees, looking down over the rocks at the shimmering river.

"Into the water?" Geo asked.

Snake shook his head. *Wait* . . . inside their heads.

A hand rose from the water. Wet and green, a foot or so from the shore, it turned, the chain and the leather thong dangling down the wrist: swinging there were two bright beads.

Iimmi and Geo froze. Urson said: "The jewels . . ."

Suddenly the big sailor sprang onto the rocks and ran toward the river's edge.

Three shadows, one white, two dark, converged above him, cutting the moonlight away. If Urson saw them, he did not stop.

Iimmi and Geo stood up.

Urson reached the shore, threw himself along the rock, swiped at the hand, and was covered by flailing wings. The membranous sails splashed in the water, there were shrieks, and one white wing arced high, then flapped down again. Two seconds later, Urson rolled from beneath the creatures still struggling half on land and half in the water. He staggered to his feet and started up the rocks again. He slipped, regained his footing, and came on, to fall into Geo's and Iimmi's arms.

"The jewels . . ." Urson breathed.

The struggle continued on the water. Something held them down, twisted at them. Suddenly the creatures stilled. Like great leaves, the three forms drifted apart, caught in the current, and floated away from the rocks.

Then two more forms bobbed to the surface, faces down, rocking gently, backs slicked wet and green.

"But those were the ones who . . ." Geo began. "Are they dead?" His face suddenly hurt a little, with something like the pain of verging tears.

Snake nodded.

"Are you sure?" asked Iimmi. His voice was slow.

Their . . . thoughts . . . have . . . stopped . . . Snake said.

Crouching in front of them, Urson opened his scarred hands. The globes blazed through the leaves. The chain and the wet thong hung from his palm to the ground. "I have them," he whispered. "The jewels!"

chapter nine

Snake picked up the beads from the calloused palm, placed one around Geo's neck, one around Iimmi's. Urson watched the jewels rise.

Then they turned into the forest; the sound of wings had stopped.

"Where do we go now?" Urson asked.

"We follow rule number one," said Geo. "Since we know Hama does have a temple somewhere, we try to find it, get the third jewel, and rescue Argo Incarnate. Then we get back to the ship."

"In three days?" asked Urson. "Where do we start looking?"

"The Priestess said something about a band of Hama's disciples behind the fire mountain—the volcano we saw from the steps in the City of New Hope." Geo turned to Snake. "Did you read her mind enough to know if she was telling the truth?"

Snake nodded.

Iimmi thought a moment. "Since the river is that way . . . we should head"—he turned and pointed—"in that direction."

They fixed their stride now and started through the pearly leaves.

"I still don't understand what was going on back at the convent," Iimmi said. "Were they really priestesses of Argo? And what was Jordde doing?"

"I'd say yes on the first question, and guess that Jordde was a spy for them for an answer to the second."

"But what about Argo . . . I mean Argo on the ship?" asked Iimmi. "And what about Snake here?"

"Argo on the ship apparently doesn't know about Argo on Aptor," said Geo. "That's what Jordde meant when he reported to the priestesses that she was bewildered. She probably thinks just like we did, that he's Hama's spy. And this one here . . ." He gestured at Snake. "I don't know. I just don't know."

When the light failed, they lay together and tried to sleep. But minutes after they had settled, and the white disk dropped from the horizon, Geo suddenly called them up again. In the distant red glow they could make out the volcano's cone.

Snake made lights with the jewels, and they began to pick their way over the land, now barer and barer of vegetation. Broken trees leaned against broken boulders. The earth grew cindery. The air bore old and acrid ash.

Soon the red rim of the crater hung close above them.

"How near are we?" Urson asked.

"I think we've already started the slope," Geo said.

"Maybe we ought to stop before we go any farther and wait till morning."

"We can't sleep here," mumbled Urson, pushing cinders with his foot. He stretched. "Besides, we don't have time to sleep."

Geo gazed up at the red haze. "I wonder what it's like to look into that thing in the middle of the night?" He began again and they followed. Twenty feet later Snake's light struck a lavid black cliff that sheared up into the darkness. Going on beside it, they found a ledge that made an eighteen-inch footpath diagonally up the face.

"We're not going to climb that in the dark, are we?" asked Iimmi.

"Better than in the light," said Urson. "This way you can't see how far you have to fall."

Iimmi started up the lip of rock. Thirty feet on, instead of petering out and forcing them to go back, it broadened into level ground, and again they could go straight toward the red light above them.

"This is changeable country," Urson muttered.

"Men change into animals," said Iimmi; "jungles turn to mountains."

Geo reached up and felt the stub of his arm in the dark. "I've changed too, I guess.

"Change is neither merciful nor just," he recited:
"They say Leonard of Vinci put his trust
in faulty paints: Christ's Supper turned to dust."

"What's that from?" Iimmi asked.

"Another one of my bits of original research," Geo explained. "It comes from a poem dating back before the Great Fire. I found it when I was doing research in the tombs."

"Who was Leonard of Vinci?" Iimmi asked.

"An artist, perhaps another poet or painter," said Geo. "I'm not really sure."

"Who's Christ?" Urson asked.

"Another god."

There were more rocks now, and Geo had to brace his stub against the wall fissure and hoist himself up with his good hand. The igneous points were sharp on his palm. The lights wavered from time to time as Snake at the lead transferred them from this hand to that. The boy rounded another jutting and the crags sent double shadows slipping down.

Reaching a fairly level spot, they turned to look behind them. They were standing on the brim of a bowl of blackness. The sky was starry and lighter than the plate of velvet vegetation circling before them. They turned again and continued.

Through the night the glowing rim dropped. With it came a breeze that pushed sulfur powder through their hair and made their nostrils sting.

"Maybe we should go around and approach it from the other side," Urson suggested. "That way the wind won't be so bad."

They set their climb at an angle now; soon the wind fell, and they could head straight up again.

The earth became scaly and rotten under their feet. Fatigue tied knots high in their guts so that what was in their stomachs hung like stone.

"I didn't realize how big the crater was," Iimmi said.

So much nearer, the red glow, cut off at the bottom by the curve of the edge, took up a quarter of the sky.

"Maybe it'll erupt on us," Urson muttered. He added, "I'm thirsty. If Hama is supposed to be behind the volcano, couldn't we have gone around instead of over it?"

"We're this far," said Iimmi. "Why turn back now?" A scab of shale skittered from under his foot. The wind shifted again and they were forced to skirt farther around the crater.

"I hope you're keeping track how far off course we've gotten," Urson said.

"Don't worry," said Iimmi.

The glow from the jewels in Snake's hands showed pale yellow growths about them on the slope like miniature bulbous cactuses. Some of them whistled. "What are they?" Urson asked.

"Sulfur cones," said Iimmi. "Deposits of sulfur get caught under the surface, are heated, and make little volcanoes all by themselves."

After another comparatively level stretch, they began the final ascent over veins of rock and twisting trails that took them up the last hundred feet.

Once Urson looked back and saw Geo had stopped some twenty feet behind them at a niche in the ledge. Urson turned around and scrambled back. There was sweat on the boy's upturned face as the big sailor came toward him, gleaming in the red flicker.

"Here," Urson said. "Give me a hand."

"I can't," Geo whispered. "I'll fall."

Urson reached down, caught Geo around the chest, and hoisted him over the rock. "Take it easy. You don't have to race with anybody." Together they made their way after the others.

Iimmi and Snake cleared the crater rim first; Urson and Geo joined them on the pitted ledge. Together they looked into the volcano as red and yellow light splashed their bellies and faces.

Gold dribbled the internal slope. Tongues of red rock lapped the sides, and the swirling basin belched brown blobs of smoke that rose up the far rocks to spill the brim a radian away.

White explosions in the white rock roared below them. Pylons of blue flame leaped, then sank back. Trails of light webbed the crater's walls. At places ebon cavities jeweled the rock.

Wind fingered the watchers' hair.

Geo saw her first, two hundred feet along the rim. Her veils, bloodied by the flame, blew about her as she approached. Geo pointed to her. The others looked up.

She stood very straight. White hair snapped at the side of her head in the warm wind. Firelight and shadow fell deeply in the wrinkles of her face. As she neared them, light ran like liquid down the side of her winded robe. She smiled and held out her hand.

"Who are you?" Geo suddenly asked.

"Shadows melt in light of sacred laughter,"

recited the woman in a sure, low voice.

"Hands and houses shall be one hereafter."

She paused. "I am Argo Incarnate."

"But I thought . . ." Iimmi started.

"What did you think?" inquired the elderly woman gently.

"Nothing," said Iimmi.

"He thought you were a lot younger," Urson said. "We're supposed to take you home." Suddenly he pointed into the volcano. "Say, this isn't any of that funny light like back in the city that burned our hands, only this time it made you old?"

She glanced down the crater wall. "This is natural fire," she assured them, "a severed artery of the earth's burning blood. But wounds are natural enough."

Geo shifted his feet and rubbed his stump. "We were supposed to take the daughter of the present Argo Incarnate and return with her to Leptar," he explained.

"There are many Argos." The woman smiled. "The Goddess has many faces. You have seen quite a few since you arrived in this land."

"I guess we have," Urson said.

"Are you a prisoner of Hama?" asked Iimmi.

"I am with Hama."

"We are supposed to secure the third jewel and bring it back to the ship. We don't have much time. . . ."

"Yes," said Argo.

"Hey, what about that nest of vampires down there?" Urson said, thumbing toward the black behind them. "They said they worshiped Argo. What have you got to do with them? I don't trust anything on this place very much."

"The nature of the Goddess is change." She looked sadly down the slope. "From birth, through life, to death"—she looked back up at them—"to birth again. As I said, Argo has many faces. You must be very tired."

"Yes," said Geo.

"Then come with me. Please." She turned and began to walk back along the rim. Snake and Iimmi started after her, followed by Geo and Urson.

"I don't like any of this," the big sailor whispered to Geo as they followed. "Argo doesn't mean the same thing in this land as she does in Leptar. There's nothing but more trouble to come out of this. She's leading us into a trap, I tell you. I say the best thing to do is take the jewels we have, turn around, and get the hell out of here. I tell you, Geo—"

"Urson."

"Huh?"

"Urson, I'm very tired."

They walked silently for a few steps more. Then Urson heaved up a disgusted breath and put his arm around Geo's shoulder. "Come on," he grunted, supporting Geo against his side as they progressed along the rocky ledge, following Argo.

She turned down a trail that dropped into the crater. "Walk carefully here," she said as they turned into the huge pit.

"Something's not right," Urson said softly. "It's a trap, I tell you. How does that thing go? I could use it now: *Calmly, brother bear . . .* "

> "Calm the winter sleep,"

continued Geo:

> "Fire shall not harm . . ."

"Says who," mumbled Urson, glancing into the bowl of flame.

Geo went on:

> "water not alarm.
> While the current grows,
> amber honey flows,
> golden salmon leap."

"Like I once said before," muttered Urson: "In a—"

"In here," announced Argo. They turned into one of the caves that pocked the inner wall. "No," she said to Snake, who was about to use the jewels for illumination. "They have been used too much already."

With a small stick from a pocket in her robe, she struck a flame against the rock, then raised it to an ornate, branching petrolabra that hung from the stone ceiling by brass chains. Flame leaped from oil cup to oil cup, from the hand of a demon to a monkey's mouth, from a nymph's belly to a satyr's head. Chemicals in the cups caused each flame to burn a different color: green, red, blue, and orange light filled the small chapel and played on the polished benches. On the altar were two statues of equal height: a man sitting and a woman kneeling. Geo and Urson stared at the petrolabra.

"What is it?" Iimmi asked when he saw where their eyes were fixed.

"There's one of those things in Argo's cabin onboard the ship," Geo said. "And look over there. Where did we see one of those before?" The opaque glass screen was identical to the one in the convent.

"Sit down," Argo said. "Please sit down."

They sank to the benches. The climb, once halted, knotted their calves and the muscles low in their backs.

"Hama has allowed you the privilege of a chapel even in captivity," commented Geo, "but I see you have to share your altar with him."

"But I am Hama's mother." Argo smiled.

Geo and Urson frowned.

"You yourselves know that Argo is the mother of all things, the begetter and bearer of all life. I am the mother of all gods as well."

"Those blind women," said Urson. "They aren't really your priestesses, are they? They wanted to kill us. I bet they were really dupes of Hama."

"It isn't so simple," replied Argo. "They are really worshipers of Argo, but as I said, I have many faces. Death as well as life is my province. The dwellers in that convent from which you escaped are a—how shall I say it?—degenerate branch of the religion. They were truly blinded by the fall of the City of New Hope. To them, Argo is only death, the dominator of men. Not only is Argo the mother of Hama, she is his wife and daughter."

"Then it's like we figured," said Geo. "Jordde isn't a spy for Hama. He's working for the renegade priestesses of Argo."

"Yes," returned Argo, "except that word 'renegade' is perhaps the wrong choice. They believe that their way is correct."

"Then they must be responsible for all that was going on in Leptar, only somehow blaming it on Hama," said Geo. "They were probably just after the jewels too. You don't look like a prisoner. You're here in league with Hama to prevent the priestesses of Argo from taking over Leptar."

"Nothing could be simpler," said the Goddess. "Unfortunately, you are wrong in nearly every other point."

"But then why did Jordde throw the jewel after us when he tore it from Argo's . . . I mean the other Argo's throat?"

"When he snatched the jewel from around my daughter's neck," explained Argo, "he threw it to the creatures of the sea because he knew they would take it back to Aptor. With it once again on the Island, the priestesses would have a better chance of getting it; my daughter, acting Argo Incarnate in the absence of her own daughter, does not know that what she is fighting is another face of Argo. As far as she is concerned, all her efforts are against the mischief Hama has caused, and truly caused in Leptar. But beyond these blind creatures is a greater enemy that she must vanquish."

"Hama?" began Iimmi.

"Greater than Hama," said old Argo. "It is herself. It is hard for me to watch her and not occasionally call a word of guidance. With the science here in Aptor, it would not be difficult. But I must refrain. Actually she has done well. But there is much more to do. She has directed you well and assigned your tasks properly. And until now you have carried them out well."

"She said we were to steal the final jewel from Hama and return with you to the ship," said Geo. "Can you help us with either of these things?"

Argo laughed. "The moment I compliment you, you completely confuse your mission. Once the jewel is stolen, whom are you supposed to take back to Leptar?"

"Argo Incarnate," Urson said.

"You said that Argo back in the ship was your daughter," said Geo, "but she said you were *her* daughter."

Argo laughed. "When my granddaughter was . . . kidnapped here to Aptor, I was already waiting for her. Look."

She turned a dial beneath the screen and lights flickered over the glass: the sleeping girl had short red hair, a splash of freckles over a blunt nose. Her hand curled in a loose fist near her mouth. A white sheet covered the gentle push of adolescent breasts. On the table beside her bed was a contraption made of a U-shaped piece of metal mounted on a board, an incomplete coil of wire, and a few more bits of metal, sitting near a crumpled paper bag.

"That is my granddaughter," Argo said, switching off the picture. "She is the one you must take back to the ship."

"How shall we steal the jewel?" asked Geo.

Argo turned to Snake. "I believe that was your task." Then she looked around at the other three. "You will need rest. After that, you can see about the jewel and my granddaughter. Come with me now. Pallets have been set up for you in the far room, where you may sleep." She rose and led them to another chamber. The blankets lay over soft boughs. Argo pointed to a trickle of water that ran from a basin carved in the rock wall. "This stream is pure. You may drink from it." She pointed to a burlap sack in the corner. "There is fruit in there if you become hungry."

"Sleep!" Urson jammed his fists into the air, yawned.

As they settled, Argo said, "Poet?"

"Yes?" Geo replied.

"I know you are the most tired, but I must talk to you alone for a moment or two."

As Geo raised himself, Urson stood up too. "Look," he said to Argo, "he needs the rest more than any of us. If you want to question him about rituals and spells, take Iimmi. He knows just as much as Geo."

Argo smiled. "I need a poet, not a student. I need one who has suffered as he has. Come."

"Wait," Urson said. He picked the jewel from Geo's chest, where Snake had returned it when they entered the chapel. "You better leave this with me."

Geo frowned.

"It may still be a trap," said Urson.

"Leave it with him," suggested Argo, "if it eases him."

Geo let the big hands lift the thong from his neck.

"Now come with me," said Argo.

They left the room and walked back through the chapel to the door. Argo walked to the entrance and looked down at the molten rock. Light sifted through her robe, leaving the darker outline of her body. Without turning, she spoke: "The fire is a splendid symbol for life, don't you think?"

"And for death. One of Aptor's fires burned my arm away."

She turned to him. "You and Snake have had the hardest time. Both of you have left flesh to rot in Aptor. I guess that involves you in this land." She paused. "You know, he had a great deal more pain than you. Do you know how he lost his tongue? I watched it all from this same screen inside the chapel and could not help him. Jordde jammed his knuckles into his jaws and, when the mouth came open, caught the red flesh with pincers that closed all the way through, and stretched it as far as it would go. Then he looped the tongue with a thin wire and threw a switch. You don't know what electricity is, do you?"

"I have heard the word."

"When a great deal of it is passed through a thin wire, the wire becomes hot, white hot. And the white-hot loop was tightened until the rope of muscle seared from the roasted stump. But the child had fainted already. I wonder if the young can really bear more pain."

"Jordde and the blind priestesses did this to him?"

"Jordde and some men on the boat that picked up the two of them from the raft on which they had left Aptor."

"Who is Jordde?" Geo asked. "Urson knew him before this as a First Mate. But Urson's story tells me nothing."

"I know the story," Argo said. "It tells you something, but something you would perhaps rather not hear." She sighed. "Poet, how well do you know yourself?"

"What do you mean?" Geo asked.

"How well do you know the machinery of a man, how he manages to function? That is what you will sing of if your songs are to become great."

"I still don't—"

"I have a question for you, a poetic riddle. Will you try to answer it?"

"If you will answer a question for me."

"Will you do your best to answer mine?" Argo asked.

"Yes."

"Then I will do my best to answer yours. What is your question?"

"Who is Jordde and why is he doing what he's doing?"

"He was at one time," Argo explained, "a very promising novice for the priesthood of Argo in Leptar, a scholar of myths and rituals like Iimmi and yourself. He also took to the sea to learn of the world. But his boat was wrecked; he and a few others were cast on Aptor's shore. They strove with Aptor's terrors as you did, and many fell. Two, however—a four-armed cabin boy, whom you call Snake, and Jordde—were each exposed to the forces of Argo and Hama as you have been. One, in his strangeness, could see into men's minds. The other could not. Silently, one swore allegiance to one force while one swore allegiance to the other. The second part of your question was *why*. Perhaps if you can answer my riddle, you can answer that part yourself. I do know that they were the only two who escaped. I do know that Snake would not tell Jordde his choice, and that Jordde tried to convince the child to follow him. When they were rescued, I know that the argument continued, and that Snake held back with childish tenacity both his decision and his ability to read minds, even under the hot wire and the pincers. The hot wire, incidentally, was something Jordde took back with him from the blind Priestess, according to him, to help the people of Leptar. It could have been of great use. But recently all he has done with the electricity is construct a larger weapon with it. Jordde became a staunch First Mate in a year's time. Snake became a waterfront thief. Both waited. Then, when the opportunity arose, both acted. Why? Perhaps you can tell me, Poet."

"Thank you for telling me that much," Geo said. "What is your question?"

She glanced down at the flame once more and recited:

> "By the dark chamber sits its twin,
> where the body's floods begin;
> and the two are twinned again,
> turning out and turning in.
>
> In the bright chamber runs the line
> of the division, silver, fine,
> diminishing along the lanes
> of memory to an inward sign.
>
> Fear floods in the turning room;
> Love breaks in the burning dome."

"It is not one that I have heard before," Geo said. "I'm not even sure I know what the question is. I'm familiar with neither its diction nor style."

"I doubted very much you would recognize it." Argo smiled.

"Is it part of the pre-purge rituals of Argo?"

"It was written by my granddaughter," Argo said. "The question is: could you explain it to me?"

"Oh," said Geo. "I didn't realize . . ." He paused. "By the dark chamber sits its twin, moving in and out; and that's where the floods of the body begin. And they are twinned again. The heart?" he suggested. "The four-chambered human heart? That's where the body's flood begins."

"I think that will do for part of the answer."

"The bright chamber," mused Geo. "The burning dome. The human mind, I guess. The line of division, running down the lane of memory . . . I'm not sure."

"You seem to be doing fairly well."

"Could it refer to something like 'the two sides of every question'?" Geo asked. "Or something similar?"

"It could," Argo said. "Though I must confess I hadn't thought of it in that way. But it is the last two lines that puzzle me."

"Fear floods in the turning room," repeated Geo. "Love breaks in the burning dome. I guess that's the mind and the heart again. You usually think of love with the heart and fear with the mind. Maybe she meant that they both, the heart and the mind, have control over both love and fear."

"Perhaps she did." Argo smiled. "You must ask her . . . when you rescue her from the clutches of Hama."

"Does your granddaughter want to be a poet?" Geo asked.

"I'm not sure what she wants to be," Argo said. "It can be very trying. But you must go to sleep now. Tomorrow you will have to complete your mission."

"Thank you," Geo said, grateful for his dismissal. "I am . . . am very sleepy."

Before going back to the room to his companions, he looked once more into the volcano. Tongues of light licked the black rock. He turned away now and walked back into the darkness.

chapter ten

Dawn lay aslant the crater's ridge. Argo pointed down the opposite slope. A black temple at the bottom sat among trees and lawns. "Hama's Temple," Argo said. "You have your task. Good luck."

They started down the cinder slope. It took them about thirty minutes to reach the first trees that surrounded the dark buildings and the vast gardens. As they crossed the first lip of grass, a sudden cluster of notes spilled from a tree.

"A bird," Iimmi said. "I haven't heard one since I left Leptar."

Bright blue and the length of a man's forefinger, a lizard ran halfway down the trunk of the tree. Its sapphire belly heaved in the early light; it opened its red mouth, its throat fluttered, and there was another burst of music.

"Oh well," said Iimmi. "I was close."

They walked farther until Geo mused: "I wonder why you always think things are going to turn out like you expect."

"Because when something sounds like that," declared Urson, "it's supposed to be a bird!" He shuddered. "Lizards!"

"It was a pretty lizard," said Geo.

"Echhh!" said Urson.

"Going around expecting things to be what they seem can get you in trouble . . . on this Island."

There was another sound from the grove beside them. They looked up. The man standing in the center raised his hand and said briskly, "Stop!"

They stopped.

He wore dark robes, and his white hair made a close helmet above his brown face.

Urson's hand was on his sword. Snake's hands were out from his sides.

"Who are you?" the man declared.

"Who are you?" Urson parried.

"I am Hama Incarnate."

They were silent. Finally Geo said, "We are travelers in Aptor. We don't mean any harm."

As the man moved forward, splotches of light from the trees slipped across his robe. "Come with me," Hama said. He turned and proceeded among the trees. They followed.

They entered the Temple garden. It was early enough in the morning so that the sunlight lapped pink tongues over the giant urns along the edges of the path. They reached the Temple.

The mirrors on the sides of the vestibule tossed images back and forth as they passed between. Beyond pillars of onyx spread the shiny floor of the Temple. On the huge altar sat an immense statue of a cross-legged man. In one monstrous black hand was a scythe. In the other, shafts of grain spired four stories toward the ceiling. Of the three eyes in the head, only the middle one was open.

As they passed, Hama looked at the jewels on Iimmi's and Geo's necks and then up at the gazing eye. "The morning rites have not yet started," he said. "They will begin in a half hour. By then I hope to have divined your purpose in coming here."

At the other side of the hall they mounted a stairway. Above the door was a black circle dotted with three eyes. Just as they were about to go in, Geo looked around, frowned, and caught Iimmi's eye. "Snake?" he mouthed.

Iimmi looked around and shrugged. The boy was not with them.

The room contained screens like the ones in the volcanic chapel and at the convent of the blind priestesses. Other equipment also: a large worktable, and on one wall, a window through which they could see the Temple garden.

Hama faced them, apparently unaware of Snake's disappearance. As he closed the door now, he said, "You have come to oppose the forces of Aptor, am I right? You come to steal the jewel of Hama. You have come to kidnap Incarnate Argo. Will you deny that is your purpose? Keep your hand off your sword, Urson! . . . Don't move. I can kill you in a moment—"

She pushed her fist from under the sheet, squinched her eyes as tight as she could, and said, "*Yahhhhhwashangnnn,* damn!" Then again, "Damn! I'm sleepy." She rolled over and cuddled the pillow. Then she opened her eyes, one at a time, and lay watching the near-complete motor sitting on the table beside her bed. Her eyes closed.

And opened again. "I cannot afford to go back to sleep this morning," she said softly. "One, two, three!" She threw the covers off, sat up, flung her feet onto the stone floor, and jumped erect, blinking hard from the shock of flesh and cold rock. She put her teeth together and said loudly, "*Gnnnnnnnnnn,*" and stretched to tiptoe.

Then she collapsed on the bed and jammed her feet under the covers again. With thirty feet of one-and-a-half-inch brass pipe, she mused sleepily, I could carry heat from the main hot-water line under the floor, which I would estimate to be about the proper surface area to keep these stones warm. Let me see: thirty feet of one-and-a-half-inch pipe has a surface area of 22/7 times 3/2 times 30, which is 990 divided by 7, which is . . . Then she caught herself. Damn, thinking about this to avoid thinking about getting up. She opened her eyes once more, put feet on the stone, and held them there while she scratched vigorously at her hair.

Then she went to the closet.

She pulled down a white tunic, wriggled into it, and tied the leather strap around her waist. Then she looked at the clock. "*Yikes*!" she said quietly, ran out the door, almost slammed it to behind her. But she whirled, caught it on her palms before it banged, then with gingerly care closed it the final centimeter. *Are you trying to get caught?* she asked herself as she tiptoed to the next door.

She opened it and looked in. Dunderhead looks cute when he's asleep, she thought. The cord on the floor ran from under the table by the Priest's bed, over the stones, carefully following the zigzag crevices. The end lay in the corner of the doorsill. You really couldn't see it if you weren't looking for it, which had more or less been the idea when she'd put it there last night before the priests returned from vespers. The far end was tied in a knot of her own invention to the electric plug of his alarm clock. Dunderhead had an annoying habit of resetting his clock every evening (in her plans for this morning she had catalogued all his habitual actions, this one observed three nights running as she hung upside down from the bulky stone portcullis outside his window) to make sure the red second hand still swept away the minutes.

She tugged on the string and saw it leap from the crevices to a straight line. It lifted from the floor as she drew tighter. The plug blipped quietly onto the floor, and the string went slack.

She pulled the string again until the slack left, and raised the end a few inches from the floor. With her free hand she plucked the cord and watched the vibration run up and down. The knot's invention was ingenious. At the vibration, two opposed loops shook away from a third, and a four-millimeter length of rubber band that had been sewn in tightened and released a fourth loop from a small length of number-four-gauge wire with a holding tonsure of three quarters of a gram, and the opposing vibration returning up the cord loosed a similar apparatus on the other side of the plug. The knot fell away, and she wound the string quickly around her hand. She stood up and closed the door. The oiled lock was perfectly silent. In fact the doorknob was still just the slightest bit greasy, she noted. Careless.

She went back to her room. Sunlight from the high window fell over the table. Glancing at her own clock, she saw it was still very early in the morning. She took the parts of the motor up. "I guess we try you out today? No?" She grinned. "Yes!" She put the parts in the paper bag, strode out of the room, and slammed the . . . whirled and caught it once more. "*Gnnnnnn*," she repeated. "*Do* you want to get caught?" Now she frowned. "Yes. And remember that too. Or you'll never get through this."

As she walked down the hall, she heard through one of the windows the chirp of a blue lizard from the garden. "Just the sound I wanted to hear." Her smile came back. "Good sign."

Turning into the Temple, she started down the side aisle. The great black columns passed her. Suddenly she stopped. Something had moved between the columns on the other side, swift as a bird's shadow. At least she thought it had. "Remember," she reminded herself, "you have guilt feelings about this whole thing, you want to get caught, and you could very easily be manufacturing delusions to scare yourself out of going through with it." She passed two more columns. And saw it again. "Or," she went on, "you could be purposefully ignoring the very obvious fact that there is somebody over there. So watch it."

Then she saw it again; somebody with no clothes on (for all practical purposes) was sneaking between the pillars. And he had four arms. That made her start to think of something else, but the thought as it arrowed toward recognition suddenly got deflected, turned completely about, and jammed into her brain: he was staring directly at her, and she was afraid.

If he starts walking toward me, she thought, *I'm going to be scared out of my ears. So I better start walking toward him. Besides, I want to see what he looks like.* She left the columns. Glancing quickly both ways, she saw that the Temple was deserted save for them.

He's a kid, she thought, three quarters of the way across. My age, she added, and again a foreign thought tried to intrude itself on her but never made it: he was coming toward her now. At last he stopped before her. His muscles lay like wire under his brown skin; black hair massed low on his forehead, and his eyes gleamed deep beneath the black shrub of brows.

She gulped. "What are you doing here? Do you know somebody could catch you in here and get mad as hell? If somebody comes along, they might even think you were trying to steal Hama's eye." *I shouldn't have said that, because he moved funny.* "You better get out of here because everybody will be up here in a half hour for morning services."

At that news, he suddenly darted past her and sprinted toward the altar.

"Hey!" she called and ran after him.

Snake vaulted the brass altar rail.

"Wait a minute!" she called, catching up. "Wait, will you!"

Snake turned as she slung her leg across the brass bar. "Look, so I gave away my hand. But that was only guilt feelings. You gave yours away too, though."

Snake frowned, tilted his head, then grinned.

"We'll help each other, see. You want it too, don't you?" She pointed up to the head of the statue towering above them. "So let's cooperate. I'll take it for a little while. Then you can have it." He was listening, she saw; she guessed her strategy was working. "We'll help each other. Shake on it?" She stuck out her right hand.

All four hands reached forward.

Whoops, she thought, *I hope he's not offended. . . .*

But the four hands grasped hers, and she added her left to the juncture. "All right. Come on. Now, I had all this figured out last night. We don't have much time. Let's go around . . ." But he reached out and took the coil of string from where she had stuck it in her belt. He walked to where the stalks of wheat spired from the altar base up through Hama's fist. With the twine in one hand, he grabbed a stalk with the other three and, hand over hand over hand, hoisted himself up to where the first broad metal leaves branched from the stalk. His dirty feet swung out frogwise; then he caught the stem with his toes and at last hoisted himself to the frond. He looked down at her.

"I can't climb up there," she said. "I don't have your elevation power."

Snake shrugged.

"Oh, damn," she said. "I'll do it my way." She ran across the altar to the great foot of the statue. Because he sat cross-legged, Hama's foot was on his side. Using toes for steps, she clambered to the dark bulge of the deity's divine bunion. She made her way across the ankle, up the shin, and back down the black thigh, till she stood at the crevice where the leg and torso met.

Out beyond the great knee, Snake regarded her from his perch in the groin of the yellow leaf. They were at equal height.

"Yoo-hoo!" She waved. "Meet you at the clavicle." Then she stuck her tongue out. The stylized ripples in Hama's loincloth afforded her another ten feet. The bulge in the contrastingly realistic belly of the god made a treacherous ledge along which she inched until she arrived at the cavernous navel. Her hands left wet prints on the black stone.

Glancing out, she saw that Snake had gotten to the next cluster of leaves.

The god's belly button, from this intimate distance, revealed itself as a circular door, about four feet in diameter. She dried her hands on her blouse, crouched before the door, and began to work the combination. She missed the first number twice, dried her hands off, and began again. According to the plans in the main safe of the Temple (on which she had first practiced combination breaking), there was a ladder behind this door that led up into the statue. She remembered it clearly and saved her life by doing so.

Because when she reached the second number, reversed the dial, and felt the telltale click at the third, she pulled on the handle—and was nearly pushed from the ledge as the door swung. She grabbed at a handle as the stone slipped from under her feet.

She was hanging five feet out in the air over the sacred groin fifty feet below.

The first thing she tried, after closing her eyes and mumbling a few laws of motion, was to swing the door to. When she swung out, however, the door swung closed; and when she swung in, the door swung open. After a while she just hung. She gave small thanks that she had dried her hands. When her arms began to ache, she wished that she hadn't, because then it would be over by now. She went over what she knew about taking judo falls. After closing her eyes, she perfunctorily attempted to reconstruct what she could of an ancient poem, about a young lady who had ended in a similar position, with the refrain "Curfew must not ring tonight. . . ."

Then the door swung closed, and someone grabbed her around the waist. She didn't open her eyes but felt her body pressed against the tilting stone. Her arms dropped, tingling, to her sides. The ligaments flamed with pain. Then pain dulled to throbbing, and she opened her eyes. "How the hell did you get down here?" she asked Snake. Snake helped her stagger through the open door. She stopped to rub her arms. "How did he know about the ladder?"

They stood at the bottom of the shaft. The ladder beside them rose into the darkness.

He looked at her with a puzzled expression.

"What is it?" she asked. "Oh, I'll be able to climb up there, never you worry. Hey, can you speak?"

Snake shook his head.

"Oh," she said. Something started at the edge of her mind again, something unpleasant. Snake had started up the ladder, which he had come down so quickly a minute ago. She glanced out the door, saw that the Temple was empty, pulled the door to, and followed.

They ascended into darkness. Time somehow got lost, and she was not sure if she had been climbing for ten minutes or two or twenty. Once she reached for a rung and her hand fell on nothing. The shock in the rhythm started her heart beating. Her arms were beginning to ache again, just slightly. She reached up for the next rung and found it in its proper place. Then the next. And then again the next.

She started counting steps again, and when seventy-four, seventy-five, and seventy-six dropped below her, there was another missing rung. She reached above it, but there was none. She ran her hand up the edge of the ladder and found that it suddenly curved, depressingly enough, into the wall. "Hey, you!" she whispered in the darkness.

Something touched her waist. "*Gnnnnggggg,*" she said. "Don't *do* that." It touched her on the leg, took hold of her ankle, and pulled. "Watch out," she said.

It pulled again. She raised her foot, and it was tugged sideways a good half meter and set on solid flooring. Then a hand (her foot was not released) took her arm, and another held her waist, and tugged. She stiffened for one instant before she remembered the number of limbs her companion had. She stepped off the ladder, sideways into the dark, afraid to put her other foot down lest she go headlong into the seventy-five-foot-plus shaft.

Holding her arm now, he led her along the tunnel. *We should be going through the shoulder,* she figured, remembering the plan.

They reached a steep incline. Now down the upper arm, she recalled. The slope, without visual orientation, made her a little dizzy. She put her hand out and ran her fingers along the wall. That helped some.

"I feel like Euridice," she said aloud.

You . . . funny . . . an echoing sounded in her skull.

"Hey," she said. "What was that?" But the voice was silent. The wall turned abruptly and the floor leveled out. They were in a section of the passage now that corresponded roughly to the statue's radial artery. At the wrist, there was a light. They mounted a stairway, came out a trapdoor, and found themselves high in the Temple. Below them the great hall spread, vast, deep, and empty. Beside them, the stems of the bronze wheat stalks rose up through the fist on which they were standing and spired another fifty feet before breaking into clusters of grain. Beyond the dark, gargantuan chest, in the statue's other hand, the giant scythe leaned into shadow.

"Look," she said. "You follow me now." She started back along the top of the forearm and climbed over the rippling biceps. They reached the shoulder and crossed the hollow above the collarbone until they stood just below the scooping shell of the ear.

"You still have the string?" she asked him.

Snake handed it to her.

"I guess my bag is heavy enough." She took the paper bag she had stuffed into her belt, tied one end of the string around the neck. Then, holding the other, she heaved the cord up and over the ear. She got the other end of the string, knotted it as high as she could reach, and gave it a tug.

"I hope this works," she said. "I had it all figured out yesterday. The tensile strength of this stuff is about two hundred and fifty pounds, which ought to do for you and me." She planted her foot on the swell of the neck tendon, and in seven leaps she made it to the lobe of the ear. She swung around using the frontal wing as a pivot. Crouching in the trumpet, she looked down at Snake. "Come on," she said. "Hurry up."

Snake joined her a moment later.

The ear was hollow too. It led back into a cylindrical chamber that went up through the head of the god. The architect who had designed the statue had conveniently left the god's lid flipped. They climbed the ladder at the side of the passage and emerged amid the tangle of pipes representing hair. Where the forehead began to slope dangerously forward, they could see the foreshortened nose and the brow of the statue's middle eye above that. There wasn't much of anything after that for the next hundred feet until the base of the altar. "Now you really can be some help," she told him. "Hold on to my wrist and let me down. Slowly now. I'll get the jewel."

They grabbed wrists, and Snake's other three hands, as well as the joints of his knees, locked around the base of five pipes that sprouted around them.

Slowly she slid forward until her free hand slipped on the stone and she dropped the length of their two arms and swung just above the statue's nose. The eye opened in front of her. The lid arched above her, and the white of the eye on either side of the ebony iris shone faintly in the half darkness. At this distance, all the features of the statue lost their recognizable human character, and she was staring into concaved darkness. At the center of the iris, in a small hollow, sitting on the top of a metal support, was the jewel.

She reached her free hand toward it as she swung.

Somewhere a gong sounded. Light flooded over her. Looking up, she saw white sockets of light shining down into her own eyes. Panicking, she almost released Snake's wrist. But a voice in her head (hers or someone else's, she couldn't tell) rang out:

Hold . . . on . . . damn . . . it . . .

She grabbed the jewel. The metal shaft in which the jewel had sat was not steady, and tilted as her hand came away. The tilting must have set off some clockwork mechanism, because the great lid above was slowly lowering over the ivory and ebony eye. She swung again at the end of the rope of bone and flesh; half blinded by the lights above her, she looked over her shoulder, down into the Temple. She heard singing, the beginning of a processional hymn.

The morning rites had started!

Light glinted on the stone limbs of the god. Figures poured into the Temple, miniature and far away. They must see her! But the hymns, sonorous and gigantic, rose like floodwater, and she suddenly thought that if she fell, she would drown in the sound of it.

Snake was pulling her up. Stone against her arm, against her cheek. She clenched her other fist tightly at her side. Another hand came down to help. Then another. Then she was lying among the metal pipes, and he was prying her fingers from his wrist. He tugged her to her feet, and for a moment she looked out over the crowded hall.

Nervous energy contracted coldly along her body, and the sudden sight of the great drop filled her eyes and her head. She staggered. Snake caught her and at last helped her back to the ladder. "We've got it!" she said to him before they started down. She breathed deeply. Then she checked in her palm to see if it was still there. It was. Again she looked out over the people. Light on the upturned faces made them look like pearls on the dark floor. Exaltation suddenly burst in her shoulders, flooded her legs and arms, and for a moment washed the pain away. Snake, with one hand on her shoulder, was grinning. "We've got it!" she said again.

They went down the ladder inside the statue's skull. Snake preceded her out the ear. He reached around, caught the cord, and let himself down to the shoulder.

She hesitated, then put the jewel in her mouth, and followed him. Standing beside him once more, she removed it and rubbed her shoulders. "Boy, am I going to have some charley horse by tomorrow," she said. "Do me a favor and untie my bag for me?"

Snake untied the parcel from the end of the cord, and together they climbed down the biceps and back over the forearm to the trapdoor in the wrist.

She glanced down at the worshipers. "I wonder which one is old Dunderhead?" But Snake was taking the jewel from her hand. She let him have it and watched him raise it up above his head.

He raised the jewel and the pearls disappeared as heads bent all through the Temple.

"That's the ticket!" Argo grinned. "Come on." But Snake did not go into the tunnel. Instead he walked around the fist, took hold of one of the bronze wheat stems, and slid down through an opening between thumb and forefinger. "That way?" asked Argo. "Oh, well, I guess so. You know I'm going to write an epic about this. In alliterative verse. You know what it is, alliterative verse?"

But Snake had already gone. She followed him, clutching the great stems with her knees. He was waiting for her at the leaves. Nestled there, they gazed once more at the fascinated congregation.

Again Snake held aloft the jewel, and again heads bowed. The hymn began to repeat itself, individual words lost in the sonority of the hall. The tones drew out, beat against themselves in echo, filled their ears, made her wrists and the back of her neck chill. They started down the bottom length of the stem, coming quickly. When they stood at last on the base, she put her hand on his shoulder and looked across the altar rail. The congregation pressed close, although she did not recognize an individual face. The mass of people stood there, enormous and familiar. As Snake started forward, holding up the jewel, the people fell back. Snake climbed over the altar rail, then helped her over.

Her shoulders were beginning to hurt now, and the enormity of the theft started chills up and down, up and down her back. The altar steps, as she put her foot down, were awfully cold.

They walked forward again, and the last note of the hymn echoed to silence, filling the hall with the roaring hush of hundreds breathing.

Simultaneously, she and Snake got the urge to look back at the height of Hama behind them. All three eyes were shut. A hundred dark robes rustled about them as they started forward again.

There was a spotlight on them, she realized. That was why the people, beyond the circular effulgence around them, seemed so dim. Blood beat at the bottom of her tongue. They walked forward among shadowed faces, among parting cloaks and robes.

The last of the figures stepped aside from the Temple door, and she could see the sunlight out in the garden. They stood a moment. Snake held high the jewel. Then they ran from the door and over the bright steps.

The hymn began again behind them, as if their departure were a signal. Music poured after them. When they reached the bottom step, they whirled like beasts, expecting the congregation to come welling darkly out after them.

There was only the music. It flowed into the light that washed around them, a transparent river, a sea.

"Freeze the drop in the hand,
and break the earth with singing.

> Hail the height of a man,
> also the height of a woman."

Over the music they heard a brittle chirping from the trees. Fixed with fear, they watched the Temple door. No one came out. Snake suddenly stood back and grinned.

She scratched her red hair, shifted her weight, and looked at Snake. "I guess they're not coming." She sounded almost disappointed. Then she giggled. "I guess we got it."

Don't move," repeated Hama Incarnate.

"Now look . . ." began Urson.

"You are perfectly safe," the god continued, "unless you do something foolish. You have shown great wisdom. Continue to show it. I have a lot to explain to you."

"Like what?" asked Geo.

"I'll start with the lizard." The god smiled.

"The what?" asked Iimmi.

"The singing lizards," said Hama. "You walked through a grove of trees just a few minutes ago. You had just been through the most frightening time in your lives. Suddenly you heard a singing in the trees. What was it?"

"I thought it was a bird," Iimmi said.

"But why a bird?" asked the god.

"Because that's what a bird sounds like," stated Urson impatiently. "Who needs an old lizard singing to them on a morning like this?"

"Your second point is much better than your first," said the god. "You do not need a lizard, but you did need a bird. A bird means spring, life, good luck, cheerfulness. To *you*. You think of a bird singing and you think thoughts that men have been thinking for thousands upon thousands of years. Poets have written of it in every language: Catullus in Latin, Keats in English, Li Po in Chinese, Darnel 2X4 in New English. You expected a bird because after what you had been through, you needed to hear a bird. Lizards run from under wet rocks, scurry over gravestones. A lizard is not what you needed."

"So what do lizards have to do with why we're here?" demanded Urson.

"Why are you here?" repeated the god, subtly changing Urson's question. "There are many reasons, I am sure. You tell me some of them."

"You have done wrongs to Argo . . . at least to Argo of Leptar," Geo explained. "We have come to undo them. You have kidnapped the young Argo, as well as her grandmother, apparently. We have come to take her back. You have misused the jewels. We have come to take the last one from you."

Hama smiled. "Only a poet could see the wisdom in such honesty. I thought I might have to wheedle to get that much out of you."

"I was pretty certain you knew that much already," Geo said.

"True." Then his tone changed. "Do you know how the jewels work?"

They shook their heads.

"They are basically very simple mechanical contrivances that are difficult in execution but simple in concept. I will explain. Human thoughts, it was discovered after the Great Fire during the first glorious years of the City of New Hope, did not produce waves similar to radio waves; but the electrical synapse pattern, it was found, could affect radio waves, in the same way a mine detector reacts to the existence of metal."

"Radio?" Geo said.

"That's right," Hama said. "Oh, I forgot. You don't know anything about that at all. I can't go through the whole thing now. Suffice it to say, each of the jewels contains a carefully honed crystal that is constantly sending out beams that can detect these thought patterns. Also the crystal acts both as a magnifying glass and a mirror, and reflects and magnifies the energy from the brain into heat or light or any other kind of electromagnetic radiation—there I go again—so that you can send great bolts of heat with them, as you have seen done.

"But the actual workings of them are not important. And their ability to send heat out is only their secondary power. Their primary import is that they can be used to penetrate the mind. Now we come to the lizards."

"Wait a minute," Geo said. "Before we get to the lizards. Do you mean they go into minds like Snake does?"

The god went on. "Like Snake," he said. "But different. Snake was born with the ability to transmute the brain patterns of his thoughts to others; in that, he has a power something like the jewels, but nowhere as strong. But with the jewels, you can jam a person's thoughts—"

"Just go into his mind and stop him from thinking?" asked Iimmi.

"No," said the god. "Conscious thought is too powerful. Otherwise, you would stop thinking every time Snake spoke to you. It works another way. How many reasons does a man have for any single action?"

They looked at him uncomprehendingly.

"Why, for example, does a man pull his hand from a fire?"

"Because it hurts," said Urson. "Why else?"

"Yes, why else?" asked Hama.

"I think I see what you mean," said Geo. "He also pulls it out because he knows that outside the fire his hand isn't going to hurt. Like the bird, I mean the lizard. One reason we reacted as we did was because it sounded like a bird. The other reason was because we wanted to hear a bird just then. The man pulls his hand out because the fire hurts, *and* because he wants it not to hurt.

"In other words," Geo summarized, "there are at least two reasons for everything."

"Exactly," explained Hama. "Notice that one of these reasons is unconscious. But with the jewel, you can jam the unconscious reason, so that if a man has his hand in a fire, you can jam his unconscious reason of wanting it to stop hurting. Completely bewildered and in no less pain, he will stand there until his wrist is a smoking nub."

Geo reached over and felt his severed arm.

"Dictators during the entire history of this planet have used similar techniques. By not letting the people of their country know what conditions existed outside their boundaries, they could get the people to fight to stay in those conditions. It was the old adage: Convince a slave that he's free, and he will fight to maintain his slavery. Why does a poet sing? Because he likes music and because silence frightens him. Why does a thief steal? To get the goods from his victim; also to deprive his victim of them."

"That's how Argo got Snake back," Geo said to Urson. "I see now. He was just thinking of running away, and she jammed his desire not to get caught; so he had nothing to tell him in which direction to run. So he ran where she told him, straight back to her."

"That's right," Hama said. "But something else was learned when these jewels were invented. Or rather a lesson history should have taught us thousands of years ago was finally driven home. No man can wield absolute power over other men and still retain his own mind. For no matter how good his intentions are when he takes up the power, his alternate reason is that freedom, the freedom of other people and ultimately his own, terrifies him. Only a man afraid of freedom would want this power or could conceive of wielding it. And that fear of freedom will turn him into a slave of this power. For this reason, the jewels are evil. That is why we have summoned you to steal them from us."

"To steal them from you?" asked Geo. "Why couldn't you have simply destroyed them when you had them?"

"We have already been infected." The god smiled. "We are a small number here on Aptor. To reach this state of organization, to collect the scattered scientific knowledge of the times before the Great Fire, was not easy. Too often the jewels have been used and abused, and now we cannot destroy them. We would have to destroy ourselves first. We kidnapped Argo and left you the second jewel, hoping that you would come after the third and last one. Now you have come, and now the jewel is being stolen."

"Snake?" asked Geo.

"That's right," replied Hama.

"But I thought he was your spy," Geo said.

"That he is our spy is his unconscious reason for his actions," explained Hama. "He is aware only that he is working against the evil he has seen in Jordde. 'Spy' is too harsh a word for him. Say, rather, little thief. He became a spy for us quite unwittingly when he was on the Island as a child with Jordde. I have explained something to you of how the mind works. We have machines that can duplicate what Snake does in a similar way that the jewels work. This is how the blind priestesses contacted Jordde and made him their spy. This is how we reached Snake. But he never saw us, never even really talked to us. It was mainly because of something he saw, something he saw when he first got here."

"Wait a minute," Iimmi said. "Jordde wanted to kill me, and he did kill Whitey, because of something we saw here. Was it the same thing? And *what* was it?"

Hama smiled. "My telling you would do no good. Perhaps you can find out from Snake or my daughter, Argo Incarnate."

"But what do we do now?" Geo interrupted. "Take the jewels back to Argo? I mean Argo on the ship. She's already used the jewels to control minds, at least Snake's, so that means she's 'infected' too."

"Once, you guessed the reason for her 'infection,'" said Hama. "We have been watching you on our screens since you landed. Do you remember what the reason was?"

"Do you mean her being jealous of her daughter?" Geo asked.

"Yes. On one side her motives were truly patriotic for Leptar. On the other hand they were selfish ones of power seeking. But without the selfish ones, she would have never gotten so far as she did. You must bring young Argo back and give the infection a chance to work itself out."

"But what about the jewels?" asked Geo. "All three of them will be together. Isn't that a huge temptation?"

"Someone must meet this temptation and overcome it," said Hama. "You do not know the danger they create while they are here in Aptor."

Hama turned to the screen and pushed a switch to the on position. The opaque glass filled with a picture of the interior of the Temple. On the great statue, a spotlight followed two microscopic figures over the statue's shoulder. They climbed over the statue's elbow.

Hama increased the size. The two made their way along the statue's forearm to the golden stalks of wheat in the god's black fist. One after the other they shimmied down the stem. At the base they climbed over the rail. The view enlarged again.

"It's Snake!" said Geo.

"And he's got the jewel!" Urson added.

"That's Argo with him," Iimmi put in. "I mean . . . *one* of the Argos!" They gathered around the screen to watch the congregation give way before the frightened children. Argo held on to Snake's shoulder.

Suddenly Hama turned the picture off. They looked away from the screen, puzzled. "So you see," said the god, "the jewel has been stolen. For the sake of Argo and of Hama, carry the jewels back to Leptar. Young Argo will help you. Though we here are pained to see her go, she is as prepared for the journey as you are, if not more. Will you do it?"

"I will," Iimmi said.

"Me too," said Geo.

"I guess so," Urson said.

"Good." Hama smiled. "Then come with me." He turned from the screen and walked through the door. They followed him down the long stairway, past the stone walls, into the hall, and along the back of the church. He walked slowly and smiled like a man who had waited long for something to finally come. They left the Temple and descended the bright steps.

"I wonder where the kids are," Urson said.

Hama led them across the garden. Black urns sat close in the shrubbery. Old Argo joined them at the crosswalk with a silent smile of recognition. They turned from the path and stepped between the urns.

Argo twisted two ends of wire together with sun-dappled hands. Snake, knees beneath his arms, set the jewel on the improvised thermocouple. Now Argo crouched too. They concentrated at the bead. The thermocouple glowed: current jumped in the copper veins, the metal core became a magnet, and the armature tugged once about its pivot, tugged once more. Brushes hissed on the turning rings. The coil whirled to copper haze. "Hey!" she whispered. "Look at it go, will you! Just look at that thing go!" Oblivious to the elder gods, who smiled at them from the sides of the stone urn, the young thieves gazed at the humming motor.

chapter eleven

Under the trees, she stood on tiptoe and kissed the Priest's balding forehead. "Dunderhead," she said, "I think you're cute." Then she blinked rapidly and knuckled beneath her eye. "Oh," she added, remembering, "I was making yogurt in the biology laboratory yesterday. There's two gallons of it fermenting under the tarantula cage. Remember to take it out. And take care of the hamsters. Please don't forget the hamsters!"

That was the last of some twenty or twenty-five good-byes. There had been the entrusting of the shell collection, several exchanges of poems, the confession of authorship to a dozen practical jokes, and again respects to old Argo and Hama.

They started along the slope of the volcano. The Temple disappeared among the trees behind.

"Two days to get to the ship." Geo squinted at the pale sky.

"Perhaps we had better put the jewels together," said Urson. "Keep them out of harm's way, since we know their power."

"What do you mean?" Iimmi asked.

Urson took the leather purse from Geo's belt. "Give me your jewel."

Geo hesitated, then took the thong from his neck; Urson put it in the purse.

"I guess it can't hurt," Iimmi said, and dropped his chain after it.

"Here's mine too," Argo said. She had been carrying the third one. She had woven the cord she used to climb the statue into a small net sack, put the jewel inside, and hung it around her neck. Now she gave it to him.

Urson pulled the purse string and tucked the pouch at his waist.

"Well," said Geo, "I guess we head for the river, so we can get back to your mother and Jordde."

"Jordde?" asked Argo. "Who's he?"

"He's a spy for the blind priestesses. He's also the one who cut Snake's tongue out."

"Cut his . . ." Suddenly she stopped. "That's right—four arms, his tongue—I remember now, in the film!"

"In the what?" asked Iimmi. "What do you remember?"

Argo turned to Snake. "I remember where I saw you before!"

"You know Snake?" Urson asked.

"No. I never met him. But about a month ago I saw a movie of what happened. It was horrible what they did to him."

"What's a movie?" asked Iimmi.

"Huh?" said Argo. "Oh, it's sort of like the vision screens, only you can see things that happened in the past. Anyway, Dunderhead showed me this film about a month ago. Then he took me down to the beach and said I should have seen something there, because of what I'd learned."

"See something! What was it?" Iimmi took her shoulder and shook it. "What was it you were supposed to see?"

"Why—?" the girl began, startled.

"A friend of mine was murdered and I almost was too, because of something we saw on that beach! Only I don't know what it was!"

"But . . ." began Argo. "But I don't either. I couldn't see it, so Dunderhead took me back to the Temple."

"Snake?" Geo asked. "Do you know what they were supposed to see? Or why Argo was taken to see it after she was shown what happened to you?"

The boy shrugged.

Iimmi turned on Snake. "Do you know or are you just not telling? Come on, now! That's the only reason I stuck with this so far. I want to know what's going on!"

Snake shook his head.

"I want to know why I was nearly killed!" the black sailor insisted. "You know and I want you to tell me!" Iimmi raised his hand.

Snake screamed. Sound tore through the distended vocal cords. Then he whirled and ran.

Urson caught him and brought the boy crashing down among leaves. "No you don't!" the giant growled. "You're not going to get away from me this time."

"Watch out!" cried Argo. "You're hurting him. Urson, let go!"

"Hey, ease up," said Geo. "Snake, you've got to give us some explanation. Let him go, Urson."

Urson let the boy up, still mumbling. "He's not going to get away again."

Geo came over to the boy. "Let him go. Look, Snake, do you know what there was about the beach that was so important?"

Snake nodded.

"Can you tell?"

Now the boy shook his head and glanced at Urson.

"You don't have to be afraid of him," Geo said, puzzled. "Urson won't hurt you."

Snake shook his head again.

"Well," said Geo, "we can't make you. Let's get going."

"I could make him," Urson mumbled.

"No," said Argo. "I don't think you could. I watched the last time somebody tried. And I don't think you could."

Late morning flopped over hot in the sky, turning to afternoon. The jungle grew damp. Bright insects plunged like tiny knives of blue or scarlet through the foliage. Wet leaves brushed their chests, faces, and shoulders.

At the edge of a rocky stretch, Urson suddenly drew his sword and hacked at a shadow, which resolved into a medium-sized cat-like animal. Blood ran over the rock and mixed with encrusted leaves in the dirt.

No one suggested using the jewels for fire. As Iimmi was striking stones over a handful of tinder, he suddenly asked, "Why would they show you a film of something awful before taking you to the beach?"

"Maybe it was supposed to have made me more receptive to what I saw," said Argo.

"If horror makes you receptive to whatever it was," said Iimmi, "I should have been about as receptive as possible."

"What do you mean?" asked Geo.

"I had just watched ten guys get hacked to pieces all over the sand, remember?" The fire flickered, caught, and held.

As they ate, Argo got out a packet of salt from her tunic, then disappeared with Snake into the woods, to come back two minutes later with a purplish vine that she said made good spice when the bark was stripped and the pith rubbed on meat. "Back at the Temple," she told them, sitting down in front of the fire, "I had a great herb garden. There was one whole section for poisonous plants: death angel, wolfsbane, deadly nightshade, monkshood, hebenon, the whole works." She laughed. Then the laugh stopped. "I guess I won't be going back there again. For a little while, anyway." She twisted the vine. "It was a beautiful garden, though." Then she let the stem untwist.

They left the rocky plateau for lower woods, and the dampness grew and the light lessened. "Are you sure we're going the right way?" Urson asked.

"We should be," said Iimmi.

"It is," said Argo. "We'll come out at the head of the river. It's a huge marsh that drains off into the main channel."

Evening came quickly.

"I was wondering about something," Geo said after a little while.

"What?" asked Argo.

"Hama said that once the jewels had been used to control minds, the person who used them was infected. . . ."

"Rather the infection was already there," corrected Argo. "That just brought it out."

"Yes," said Geo. "Anyway, Hama also said that he was infected. When did he have to use the jewels?"

"Lots of times," Argo said. "Too many. The last time was when I was kidnapped. He used the jewel to control pieces of that thing you all killed in the City of New Hope to come and kidnap me and then leave the jewel in Leptar."

"A piece of that monster?" Geo exclaimed. "No wonder it decayed so rapidly when it was killed."

"Huh?" asked Iimmi.

"Argo—I mean your mother—told me they had managed to kill one of the kidnappers, and it melted the moment it died."

"We couldn't control the whole mass," she explained. "It really doesn't have a mind. But, like everything alive, it has, or had, the double impulse."

"But what did kidnapping you accomplish, anyway?" Iimmi asked.

Argo grinned. "It brought you here. And now you're taking the jewels away."

"Is that all?" asked Iimmi.

"Well, jeepers," said Argo. "Isn't that enough?" She paused

for an instant. "You know, I wrote a poem about all this once, the double impulse and everything."

Geo recited:

> "By the dark chamber sits its twin,
> where the body's floods begin,
> and the two are twinned again,
> turning out and turning in."

"How did you know?"

"The dark chamber is Hama's Temple," Geo said. "Am I right?"

"And its twin is Argo's," she went on. "They should be twins, really. And then the twins again are the children. The force of age in each one opposed to the young force. See?"

"I see." Geo smiled. "And the body's floods, turning in and out?"

"That's sort of everything man does, his going and coming, his great ideas, his achievements, his little ideas too. It all comes from the interplay of those four forces."

"Four?" said Urson. "I thought it was just two."

"But it's thousands!" Argo exclaimed.

"It's too complicated for me," said Urson. "How far do we have to go to the river?"

"We should be there by evening," Iimmi calculated.

"And we're headed right," Argo assured them again. "I think."

"One more thing," asked Geo. The ground beneath the fallen leaves was black and spongy now. "How did your grandmother get to Aptor?"

"By helicopter," Argo said.

"By what?" asked Iimmi.

"It's like a very small ship that flies in the air, and it goes much faster than a boat in water."

"I didn't mean the method of transportation," said Geo.

"When she had decided her daughter was reigning steadily in

Leptar, she just went to Aptor permanently. I didn't even know about it until I was kidnapped. I've learned a lot since I came here."

"I guess we have too," said Geo. "But there's still that one thing more, at the beach."

"Then let's hurry up and get there," said Urson. "We're slowing down, and we don't have much time."

The air was almost drenched. The leaves had been shiny before. Now they dripped water on the loose ground. Pale light lapsed through the branches, shimmered from leaf to the wet underside of leaf. The ground became mud.

Twice they heard a sloshing a few feet away and then the scuttling of an unseen animal. "I hope I don't step on something that decides to take a chunk out of my foot."

"I'm pretty good at first aid," Argo said. "I'm getting chilly," she added.

Urson humphed now as the trees thinned around them. The muddy forest floor for yards at a span was coated with water that became mirrors for the trees stuck in its surface.

"Start watching out for quicksand," Geo said. They went more cautiously now. "Just keep within grabbing distance of a tree."

"They're getting sort of far apart," said Argo.

Just then Geo, who was a bit ahead of the others, cried out. When they reached him he had already sunk knee-deep. He threw himself to the side and his good arm wrapped around the trunk of a thin black tree. He tried to grab on with his nub too, but he just scraped it on the bark.

"Hold on!" Urson called. He skirted the pool and grabbed the trunk of the tree with one hand and Geo with the other. Geo came up, coated to the thigh with gray. As Urson helped him to more solid ground, the tree they had grabbed suddenly tilted and then splashed forward in a medusa of roots. A nameless animal slithered from the matted, dripping stalks. Then the whole thing slipped beneath the mud and there were only ripples.

"You all right?" Urson still supported him. "You sure you're all right?"

Geo nodded, rubbing the stump of his arm with his good hand. "I'm all right," he said. They gathered together and began once more through the mud. The trees gave out.

Geo suddenly saw the whole swamp shiver in front of him. He splashed a step backward, but Urson caught his shoulder. Ripples appeared over the water, spreading, crossing, webbing the whole surface with a net of tiny waves.

And they rose: green backs broke the water. They stood now, torrents cascading their green faces, green chests. Three of them, then a fourth. Four more, then many more. Their naked bodies were mottled green.

Geo felt a tugging in his head, at his mind. Looking around, he saw that the others felt it too.

"Them . . ." Urson started.

"They're the ones who . . . carried us. . . ." Geo began. The tug came again, and they stepped forward. He put his hand on his head. "They want . . . us to go with them. . . ." And suddenly he was going forward, slipping into the familiar state of half consciousness that had come when he had crossed the river, to the City of New Hope, or when he had first fallen into the sea.

Wet hands fell on their bodies and guided them through the swamp. They were carried through deeper water. Now they were walked over dry land where the vegetation was thicker. Slimy boulders caught shards of sunset on their wet flanks.

Dripping canopies of moss looped the branches. Water rose to their knees, their stomachs, their necks. A bright wash of pebbles and shells resolved through the water, as if their eyes had been pushed close to the sea bottom, sensitized to new light. The air was white, static, and electric. Then it slipped through blue to black. There were red eyes in the blackness. Through a rip in the arras of vegetation, they saw the moon push between the clouds, staining them silver. A rock rose against the moonlight where a naked man stared at the white disk. As they passed, he howled (or anyway, opened his mouth and threw his head back. But their ears were full of night and could not hear) and dropped to all fours. A breeze blew in the sudden plume of his tail, in the scraggly hair of his underbelly, and light lay on the points of his ears, his lengthened muzzle, his thinned hind legs. He turned his head once and scampered down the rock and into the darkness. A curtain of trees swung across the open sky. Eyes of flame glittered ahead of them. Water swirled their knees once more, then went down. Sand washed from beneath their feet along the dark beach. The beating of the sea, the rush of the river. Wet leaves fingered their cheeks, tickled their shins, and slapped their bellies as they moved forward. All fell away.

Light flickered on the wet rocks as they entered the largest cave. Their eyes focused once more. Foam washed back and forth over the sandy floor, and black chains of weeds caught in crevices on the stone, twisted on the sand with the inrush of water. Webbed hands released them.

Brown rocks rose around them in the firelight. They raised their eyes to a rock throne where the Old One sat. His long spines were strung with shrunken membranes. His eyes, gray and clouded, were close to the surface of his broad-nostriled face. Water trickled over the rock where he sat. Others stood about him.

They glanced at one another. Outside the cave it was raining hard. Argo's hair, wet to dark auburn, hugged her head, with little streaks down her neck.

A voice boomed at them, with more than just the natural sonority of the cave: "Carriers of the jewels," it began. Geo realized that it was the same hollowness that accompanied Snake's soundless messages. "We have brought you here to give a warning. We are the oldest forms of intelligence on this planet. We have watched from the delta of the Nile the rise of the pyramids; we have seen the murder of Caesar from the banks of the Tiber. We watched the Spanish Armada destroyed by England, and we followed Man's great metal fish through the ocean before the Great Fire. We have never aligned ourselves with either Argo or

Hama, but rise in the sexless swell of the ocean. We come only to touch men when they are bloated with death. You have carried and used the jewels of Aptor, the Eyes of Hama, the Treasure of Argo, the Destroyers of Reason, the playthings of children. Whether you use them to control minds or to make fire, all carriers of the jewels are maimed. But we can warn you, as we have warned Man before. As before, some will listen, some will not. Your minds are your own, that I pledge you. Now I warn you: cast the jewels into the sea.

"Nothing is ever lost in the sea, and when the evil has been washed from them with time and brine, they will be returned to you. For then time and brine will have washed away your imperfections also.

"No living intelligence is free from their infection, nothing with the double impulse of life. But we are old and can hold them for a million years before we will be so infected as you are. Your young race is too condensed in its living to tolerate such power in its fingers now. Again I say: cast them into the sea.

"The knowledge man needs to alleviate hunger and pain from the world is contained in two temples on this Island. Both have the science to put the jewels to use, to the good uses possible with them. Both have been infected. In Leptar, however, where you carry these jewels, there is no way at all to utilize them for anything but evil. There will be only the temptation to destroy."

"What about me?" Argo piped up. "I can teach them all sorts of things in Leptar." She took one of Snake's hands. "We used one for our motor."

"You will find something else to make your motor run. You still have to recognize something that you have already seen."

"At the beach?" demanded Iimmi.

"Yes." The Old One nodded, with something like a sigh. "At the beach. We have a science allowing us to do things that to you seem impossibilities, as when we carried you in the sea for weeks without your body drowning. We can enter your mind as Snake does. And we can do much else. We have a wisdom far surpassing even Argo's and Hama's on Aptor. Will you cast the jewels into the sea and trust them with us?"

"How can we give you the jewels?" Urson demanded. "First of all, how can we be sure you're not going to use them against Argo and Hama once you get them? You say nobody is impervious to them. And we've only got your say-so on how long it would take you to fall victim. You can already influence minds. That's how you got us here. And according to Hama, that's what corrupts. And you've already done it."

"Besides," Geo said, "there's something else. We've nearly messed this thing up a dozen times trying to figure out motives and countermotives. And it always comes back to the same thing: we've got a job to do, and we ought to do it. We're supposed to return Argo and the jewels to the ship, and that's what we're doing."

"He's right," said Iimmi. "Rule number one again: act on the simplest theory that holds all the information."

The Old One sighed a second time. "Once, fifteen hundred years ago, a man who was to maneuver one of the metal birds that was to drop fire from the sky walked and pondered by the sea. He had been given a job to do. We tried to warn him, as we tried to warn you. But he jammed his hands into the pockets of his uniform and uttered to the waves the words you just uttered, and the warning was shut out of his mind. He scrambled up over the dunes on the beach, never taking his hands out of his pockets. He drank one more cup of coffee that night than usual. The next morning, at five o'clock, when the sun slanted red across the airfield, he climbed into his metal bird, took off, flew for some time over the sea, looking down on the water like crinkled foil under the heightening sun, until he reached land again. Then he did his job: he pressed a button that released two shards of fire metal in a housing of cobalt. The land flamed. The sea boiled in the harbors. And two weeks later he was also dead. That which burned your arm away, Poet, burned his whole face away, boiled his lungs in his chest and his brain in his skull." There was a pause. "Yes, we can control minds. We could have relieved the tiredness, immobilized the fear, the terror, immobilized all his unconscious reasons for doing what he did, just as man can now do with the jewels. But had we, we would have also immobilized the . . . humanity he clung to. Yes, we can control minds, but we do not." The voice swelled. "But never, since that day on the shore before the Great Fire, has the temptation to do so been as great as now." The voice returned to normal. "Perhaps," and there was almost humor in it now. "Perhaps you are right. Perhaps the temptation is too great even for us. Perhaps we have reached the place where the jewels would push us just across the line we have never crossed before, make us do those things that we have never done." Another pause. "There, you have heard our warning now. The choice, I swear to you, is yours."

They stood silent in the high cave, the fire on their faces weaving brightness and shadow. Geo turned to look at the rain-blurred darkness outside the cave.

"Out there is the sea," said the voice again. "Your decision quickly. The tide is coming in. . . ."

It was snatched from their minds before they could articulate it. Two children saw a bright motor turning in the shadow. Geo and Iimmi saw the temples of Argo in Leptar. Then there was something darker, from Urson. And for a moment, they all saw all the pictures at once. And then they were gone.

"Very well, then," boomed the voice. "Keep them!"

A wave splashed across the floor, like twisted glass before the rock on which the fire stood. Then it flopped wetly across the burning driftwood. They were hissed into darkness. Charred sticks turned, glowing in the water, and were extinguished.

Rain was buffeting them, hands held them once more, pulling them into the warm sea, the darkness, and then nothing. . . .

Snake was thinking again, and this time through the Captain's eyes:

The cabin door burst open in the rain. Her wet veils whipped about the doorframe; lightning made them transparent. Jordde rose from his seat. She closed the door on thunder.

I have received the signal from the sea, *she said*. Tomorrow you pilot the ship into the estuary.

The Captain's voice: But, Priestess Argo, I cannot take the ship into Aptor. We already have lost ten men; I cannot sacrifice . . .

And the storm. *Jordde smiled*. If it is like this tomorrow, how can I take her through the rocks?

Her nostrils flared; her lips compressed to a chalky line. She regarded Jordde.

The Captain's thoughts: What is between them, this confused tension. It upsets me deeply, and I am tired. . . .

You will pilot the boat to shore tomorrow, *Argo hissed*. They have returned with the jewels!

The Captain's thoughts: They speak to each other in a code I don't understand. I am so tired now. I have to protect my ship, my men; that is my job, my responsibility.

Argo turned to the Captain. Captain, I hired you to obey me. You promised this when you took my commission, and you knew it involved danger in Aptor. You must order your Mate to pilot this ship to Aptor's shore tomorrow morning.

The Captain's thoughts: Yes, yes. The fatigue and the unknowing. But I must fulfill, must complete . . . Jordde, *he began*.

Yes, Captain, *answered the Mate, anticipating.* If the weather is permitting, sir, I will take the ship as close as I can get. *He smiled, a thin curve over his face, and looked back at Argo.*

chapter twelve

Roughness of sand beneath one of his sides, and the flare of the sun on the other. His eyes were hot and his lids orange over them. He turned over and reached out to dig his hands into the sand. One hand closed.

He opened his eyes and rolled to his knees. The sand grated under his kneecaps. Looking out toward the water, he saw that the sun hung only inches above the horizon. Then he saw the ship.

It was heading toward the estuary of the river down the beach. He stood up and looked around. He was alone. The estuary was to his left. He began to run toward where the rocks and vegetation cut off the end of the beach. The sand under his feet was cool.

A moment later he saw Iimmi's dark figure run from the jungle, heading for the same place. Geo hailed him. Panting, they joined each other. Together they continued toward the rocks.

As they broke through the first foliage, they nearly bumped into red-haired Argo, who stood, knuckling her eyes, in the shadow of the broad palm fronds. When she recognized them, she joined them silently. Finally they reached the outcropping of rocks a few hundred feet up the riverbank.

The rain had swelled the river's mouth to tremendous violence. It vomited brown water into the ocean, frothed against rocks, and boiled opaquely below them. It was nearly half again as wide as Geo remembered it.

Although the sky was clear, beyond the brown bile of the river, the sea snarled and bared its ivory froth to the early sun. It took another fifteen minutes for the boat to maneuver through granite spikes toward the rocky embankment.

Staring down into the turbulence, Argo whispered, "So fast . . ." But that was the only human sound against the roar.

The boat's prow bobbed in the swell. At last her plank swung out and bumped unsteadily on the rocks. Figures were gathering on deck.

"Hey," Argo said, pointing toward one. "That's Mom!"

"Where the hell are Snake and Urson?" Iimmi asked.

"That's Snake down there," Geo said. "Look!" He pointed with his nub.

Snake crouched near the gangplank itself. He was behind a ledge of rock, hidden from those on the ship, but plain to Geo and his companions.

Geo said: "I'm going down there. You stay here." He ducked through the vines, keeping in sight of the rocks' edge and the heaving foam. He reached a sheltered rise, just ten feet above the nest of rock in which the four-armed boy was crouching.

Geo looked out at the boat. Jordde stood at the head of the gangplank. The eighteen feet of board was unsteady with the roll of the ship. Jordde held a black whip in his hand; the end went to a box strapped to his back. With the lash raised, he stepped onto the shifting plank.

Geo wondered what the contrivance was. The answer came with the hollow sound of Snake's thoughts:

That . . . is . . . machine . . . he . . . used . . . to . . . cut . . . tongue . . . with . . . only . . . on . . . whip . . . not . . . wire . . . So Snake knew he was just behind him. As Geo tried to understand exactly the implications of what Snake had said, suddenly, with the speed of a bird's shadow, Snake leaped from his hiding place and landed on the end of the plank, recovered from his crouch, and rushed out toward Jordde, apparently intending to knock him from the board.

Jordde raised the lash and it fell across the boy's shoulder. It didn't land hard; it just dropped. But Snake reeled and went down on one knee, grabbing the sides of the plank. Geo was close enough to hear the boy scream.

"I cut your tongue out once with this thing," Jordde said matter-of-factly. "Now I'm going to cut the rest of you to pieces." He adjusted a control at his belt and raised the lash again—

Geo leaped for the plank. The sudden swell of anger and fear defined the action, but once on the end of the plank, facing Jordde over crouching Snake, he wondered how wise it had been. Then he had to stop wondering and try to duck the falling lash. He couldn't.

It landed with only the weight of gravity, brushing his cheek, then dropping across his shoulder and down his back. He screamed: it felt as if the whole side of his face had been seared away, and an inch-deep crevice burned into his shoulder and back the whole length it touched him. He bit white fire, trying not to leap aside into the foaming chasm between rocks and boat. As the lash rasped away, sweat flooded into his eyes. His good arm, which held the edge of the plank as he crouched, was shaking like a plucked string on a loose guitar. Snake staggered back against him, almost knocking him over. When Geo blinked the tears out of his eyes, he saw two bright welts on Snake's shoulder. Jordde stepped out on the plank, smiling.

When the line fell again, he wasn't sure just what happened. He leaned in one direction. Snake was a dive of legs in the other, then only four sets of fingers over the edge of the plank. Geo screamed again and shook.

Two sets of fingers disappeared from one side of the board and reappeared on the other. As Jordde raised the lash a fourth time to rid the plank of this one-armed nuisance, the fingers worked rapidly forward toward Jordde's feet. An arm rose from beneath the plank, grabbed Jordde's ankle, and the lash fell far of Geo. He was still trembling, trying to move back off the unsteady plank and keep from vomiting at the same time.

Jordde lost his balance, but turned in time to grab the rail of the ship's gate. At the same time, one leg, then the other, came over the side of the plank. Snake rolled to a crouch on top of the board.

Geo got his feet under him and stumbled off the plank. Back on the rocks, he sat down hard. He clutched his good arm across his stomach, and without lowering his eyes, leaned forward to cool his back.

Jordde, half seated on the board, lashed the whip sideways. Snake leaped a foot as the line swung beneath his feet. All four arms went spidering out to regain equilibrium. The whip struck the side of the boat, left a burn on the hull, and came swinging back again. Snake leaped once more and made it.

Suddenly there was a shadow over Geo, and he saw Urson stride up to the end of the plank. His back to Geo, the big sailor

crouched bearlike at the plank's head. "All right, now try someone a little bigger than you. Come on, boy; get off there. I want
my chance." Urson's sword was drawn.

Snake turned, grabbed at something on Urson, but the big
man knocked him away as Snake leaped diagonally onto the
shore. Urson laughed over his shoulder. "You don't want the ones
around my neck," he called back. "Here, keep these for me." He
tossed Geo's leather purse from his belt back to the bank. Snake
landed just as Jordde flung the lash out again. Urson must have
caught the line across his chest, because his back suddenly stiffened. Then he leaped forward and came down with his sword
so hard that had Jordde still been there, his leg would have been
severed. Jordde leaped back onto the edge of the ship, and the
sword sliced three inches into the wood. As Urson tried to pull
the blade free, Jordde sent his whip singing again. It wrapped
Urson's midsection like a black serpent; and it didn't come loose.

Urson howled. He flung his sword forward. The blade sank
inches through Jordde's abdomen. The Mate bent forward with
a totally amazed expression, grabbed the line with both hands,
and tugged backward, screaming.

Jordde took two steps onto the plank, mouth open, eyes
closed, and fell over the side.

Urson, without stopping his own howl or letting go of the
line, heaved backward, and toppled from the other side. For a
moment they hung with the whip between them, over the board.
The ship heaved back and then rolled to. The plank swiveled,
came loose; and, with the board on top of them, they crashed
into the water.

Geo and Snake scrambled to the rocks' edge. Iimmi and Argo
were coming up behind them.

Below them, the tangle of limbs and board bobbed in the foam
once. The line had somehow looped around Urson's neck, and
the plank had turned up almost on end. They went under again.

With nothing between it and the rocky shore, the boat began
to roll in. With each swell, it came in six feet and then leaned
out three. Then it came back another six. It took four swells,

the time of four very deep breaths, until the side of the boat was grating up against the rocks. Geo could hear the plank splintering in the water.

But the river's rush blanketed anything else that was breaking.

Geo took two steps backward, clutched at his stubbed arm, and threw up from pain and terror.

Somebody, the Captain, was calling. "Get her away from the rocks! Away from the rocks, before she goes to pieces!"

Iimmi took Geo's arm. "Come on, Geo!" He managed to haul him onto the ship. Argo and Snake leaped on behind them. The boat floundered away from the shore.

Geo leaned against the rail. Below him the water turned on itself in the rocks, thrashed along the river's side, and then, as he raised his eyes, stretched out along the bright blade of the beach. The long sand that rimmed the Island dropped away from them, a stately and austere arc gathering in its curve all the sun's glare, and throwing it back in wave and on wave.

His back hurt, his stomach was shriveled and shaken like an old man's palsied fist, his arm was gone, and Urson . . . "Captain," Geo said. He turned from the rail, his good hand going to his nub. Then he bawled, "Captain!"

The little redhead caught his shoulder. "It . . . it won't do any good!"

"Captain!" he called again.

The elderly, gray-eyed man approached him. "What is it?"

He looks tired, Geo thought. *I'm tired.*

Iimmi was by his shoulder now. Geo was quiet until Iimmi said, "Never mind, sir. I don't think you can do anything now."

"Are you sure?" the Captain asked, looking at the shocked black hair, the bruised face, the deep eyes. "Are you . . ."

"Never mind," Geo said. He turned back to the rail. Below them, splinters of the plank were still washing up to the boat's hull and falling back into the white froth. Only splinters. Only . . .

Then Argo said, "Look at the beach!"

Geo flung his eyes up and tried in one moment to envelop whatever he saw, whatever it would be. Beneath the water's roar was a still tide, a tide of quiet. Sand along the naked crescent was dull at some depressions, mirror bright at certain rises. At the jungle, multitextured ripplings sped over the leaves and fronds covering the foliage-thick limbs. Each fragment in that green tapestry hung there in the sun was one leaf, he reflected, with two sides, a system of skeleton and veins, as his arm had been. And one day would drop off too.

Now he looked from rock to rock. Each one was different, differently shaped, distinctly lined, losing detail as the ship floated farther, like the memory of his entire adventure was losing detail. That boulder there was like a bull's head half submerged. Those two flat ones together on the sand looked like an eagle's opened wings. And the waves, measured and magnificent, followed one another onto the sand, like the varying, never duplicating rhythm of a fine poem: peaceful, ordered, and calm. He tried to pour the chaos of Urson's drowning from his mind onto the water. It flowed into each glass-green trough that rode up to the still beach. He tried to spread the pain in his own body over the foam and shimmering green. And was surprised because it fit so easily, hung there so well in the sea's web. Somewhere, understanding was beginning to effloresce with the water, under the heightening sun.

Geo turned away from the rail. The wet deck slipped under his bare feet. He walked back toward the forecastle. He had released his broken limb, and his hand hung at his side while he walked.

Later in the evening, he came on deck again. The veiled Priestess stood by the railing. When he approached, she turned to him and said quietly, "I did not want to disturb you for a report until you had rested some."

"I've rested," he said. "We've returned your daughter to you. You can get the jewels from Snake. He'll give them to you now. You can get your daughter to explain everything about Hama."

"She has already," answered the Priestess, smiling. "You've done very well, Poet, and bravely."

"Thank you," Geo said. Then he turned back to the forecastle.

When Snake came down that evening, Geo was lying on his back in the bunk, following the grain of the wood on the bottom of the bed above his. His good arm was behind his neck now. Snake touched Geo's shoulder.

"What is it?" Geo asked, turning on his side and looking from under the bunk.

Snake held out the leather purse to Geo.

"Huh?" Geo asked. "Didn't you give them to Argo yet?"

Snake nodded.

"Well, why didn't she take them? Look, I don't want to see them again."

Snake pushed the purse toward him again and added: *look . . .*

Geo took the purse, opened the drawstring, and turned the contents out in his hand: there were three chains. On each, a gold coin was fastened by a hole near the edge. Geo frowned. "How come these are in here?" he asked. "I thought . . . where are the jewels?"

In . . . ocean . . . Snake said. *Urson . . . switched . . . them . . .*

"What are you talking about?" demanded Geo. "What is it?"

Don't . . . want . . . tell . . . you . . .

"I don't care what you want, you little bastard!" Geo grabbed him by the shoulder. "Tell me!"

Know . . . from . . . back . . . with . . . blind . . . priestesses . . . Snake explained rapidly. *he . . . ask . . . me . . . how . . . to . . . use . . . jewels . . . when . . . you . . . and . . . Iimmi . . . exploring . . . and . . . after . . . that . . . no . . . listen . . . to . . . thoughts . . . bad . . . thoughts . . . bad . . .*

"But he . . ." Geo started. "He saved your life!"

But . . . what . . . is . . . reason . . . Snake said. *at . . . end . . .*

"You saw his thoughts at the end?" asked Geo. "What did he think?"

You . . . sleep . . . please . . . Snake said. *Lot . . . of . . . hate . . . lot of . . . bad . . . hate . . .* There was a pause in the voice in his head. *And . . . love . . .*

Geo began to cry. A bubble of sound in the back of his throat burst, and he turned onto the pillow and tried to bite through the sound with his teeth and tried to know why he was crying; for the tiredness, for the fear, for Urson, for his arm, and for the inevitable growth, which hurt so much . . . his body ached; his back hurt in two sharp lines, and he couldn't stop crying.

Iimmi, who had taken the bunk above Geo's, came back a few minutes after mess. Geo had not felt like eating.

"How's your stomach?" Iimmi asked.

"Funny," Geo said. "But better, I guess."

"Good," said Iimmi. "Food sort of weights you down, once it gets inside; sort of holds you down to earth."

"I'll eat something soon," Geo said. He paused. "Now I guess you'll never find out what you saw on the beach that made you dangerous." The slosh of water on the hull outside was just audible; they were veering toward Leptar now.

Then Iimmi laughed. "I found what it was."

"How?" asked Geo. "When? What was it?"

"Same time you did," Iimmi said. "I just looked. And then Snake explained the details of it to me later."

"When?" Geo repeated.

"I took a nap just before dinner and he went through the whole thing with me."

"Then what was it you saw, we saw?"

"Well, first of all, do you remember what Jordde was before he was shipwrecked on Aptor?"

"Didn't Argo say he was studying to be a priest? Old Argo, I mean."

"Right," said Iimmi. "Now, do you remember what your theory was about what we saw?"

"Did I have a theory?" Geo asked.

"About horror and pain making you receptive to whatever it was."

"Oh, that," Geo said. "I remember. Yes."

"You were also right about that. Now add to all this some theory from Hama's lecture on the double impulse of life: sift together; mix well. It wasn't a thing we saw; it was a situation, or rather an experience we had. Also, it didn't have to be on the beach. It could have happened anywhere. Man, with his constantly diametric motivations, is always trying to reconcile opposites. Take Hama's theory one step further: each action *is* a reconciliation of the duality of his motivation. Now, take all we've been through—the confusion, the pain, the disorder; reconcile that with the great order obvious in something like the sea, with its rhythm, its tides and waves, its overpowering calm, or the ordering of cells in a leaf, or a constellation of stars. If you can do it, something happens to you: you grow. You become a bigger person, able to understand, or reconcile, more."

"All right," said Geo.

"And that's what we saw, or the experience we had when we looked at the beach from the ship this morning: chaos caught in order, the order defining chaos."

"All right again," Geo said. "And I'll even assume that Jordde knew that the two impulses of this experience were something terrible and confused, like seeing ten men hacked to pieces by vampires, or seeing a film of a little boy getting his tongue pulled out, or coming through what we came through since we landed on Aptor, as well as something calm and ordered, like the beach and the sea. Now, why would he want to kill someone simply because he might have gone through what amounts, I guess, to the basic religious experience?"

"You picked just the right word." Iimmi smiled. "Jordde was a novice in the not-too-liberal religion of Argo. Jordde and Snake had probably been through nearly as much on Aptor as we had. And they survived. And they also emerged from that jungle of horror onto that great arching rhythm of waves and sand. And they went through just what you and I and Argo went through. Little Argo, I mean. And it was just at that point when the blind priestesses of Argo made contact with Jordde. They did so by means of those vision screens we saw them with, which can receive sound and pictures from just about anyplace, but can also project at least sound to just about anywhere too. In other words, right in the middle of this religious or mystic or whatever you want to call it experience, a voice materialized out of thin air that claimed to be the voice of the Goddess. Have you any idea what this did to his mind?"

"I imagine it took all the real significance out of the whole thing," Geo said. "It would for me."

"It did," said Iimmi. "Jordde wasn't what you'd call stable before that. If anything, this made him worse. It also stopped his mental functioning from working in the normal way. And Snake, who was reading his mind at the time, suddenly saw himself watching the terrifying sealing-up process of a more or less active and competent, if not healthy, mind. He saw it again in Urson, slower this time. But the same thing. It's apparently a pretty stiff thing to watch from the inside. That's why he stopped reading Urson's thoughts. The idea of stealing the jewels for himself was slowly eating away the balance, the understanding, the ability to reconcile disparities, like the incident with the blue lizard; things like that, all of which were signs we didn't see. Snake contacted Hama by telepathy, almost accidentally. But Hama's information about the aims of the blind priestesses, to get the jewels for themselves, was something to hold on to for the boy: the second part of his impulse to serve Hama, the first part being the awful thing that had happened to Jordde's mind at contact with the blind priestesses."

"Still, why did Jordde want to kill anybody who had experienced this, voice of God and all?"

"Because Jordde had by now managed to do what a static mind always does. Everything became equivocated with everything else. The situation, the beach, the whole thing suddenly meant for him the revelation of a concrete God. He knew that

Snake had contacted something also, something which the blind priestesses told him was thoroughly evil, an enemy, a devil. On the raft, on the boat, he religiously tried to 'convert' Snake, till at last, in evangelical fury, he cut the boy's tongue out with the electric generator and the hot wire the blind Priestess had given him before he left. Why did he want to get rid of anybody who had seen his beach, a place sacred to him by now? One, because the devils were too strong and he didn't want anybody else possessed by them; Snake had been too much trouble resisting conversion. And two, because he was jealous that someone else might have that moment of exaltation and hear the voice of the Goddess also."

"In other words, he thought what happened to him and Snake was something supernatural, actually connected with the beach itself, and didn't want it to happen to anybody else."

"That's right." Iimmi sat on the bunk's edge. "Which is sort of understandable. They didn't come in contact with any of the technology of Aptor, and so it might well have seemed that way."

Geo leaned back. "I can see how the same thing almost . . . almost might have happened to me. If everything had been the same."

Geo closed his eyes. Snake came down and took the top bunk; and when Geo slept, Snake told him of Urson, of his last thoughts, and surprisingly, things he mostly knew, about hate, a lot of hate, and about love.

Emerging from the forecastle the next morning, bright sunlight fell across his face. He had to squint. When he did so, he saw her sitting cross-legged on the stretched canvas tarpaulin in one of the suspended lifeboats.

"Hi up there," he called.

"Hi down there. How are you feeling?"

Geo shrugged.

Argo slipped her feet over the gunwale and, with paper bag in hand, dropped to the deck. She bobbed up next to his shoulder, grinned, and said, "Hey, come on back with me. I want to show you something."

"Sure." He followed her.

"I bet you must be looking forward to school," she said as they walked. "You and Iimmi might turn up in some of the same classes, now that you know each other."

"Maybe," said Geo.

"My, are you glum!" She pulled a long face under short shocks of red hair.

"I hope Iimmi and I do get into some classes together," Geo said.

"That's more like it." Suddenly she looked serious. "Your arm is worrying you. Why?"

Geo shrugged again. "I don't feel like a whole person. I guess I'm not really a whole person."

"Don't be silly," said Argo. "Besides, maybe Snake will let you have one of his. How are the medical facilities in Leptar?"

"I don't think they're up to anything like that."

"We did grafting of limbs back on Aptor," Argo said. "A most interesting way we got around the antibody problem too. You see—"

"But that was back in Aptor," Geo said. "This is the real world we're going into now."

"Maybe I can get a doctor from the Temple to come over." She shrugged. "And then, maybe I won't be able to."

"It's a pleasant thought," Geo said.

When they reached the back of the ship, Argo took out the contraption from the paper bag. "I salvaged this in my tunic. Hope I dried it off well enough last night."

"It's your motor," Geo said.

"Uh-huh." She set it on a low set of lockers by the cabin back wall.

"How are you going to work it?" he asked. "It's got to have that stuff, electricity."

"There is more than one way to shoe a centipede," Argo assured him. She reached behind the locker and pulled up a strange gizmo of glass and wire. "I got the lens from Mom," she explained. "She's awfully nice, really. She says I can have my own laboratory all to myself. And I said she could have all the politics, which I think was wise of me, considering. Don't you?" She bent over the contraption. "Now, this lens here focuses the sunlight—isn't it a beautiful day?—focuses it on these here thermocouples. I got the extra metal from the ship's smith. He's sweet. Hey, we're going to have to compare poems from now on. I mean I'm sure you're going to write a whole handful about all of this. I certainly am. Anyway, you connect it up here."

She fastened two wires to two other wires, adjusted the lens; the tips of the thermocouple glowed beneath the glass. The armature tugged about its pivot.

Geo looked up to see Snake and Iimmi leaning over the rail on the cabin roof.

"Hey," Argo called. "Move out of the light!"

Grinning, they moved aside.

Brushes hissed on the turning rings. The coil whirled to copper haze. "Look at that thing go!" She stepped back, fists proudly on her hips. "Just look at that thing go!"

New York
February 1962

the ballad of beta-2

Oh, one came back to the City,
Over sand with her bright hair wild,
With her eyes coal black and her feet sole sore,
And under her arms a green-eyed child.

—FROM "THE BALLAD OF BETA-2"

chapter one

"Quite simply, the answer is: because they are *there*!"

White light from the helical fixtures struck down at the professor's bony face.

"But—" began Joneny.

"But no," the professor interrupted. They were alone in the office. "It isn't that simple, is it? The reason is that many of them were once there, and they did something that had never been done before—that will never be done again—and because remnants of them are still there now. *That* is why you will study them."

"But, sir," Joneny persisted, "that's not what I asked. I'm requesting a personal dispensation that will exempt me from research work on this unit. I expect to be held accountable for all examination questions on the Star Folk; but I'm already an honors student, and on the strength of that, I'm asking to skip the detail work on them. I'm perfectly willing to put in the time on my thesis topic, the Nukton Civilization of Creton III, or anything else that's reasonable, sir." Then, as an afterthought: "I realize it would be a privileged exemption that only you can grant."

"That's quite correct," the professor said coolly; he leaned forward. "On the strength of your 'honors,' Joneny—and you're more than a good student, you're an amazing one—I'll listen to your objections. But I have to admit that there's something about your request that annoys me."

Joneny took a breath. "I just don't want to waste my time on them, sir. There's so much needed research in a field like Galactic Anthropology; and, as far as I can see, the Star Folk are a dead end, with no significance at all. They were a very minor transition factor that was eliminated from the cosmic equation even before the terms were fully written out. Their 'contributions to the arts' are entirely derivative—and they produced nothing else. All that remains of them is a barbaric little settlement, if you can call it that, which the Federation sentimentally allows to exist out near Leffer VI. There are too many cultures and civilizations crying to be researched for me to waste time poking through dozens of chrome-plated eggshells, documenting the history of a . . . a bunch of chauvinistic, degenerate morons. And I don't care what anyone says, sir. That's all they are!"

"Well," the professor said. "Well. You are vehement on the subject." He glanced at the screen on his desk, flicked a few notes across it, then looked sternly at Joneny. "I am not going to grant your request. But I'll tell you why. In fact, I'll even argue with you—because of your 'honors' status. You say that the culture of the Star Folk was an insignificant transitional factor, superseded before its purpose was achieved. Why?"

"Because, sir . . ."—Joneny was prepared for that question— "they left Earth for the stars in their ships early in 2242, expecting to cruise through space for twelve generations before reaching an uncertain destination. They'd been gone only sixty years when the hyperspace drive became a large-scale reality. By the time the ten remaining generation-ships arrived in the Leffer system, Earth had already established a going-business of trade and cultural exchange, already a hundred or so years old, with scores of planetary systems. And it was just as well too, because the level of *civilization* on the starships was at a primitive-barbaric stage; and the descendants of the Star Folk who had left Earth with such exalted goals would never have been able to survive on alien planets, much less make friendly contact with any of their cultures. So the ten ships were herded into orbit around Leffer and, with the imbecilic remnants of their population, allowed to dodder toward extinction. From all reports, they are as contented as such creatures can be; I say leave them there. But I personally am not interested in knowing much more about them." Certain that he had made his point, he waited for the professor's—perhaps reluctant—acquiescence to his request; but the silence lengthened.

When the professor spoke, it was in a tone more distant than before. "You assert that they produced no significant contribution to the arts. Are you completely familiar with *all* the records?"

Joneny's face reddened. "I'm hardly an expert, sir. But again, you'd think that in twelve generations there would be one poem, one painting, something—other than those insipid, maudlin, derivative exercises in nostalgia."

The professor raised a quizzical eyebrow.

Joneny went doggedly on. "I've looked through the collection of their ballads Xamol Nella made in '79, and there's not a single metaphor or simile in any of them that could be called original or even relevant to life on a starship. There's nothing but semi-mythical folktales couched in terms of sand and sea and cities and nations—some of them very interesting, no doubt, but complete fantasies with no relation to the people living and dying on the ships. I couldn't be less interested in such cotton-candy effusions."

The professor raised his other eyebrow. "Oh? Well, before I give you your assignment, I want to stress what I said in the beginning: the Star Folk did something never done before or since. They traveled through space—a lot of it—for a very long time. No one else has ever really been there, because the hyperspace drive actually takes you *around* interstellar space." He laughed softly. "So perhaps they did find all the sand and sea and cities and nations there." He raised a hand as Joneny started to object. "You haven't been there, so you can't disprove it. At any rate, they made what is perhaps the most dangerous journey imaginable, and for that alone they deserve to be studied."

"What could be safer than interstellar space, sir?" Joneny's tone was slightly contemptuous. "There's nothing in it."

Both the professor's eyebrows fell. "Even if we knew that to be true—which we do not—what in blazes makes you think it

would be safe for Earthmen in Earth starships? It's within the
realm of possibility that there were others. I remind you that
although twelve ships left Earth, only ten reached the Leffer system, and two of those arrived empty. Perhaps there was something in the 'safety' of interstellar space—in the sand and the
sea—which we do not know about yet." Bony fingers pushed
buttons below the screen. More notes flicked across. "You say
you are familiar with the Nella's ballad collection? Then no
doubt you know 'The Ballad of Beta-2.'" I want a complete historical analysis of that ballad—from primary sources. That will
be your detail assignment for this unit."

"But, Professor—!"

"Dismissed."

chapter two

Joneny scanned Xamol Nella's laconic footnote: * "Beta-2
was one of the starships that arrived at its destination, the Leffer system, empty. The ballad is extremely popular among the
remaining Star Folk. (See Appendix for music.) Note the irregular repetition of the refrain, an original feature of many of the
Star Folk ballads, as well as the slightly elliptical syntax."

That's really straining for originality, Joneny thought as he
turned back to the ballad's text:

> Then came one to the City,
> Over sand with her bright hair wild,
> With her eyes coal black and her feet sole sore,
> And under her arms a green-eyed child.

Three men stood on the City wall,
One was short and two were tall,
One had a golden trumpet clear
That he shouted through so all would hear

That one had come to the City,
Over sand . . . etc.

A woman stood by a Market stall,
The tears like diamonds on her cheek,
One eye was blind, she could not speak
But she heard the guards of the City call

Out: *One has come to the City,*
Over sand . . . etc.

One man stood by the courthouse door
To judge again as he'd judged before,
When he heard the guards of the City cry,
He said, "She's come back to the City to die."

Yes, she's come back to the City,
Over sand . . . etc.

Another man stood on Death's Head hill,
His face was masked, his hands were still.
Over his shoulder he carried a rope,
And he stood stock quiet on Death's Head slope.

Three at the City wall cried: "Away!
Come back to the City another day."
But down below the woman stood:
I came back like I said I would;

Yes, I've come back to the City,
Over sand with my bright hair . . . etc.

A time you gave me to travel far,
Find the green-eyed one who made you what you are.
Well, I've searched a City and the desert dunes,
And I've found no man who caused our ruin.

But I've come back to the City
Over sand . . . etc.

She walked through the gates and the children cried,
She walked through the Market and the voices died,
She walked past the courthouse and the judge so still,
She walked to the bottom of Death's Head hill.

Down from the hill came the man with the rope,
Met her at the bottom of Death's Head slope,
She looked at the City and she turned and smiled.
A one-eyed woman held her green-eyed child.

Fire and blood, meat, dung, and bone—
Down on your knees; steel, stone, and wood
Today are dust, and the City's gone,
But she came back like she said she would.

Yes, one came back to the City,
Over sand, with her bright hair wild,
With her eyes coal black and her feet sole sore,
And under her arms a green-eyed child.

A complete historical analysis from primary sources meant he would have to visit the starships in person and find out what he could about the ballad from at least three different Star Folk. The "lab period" was twenty-four hours, but he could get a Time Adjustment through the Clearing Center of the University— which would mean that he could spend up to a week out at the starships while only twenty-four hours passed on campus.

Joneny had no intention of spending more than the minimum requisite time on this research project. And, in order to make his task as easy as possible, he'd decided to preface his jaunt with a couple of hours more in the library.

As a start, he rescanned the Introduction to the Nella *Star Folk Ballads*. He found something vaguely interesting: "Of course I did not actually go inside the starships, because of time limitations and cultural incompatibility; but a robot recorder was allowed entry, and a fair amount of cooperation was shown. The recorder transmitted a printed copy of the words and lead sheets of the music and, of course, made a permanent recording. The only changes I have made are where an obvious mispositioning of words or phrases occurred. This project was carried out rather hurriedly, and such mistakes could be, I must point out, either a fault in the recorder's copying device or simply a mistake on the part of the singer. Consult *Variorum Edition* for any discrepancies."

Joneny sat back, feeling a conscientious researcher's anger. Robot recorder, no actual entrance, the entire collection probably made in less time than he was going to spend on a single ballad. He could reconstruct it easily: Nella, somewhere in the vicinity of Leffer, suddenly getting the idea of sending his recorder in to see what he could pick up from the starships (probably did it while making some repairs or stuck in quarantine); leaving the machine on for six or seven hours; and then turning up with what appeared to be a scholarly collection of inaccessible folk songs. Such slipshod investigation infuriated Joneny, and he was sure that there was a lot of it in the inexhaustible archives of the Galactic Anthropology Library.

For the hell of it, he consulted the *Variorum Edition* anyway. The only lines of "The Ballad of Beta-2" that Nella had amended occurred in the seventh stanza. The recorder had given the lines as:

> "She walked through the gates and the voices cried;
> She walked through the Market and the children died."

Well, that was an obvious correction—or was it? Joneny frowned. No, he decided, Nella was probably right; otherwise it was a little too surreal—and that was the antithesis of everything he believed about the Star Folk.

There was a pleasant sort of simplicity about the song, he realized as he reread it slowly and carefully; too bad it wasn't about anything.

He went to the catalogue and selected a couple more crystal records on the Star Folk. There were only a half dozen or so to choose from, and he looked for a blue one (indicating a firsthand account). To his surprise, there was only one. Suspecting an error in the catalogue, he checked with the librarian and found that it *was* indeed the only blue.

It was without a title, and when he slipped it into the player, he was surprised to find that it was a recording of the primary contact when the almost-forgotten starships hove into the ken of the Federation, ninety years before.

The voice was that of an Earthman, speaking in the heavily consonanted and jarring-syllabled High Centaurian (an extremely compressed language and therefore eminently suitable for official reports), on the initial contacts and the first belligerent repulsion by the Star Folk:

. . . finally hypnotic vibrations had to be used. Even so, entry has been extremely difficult. Deëvolution is at an advanced stage. The sleeping creatures, slumped over their weapons on the floor of the inner locks, are hairless, naked, pale-skinned and fragile. Despite their frantic (one might say "heroic") efforts to keep us out, they caused us no casualties, and the probe shows that they are not basically hostile. However, they are so enslaved by an incredible my-thology that has sprung up among them, based on indeci-pherable incidents of their crossing, that we feel it advisable to leave them alone. Their technical means would not suffice for an interplanetary jump of more than six or seven million miles. There appears to have been some intercourse

between ships by radio contact and, it is surmised, by
occasional parties making the crossing from one to another.
[*There was an extended silence; then the voice continued*:]
They still have writing and, despite the polyglot nature
of the original population, it is English, but an English
difficult to follow because of orthographic changes and
because the text seems to be composed entirely of euphe-
misms. A great many of the reports we have studied had to
do with trouble in the "Market," which we assumed to be
the hydroponic gardens or one of the other food-supplying
devices on the ship. It took semanticist Burber an hour to
discover that this was a reference to the complex breeding
and birth process that was devised for the starships. To
keep the population stable, birth was to continue artificially
in a mechanical "birth bank," or rather "birth market,"
where the prospective parents would receive their children.
It was intended as a means of keeping the race fairly con-
sistent and of safeguarding it against too many radiation
deformities. From the appearance of these poor folk, it was
not entirely successful.

Joneny flipped the switch and reread the two corrected lines
in the ballad. So that's what the "Market" was. Then perhaps
"Market" did belong with "children." Undoubtedly the correction should have been:

> "She walked through the gates and the voices died,
> She walked through the Market and the children cried."

Or maybe the original way. But if so, why?
He went rapidly but thoroughly through the reports of the
individual ships and concentrated especially on:

. . . Beta-2 we have found to be completely empty. The
long corridors are deserted, the blue lights still burning.
Doors stand open, tapes are in machines only half played,

and utensils lie as if thrown down because of some inter-
ruption. At the Death's Head there is a sight that reminds
this reporter of pictures and descriptions of the Auschwitz
atrocities during the so-called Second World War. It is completely jammed with skeletons, as though the population
had been seized with a sudden suicide craze or else some
unbelievable mass murder had been committed. Again it
was semanticist Burber who called attention to the fact that
all the skeletons were those of adults. This led to an examination of the Market, which proved to be hopelessly non-
functional. Many of the tiny glass cells in which the fetuses
developed had been ruthlessly smashed. Obviously there is
a connection between the two horrors, but time does not
allow a thorough study. Hypnotic probing on the other
ships revealed an awareness of serious trouble on Beta-2
some generations back; but the exact nature or extent of it
is hazy, inexact, and clouded by legend. . . .

Again he stopped, then ran rapidly through the brief remaining text for further mentions of the Death's Head: "Death's Head
unit," "put into the Death's Head," and even "Death's Head
slope," but no clear explanation.

He chose another crystal, the transcription of an ancient
microfilm—a report on the construction of the starships in the
days before interstellar travel:

. . . is provided with a Death's Head unit that acts as a
reconverter of waste material. It can also be used as an
instrument for capital punishment in those extreme cases
that cannot otherwise be dealt with in such a limited community.

With something very like interest, Joneny turned again to the
copy he had made of the ballad. There had been Market trouble
on Beta-2. The Death's Head could be used for capital punish-

ment. Perhaps there was a meaning to the original version of stanza seven, the way the robot had first recorded it.

> "She walked through the gates and the voices cried,
> She walked through the Market and the children died,
> She walked past the courthouse and the judge so still,
> She walked to the bottom of Death's Head Hill."

At least he had something to start with.

chapter three

He sat back in the drive-hammock, staring at black view screens dead to hyperspace. He was, he realized, bypassing in seconds the immense void through which the starships had crept laboriously at a few thousand miles a second for a handful of centuries. Despite stirrings of an excitement that he refused to acknowledge, he still saw himself—a potential galactic anthropologist—on his way to track down a minute, trivial incident pertaining to a cultural dead end.

How he yearned for the city of Nukton on Creton III, for its silvered halls, its black-stone parks—the relics of that tragic race, who produced amazing architecture and music, the more amazing since it had never developed any form of speech or other means of immediate communication. Its phenomenal degree of advancement was something *worth* studying exhaustively.

The slight blurring of sight as his cruiser left hyperspace snapped him back, and he leaned forward in the hammock.

Up in a corner of the screen in front of him was the greenish glow of Leffer. Close to him, hanging like a cluster of crescent moons, were the starships. He counted six, like fingernail parings on dusky velvet. Each sphere, he knew, was some twelve miles in diameter. The other three, he reasoned, must be in eclipse. As he watched, the pattern of their movement—like a stately dance— became evident. They had been driven into a very close, delicately balanced orbit at a forty-mile distance from one another, the whole complex put in a ten-year orbit some two hundred million miles from Leffer itself.

Slowly another crescent appeared, while another, opposite, faded. He switched the view screen to a higher wavelength and the field of black became Prussian blue, with the crescents appearing as faintly green rims of shadowy spheres. Joneny's cruiser was a compact fifty-foot chrono-drive, with a six-week time margin—which wasn't much for star-hopping. However, they didn't allow students more, claiming that such unreliable "youngsters" were always producing paradoxes that annoyed the hell out of the Clearing Center. Some of the big ships were given a couple of years to play around with, which was a little more reasonable; for in the shorter time, if you got yourself into some catastrophic situation with a critical moment more than six weeks in the past, you were simply out of luck. You had a choice of oscillating back and forth between critical moment and climax while broadcasting wildly for help until someone came along and got you (which wasn't very likely to happen), or you just went through with it and *hoped*—and there wasn't much hope in a spatial catastrophe. As a result, the powers that be were always complaining about the number of accidents involving students. The whole setup was unfair.

At a thousand miles' distance, he cut his speed to two hundred miles an hour and crept along beside them, wondering how he was going to find out which was Beta-2. And what to do first: identify and explore the abandoned Beta-2, or talk (if they would talk) to the inhabitants of one of the other ships?

A further question nagged at him, although it had nothing to do with his research—directly. The last thing he had learned from the library crystals concerned the other empty ship, the Sigma-9:

> . . . completely gutted, [*ran the voice on the crystal*]. There is a great, irregular section of the hull ripped away and the skeletal interior glints under the light of Leffer with a strange iridescence. The remainder of the hull is cracked nearly in two. There is no chance that there are any survivors. It is amazing that the momentum and the automatic drive mechanism kept such a twisted wreck in flight to the ultimate goal.

He increased the magnification on the view screen until the spheres filled the whole wall. As he watched, another ship emerged from the cluster. There was no difficulty in identifying it as Sigma-9. It looked like a crushed eggshell, with a fine spider-webbing of girders feathering the edges of the cracks. The main damage was indeed an enormous area missing from the hull, from which fissures radiated in all directions, a dangling fragment here and there.

His first thought was that there must have been a tremendous explosion inside the ship, but reflection on the way that it had been constructed convinced him that any explosion of a magnitude sufficient to tear out such a large section of the hull would have forced the remainder apart. Laws learned in his course in collidal physics ruled out any exterior impact. It was, in fact, a completely impossible kind of wreckage. But there it hung, directly in front of him.

He let the mechano take him into the cluster and switched the screen to normal magnification, watching the great spheres grow. When he was seventy miles from the nearest one, he stopped the cruiser again and studied it, without result. Finally, at a speed of only seventy miles an hour (giving himself time for further reflection), he moved in. At the forty-two-second mark, he jammed the Time Stop.

And time stopped.

For all practical purposes, he was in an envelope of chronological stasis, his cruiser perhaps ten feet above the surface of a starship. He switched the screen to mobile vision, and the image grew until it surrounded him. He lowered the point of view until he seemed to be standing on the hull. Then he looked around.

The horizon was frighteningly close, and the plates he had expected to be smooth and even looked like gnawed cheese, rotten, crystallized into ruts and flaking mounds, green with a color of their own, deeper than the light lent by the far sun. He looked up.

And stopped breathing. Fourteen times the size of the appearance of the moon from Earth hung the Sigma-9. He knew that nothing moved in this stasis. He knew he was safely in his ship, minutes away from a dozen stars and their safe planets. Yet the looming, gutted wreck seemed to be careening toward him through the blackness, shimmering.

He screamed, threw one hand over his eyes and jammed the other against the mobile vision switch. Quivering, he was back in his ship; the view screen was only a six-foot window in front of him once more.

No. The mind was still not ready for unlimited space. Even the edge of an air-helmet window was something real to hang on to. But the wreck itself, shimmering with green fire—it was something so terrible that he had been unable to watch it directly for more than seconds before he felt it was falling to engulf him . . . shimmering?

Joneny took his moist palm off the hammock arm. Shimmering? It must have been part of the optical illusion of the wreck's falling. He was in time stasis. Nothing could be shimmering. But he remembered the gaseous green glow that seemed to spark over the wreck. He swung the view screen up to take another look at Sigma-9, this time from the psychological safety of his seat. Green and broken, it *shimmered* against space.

Panic caught his stomach. Something must be wrong with the time margin. His eyes flashed over dead warning lights. Nothing was out of place. He was about to jettison himself into hyperspace before something went really haywire, but his hand stopped. There was Leffer. He switched on a filter and increased magnification.

A sun's surface under time stasis looks very different from the view under normal time flow. Something known as Keefen's effect makes it look like a rubber ball dipped in glue, then rolled in parti-colored glitter. Each color shines out in a separate dot, distinct and prismatic; under ordinary chronology, it has the texture of fluorescent orange peel. Keefen's effect was in full display.

So he *was* in time stasis. But something was going on around Sigma-9 that didn't care.

At a crawl of fifteen miles an hour he switched back to normal time flow and began looking for an entrance. It was a corroded blister on the hull, and he hovered above the lock, for the hell of it, broadcasting his identity beam to see what it netted. To his surprise a voice came through his speaker in accented English:

"Your ears are unplugged, but your eyes are black. Your ears are unplugged, but your eyes are black. No admittance while your eyes are black. Please identify yourself. Over."

The static voice was from an automatic answering station, but its message left him bewildered. He sent out his identity beam again and this time spoke as well: "If this is a robot answering, please get a human agent to let me in. I'd like to talk to a human agent."

"Your ears are free of wax, free and unplugged," came the voice again. "But your eyes are blind. We can't see you at all."

Then Joneny got the idea. The robot could apparently discern articulation changes. He wants my visual as well, Joneny thought. He put an image of himself through on a simple ban and waited for a return picture on the screen.

"Your eyes see clearly. Just a moment and we will give you an entrance pattern."

In a corner of the viewing screen the flickering black-and-white pattern appeared, a series of white circles and black lines. Across it was written in block letters:

YOU ARE NOW ENTERING THE CITY OF GAMMA-5

Below, one of the blisters began to turn. The shuttle ships it had been built to accommodate were almost three times the size of Joneny's little cruiser. Shalings from the crystallized hull broke off in chunks and a drift of fine powder. Rotating, it sunk and divided into thirds, slipping back into the ship's hull. A mechano maneuvered Joneny's cruiser over the tunnel. As the ship turned, Joneny glimpsed the Sigma-9 on the view screen and remembered what he had said to the professor: "What could be safer than interstellar space, sir?" The ships had supposedly indestructible drives and hulls of immense strength. What had chewed up the plating—or had smashed the Sigma-9 like a porcelain shell? He resolved his curiosity by determining to consult his ship's tiny iridium cell computer on the problem and see if it could suggest any answer from a measurement of the stresses and strains still held in the shattered metal. Before he was finished, he would go over and make an extensive investigation. Even the first reporters had done no valuable research. As the triple doors of the first lock closed, he made a disgusted sound and waited for the landing process to finish.

The ship jarred and the indicator light for the repeller field flashed. These locks were designed to hold much bigger ships: the grapplers were groping in thin vacuum. The field held the ship centered in the lock, but the grapplers were too short. He increased the consistency of the repeller field to that of titanium steel twenty feet out from his cruiser in all directions. Let them sink their claws into that.

Clunk

They did.

A voice came through the speaker:

"Prepare for debarkation."

Here goes nothing, Joneny thought. The pressure in the lock

was Earth normal. What about the rest of the starship? The robots should have sense enough not to allow admittance if there was anything wrong. Just in case he slipped a pressure gell in with his survival kit. He checked the power pack on his belt, tied his left sandal thong, which had come undone, and went to the door.

Selector fields had made double airlocks obsolete. The iris of metal rolled away and he was looking across the inside of the starship's lock to where the flexible entrance tube had stuck against the side of the repeller field.

Though Joneny's ship had a comfortable semblance of gravity, the starship was in free fall. He launched himself across and felt weight leave him. Then the round end of the tube moved up to engulf him like the mouth of a lamprey eel. The light was a soft blue-white. Inside the tube he brought himself to a halt by pressing a button on his power belt. He caught hold of the rail running down the side of the tube and hauled himself along.

Rectangular windows looked out into the rest of the lock, ill lit with the same blue-white. Fifteen feet later the ribbed wall turned to smooth steel and the windows ceased. He'd come to the body of the ship. He turned as a faint sound behind him lisped through the tube. A triple jaw clamped over the mouth of the passage. It was comparatively cool in the tube and a breeze was coming from someplace. He reached the end.

Running off in both directions was a triangular corridor. A spiral bar wound through the middle. An arrow pointing one way read, RECREATION HALL, and one pointing the other read, NAVIGATION OFFICES. Joneny's English was of the scholarly type: conversationally adept, but including few technical words, since they had almost all been superseded. He was acquainted with a good number of Latin and/or Indo-European roots that were supposed to help one out of obscure translation situations.

After racking his mind, he decided that the Navigation Offices would prove more interesting. He was a little curious to see what they *re-created* down the first corridor, as well as what sort of re-creation system they could have. But the idea of *sacrifices to the sea* left him completely bewildered—so he headed in that direction.

A moment later he came to a small room. A large post rose in the center. Around the wall were screens, dials, and seats before numerous desks. The bulkhead was metal, so Joneny put a light magnetic field on his sandal soles, drifted to the floor, and went *click*. He glanced at the desks. Obviously this part of the ship had had gravity at one time.

"Just a moment," a voice said through a speaker. "I will try to locate a human agent to deal with you as requested."

"Thanks," Joneny answered the robot. It had certainly taken its time. "Where is everybody around here?"

"Too complicated a question. I will try to locate a human agent." After five seconds of silence, the speaker said, "No human agent can be found who will respond. Apologies, sir."

"Aren't there any people left alive on this ship?" asked Joneny.

"People are alive," answered the robot. The flat automaton voice sounded unintentionally menacing.

On the desk was a pile of books. *Books!* Real books were Joneny's delight. Heavy, cumbersome, difficult to store, they were the bane of most scholars. Joneny found them entrancing. He didn't care what was in them. Any book today was so old that each word glittered for him like the facet of a lost gem. The whole conception of a book was so at odds with this compressed, crowded, breakneck era that he was put into ecstasy by the simple heft of it. His own collection, some seventy volumes, was considered a pretentious luxury by everyone at the University. The glory of the collection, each page sealed in plastic, was the Manhattan telephone directory for 1975.

He clicked toward the desk and lifted the top volume. It came away with a tug and a *tsk* as the magnets came loose. He opened it; the pages were thin sheets of metal, silver under the blue light. The writing was machine made. It was a logbook or diary, each entry timed and dated. Turning to the middle of the book, Joneny read at random:

Have been in the desert now for thirty-nine hours. Don't
know whether the ship can take much more of this. Sand
count varies between fifteen and twenty-two. The terrifying
thing is that we have no way of knowing how long it will go
on. The first desert we encountered twelve years ago took
us fourteen hours to get through. Two years later we left
the sea again to travel through light sand for nearly eleven
months. The wear on the ship was incredible. Much more
of this, it was decided back then, and the ships would not
make it through the third generation. Then again there was
sudden clear sailing with nothing but ocean for almost six
years. Next there was a sandstorm of tremendous intensity for almost three hours where the count was over one
hundred fifty—which did almost as much damage as the first
fourteen-hour one we passed. How long will this one last?
Another hour? A year? A hundred years? Five hundred?

A later entry:

Sand count has remained fairly steadily at six for the past
nine days. That is something to be thankful for, but even at
one or two for an extended enough time, it will prove fatal
to us. Married this evening: Afrid Jarin-6 and Peggy Ti-17.
There was a celebration at the Market. I left early, slightly
drunk. They have selected fetus BX-57911, containing
some of my genes. Peggy said jokingly, "Since you're going
to be the godfather, you might as well have a hand in its
genetics." I guess because it's still primarily Afrid's and Peggy's, Afrid took the joke very well. I left feeling depressed.
Kids like them, who came out of the Market themselves,
seem so flat and bland to us who remember Earth. Of
course they have been told nothing about the real danger
of the desert. They can milk so much pleasure out of so
little; they believe so strongly in the successful outcome of
our voyage that it would be cruel to blight what little they

can enjoy by the truth about the sand. I knew it would only make me feel worse, but I gave Leela a call over in Beta-2. "How you doing, Captain?" I asked.

"Fine, thanks, Captain."

"Want to come over here with me and raise a kid?"

"You're drunk, Hank," she said.

"Not very," I told her. "I'm serious. Why don't you chuck Beta-2 City to your next in command, take a shuttle boat over here, and I'll resign to an advisory position and you and me will live in idyllic free fall in the Center Section for the rest of our natural lives—which may not be very long; so think it over, Lee."

"This desert got you down, Hank?"

"Lee, it's such a waste! How the hell did we know we were going to run into this sort of nonsense? If we had known, maybe we could have prepared for it. But at this rate we'll be running through meson fields as thick as this or thicker all the way out, and they eat through the hull just like a file."

"Or we could come out of this one in ten minutes and not hit another one the whole time left. We don't know *what's* out there, Hank."

"Hell, a purple dragon with crepe-paper wings may be out there too, waiting for jelly beans like us to roll by. But it's not likely. The only thing that *is* likely is that we'll be gnawed up by these damn meson fields until there isn't a scrap of anything resembling a starship left. The outside viewscope already shows that the hull looks like a road map of the North Atlantic states. Three hundred years of this and we'll be lucky if a lump of Swiss cheese gets to Leffer. Lee, come over and spend the time with me."

"Hank," she said. (I couldn't see her. We always talked to each other with our eyes black. I hadn't seen her in person since she was twenty-two. The idea of her pushing seventy now made me feel funny.) "Hank, suppose we do get out of the desert. I've got at least ten years of teaching to do if these kids are to get through the next three hundred years alive and look like something Earth would be proud of. By then we'll both probably be ready for the Death's Head."

"There're others to teach them, Lee."

"Not enough. You know that."

I was quiet for maybe six seconds. "Yeah, I know that."

Then she surprised me, and I realized in a moment how much all this sand count business was taking out of her. She said very quickly: "The next time the sand count reaches a hundred and twenty-five, I'll come to you, Hank." And she switched off. I feel like a little less than two cents.

The entry ended and Joneny glanced at the next: "Sand count up to eleven," and the next, "Sand count down to eight," and the next, "Sand count down to seven," then: "Sand count steady at seven." For almost a month it continued there. Then an alarmed: "Sand count up to nineteen." "Sand count up to thirty-two." An hour later: "Sand count up to thirty-nine." An hour on: "Sand count seventy-nine." And the next hour:

How it happened, or why, I don't know. I'd been watching the needle creep up for the past three hours. Sand count ninety-four; sand count one hundred seventeen. I felt like I was nothing but sweat sherbet, frozen and useless. Then the damn inter-vessel phone was shouting at my elbow. When I punched the switch, I heard Lee's voice: "Oh, for God's sake, Hank, what are we going to do? What's happening? Why?"

"Lee, I—I don't know."

"Jesus Christ, Hank, sand count one hundred thirty-eight, one forty-nine. Oh, Hank, we had a dream, a dream about the stars! And now we won't get there. Oh, God, we won't get there!" She was crying. I was just numb. When I looked at the meter, the needle was moving with the speed of a second hand on a watch.

"It's a hundred and ninety-six, Hank. I'm coming over. I'm coming over to you, Hank." I could hardly hear her for the tears.

It was at two hundred and nine. "You're crazy," I cried back at her. "Even the shuttle boat would be eaten up before you got two hundred miles. Oh, goddamn it, Lee, we won't make it."

She was still crying, "I'm coming to you, Hank," and the needle soared somewhere up past three hundred. Then—it just reversed itself and whipped back down to zero, pausing for about three seconds at forty-five before it slipped off the other end of the scale. My first thought was that the meter had broken.

I could just hear Lee trying to catch her breath on the other end of the phone. "Hank?"

"Lee?"

"We're out of it, Hank." Nothing was broken, except maybe something inside me. "We're in the sea again. It's clear sailing, Hank." Then she said, "I am coming to see you. I won't stay, but I want to see you."

Joneny turned the page and read on.

For half an hour the exhaust from her shuttle boat was like a wisp of wild hair blowing brightly on the viewscope. She came in with her eyes clear and her ears open and I went down to the tube to meet her. I saw her walk in. She must have seen me and paused for a moment. I think she raised her head, and I saw her brown eyes sparkling, and her black hair shaking to her shoulders. I saw the slightly pugged nose and the clear alabaster skin and the smile on lips just a trifle full. Then she came toward me—and I realized what I *had* seen.

"Hank," she said when she had walked—very slowly—

along three quarters of the way. Now I went toward her. Her hair was short, white, her eyes were wide, and there was no smile on her face. She breathed hard. "Hank?" It was as though she didn't believe it was me. Then she said, "Hank, you're going to have to get me out of this gravity before I have a stroke."

"Huh?"

"I haven't been well recently and I've been keeping to the free-fall section."

"Oh, yeah. Sure," I said.

"I'm afraid my feet are killing me." She gave a little laugh.

The voice was hers. I had followed its aging over the forty years that separated us from Earth. But when I put my arm around her shoulder to help her, the skin was like loose cloth over her bones. We got to the edge of the tube and into the lift. When we reached the free-fall section, she got a hell of a lot more relaxed. Once she stopped and looked at me. "I guess . . . you've come through in a little better shape than I have, Hank. Well, they say pretty women age quickly. And I used to be . . . be very pretty, wasn't I, Hank?" She laughed again. "Oh, forget it, Hank. Boy, now I know what it means to have sore feet."

"Sore feet?" I asked.

"Hasn't that gotten around this City yet? That's what the kids say now when somebody's been in free fall too long and they come into a gravity section. Don't worry. It'll get here. It's funny the way we pick up the kids' expressions. They pick 'em up from us, make up new meanings. Then we get 'em back again. They affect us almost as much as we affect them." She sighed. "We've put so much Earth into them, they want everything to be Earth again. So they keep giving Earth names and Earth phrases to things that belong out here. Do you think we'll make it, Hank?"

I didn't say anything. I wanted to, but I couldn't. She waited with a smile sitting so strangely on the loose skin of her lips. Then the smile went and she looked down at her wrinkled hands. When she looked up, there was something like fear in her expression.

"Lee, we're old now, aren't we? It doesn't seem so long." I said it almost like a question, as though perhaps she could explain to me how it had happened.

When she did speak, she just said, "I think I better go back now."

We exchanged two more words, just at the shuttle boat door, and both of them were "Good-bye." I took her in my arms, and she held on to my shoulders as tight as she could. But it wasn't very, and I let her go quickly. Then she was just a wisp of silver light on the view screen.

I was in a bad mood for the rest of the day and the kids avoided me like plague. But that evening I put in a call to Beta-2 City.

"Hey there, Captain," I heard a familiar voice say.

"Hello, Captain," I answered, and we laughed. Then we did something we hadn't done for a long time. We talked for an hour and a half about the stars.

Joneny closed the book. Sand and desert: meson fields! And "City" was part of the starship's title. Bright hair: the exhaust from a shuttle boat. Sore feet, eyes black; of course "The Ballad of Beta-2" was from a time much later than that of Hank and Leela, the first captains of the starships. But almost everything, at least in the chorus, made some some sort of sense now. He let the words run through his mind once more, his concentration drifting inward, losing focus upon the dials and screens, even the logbook in his hand:

> Then came one to the City,
> Over sand with her bright hair wild,
> With her eyes coal black and her feet sole sore,
> And under her arms a green-eyed child.

Then someone said, "Hello."

chapter four

Joneny whirled and nearly tore himself loose from his magnetic couplings with the floor. The book flew from his hand and bounced away.

The boy was holding the edge of a circular doorway with one hand. Now he reached out with his skinny foot and caught the book in his toes. "Here," he said, giving the book a shove so that it went floating end over end back to Joneny.

Joneny caught it. "Thank you."

"Any time." The boy was thin, naked, with luminously white skin. Joneny would have put his age at fourteen or fifteen, except that his hair, fine and pale and long, had receded at the temples like an old man's, throwing off the whole character of his face. The nose was flat, the lips were thin, and the features were all dominated by immense shell-green eyes. "What are you doing?"

"Just . . . eh . . . looking around," answered Joneny.

"For what?"

"Eh . . . whatever I can . . . well, find." Joneny was surprised and a little put off.

"You found that?" The boy gestured with his foot toward the book.

Joneny nodded cautiously.

"Can you read it?"

Joneny nodded again.

"You must be pretty smart," the boy grinned. "I can read it too, I bet. Give it here."

Joneny couldn't think of anything else to do, so he tossed the diary back. The boy grabbed it with his toes again, opened the cover with his other foot, reached down and turned the first page with his free hand. "This is the Logbook of Gamma-5 City, sole property of Captain Hank Brandt, begun in the year—"

"All right, all right," Joneny said. "I believe you." A thought struck him. "Where did you learn to talk?"

"What do you mean, where?" the boy asked. His green eyes widened in surprise.

"Your accent," Joneny said. "You're speaking pretty modern English." It was a lot more modern than the clipped distortions of the robot speaker that had guided him in.

"I just—" He paused. "I don't know where I learned. Just"—he looked around—"here."

"Where are all the others?" Joneny asked.

The boy let go of the door and began to turn over slowly in the air, the book still in his toes. "Other what?"

"The other people."

"On the ships," the boy said. Then he added, "There're no people on Sigma-9 City or Beta-2 City, though."

"I know that," Joneny said, mustering an imitation of patience. "Where are the people on this ship?"

"Mostly in the center section, at the Market, in the Fishstore, in the Mountains, or down in the Poolroom."

"Will you take me to them?" Joneny asked.

The boy was almost right side up again. "Are you sure you want to go?"

"Well, why not?"

"They won't like you very much," the boy said to him. Now he reached with his hand and grabbed back on the rim of the entrance. "They almost killed the last visitors they had. Those stun guns are still pretty powerful."

"What visitors were those?"

"About ninety years ago some people tried to get in."

To be sure, thought Joneny, the primary contact from the Federation explorers. Suddenly the boy launched from the ceiling. Joneny ducked back and nearly lost his couplings again. But the boy had aimed to miss him and simply placed the book on the table once more. *Tsk* went the magnets. The boy grabbed the edge of the desk with one hand and one foot. Those agile, pre-hensile toes, Joneny saw at close range, were over half the length of his fingers. "Then what are you doing here?" Joneny asked.

"The robot mechano told me you were here. So I came up."

"Isn't there anybody older than you around, somebody in charge who can perhaps give me some more information?"

"I don't think the people in charge are going to help you very much."

"Well, where are they?"

"I told you, down at the Market and in the Poolroom." He turned to the wall and switched on a dial. "Here, I'll show you."

A gray screen erupted into colors that formed at last into the view of a large chamber. The particular room, Joneny noted, had gravity, though not much. The floor was covered with water that bubbled and lapped in slow-motion waves. Transparent plastic tubes crossed and recrossed the room. Immense bus bars of varying sizes stood in the water, and there was a bank of good-sized waldos along one wall. Through the tubes loped men—or men and women, he couldn't tell: their eyes were small and pink, probably half blind. They were bald. Their ear trumpets had grown to their skulls. Round-shouldered, with nubby, nail-less fingers, they paused and groped mechanically at instrument dials and nobs, raising and lowering the rods in and out of the pool below them. Suddenly Joneny remembered the description that the Primary Contact had given of the Star Folk. These people were a lot closer to what had been reported than this green-eyed boy with him. Joneny glanced at the boy's hands and feet. The nails, though bitten, were perfectly in evidence. The boy also had hair, while these . . . people were completely naked.

"That one's in charge." The boy pointed. As he spoke, the figure on the screen gave one of his companions a blow on the back of the head. The companion staggered away, regained his balance, and went off toward an instrument board. "I don't think he'd be too interested in helping you. That, incidentally, is the Poolroom. I don't like to go in there."

Joneny looked at the figures all firmly anchored to the floor, then regarded the boy so adept at free fall. "You get sore feet?"

"You said it."

"What are they doing?" Joneny asked, turning back to the screen.

"Taking care of one of the temporary reactors. It's got to be kept underwater. It maintains the spin of that whole section of the ship."

Like a gyroscope spinning inside a beach ball, reflected Joneny. And an underwater reactor! Just how primitive were these ships anyway? With that many moving parts, it was a wonder they were around at all.

"Why don't you look like them?" Joneny asked as the boy switched off the screen. He might as well come right out and ask.

"I come from another City," the boy said.

"Oh," said Joneny. Apparently, then, this degeneration hadn't taken place on all the other ships. "Isn't there anyone around who can help me?"

"Help you do what?"

"Help me get some information."

"Information about what? You're not very clear."

"About a song," Joneny said. "A song about Beta-2."

"Which song?" the boy asked. "There're more songs about that City than all the rest put together."

"Do you know them?"

"A lot of them," said the boy.

"This is 'The Ballad of Beta-2.' It starts off, 'Then came one to the City . . .'"

"Oh, sure. I know that one."

"Well, what the hell is it about?"

"Leela RT-857."

Could it be one of the descendants of the woman Hank Brandt had been in love with? "Who was she?"

"She was captain of Beta-2 City when"—he stopped—"when everything—when . . . I don't know how to say it."

"Say what?"

"When everything changed."

"Changed? What things changed?"

"Everything," the boy repeated. "That's when Epsilon-7 City and the Delta-6 were attacked, and the Sigma-9 was crushed, and we were stuck in the desert and the Market crashed, and . . . everything changed."

"Attacked? What do you mean, changed?"

The boy shook his head and shrugged. "That's all I know. I can't explain it anymore."

"What were they attacked by?"

There was only silence. The green eyes were wide and bewildered.

"Can you tell me when this happened?"

"About two hundred and fifty years back," the boy said at last. "The Cities were still a hundred and fifty years out. And Leela RT-857 was captain of Beta-2 City."

"Then what happened?"

The boy shrugged. "Just like it says in the song, I guess."

"And that's just what I'm trying to find out." Joneny thought for a moment, again remembering the verses. "For instance, can you tell me who the one-eyed woman was?"

"Her name was Merril. One-Eyed Merril. And she was . . . well, one of the One-Eyes."

"Who *are* the One-Eyes?"

"They're dead now," the boy said after a minute. "They could have helped you. But they're all dead."

"But what did they do?"

"They kept us from the others. They tried to teach us. They tried to make it so we would know what to do. But they got killed finally by the others, the ones you saw."

Joneny frowned. Something was beginning to clear, but he wasn't sure what it was. "Maybe there's somebody back at your City who can tell me just exactly what this is about. Why don't we go back there?"

The boy shook his head. "Nobody there can help you."

"How can you be sure? Do you know everybody on the ship?"

Joneny didn't expect an answer, but the boy nodded.

"How many of you are there?"

"Many."

"Let's give it a try," Joneny insisted.

The boy shrugged.

"They won't be hostile to me, will they?"

"No, they won't be hostile."

"Fine," Joneny said. He was excited by the idea of something to be uncovered on one of the other ships. His magnetic soles, however, were weaker than he thought, for when he turned, he came loose and drifted away from the floor, helpless.

The boy, still holding the desk, swung his leg out and offered, "Here, grab my arm."

Joneny flailed at the boy's ankle, caught, and was pulled back down to where his sandals clicked onto the bulkhead.

"You're not very used to free fall, are you?" the boy said.

"I'm a little out of practice," Joneny said, releasing the kid's foot and righting himself. "That's your idea of an arm?"

"What do you call it?" asked the boy a little indignantly.

"I call it a leg," laughed Joneny.

"Sure," said the boy. "But a leg *is* an arm, isn't it?"

"I suppose, technically speaking, you could call anything that sticks out—Oh, never mind." It really wasn't worth going into. As they started for the door, Joneny reflected: now here's a piece of information that could have nothing to do with the ballad. Legs and arms were both arms: that was quite logical when, under free fall, hands and feet had developed almost equal dexterity. *Under her legs was a green-eyed child?* That was safely in the realm of nonsense.

Only something from way back in a semantics course he had taken was jabbing at his mind. What did they call it? Denotative instability? The spiral of decreasing semantic functionality . . . something like that. Then it hit him. In an environment where there is no gravity, or little enough gravity to develop this much dexterity in hands and feet, words of vertical placement—up, down, under, over, above, below—would rapidly lose their precise meanings. According to the spiral, before the words disappeared from the language altogether, they would stay on awhile as subtle variants of words with more immediate meanings—inside, through, between. (Two fine examples of the spiral of decreasing semantic functionality that Joneny was completely unaware of were *recreation hall* and *navigation offices*.) *Between*, thought Joneny. *Between her legs was a green-eyed child*. He stopped as they were about to enter the tube to the cruiser. The boy stopped too, looked puzzled, and blinked at him with his wide green eyes.

It was impossible; they were all born from the Birth Market. But there had been a Market crash, and everything changed. "Which City did you come from?" Joneny asked suddenly.

"Sigma-9."

Joneny stopped. Before them, the triple door to the flexible portion of the tube sank back into the wall.

"Which lock is your shuttle boat in?" Joneny asked.

The boy shook his head.

"Which lock?" Joneny demanded.

"No shuttle boat—" the boy began.

"Then how the hell did you get over here?"

"Like this," the boy said.

Then there wasn't any boy there anymore. Joneny was floating alone in the tube. He blinked. He decided he was crazy. Then he decided he was sane and that something strange was happening. But if this was a fantasy of his own imagining, why was he aware of the contradictions in it? The boy had said there were "many" on Sigma-9, and he had also said there were no people on it. Suddenly Joneny turned and pulled himself back to the navigation offices. Launching himself into the room he shouted at the robot mechanism: "Connect me with somebody who can give me some cogent information about what's going on here!"

"I am sorry," came the clipped, archaic voice. "I have called all over the City, sir, and no human agent has responded to my announcement of your presence." It was repeated: "No human agent has responded to your presence."

Joneny felt chills unraveling up his spine.

chapter five

Once more in his chrono-drive, sitting back in his hammock, Joneny watched the twisted shell of Sigma-9 grow in his viewscope. The crushed surface plates had been chewed up and spit out by a mad rush through how many millions of miles of meson showers—those tiny particles bigger than electrons, but most smaller than nucleons, that came in a staggering quantity of which masses, spins, and charges—yet what had caused the catastrophe had been something else.

Automatically he slowed as the webbing of bare girders flashed brightly in the direct light from the sun. He passed over the wreck, and a gaping darkness veered beneath. From the distance, the shimmer that played over this ruins was invisible. He switched on the iridium cell computer and let it record the twists and wrenches in the metal. It might be able to reconstruct the catastrophe. He drifted out over the edge of the gaping hull, a blister of blackness beneath. Slowly the mechano took him down into the pit. The view screen went black as they cut into the shadow. He swept the selector up and down the spectrum. At the violet end of the band there was enough hazy light to determine the details of the wreck. Girders, melted to blobs on the ends, spider-webbed in a blue underwater fog. Hunks of refuse moved about lazily, caught by the faint gravity of the ship's mass.

A section of corridor was split below him like a length of rubber tubing. As he swung his viewscope around the depths of the Sigma-9, he stopped. Deep in the marine blue was a faint red. He looked over the dials. No particular radiation to worry about. Double-checking, he found it higher to the left. He wondered again what that shimmering had been. He sank farther into the ship. Once he switched to natural light, but immediately the screen went black.

The computer was chuckling away but so far had arrived at no conclusion. He got out a pressure gell as the ship finally anchored itself to a strut. The gell was a mobile force bubble composed of a complex arrangement of geodesically crystallized plasmas. It held about six hours' worth of air, could be moved from his power belt, as well as be adjusted to become opaque to almost any frequency of radiation. Delicate work could be done at the edges of the gell by forming the skin into gloves.

The bubble wavered on the floor, growing. He stepped forward, and it surrounded him with just a tingle on his skin before the plasmas sealed.

He walked toward the door, the bubble rolling with him. It was like walking inside a balloon. The sphincter of metal wings that was the airlock pulled away in a circular opening on total black. He touched his belt and the light-frequency differential plunged into far violet: the ship behind him darkened at the same time the scene outside the lock began to glow like blue, milky mist.

The ship had anchored on a wall of girders that jutted out three hundred yards into the body of the wreck in a huge octagonal web. A bank of corridors twisted out into the cavity like arteries severed in meat. Raising his eyes, Joneny saw a sectioning of the ripped outer hull. Lowering them, he could see where the red glow leaked from behind twisted girders and burst chambers.

· Launching from the lock and hovering in the blue, he looked at his own cruiser, a thin, seamless, silver-blue oblong. But when he glanced over the octagonal web floating beside him, he grabbed his belt and brought himself to a quick stop, banging into the bubble's transparent wall. Something was climbing over the girders.

It stood up and waved at him.

The boy, still naked, seemed to have no protection from the hard vacuum of the gutted starship. The shifting of his fine hair increased the submarine illusion. The boy was about thirty feet away, and from this distance (and under this particular frequency of light that the pressure gell was translating), his eyes were black. He waved again.

Joneny's mind jutted toward half a dozen different conclusions, several of which involved doubts of his own sanity. He rejected them all and at last merely waved back—because there was nothing else to do. Just then the boy left the girder and sailed through the space between them. With hands and feet he caught the surface of the gell and perched there like a frog. Then he was—half inside; and then *all* the way in. "Hello."

Joneny's back was pressed against the curved inside of the gell and his hands spread-eagled over the transparent plasma. And he was sweating. "What—" he began. Impossibilities fluttered in his mind like moths. He tried to shake them clear. People leaping across hard vacuum, climbing through pressure gells, disappearing, appearing: impossible—

"Hello," the boy repeated, green eyes blinking.

Now Joneny repeated: "Wha—"

"You okay?"

"What *are* you!" Joneny finally got out, and peeled himself from the wall.

The boy blinked again and shrugged.

Joneny wanted to scream, "Get out of here"; cover his eyes until the apparition went away; go home. He didn't. The same passion that made him collect impossibly cumbersome books in a world of recording crystals made him look closely at the impossibilities around him now.

He saw fifteen of them right off. They were standing on the web of girders, some upside down, some sideways, all naked, all watching him and, from what he could make out, all duplicates of the boy who shared the gell with him.

"I figured you were going to come out here," the boy said. Then he asked, "Are you sure you're all right?"

"My adrenaline count I'm sure is way above normal," Joneny

said as calmly as he could. "But that is because I am in a situation in which lots of things are happening I don't understand."

"Like what?"

"Like *you*!" Some of Joneny's calmness went.

"I told you, I don't know what I am. I don't know." It took Joneny a moment to see through his own upset and realize there was genuine perturbation in the boy's face. "What are you?" the boy asked.

"I'm a student of galactic anthropology. I'm a human being. I'm flesh and blood and bone and hormones and antibodies that can't jump a hundred miles of cold space without protection, that can't disappear and reappear, that can't walk through a crystallized pressure gell. I answer to the name of Joneny Horatio T'waboga, and I may be stark, raving mad."

"Oh."

"Do you want to give it a try now?"

The boy looked blank.

"Well what's your name?"

The boy shrugged.

"What do people call you?"

"The people call me the Destroyer's Children."

Joneny, as has been pointed out, was not semantically alert enough to catch all he had been told by that statement; it floated on the surface of his mind, and out of the corner of his eye he saw the red glow in the labyrinthine ruin. "What's that?" he asked, again because he could think of nothing else to do.

"A Death's Head," the boy told him.

Now his eye caught again the boy's duplicates on the webbing. One leaped off and sailed by ten feet away, peering back over his shoulder until he grew too small to make out. "What about them?"

"Huh?"

"Are they Destroyer's Children too?"

The boy nodded. "Yeah. They're the rest of me."

Again Joneny turned his mind away from the syntactical discrepancies that would have given him many of the answers he sought. Now he looked back at the Death's Head.

He touched his belt and the gell began to drift toward the glow, gaining speed. He wouldn't have been shocked if the boy had simply slipped out of the gell once it started moving, but he came along predictably inside the bubble.

"Incidentally," Joneny said, "how much air do you breathe? This has only got six hours for one person, and I didn't bring a renewer."

"It depends," the boy said. "I don't have to breathe any."

"Then don't."

"All right. But then I won't be able to talk."

"Well, breathe when you want to say something, okay?"

"Okay."

They neared a wall of refuse. The junk floated closely, but there were paths through. "Which way?" Joneny asked.

"You can go through a corridor," the boy said. Then he added in a strangled voice, "I . . . just . . . used . . . up . . . two . . . seconds . . . of . . . air."

"Huh?" asked Joneny. "Which corridor?"

"You can go through that one," the boy said. "One . . . and . . . a . . ., quarter . . . seconds . . . more . . ."

Joneny moved the gell into the end of a tubular corridor that had been crushed and broken open. The walls were bare and set with free-fall handholds. They passed a place where another corridor had joined this one. The intersection was ripped raggedly at the seam.

"Where are we heading for now?" he asked again over his shoulder.

"We'll be coming to the Mountains soon." The strangled voice once more: "One . . . and . . . a . . ."

"Oh, cut it out," Joneny said. "I don't care what you use up. I don't intend to stay that long anyway."

"I was just trying to be helpful."

They turned another corner, passed the next section where the wall had been ripped, and sailed down the straightaway. At the end of the corridor, Joneny brought them to a halt and gasped.

Before them in blue mist a vast auditorium rolled away. In the center, above a raised dais, was a huge sphere. Even at this distance and in this light, Joneny could see etched on the surface a representation of the lands and oceans of Earth. The scooped immensity of the hall, the rings of seats, the isolated globe, gave the place a comprehensible air of hugeness, completely different from his glimpse of empty space in which the wreck hung. This feeling of contained size was calming, nearly religious. "What's this? Is it the Death's Head?"

"It's the Courthouse," said the boy.

"The Courthouse?" Joneny looked from the smooth, vaulted ceiling down to the tiered seats, at last back to the globe. "What happened here?"

"Trials." He added, "Of criminals."

"Were there many criminals onboard the starships?"

"Not many, at least at the beginning. Toward the end there were a lot more."

"What did the criminals do?"

"Mostly went against the Norm."

"The Norm?"

"That's right. You can hear the records if you want. They were all recorded."

"Does the mechanism still work?"

The boy nodded.

"Where is it?"

"Down there." The boy pointed toward the dais.

Joneny touched his belt, and the gell floated down over the seats toward the globe. He paused just above the stage, adjusted the gell for hyper-malleability and magno-permeability. His sandal soles clicked as he hit the floor, a drop of an inch, and stuck there through the pliable surface of the gell.

When he glanced toward the boy, he saw that he was hovering on the other side of the dais now, outside the bubble. The boy motioned to him, and Joneny carefully walked the bubble around the edge of the dais. When he reached the other side, there was a small pop as the boy stuck his head inside (Joneny jumped a little) and said, "The index is right there." He popped out again.

Joneny reached for the slanted desk through the bubble's skin, which molded to his hands. He ran his fingers around the edge of the desk till he found a catch. He pushed it, pulled at the desk-top; it came up. Revealed was a complicated mosaic. Bending closer, Joneny saw that it was actually a matrix of pentagonal labels, each holding two names. The top of the desk slid back down into an envelope. Joneny squinted in the blue:

45-A7 Milar vs. Khocran; 759-V8 Travis vs. The Norm; 654-M87 DeRogue vs. Blodel; 89-T68L One-Eyed Davis vs. The Norm.

The tray of labels was on a very long conveyor that moved upward. It was arranged in some sort of five-coordinate index system that was roughly chronological. As he perused the labels, one thing became quite clear. There was a marked increase of trials between One-Eyed Someone-or-Other and The Norm. Joneny came to the place where the crystal labels stopped. The last trial was 2338-T87 One-Eyed Jack vs. The Norm.

Joneny looked up as the boy popped inside the gell again. "What do you do with these?" Joneny asked.

"How do you mean? Just press one and it'll play back."

"Press?"

"With your finger or your toe or your elbow," the boy said a bit impatiently. "Just press it."

Joneny reached out and pressed the last labeled pentagon—and stepped back as a roar swelled around him. The sound was being transmitted through the soles of his feet. The whole floor of the dais was acting as the vibration plate for some sort of loudspeaker. The roaring was the sound of many people talking at once.

A staccato tattoo rang out above it, and an elderly baritone, oddly accented, cried out, "Order in the court! Silence! Please!

Order in the court." The roaring stilled, became the rustling of someone here twisting in a chair, someone there coughing behind a fist.

Joneny looked across the empty chairs in the blue auditorium.

"Order in the court," the voice repeated unnecessarily. The baritone voice paused, then went on: "There has been a slight deviation from normal proceedings. Captain Alva, before we make the official opening, you may make your statement."

"Thank you, judge." It was the voice of a younger man. Also a very tired man, Joneny thought. His phrases were measured, with long pauses between. "Thank you. Only it isn't exactly a statement I want to make. It's a request—of the Court, and an appeal to the leniency of the citizens of the City of Sigma-9. I would like to request that this trial not take place . . ." In his pause a murmur began among the people. ". . . and that One-Eyed Jack, in fact all the One-Eyes remaining in Sigma-A-9, be placed in the custody of the City's navigation staff, with myself fully and finally responsible for their conduct." The murmur broke out into expletives of indignation. Above them the judge's gavel crashed and the judge's voice cut sharply over the noise:

"Captain Alva, this is most—"

And above even this the captain's voice came sharply: "I make this request, not only in my own name, but with the full consent and encouragement of the Captains of every other City in the Nation. We have been in radio contact with one another constantly since the tragedy of Epsilon-7. Captain Vlyon of Alpha-8, Captain Leela of Beta-2, Captain Riche of Epsilon-6—every single Captain of every City in the Nation has begged me to make this request, Your Honor, and they are all making similar requests of the courts of their respective cities."

The crowd sounded chaotic. The gavel pounded again. When something like order was regained, the judge's leveling voice led over the noise: "Captain Alva, may I remind you that, as Captain of this City, you are in charge of its physical welfare. But there are other issues involved here; and as the Spiritual Head of the City, as the repository for moral cleanliness, and as representative of the Norm, I must certainly, in the name of the City, refuse your request. I most certainly must refuse!"

The murmur rose again, this time an inrush of relief. Not so heavily the gavel sounded; more responsively, silence came.

"To continue with the formal opening of the trial: Case 2338-587 Jackson O-E-5611, physical and mental deviate of the first magnitude, alias One-Eyed Jack, versus the Norm. Are you in Court, Jackson?" Momentary silence. "Are you present at court, Jackson?"

A voice came back, curtly, shrill, yet with the same tiredness Joneny had heard in the Captain's words. "You have eyes. Can't you see I'm here?"

"I must ask you to follow the forms prescribed by the Norm and not to ask impertinent, irrelevant questions. Are you present at court?"

"Yes. I am present at court."

"Now, will you describe, please, your deviation from the Norm as you understand it."

A hiss of air drawn quickly between teeth. "This is not an irrelevant question. It is a declarative statement—you have eyes and you can see."

"Jackson O-E-5611"—a defensive listlessness oozed into the judge's voice—"the code of the Norm requires that a deviate, to be held responsible, have understanding of his deviation. Now, will you please describe your deviation as you see it to the court."

"I had the misfortune to emerge from the Market with a full set of brains in my head. That's not normal around this place. Or perhaps I'm a deviate because there was a certain amount of information about Earth and our goals that I felt was important to study without the permission of the Norm. Or because I decided it was worth joining others like me to pursue these studies. But to you that makes me a One-Eyed monster who's got to be exterminated before he thinks in the wrong direction and corrupts somebody."

"Obviously Jackson is not aware of his deviation. That relieves him of having to sign his own reconversion certificate.

There will be no difficulty now in returning you to the Death's Head."

"For God's sake, I've got arms, legs, hands, feet. My eyes see, my ears hear. All right. You tell me what's wrong with me."

"Will the medical examiner please make her comparative Norm report?"

There was a rustling of papers; someone rose to standing. A contralto voice said, "Medical report, taken two days ago, of Jackson O-E-5611 correlated with the Norm of the City of Sigma-9."

"Go on, Dr. Lang."

"Thank you. Jackson O-E-5611, height six feet, one and a half inches: the Norm for the City of Sigma-9 is five feet nine and three-quarter inches. Of course this discrepancy does not indicate anything definite, but it is a deviation, nevertheless. Jackson O-E-5611 is a chronic nail biter and has been so since early childhood. This is quite far away from the Norm, a condition that exists in less than 5 percent of the population, definitely marking him for consideration."

"I notice you are skipping the more standard criteria, Dr. Lang," the voice of the judge interrupted.

"Yes, your Honor. But, as you advised me earlier, in view of the destruction of Epsilon-7 so short a time ago, I thought I might skip to the more drastic deviations."

"Very well. I just wanted it on record that I did so advise you. I saw Captain Alva about to raise an objection."

The Captain's voice: "Not an objection, Your Honor. I only wanted to say that the destruction of the City of Epsilon-7 is exactly the reason why I and the other Captains believe that—"

"Very well," interrupted the judge's voice, "then Dr. Lang will give a thorough report on the deviation."

"Your Honor, that wasn't my object—"

"I have requested a thorough report from Dr. Lang. I can see no other reason for you to object. Proceed, Dr. Lang."

"But, Your Honor—"

"Dr. Lang, if you will."

A murmur in the audience again, then the contralto voice went on. "Weight, 169 pounds as compared to the Norm of 162. I might well mention that this difference is only significant when looked at along with the height, where it becomes apparent that the subject, though above the Norm, is still underweight for his own physical development."

Jackson's taut voice jutted in, "Isn't that a hell of a complicated way of saying I haven't had a decent meal in three months, thanks to the hounding of your goon squad?"

"Jackson!"

Dr. Lang went on, "He conforms quite well to the Norm in dexterity. He's right-handed, and the Norm is 89 percent of the City's population also right-handed."

Again Jackson's voice, sharp and darting: "I notice you hold your stylus in your left hand, Dr. Lang. Would you say that marks a significant deviation?"

"Jackson, need I remind you that in several Cities, One-Eyes are not allowed to speak at their own trials, and occasionally not even allowed to attend them. I would dislike to find such an arrangement a temporary necessity."

"Captain Alva . . ." The tautness had gone from Jackson's voice; pleading replaced it.

"Jackson, I'm doing everything I possibly—"

"There is a slight difference in length of limbs, right arm nearly a centimeter and a half longer than the left. The Norm is a discrepancy of only a centimeter. Legs are identical length. Norm of Sigma-9 is a two-millimeter extension of left leg over right. Note the gauntness of his face, for which I have no figures, but it is definitely away from the Norm. His nose has been broken twice. The percentage of the population to break bones is 1.6 percent. This puts him quite definitely out of the Norm. A small birthmark on his right shoulder is completely away from the Norm. In situations of great strain, artificially induced, his perspiration index is 9.75 as opposed to 8.91 for the Norm. There is also a marked . . ." and the contralto voice continued to outline a list of glandular secretions, submetabolic functions, and tropal differentiations that sounded like the cataloguing process a modern biologist might go through in defining a newly discovered life-form; nothing less, mused Joneny, could merit such detail. After fifteen minutes she paused; then, in a staccato epilogue, in which Joneny could hear the lack of conviction, Dr. Lang declared: "And due to the extremity of our situation, I believe all this taken together is deviation enough to recommend reconversion in the Death's Head."

Approving whispers rose and fell.

"You may, if you really want to, question Dr. Lang on her findings," said the judge. "If you want to take the time."

"Yes, I want to." The answer was quick and desperate.

"Go on. But the questioning is only a formality."

"You've reminded me of a lot of things today, Your Honor." There was an expectant pause, but the judge was silent. "Dr. Lang, you're a woman of science. You deal closely with the biology staff and the Market Research staff; you're friendly with many of the Navigation Officers."

"That's right."

Dr. Lang's voice was overriden immediately by the judge's: "I don't see what this has to do with—"

"Please let him go on," from Captain Alva.

Silence. Then Dr. Lang repeated, "That's right. I am."

"Do you remember, Dr. Lang, two years ago when a thirteen-year-old girl named Tomasa was discovered to have the first case of carcinoma of the pancreas on record in the ten generations of the City's history?"

"I remember."

"And how was Tomasa's life saved?"

"By an ancient technique of radio-microsurgery."

"Where did you find out the existence of this technique and its application?"

"From an old woman named—"

"—named Mavle TU-5, who six months later was condemned as a One-Eyed deviate and executed in the Death's Head!"

"I fail to see what this has to do with—" began the judge.

Disorder had begun again and the gavel now covered the voice, rapping loudly. But the moment a sort of silence was restored, Jackson's voice came again: "Captain Alva, when the gyroscopic centering for the multiple gravity distributor failed, didn't you come to Ben Holden I-6 for a two-week cram course in general relativistic physics before you even dared to open the housing?"

From the judge: "This has nothing to do with your case! You were asked only to question Dr. Lang's report on your deviation!"

"For the love of knowledge, I *am* questioning. I'm telling you we're not a bunch of mutant monsters. I'm telling you we're only people who are trying to guard what's left of wisdom in this barbaric cave you call a City. Your beloved Norm! To close off twenty people in a section and gas them for their love of history; to chase a man out of hiding with a herd of specially bred twenty-pound rats because he knows multiple calculus; to inject a woman with half a dozen pathological viruses until she confessed Gödel's incompleteness theorem and then sentence her to the Death's Head as an unredeemable mutant; what Norm does this conform to? Does this meet any standard of human—"

"Silence!" The gavel thundered. Then, slow but mounting: "Our ancestors charged us with bringing *human beings* to the stars. And no deviation will be tolerated. How long ago was it that One-Eyed conspirators took over Epsilon-7 and destroyed it?"

Three voices attempted to interrupt—the Captain's, Jackson's, and Dr. Lang's: "But your Honor, we don't—"

"That the last communication came from One-Eyes is proof enough that they were the last ones in charge, and therefore that they must have overthrown the leadership of the Norm. Fifteen thousand people on Epsilon-7 all dead: the Sigma-9 will not be next. In view of the threat such deviation poses, I cannot but give my assent to Dr. Lang's recommendation of death by—"

"Excuse me, your Honor!" It was Captain Alva's voice, desperate. "I've just received a message from the communications gate. Static has blanketed our connection with Delta-6. Faint messages are coming through asking for assistance. They seem to have—"

A sound like an explosion, only it didn't stop.

Joneny jumped. At first he thought the people in the court had rioted. Then he realized it was raging static. He punched the label again; the static stopped. Confused, with long rollings of terror in him, he stepped back from the trial index, pulling his thoughts to the present. The auditorium before him was no longer empty.

He started. Nearly a quarter of the seats were filled with azure-skinned youngsters, boys, all of whom had been paying silent attention to the record of the trial. As Joneny watched, openmouthed, several of the audience, now that the recording was over, floated from the seats and listed to one side or the other. Joneny looked around for his guide and found him at last, stretched out across the upper surface of the gell.

"What—what are they?" Joneny motioned again to the figures in the auditorium.

The boy stuck his head in and said, "I told you. They're the rest of me . . . the Destroyer's Children."

"Then what are you?"

The boy slipped the rest of the way into the gell, shrugged, and when Joneny glanced at the auditorium again, it was empty.

"Didn't you say you wanted to go to the Death's Head?"

Joneny shook his head, not in negation but to clear it. He was still trying to figure out why the ending of the last trial record was so sudden, as well as make some judgment on the situation between the One-Eyes and the Norm. And there was no explanation for these green-eyed youngsters who seemed so capable of navigating in a vacuum.

"You said you wanted to see it."

"Huh?" Nothing would resolve. "Oh, yes. I guess so."

"You just follow me," the boy said; then he added in what seemed a consoling tone, "You'll see."

The boy popped out of the bubble. Nervously Joneny propelled the gell after him.

chapter six

So this was what the ballad meant by "Death's Head hill."

The gell, with Joneny inside, had just entered a room larger than the auditorium. The walls curved toward a vaulted peak. The blue glow was replaced by crimson. The floor sloped upward; the ceiling came down and joined in an immense funnel that was stopped by a skull-shaped grate. The wide door at the bottom where the mouth would be increased the resemblance. Joneny stood at the bottom of the curved metal slope and stared for a full minute.

At last his gaze fell away from the heights and he caught sight of an alcove at the bottom. At the back of the alcove was a door. His sandals clicking on the plates, he started toward it. A moment later he pushed open the door and blinked as the light went again to blue. It was a living apartment; it had not been set up for free fall, which reigned in this part of the ship now. Books had drifted from shelves and settled like barnacles on the walls. A lamp had done the same. As Joneny stepped in, the bulb, disturbed after aeons, blinked on and went out again. *Who had lived here?* Joneny wondered.

His eyes roamed the books: *Moby-Dick; Les Illuminations; Voyage, Orestes; The Worm Ouroboros.* He had read none of them and had heard of only one.

Across the room was another door. He gloved the gell again and pulled it open. One instant he was terrified that the black thing billowing out was alive. But it was only cloth. Surprise still held, but he reached out and took the suit of clothing from the closet and spread it. There was something on the shoulder, and when he pushed back the black folds, he saw it was a rope—a rope had been coiled about one shoulder like an emblem.

Without bellying, the cloth waved and floated, and a part of the suit he hadn't seen rose into sight from behind the collar. It was a black hood that would mask the entire face save two ominous eyeholes.

Joneny frowned. He put the suit back in the closet and shut the door. One sleeve caught outside and flapped slowly in the windless space like a truncated arm. Again he looked at the books quivering among the shelves.

One was large, black, and familiar. It was the same sort of book that Captain Hank Brandt had kept his log in. Joneny pulled it to him and opened the silvered pages. It was no diary. The entries were statistically terse. On the opening page the epigraph:

> Lord, what do I here . . .

Then:

Executed today at 2:00 P.M. . . . name and date. *Executed this morning at* 6:30 . . . name and date. *Executed this afternoon* . . .

The book was only half filled. Joneny turned to the final entry: . . . *this evening at* 11:45, *One-Eyed Jackson-O-E*-5611.

The words that started in his mind were also sounding inside the gell. He turned to listen to the boy singing to an odd, bare melody:

> "Another man stood on Death's Head hill,
> His eyes were masked, his hands were still.
> Over his shoulder he carried a rope,
> And he stood stock quiet on Death's Head slope."

Joneny let the book float away, went to the door of the executioner's apartment, and looked toward the Death's Head.

The Destroyer's Children, several hundred of them now, all

standing over the floor that sloped toward the skull, turned and looked at him. Their lean bodies cast thin shadows in the crimson vault.

Joneny turned back again. The boy was outside the bubble now. The words *What are you?* came into his mind again, but before he said them, the boy shrugged again. Joneny thought about this for three whole seconds before he asked, "You can read my mind, can't you?"

The boy nodded.

"Is that why you speak so well?"

The boy nodded again.

"And you say you don't know what you are," said Joneny trying to control both voice and thoughts.

A third time the boy nodded.

"Why don't we try to find out?" He motioned for the boy, who came forward and stepped (pop) into the bubble. "Let's go back to my ship, all right?"

"All right," the boy said.

They made their way from the Death's Head, along the blue corridor, through the courthouse, and out into the hollow wound of the starship in which Joneny's cruiser hung against the girders.

The gell plunged through the open space toward the silver oblong. A few yards from the door, Joneny slowed. "I want you to stay outside the ship until I call you in."

"Okay."

Joneny moved the gell forward, and the boy *popped* out the back wall. The selector field passed the gell and Joneny felt gravity strike him again. He collapsed the bubble around him and kicked it into the corner like a pile of cellophane. Then he looked out the door again. In the light from his cruiser, some twenty feet away, the boy waved at him. Joneny waved back and went to the controls.

Once more he glanced at the boy before he jammed the ship into time stasis. Again he went to the door and looked out.

Nothing in that blackness should be able to move now, reflected Joneny, for, relatively speaking, everything outside the ship was caught in time, though one could also say that it was Joneny's cruiser that was caught.

"You can come in now," he said. Joneny was expecting one of two things to happen. Either the boy would stay put, suspended and immobile. Or he would come drifting in through the door: Joneny rather hoped for the latter. It would correlate with the strange flickering he had seen before on the Sigma-9 that also ignored time stasis. It would be at least a stab in the definition of just what the boy's lack of humanity was, and his ignorance (in the sense of ignoring) of time would make his disregard of space less strange.

Joneny expected one of these two things to happen.

Neither of them did.

Instead, everything exploded.

Outside the door a wave of purple light rolled across the girders. The gravity of the cruiser went crazy; he got heavier and lighter in sickening waves. The figure of the boy erupted into a geyser of green sparks, which swept for the door of the cruiser and missed.

Every loudspeaker in the ship began to moan in different keys. As Joneny stumbled for the controls, something happened to his eyes. The room went double, quadruple, octuple, and his hand, searching for the switch to throw the ship back into normal time, was lost among infinite decisions and choices. Then his head twisted.

He was falling, orbiting great pulsing luminosities of thought. A white light glowed before him so beautifully he wanted to cry. He turned from it and was confronted by blindingly cool green, which was very funny. He slid toward it and was enveloped in sad heat. A face rolled toward him down a long hall, the face of a man with green eyes, dark hair, high cheekbones. The face rolled over him, and he reached out to push it away, but his hand kept going, for miles and miles, until it fell on the time margin switch.

And he was standing before the control board, slightly nauseated, but all right. He sank in the hammock and turned to face the door, just in time to see the boy step through.

"What happened?" Joneny asked.

"You—you called me in. But I couldn't . . ."

"Couldn't what?"

"I couldn't hear you. So my . . . father . . . father? . . . you don't have the words. My father told me you called."

"What are you talking about?" asked Joneny.

"My . . . father . . . but not father. The Destroyer."

"What's the Destroyer?"

"He's where—where I came from."

"When I asked you where you came from before, you said from this starship, Sigma-9."

"That's right. That's where my father is."

"Whereabouts in the ship is he?"

The boy frowned. "All over it."

Joneny closed the portal. "I'm going over to Beta-2," he said. "Maybe I can find something there." He tried to put off the paralysis that the last strange incident had pushed him toward, detached the cruiser, and aimed for the rent in the hull of the Sigma-9.

The iridium cell computer, which had been humming all this time, suddenly flashed its completion light. Joneny opened the tape case and ran the answer through his fingers. All that the computer had been able to come up with was that the Sigma-9 had been torn open—torn open from the outside, the way one might tear off the skin of an orange!

"Hey, stop," the boy said. They were halfway between the two ships.

"Stop what?"

"Stop your ship."

"For what?"

"You'll see. Just stop it."

Joneny turned the ship into a slowing spiral.

"Now put it in time stasis."

Warily Joneny put the ship in stasis. Nothing happened.

"Now look back at Sigma-9 and you'll see my father."

Puzzled, Joneny turned the view screen back toward the wreck they had just left. As before, it glowed and shimmered in complete disregard for their chronological position.

"The flickering," the boy said, pointing. "That's it."

"That's what?"

"That's the Destroyer."

chapter seven

Beta-2 was silent. The locks opened without any address from the robot mechanism. Here the corridors, though filled with air, were without gravity. "I'm looking for records," Joneny told his companion as they threaded the triangular halls.

"Here," the boy said.

They turned into a room that must have been the ship's library. "These are the rest of the records," said the boy, going to one wall of books behind glass. Joneny opened the case door. Black tomes ranged along the shelves, logbooks for the duration of the crossing. Joneny took first one out, then another. There were records of the Market, food production; he had absolutely no idea where to begin when the boy picked one and handed it to him.

"This one was my mother's."

Before the thought sank and bloomed to meaning, the cover fell open and he read: "This is the Logbook of Beta-2 City, the sole property of Captain Leela RT-857."

"Mother?" Joneny remembered his new interpretation of the lines:

Under her arms a green-eyed child.

The boy nodded. "Turn to when the first ship was attacked." He reached over Joneny's shoulder and flipped the pages. It was near the end:

The report came in this afternoon that we had left the sea and entered light sand. The count from the first half an hour was in the high thirties, which caused me that odd paralytic alarm I have been so subject to lately with all the nonsense over the One-Eyes. But it dropped to three and has been there for the last couple of hours. Any sand is dangerous, but as long as it stays down there, we can sustain it for a few years. The uncertainty of when it will increase or end is unsettling.

Earlier this evening I left the staff meeting and decided to visit the One-Eye quarter. Passing through the City Concourse, I met Judge Cartrite.

"What brings you to this part of the ship?" he asked.

"Just walking," I said.

"Taking stock of all your charges, Lee?" He gestured to the people around us.

"Just walking, Judge."

"Well, you seem to be going in my direction. We'll go together a ways and give a picture of official solidarity."

"I'm turning off shortly," I told him. But he accompanied me across the walkway.

"Have you heard anything about the new ritual group they've started over in Quadrant Two? They're evolving some elegant complexities on some of the rituals I initiated back ten years ago. It makes a man feel he's accomplished something. You know"—and the tone of his voice dropped—"I hardly ever hear of any of the City's officers attending the ritual groups. You ought to encourage them to go, Lee. Solidarity again."

I smiled at him. "We're a busy bunch, Judge. And let's

face *it*, the rituals are mostly time consumers." I smiled—to avoid spitting, I think.

"They mean a great deal to a lot of people."

"I'll put up a notice," I said. I'd like to paste it over his face.

Judge Cartrite grinned. "Can't ask more than that." As we reached the other side of the concourse, he stopped. "Do you turn off here?"

"I'm afraid I do." I left him at the lift to the administrative sphere.

The tall corridor was empty. My feet echoed. Then the hall ended at the web, spreading out in front of me, dim and huge, run through with catwalks and free corridors. It's such a tangle that you can't really see more than a hundred yards into it. I remembered as I stood on the edge of that spreading gulf how as children we had played near the exit. We were always terrified of getting lost inside. But now I took a short breath and pushed off. Gravity left me and I was floating toward the tangle of beams that was the web. It takes skill to leap from normal gravity into free fall. A lot of people never learn to. More than one body has gone into the Death's Head with its neck broken from a head-on crash with anything from a bus bar to a plate wall. I caught myself against a ground sheet and pulled around on the handholds. It's pointedly obvious that this section of the ship was not intended to be lived in; certain repairs for the rest of the ship must be made here, but the hidden ways and mechanical caverns, niches and paths of the center are never used by people of the City. Nevertheless, it holds some six or seven hundred inhabitants. From the other side of the plate I could see the housing for the little detractor gyro, a riveted sphere of metal seventy-five feet in diameter. I launched for one of the guy cables. It sailed up to me. I caught it and pulled myself down to the surface. Just from playing at the very edges of the web with other children of the City, I had learned that one magnetic boot was useful. Two were a nuisance. So now I stood, anchored by one foot to the housing.

I beeped a few times on my belt communicator, just to let them know I was there, when a soft, familiar voice behind me said, "What are you doing that for?"

I avoided the impulse to whirl—and perhaps tear loose from my position. The voice chuckled, and I tried to look over my shoulder. "Every time I come here, Ralf tells me you know I'm here as soon as I leave gravity; but just in case, I like to let somebody know. I haven't got time to stand around on one leg all day."

The voice chuckled again.

"That *is* you, Timme?" I was turning slowly; and he, who could maneuver five times as fast as I could, was keeping out of my field of vision.

"Here I am," he said.

I turned quickly the other way and he was floating in front of me, still chuckling.

Timme is maybe seventeen or eighteen. He's a dark boy, his hair uncut, black, his clothes nondescript rags. Timme is missing an arm and his left sleeve is just knotted at his shoulder. "You want to go to Ralf's?"

"That's what I came here for."

"Aye, aye, Captain Lee." He nodded slightly with his vaguely mocking smile.

With his one hand he untied a coil of rope from his waist and threw me an end. I made a loop in it, slipped it around my back and under my arms, and held on in front.

Timme looped the rope a couple of times around his wrist—which always struck me as a trifle insecure—and said, "Kick free!" I let go my hold with my boot. "We go that way," he said, pointing off between two large columns with a ten-foot space between them; then, crouching like a frog, he leapt off from the housing—in the entirely wrong direction! This is the thing that always confuses me about free-fall travel: how can they calculate the whole business? The rope went taut, I was pulled along (nearly three times as fast as I'd ever dare go myself), but when Timme reached the end, the rope made him swing around, and our whole trajectory changed. The two of us on the ends of the rope were a complex rather than a simple weight, and together we were spiraling directly toward the space between the bars.

The trip into the web probably beats what our ancestors called a roller-coaster ride hands down. Every five or six seconds Timme would kick off from another plate or strut, and we would shoot in another direction.

Then we were in the clear again. Rotating before us was the Ring. Amidst the confusion of the web, a circular path three hundred feet in diameter had been discovered that would admit objects throughout its circumference of thirty or forty feet. In it the One-Eyes had constructed a metal ring, rotated by the City's excess power, on which were attached small dwellings where four fifths normal gravity was maintained. The houses themselves, terribly flimsy contraptions that occasionally broke loose and caused a bit of damage, flung out like seats in the old pictures of a Ferris wheel. I'm sure boarding a moving train was no more difficult than getting into the Ring. I always did it with my eyes closed and simply let myself be pulled.

Timme launched himself toward the whirling sheet-metal shacks, and I held on and closed my eyes. A moment later I was hauled, pulled, pushed into gravity again. In general the One-Eyes, even those who are physically deformed like Timme, have developed a physical dexterity that leaves the less adventurous majority of the City's population aghast. I'm sure that's one reason for so much of the fear.

When I opened my eyes, Timme was closing the trapdoor. I was sitting on the floor, and Merril was standing over me, saying, "Well, Captain Lee, what brings you here this evening?"

"I wanted to talk to you and Ralf about a number of things. Do you know about the desert we've entered?"

She gave me her hand as I stood up. "Yes. But there's nothing that can be done. Would you have come all the way out here just to tell us something our instruments show as well as yours?" There was the same slightly mocking tone that Timme used.

"There's more than that," I said. "Is Ralf here?"

Merril nodded. The two of them, Ralf and Merril, were more or less the leaders of the One-Eyes, though the fabric of their society was so amorphous, vertically and horizontally, that perhaps the term was too—precise.

"Come with me," she said. "He got your beeps; we were expecting you."

We went down a low-ceilinged corridor. Through a window, light from outside shifted across the far wall to remind us of the whirling frame we were on. As we stepped into the next room, Ralf looked up from his desk, smiled, and rose.

"Captain Leela, what can I do for you?"

We were in an informal office with a few filing cabinets along the walls. Two paintings hung in the office. One was *Assumption of the Virgin* by the old earth painter Titian. The other was done by a second-generation artist of the City: abstract, troubling darknesses lapping one another, full of blacks and greens.

"What can you do for me?" I asked. "Talk to me like intelligent people, in sentences I can put in logical order. Maybe even say a few funny things about the more ludicrous stupidities of the City, maybe drop some advice my way."

"Is it that bad?"

I sat down in the hammock suspended across the office. Merril took a seat near the filing cabinet. Timme, I saw, had sat quietly in a corner on the floor, though nobody had invited him to stay. But then, neither Ralf nor Merril seemed to want him to go, either.

"While I was coming here, I ran into Judge Cartrite. He suggested that the official staff start attending the rituals. Hell, it's all I can do to keep them away now."

"What do the rituals do?" Timme asked from the corner.

"Fortunately you'll never have to be bothered with them," Ralf told him. "That's one of the advantages of living out here with us. You came here when you were only three. But some of us who took a little longer to get here know a little too much about what they do."

Timme—Ralf told me this last time I visited him—had fallen into the web as a child and floated around for more than thirty hours before he was discovered. He had eventually been sucked to one of the great ventilator ducts that drew in air at seventy miles an hour. His arm had been squeezed between two grill blades and chewed off by the fan above his elbow. Instead of sending him back to be persecuted by the Norm, which was going through a particularly rigid enforcement on children that year, they kept him among the One-Eyes and nursed him back to health.

"A lot of people get together and do perfectly meaningless things for hours at a time, for which impossible reasons have been calculated: standing on their heads for five minutes in the corner and then drinking a glass of pink-colored water seventeen times in succession, in honor of the seventeen times an hour the Poolroom revolves to maintain gravity, and the pink liquid in honor of the red shift of Sol—"

Timme laughed. "No, I know what they do, or some of the things. But I mean, what do they do it for?"

"Damned if I know," I said.

"Is that true?" asked Merril.

"What do you mean?"

"Why do you think they have the rituals?"

"Because they have nothing better to do. They need something to occupy their minds, and they haven't got the guts to come out here in the web and struggle for themselves."

Ralf laughed now. "If they all migrated out here, Leela, there would be no struggle. We'd all die. In our own way we live off you people in the official quarter of the City. We struggle, do perhaps a little unofficial stealing from the surplus farm stores, bargaining with your people when there's some specialized knowledge we have that you don't. All we are, Lee, is the people rituals couldn't work for, the ones who'd go a little crazy if we didn't reconstruct the City's radar sector in miniature—for a hobby; make improvements on a model hydroponics garden—not for food but for fun; or put colors and shapes on canvas simply as an organization of forms. Maybe it's just different rituals."

Just then Timme stood up. "Isn't it about time for Hodge to come over?"

"That's right," Merril said. "He'll make it to the edge of the track. Just go out to bring him over to the Ring."

Timme bounced out the door.

"Hodge?" I asked.

"Uh-huh." Merril nodded.

"Does he come to visit you too?"

"He gets lonely," she said. "Probably lonelier than you do."

"That's funny," I said. "Sometimes I've seen him walk in the concourse. Nobody talks to him, everyone backs away. But he walks around looking at things, at people . . . I don't *think* anyone talks to him. But if that's true in the official quarter, I'm surprised anyone even allows him in here."

"Why?" Merril asked, with the slight smile again.

I shrugged. "Well . . . because he's been responsible for so many of your people's . . . I mean, whenever the legal department takes it into its head to start enforcing the Norm—" I stopped.

"Responsible?" questioned Merril.

I shrugged. "I see what you mean. He's only carrying out orders."

"Hodge is a very lonely man," Ralf said. "Most of us

are lonely out here in the web. Yes, maybe there should be that sort of fear, but we're also a pretty suicidal bunch as well."

"Hodge comes out here twice a week," Merril said. "He spends the evening with us, eats here, plays chess with Ralf."

"Twice a week?" I said. "I'm surprised when he comes to the official sector twice a year."

"You know, sometimes I've thought that you and Hodge have a lot in common."

"How do you mean?"

"Well, you are the only two people who aren't allowed to choose mates and go to the Market and raise children."

"With the exception," I reminded him, "that I can resign and play mother any time I want, where Hodge is stuck with his job for life."

Ralf nodded. "Then, also, you both are, in your ways, responsible for the entire ship, not just your sector. Even Judge Cartrite doesn't have any real control over the One-Eyes, except when he catches us. But we're bound to obey you as much as anyone else in the City."

"I know," I said. Then I said, "The responsibility: Ralf, Merril, that's what I really wanted to talk to you about. Somehow I feel that even by letting the rituals go on, I'm betraying that responsibility. Oh, a couple of times when we've argued, you've told me that we all have our rituals, from my duties as Captain to some poor creature who pushes a small steel ball up a metal ramp with his nose in honor of the Journey to the Stars, to your studies in Ancient Earth political sciences. But there has to be some way to distinguish between them. I look at the kids walking around the official sectors, and then I look at Timme. One-Arm and all, Timme is alive, alert; you can see it in his face. There's a kid Parks is training in Market Research, a bright boy, but every response comes out in slow motion. Parks tells me the boy's appalled at the lack of interest we show in the rituals—thinks we're all oafish brutes with no interest in the higher things."

Ralf waited for me to go on as I turned in my seat.

"What it all comes down to is that *someday*—and this seems to be the thing they've all forgotten—someday there won't *be* any more Cities. There will be a bright new world hanging in the night before us, with natural forces to fight and food to be searched for, tracked, and hunted, not handed to us on a conveyor belt from the hydroponics garden. All right, you and I will never see it, but it's not five or six hundred years from now anymore; it's only a hundred and fifty, two hundred years away. And one and the other considered, I'd rather turn Timme out on a new world to struggle for his own than Parks's little bright-eyed boy. If I let the City become a bunch of blank-faced ritual followers, then I'm not fulfilling my responsibility."

There was silence for seconds as Ralf thought. I wondered what answer he might make. Merril did not seem to have one.

Just then Timme called in, "Here's Hodge."

I turned as Hodge reached the door. He was tall, with high cheekbones and deep eyes. The black hood was pushed back from his face, and as he stopped on the threshold, the emblem of rope he carried over his shoulder swung around against his chest. His black uniform made me conscious of all the other colors in the room; even the paintings, which I had thought somber, now seemed very bright.

We talked a little more, and when dinnertime came, I excused myself, and Timme took me through the hectic journey back to the mouth of the web. This time I kept my eyes open. I saw many of the One-Eyes making the fantastic leap onto the Ring, as though they were stepping off a curb.

Timme, as he towed me along, guessed my thought. "You know Hodge can get around the web almost as well as a One-Eye," he said. "But he still needs help over the jump. Just takes practice, though."

He cut me loose and gave me a shove into the corridor. Gravity returned, and I staggered forward. Then I turned, waved good-bye to Timme, and started back to my office.

chapter eight

*S*econd *entry:*

Parks woke me up at three thirty this morning to give me the first report. He was on Night Watch in the Market, so of course he noticed it first. I got out of my bed, went over and jammed the receive button on the emergency intercom. "What the hell's the matter?" I said. "Has the sand count gone up again—"

"Captain, this is Parks down in the Market."

"What in the world do you want at this hour of the morning?"

"I just checked the sand count, Captain. It's been steady. But there's something else, even worse—"

"Huh?"

"The hard radiation all over the City has just tripled. It's not enough to bother anyone where you are, but I'm worried about its effect on the fetuses down here. I've tried to shield the stalls off, but I don't know how much good it's doing."

"What's gone wrong? Have you found out which one of the reactors is haywire?"

"That's just it. None of them. It's coming from outside the City."

"Are you sure? Have you contacted any of the other Cities to see if they've registered the same thing?"

"I wanted to call you first, Captain, and see what you said."

"Then I'll call up Epsilon-6 and see what's going on."

"Right, Captain. Can I listen in?"

I got the Nine and waited for about five minutes for Riche to answer. Finally his voice came over: "Leela, well how's my girl today?"

"She's puzzled," I said. "We've got radiation flooding our City. As of yet it's not very high, but it's coming from outside, so they tell me."

"You too?" His voice grew a bit worried. "About twenty minutes ago somebody over here woke me up to tell me the same thing. I told him to go check everything from top to bottom and then went back to bed. I had a hard night over here arguing with Judge Philots. Somebody in one of the free-fall sectors pushed off too hard and smashed his head. Two One-Eyes found him and tried to help him, but he died. Now the good Judge wants to press charges on them for interfering with a citizen. So I yelled at him all evening till he got tired. But I'm bushed too. What about this radiation business? I knew we'd hit light sand yesterday—"

Suddenly there was a burst of static in which I could detect voices that lasted for nearly a minute. Then it stopped and Captain Riche said, "Hey, what happened?"

"I don't know," I said. "Everything's all right over there?" But in the middle of my sentence the static started again, and this time the attention lights all over my desk began to blink at me.

I answered the closest one.

Meeker from Communications answered, "I don't know, but whatever it is, it's happening on Epsilon-7. They're trying to contact us, but something's way the hell wrong."

"Switch me on, will you?"

"Okay."

The static returned, and with it the unintelligible voices. Meeker overrode it once more with: "Turn on your video, Captain, and I'll relay what I'm getting."

I switched on the large screen above my desk. It went from gray to black, and a handful of luminous disks appeared against the far speckling of stars. It was the radio view of all the cities.

Somehow they cut through the static and the voices— which I now realized was one voice echoing back on itself again and again—were briefly intelligible:

". . . Epsilon-7; this is Epsilon-7, emergency red, emergency red, can anyone read me, can anyone read me . . . Epsilon-7—"

The other Cities must have all been tuned in by now. Finally another voice came over, static-free: "This is Captain Vlyon of Alpha-8. I read you clearly. Go ahead." Apparently Alpha-8 was having a lot less trouble with interference than we were.

"Thank God. This is One-Eyed Pike, calling from the One-Eyed Quarter of Epsilon-7. The rest of them are dead, the whole official quarter. I don't know, they went crazy or something. Someone came, or something, a man with green . . ." Static again, and when it cleared Captain Vlyon was saying: "I'm sorry, I don't understand your story. Please calm down, Pike, and tell me again."

"The whole damn ship nearly exploded, I think. Maybe forty minutes ago. It was night cycle in the City, but there was a huge jerk—everybody woke up. A couple of people got hurt, and then they started to go crazy, because they didn't know. And in the Concourse—I didn't see, but they told me—a figure, all on fire, with green eyes began to walk. No, I don't understand it. But they died. Twenty minutes ago, a group of us tried to get into the official sector, and there were corpses all over—just dead, all over, and a few screaming still, trying to tell us, and then we saw a light, and we fled back here."

"Now look a minute, Pike—"

"Now *you* look! Goddamn it, you come here and get us out! We're hiding out in the web, but you can take the shuttle boats across. For God's sake, come over here and get us out of this—" Over Pike's voice came a scream; then Pike cried out. Then I saw why Meeker had put me onto visual.

One of the circles—Epsilon-7—wasn't right. There was a nimbus around it and the ship was quivering. Then suddenly the radio went dead, and on the screen Epsilon-7 began to break up. First it crushed in; then five or six fragments sped off in different directions as though they had been hurled. What was left just cracked apart like an eggshell. Within five minutes the twelve-mile hunk of metal was torn to bits in front of my eyes and the pieces scattered through space.

By now there must have been people on all eleven remaining Cities watching what I had just seen. For ten minutes there was silence. I was beyond speech.

Finally Captain Alva's voice came through. "Captain Vlyon, are you still there? What happened?"

A very strained voice came back. "Yes. I'm . . . still here. I don't . . ."

He didn't finish. I felt that perhaps Captain Vlyon was not the same man whose voice we had heard before; I don't mean anything mysterious. Were any of us the same?

"I don't know . . ." he whispered.

Third entry:

The shock had worn off, and in the cessation, the rumor has fled over the City. Light sand continues, but compared to the destruction of a City, that's no problem. There is a still panic, with no way to protect ourselves. Judge Cart-rite greeted me affably this morning: "Well, at least one good thing has come out of this. A good many people have returned to the rituals."

I suppose he expected me to be overjoyed. Meeker and three other communication engineers in three other Cities had enough presence of mind to record everything that went on that evening. Communications was busy all morning making a detailed comparison, as well as trying to unscramble some of the staticked-out sections. They cleared up perhaps ten more words by the end of the afternoon, which added nothing to what we already know. There was a depressing intercity conference that afternoon, during which we were supposed to offer suggestions.

First, five minutes of silence; then fifteen minutes of embarrassed, preposterous speculation. Finally the meeting was abandoned.

It was nearly dinner hour when Captain Alva called me again.

"What's happened now?" I asked. "Something come up?"

"Just more trouble. Somehow the rumor got out that the One-Eyes on Epsilon-7 had taken it over and managed to blow it up."

"What?"

"Oh, it's nothing serious, but there's talk of putting rigid enforcement on the Norm again."

"Who came out with that idea?"

"I don't know. The idea that the City could just go up like that is too much for most of them. You can almost watch each person turning around and around, looking for someone to blame it on. The One-Eyes are the easiest."

"But why?"

"Oh, the reasoning works something like this: the last report we got from Epsilon-7 came from a One-Eye, so therefore they were the last people in charge of the City; therefore they must have taken it over from the officers and so on and so forth."

"And managed to destroy the whole City?"

"Don't ask me. One of the ritual groups here has already incorporated it; they get themselves high on ether, then all stand around while their leader puts out the left eye of a large doll. Then everyone moans and has visions of destruction."

"Ether?" I asked. "I don't like that at all."

"Neither do I. As far as I'm concerned, the rituals can get as involved as they want to, but I draw the line at the use of narcotics."

I agreed with him. "I just hope this ritual business doesn't get completely out of hand. This afternoon I got a complaint from Parks—he's my head Market Research man—about the kid he's training to be his assistant. Parks told me that the kid always brought a little pad of paper and pencil to work with him and would take it out and doodle on it occasionally. Parks always thought the kid was using it to figure out something. But when the kid came in today, Parks couldn't get any work out of him. He just sat there and doodled, and when Parks asked him why, he said that his ritual group always wrote down certain signs when certain categories of thoughts entered their heads. He wouldn't say what they were, but apparently he was thinking them all the time and had to sit in the corner making circles, crosses, and parallelograms."

"I can believe it," Captain Alva told me. "This whole business has me worried—which is the euphemism of the day."

Fourth entry:

I had been at work in my office for perhaps fifteen minutes when Judge Cartrite sent through a request to see me.

"Come right in," I said into the intercom, and a moment later the judge entered.

"Good morning, good morning. I just thought I would

stop up and check through you before I got busy. There'll
be a lot of changes to be made now, a lot of lax laws will
have to be enforced more strictly."

"What do you mean?"

"Well, has it or hasn't it been adopted as the official
explanation of the catastrophe of Epsilon-7?"

I put my fingers together and leaned back. "As far as
I know, there has been no vaguely plausible explanation
advanced."

"Oh, come now," said Judge Cartrite. "You don't mean
you haven't heard. That's why I came to see if it was official. It's all over the City."

"What's all over the City?"

"That the One-Eyed sector of Epsilon-7 tried to take
over their City, slaughtered the population, and blew up the
ship."

"Nothing of the kind has even been considered."

"Well then, perhaps you ought to—"

"And it's preposterous."

"Are you sure you can say that?"

"I am. Here, I want you to listen to a transcription of
everything that came across from Epsilon-7 the night she
went."

I called Meeker and got him to pipe up the playback on
both sound and video. The judge sat through it perfectly
still. I'd seen it fifteen times, so I'd forgotten what a shock
the first run-through could be. He was silent and his face
was drawn. At last he muttered, "Well . . ."

"Did that sound like a man who had just taken over a
ship to you?"

"Well," he repeated. "Perhaps it . . . wasn't real, or was
fixed or something. After all, what *did* take over the ship,
then? The green man with the flaming eyes, or whatever
that nonsense was?"

After the judge left, Parks gave me a ring. "You know,
Captain, the radiation is still pretty high. The mutations

that are going to come out of this will set the Norm jumping something awful."

"I'll come down and take a look."

"Not that there's anything anybody can actually do,"
Parks said. Then he added, "But it would make us feel better."

The Market is bright with fluorescent fixtures, and stall
after stall is sided with glittering tubes where infants are
brought to term. The front of the Market holds the genea-
logical files, which have the chromosome pattern of every
person in the City.

Parks's assistant sat at the desk, blond head down, absorbed in his pad. A moment later Parks came up. "Hello,"
he said, smiling. He saw me glance at his assistant and made a
hopeless gesture. "Ignore him. I'll show you what I've done."

We went toward the back. "I've put lead foil around the
early blastulas. They need it most. I don't think anything
over four months will be affected, but it's still going to be
nip and tuck." One section of the glittering rack was dark
where the tubes had been wrapped in lead.

Looking at the dull, crinkled foil, I suddenly felt the
heaviness of the responsibility to these born and unborn
thousands hurtling between stars, lost somewhere in
timelessness, sea and desert, life and catastrophe, spinning
around one another like dots on dice.

"Well," I told Parks, "like you said, there's not much I
can do. This place is depressing. Or maybe it just brings out
the mother in me."

Parks laughed. I left the Market and went back up to my
cabin.

Fifth entry:

Captain Alva called this evening from Sigma-9, very upset.
"Lee, what's your situation with the One-Eyes."

"Cartrite's been annoying the hell out of them," I told him.
I heard his breath whistle through the speaker. "It's

worse over here," he said. "I'm going to ask something strange of you right now."

"Go ahead," I said, question mark implied.

"Will you join with me in an official request to the judicial offices of all the Cities not to persecute the One-Eyes. I'm asking all the captains to do the same. The way things are going here, they'll be extinct in no time, and when their knowledge is gone, so is all humanity."

"We're not supposed to meddle with the judicials," I mused.

"Lee—"

"Shut up, Alva, I'm just thinking out loud. But we're not that far away from where you are. If you already had the consent of the other captains, I'd feel better about the whole thing. Oh, hell, what am I, a woman or a mouse? Sure, you've got my consent, Captain Alva; just send a wording of the statement to me before you present it."

"Thanks, Lee." The gratitude in his voice reflected the relief even I felt. "You're the third captain who's gone along with me."

"I think you'll get us all," I told him, "if the condition in this City is any indication." Then I added, "I hope it does some good."

I heard Alva sigh. It was a long sigh; I bet it sent the stars outside shaking. "I hope so too, Lee."

Sixth entry:

They're gone. Must I cry, rage; the City of Delta-6 is destroyed. This time it took ten hours. It began with a blast of static that wiped out the broadcast of One-Eyed Jack's trial, which we were all monitoring over in Sigma-9. Faint signals started coming through, panic had broken out on the ship, then a call for help from Communications. Then more static. Apparently the green-eyed being was back. It was fantastic. I don't know how to take it seriously. It would be easier to think it some cosmic joke. But it's real, and the lives of all the citizens of the City depend on perceiving that reality correctly. Toward the end, the only communication was from the One-Eyes. Help, help, and help again. Some green-eyed being who stole their sanity as well as their organization marched among the survivors on that ruined ship for ten hours, and at the end, there was destruction. At the end, I relayed to Captain Alva: "Can't we do something? What if I go over there?"

"Don't be silly, Lee. What can you do?"

"At least find out . . . at least . . ."

Over the intercom someone was screaming.

"If you die, will that do any good, Lee?"

"It will if I can find out what's killing off the rest of them."

Then on the vision screen, the ship began to break apart. God, the screaming—

chapter nine

Skip the next couple of pages," the boy said.

So Joneny turned them over. His eyes caught up the words again at:

. . . so that when I heard Captain Alva shrieking over the clattering speaker, "Help, oh, for God's sake, will somebody help us," what could I do?

I radioed down to Meeker, "Get an intercity ferry ready. I'm going over there to take a look."

"But, Captain," Meeker said, "if you get caught—"

"The last one lasted ten hours. That should give me time enough to get there and back."

"The one before that lasted sixteen minutes. This one could be longer, shorter, or the same. And what about the sand count—"

"I'm going, Meeker. Get the shuttle ready."

When I was swinging out of my office five minutes later, suddenly someone from an adjoining corridor barked, "Captain!"

"What is it, Judge Cartrite?"

"Meeker just informed me you were heading over to Sigma-9."

"And what the hell business is it of yours?" I snapped.

"Captain, I forbid you to go. And if you do go, I certainly forbid you to come back."

That brought me up short. "And where do you come off with the authority to say what I can or cannot do?"

"If you remember, I have charge of the responsibility of morals on this ship. I feel that if you returned from Sigma-9 it would be demoralizing. . . ."

"For God's sake, Judge, what are you afraid of?"

"Suppose you bring the Destroyer back with you?"

"The Destroyer?"

"Yes, the green-eyed creature that is wrecking—"

I interrupted him. "Well, at least you're off blaming it on the One-Eyes. I'm going, Judge."

I wasn't paying too much attention to him because I was both frightened and furious.

I got to the boat, locked the locks behind me, unplugged my ears, opened my eyes, and radioed myself clear. The triple ports swung back and I barreled out into the sand. The meter read three point seven. The Sigma-9 grew in the view screen like a shimmering egg.

The robot receiver announced: "Your ears are unplugged"— I switched on my radio—"and your eyes are seeing."

The hatch opened up, and as I drifted into the lock, the sand meter swung down. The tunnel attached itself, and as I stepped out, my stomach retreated against my backbone in fear of what I might find. I felt a slight mental tingling, which I assumed at first was part of my own anticipation. I walked up the empty corridor and the tingling grew stronger until, as I was walking toward the navigation offices, I realized there was something ringing in my head like a buzzer. I turned toward the City Plaza, wondering where on the road to destruction I was.

Suddenly I saw a few people ahead. They were staggering silently away from me. One fell, then two more. The others wove to the side; one leaned against a column for a moment, then slipped to the ground as well.

I tried my belt radio, thinking maybe I could zero in on where the remaining forces of the City were held up. When I turned the switch, the buzzing left my head and became real. Just as I was trying to figure out what to do, the hum on the speaker began to rise and fall and then resolved itself into a voice. *"Who are you?"*

"Huh?" I said in surprise, and wanted to know—though I didn't say it—who the hell are you?

"I am the Destroyer. Your people call me the Destroyer. Who are you, come to hunt the Destroyer?"

It was weird. I thought maybe somebody who'd lost their nuts had gotten hold of what communications devices were left.

"Where are you?" I demanded. The radio wasn't two-way, but in my frustration, I guess I must have forgotten it. I remember I called out, "Where are you? I'm trying to help you!"

And the radio blared out in the oscillating voice: *"I'm here."*

Then it happened. I think most of it happened in my head. Things just went crazy—emotions, thoughts, impressions—and through the whirling chaos around me, something great and shimmering staggered into the concourse, the form of a man—naked, huge, but like some sort of ghost, with flowing eyes.

The thing startled me, so I just cried out, "Stop that!"

And it stopped. My head jarred back into place on my shoulders, and I could see the figure glittering, fading, disappearing, and reaffirming itself across the shattered wreckage over the plaza.

"*I am here,*" it repeated, but this time the voice reverberated from the vague area of its head.

"What are you doing!" I demanded, and was only then struck by the impossibility that I had all along been communicating.

"*Help me,*" it said. "*I—I don't know.*"

"You're killing us," I cried. "That's what you're doing!"

"*I approached slowly,*" it said. "*Very carefully into their minds—but they died screaming. Their minds are not big enough.*" It swayed and staggered, gaining form and losing it like a dream.

My heart was pounding, though I was beginning to recover. "But you're not killing me," I said.

"*You told me to stop. I'm not in your mind now, just the image in your eyes and ears.*"

I wasn't too sure what it was talking about, so I said, "Well, bring your image a little closer; but don't do anything that will . . . hurt my mind. I want to see you."

Three steps carried him across the floor till he stood, green-eyed and towering, above me.

"*You don't really see me,*" he said. "*I took this image from their minds, to try to come closer with. But their minds break up even when I come slowly.*"

"And what about me?" I asked, unsure what I was really talking about.

"*I came to you fast, and you yelled stop; so I stopped.*"

"Oh," I said, "well, thanks." I remembered what coming fast had meant. Suddenly I remembered. "Where is Captain Alva?"

"He's dead, and so are most of the others . . . there; they are all dead now."

"All . . . ?"

"They didn't say stop."

Suddenly it hit me. "Well then, you *stay* stopped, damn you! All? What in the—Don't move ever again! Why didn't you stop anyway? What the hell do you think you are?" I screamed it, and maybe some more besides; I don't remember. When I stopped, I was quivering, both mad and scared.

It didn't say anything; it just shook there in front of me. At last I could only ask, "What *are* you?"

And more softly, as if it had understood on a deeper level, it repeated, *"I don't know."*

Then it occurred to me to ask: "Where are you from?"

"Outside, outside the City. I exist in the—the sand, you call it, the meson fields outside the starships."

"You're—" The idea came to me as something too big trying to fit in the too-small space of my head. "You're . . . a living being from the sea and the sand?"

He nodded.

I had been going up until now on a hysterical drive that had battered up against what it met without question. But now the impossibilities began to flood my mind and I struck at them with questions.

"But who—how—how can you communicate with me?"

"I can't, really," it explained. *"I took apart their minds, and I know your words and your images, but your minds are too small for me. I can't really communicate with you, but I know what you are thinking. I took the image so you could see something of me. But I took the image from your people."*

I let the breath, which had somehow stopped, come back into my lungs. "I see."

"*I did not realize,*" it went on, "*that you were alive until just now when you told me to stop. That was the first time any of you addressed me directly.*"

Again I nodded.

"*The image comes to me of one of your people breaking open an anthill to see what is inside. That is how I broke open your ships. I saw the confusion, but I did not realize it was wrong until you told me.*"

"You are a very different sort of life-form than we are," I said. "Are your people common all over interstellar space?"

"*No people. There is only me.*"

"You must be very lonely," I said.

"*Lonely?*"

And I actually heard the rising inflection of interrogation.

"*I . . . lonely,*" and then something odd happened. The room began to quiver around me, and for a moment I thought the chaos was going to begin.

"*Yes, I am very lonely. But I did not know it until you told me the word.*"

The quivering began again, and there was a shift in color values.

"For pity's sake," I called out, "what's happening to you?"

And from the green eyes I suddenly saw tears flowing, flooding over those shimmering cheeks.

"*You see, I am doing what you would call crying.*"

"Try and control yourself," I said. "I . . . understand. . . . It would be hard to discover that you were all alone. You discover that as soon as you meet somebody."

"*Yes.*" There was a pause. "*As soon as you meet somebody who is not alone, like you.*"

"You don't think I'm alone?" I said.

Again a pause, and the colors returned more or less to normal. "*You are, I see from your mind, but not as much as I am.*" Again the pause, then the quivering, then the kaleidoscope. It said, "*I love you.*"

"What?"

The words repeated, and there was less sensory confusion.

"You love me?" I asked. "Why?"

"Because you are a power among your people, you are alone and not alone."

It was complete confusion, and at the same time I thought I saw.

"That's . . . very flattering."

"Will you love me?"

That brought me up short. I had been feeling all sorts of empathy with this creature, had begun to understand, if not forgive its destruction, but this . . . ?

"I don't even know what that would mean," I said. "I don't want to laugh at you, but I couldn't even begin to comprehend what loving you would mean."

"The word is from your mind," came its answer. *"If I give you something that you want very much, will you love me?"*

"I still don't . . ."

It interrupted me: *"More than anything else, you want descendants who will be able to live among the stars, and you know as well that most of your people could not do so now. I will promise you that I will break apart no more of your ships, and that your progeny will be able to live among the stars, as well as communicate with me, throughout all time."*

I guess everybody has a pressure point that you just have to touch to make everything go bang. The colors changed this time because my irises suddenly opened. The quivering was inside me. I don't know what the emotion was.

It said, *"You love me,"* and opened its great glittering arms. *"Come,"* and I started forward.

What happened next—oh, all the powers and audience of the stars, what happened? I don't know—the colors, the pain, the sensations that caught me up and broke me

apart in swirls of metallic ice, that burned me with myriad
thoughts, complete and incomplete. The colors? Breaking
from white through red, down through cascading green,
soaring through gold that glittered and turned to emeralds,
emerald as his eyes. The pain? Transparent as pleasure,
loosed in my knees and cool in my loins, to surge again and
flood the whole column of me, explode and glisten on my
fingers, writhe in the center of tension, wave upon wave,
on a clean beach. The sensations? They rose, rose, fell, and
rose again, mounting till I screamed and laughed and covered my mouth with open fingers, as the whole musculature
of my body tensed and flattened against itself, quivering
toward a release that came surging forward through my
pelvis from the base of my spine to flower there, burn, and
bloom. . . . I held all his flickering presence, gentle as mist
in my arms, hard as metal.

Next entry:

The Sigma-9 tore apart, heaving, two minutes after my
intercity shuttle took off. The radio interference knocked
my eyes coal black and something was goofy in the gravity
spin, so I drifted all the way back in free fall, feeling as if I
had a stiff hangover.

I radioed for entrance, and after the robot went through
its little bit, suddenly a voice cut in. "This is Smythers of
the judicial office, Captain Lee. Judge Cartrite has told us
we are not to allow you entrance to the City."

"You *what*?"

"I said Judge Cartrite doesn't want—"

"You open that damn lock this instant, or when I get in
there I'll tear you to pieces."

"I'm sorry—"

"Put Cartrite on the phone. He's been waiting for me to
jet outside the City, but he's out of his mind if he thinks he
is going to keep me locked up here."

"We have two others here and the three of us are to examine you. Maybe if you went away and came back some other time, Judge Cartrite—"

"Have you all gone *nuts*?"

"No, Captain, but our rituals—"

"I don't give a damn about your rituals!"

"Captain," it was another voice, "can you tell me what note this is?"

Something that sounded for all the world like a trumpet rang through the speaker.

"No, I can't," I said. "Why should I?"

"Well, it's part of the ritualistic examination Judge Cartrite set up for your entrance. The note of the trumpet signifies the call that came to our ancestors—"

"I'll kill you," I said. "When I find out who you are, I'm going to declare you insane and have you put in the Death's Head. Now let me in. I said I was coming back and I've come back. Suppose I told you I've found out what caused the wreck of the other cities. Suppose I told you that I can stop it from happening here . . . *if* you let me in."

There was silence.

"You've found the green-eyed leader of the rebellious One-Eyes?"

"You haven't brought him back with you?" demanded the other.

"Of course I haven't," I snapped. "And it's no man, one- or two-eyed."

"Well, what was it?" asked the third lawyer, the one with the trumpet.

"Why don't I just sit here and let you guess until you decide time is running out."

"I'm going to get Judge Cartrite," I heard one say, and tootle his trumpet.

Two minutes later, before the judge got there, one of them—you could hear him gnashing his nails—said, "I'm going to let her in."

And the triple lock rolled back. I figured they'd be crying before the judge got through with them, but I didn't really care.

Twenty minutes later I was talking to Judge Cartrite on the phone, and I told him enough that I think his hair began to singe. But I didn't let the cat out of the bag. For the next week I kept to my quarters. The first day my feet were sore from the no gravity of the ride back, but after that I was just being careful.

Finally I went down to the Market. "Parks," I said. His assistant was doodling over at the desk. Behind us the rows on rows of embryo flasks were banked to the ceiling. "Parks, I've got a problem; maybe you can help me."

"What is it, Captain?"

"I'm pregnant, Parks."

"You're *what*?"

"I said I am going to have a baby."

He sat down on the desk. "But . . . how?"

"That's a very good question," I said. "And I'm not too sure of the answer. But I want you to get it out of me."

"You mean an abortion?"

"Hell, no," I said. "I want you to remove it with tender loving care and get it into one of those embryo flasks of yours."

"I still don't see. . . . I mean everybody on the ship is kept harmonally sterile. How did you . . ." Then he said, "Are you sure?"

"Examine me," I said.

He did and told me, "Well, I guess you are. When do you want it transferred?"

"Right away," I said. "Keep it alive, Parks. I'd bring it to term myself, but there's nobody in the whole nation that has the muscle left to go through labor and come out alive."

"It'll be alive," said Parks.

I had a local anesthetic and watched the whole business

through a series of mirrors. It was fascinating; and when I was finished, I was hungry as could be. I went upstairs, had dinner in my room, and thought some more.

While I was thinking, Parks suddenly buzzed me from the Market. "Captain Lee, Captain Lee—" and then he got caught on something that sounded like choking.

"Is the kid all right?" I demanded.

"Oh, yeah, he's fine. But Captain, the rest, they're dying. They're dying all over the place. I've lost half the supply already."

"Has the radiation on our ship gone up?" My first thought was that the Destroyer had broken its promise and moved in on us. But the wreck of the Sigma-9 still drifted along with us.

"It's you, Captain. Check yourself, that's all I can think of. I checked your embryo, and it's soaked with radiation. I can't understand why it's still alive. But it is, and doing very well. But some time or other, this place was blasted by enough hard gamma to upset everything and kill off half the stores here. Even I'm feeling a little woozy and had to undergo decontamination."

"I see," I said. "I'll call you back and tell you what I find."

I switched off and turned to the scintillator. It said that I had been dead since I arrived on the ship. I was going to phone Parks when I was interrupted by a *beep*. Judge Cartrite's face came together on the screen.

"Captain, I'm sorry to bother you, but I thought this was something I'd better see to in person."

"What is it?"

"I'm afraid I'm going to have to place you under arrest."

"Arrest? For what?"

"Leela RT-857 vs. The Norm."

"And aside from the trivia, how do I differ from the run of the mill?"

"It's not trivial, Captain. You were pregnant. And in this City that's unforgivable as well as illegal."

"Who told you?" I wanted to know. I couldn't imagine Parks giving out something like that.

But the answer when it came was all too believable. "Parks's new assistant overheard."

---

chapter ten

After a few more lines, the entries stopped.

Joneny closed the book. The boy, still in Joneny's gell, was holding another book, a similar diary. "This one is Hodge's," he said. "Hodge, the executioner."

Joneny took it, frowning, and as he turned through the laconic mentions of death after death, verses of the ballad threaded through his mind once more:

> "She walked through the gate and the voices cried,
> She walked through the Market and the children died,
> She walked past the courthouse and the judge so still,
> She walked to the bottom of Death's Head hill."

And the one-eyed woman who held her green-eyed child? The last few pages were in more detail. Hodge had written:

The trial is over now. It went very quickly. There was no defense. I was not there, but I heard.

I see her in the death cell every few hours when she walks slowly in front of the long thin window. Death is heavy on her shoulders. I do not think she is afraid. Once she stopped and called to me. I came over, opened the little door in the top so I could hear better, and she said: "Hodge, what's happening in the rest of the City?"

"It's in chaos," I told her. "The rituals have gotten out of hand, and people have raided the web and are killing the One-Eyes. They go out in hunting parties now, with gas and spears. Ralf is dead, I know. I don't go there anymore."

She had looked calm before, but her face seemed struck now. "Can you get Parks here to see me?" she said softly.

"I'm not supposed to," I said. "But I will, Captain."

Parks, from the Market, hurried up there so fast he was panting. He looked at me like he wanted me to go away, but I couldn't do that. So finally the Captain told him to go ahead anyway, that I could be trusted. When she said that, he glanced at me with hate and said, "Trusted to kill you?"

"That too," said the Captain. "Go on, Parks, what about the child. Is it safe?"

He nodded. "They tried to break in, and a lot of the tubes were smashed. But after the first attack . . . well, I got an idea. You see, Captain, someone's with us now."

She frowned.

"After one of the raids on the web, when Ralf was killed, Merril came to us in the Market. She knows I'm friendly, anyway. And, well, the same way we took it out of you, we put it into her. She'll hold it up until a week or so before normal labor would occur, and then we'll remove it by Cesarean. At least it will be in a mobile container, and the stupid tube-smashing parties won't get it."

"Good," I said.

"Just what does that child mean, Captain?" Parks asked. "There's something special about it, isn't there? It has to do with what happened on the Sigma-9?"

"That's right." And then she told him. It didn't make too

much sense to me. But she said a lot of scientific-sounding things, and at the end Parks said, "Then we *will* make it to the stars," very slowly, very softly. Then, "They won't get at it. The One-Eyes who're left will raise it. Merril thought it was something like that. But I didn't realize—" He stopped. "Merril cried for you, Captain. When we were in the Market, there, talking about your execution, she—we cried."

She just held on to the edge of the window, hard, and a muscle in her jaw jumped a few times. All she said was, "Make sure it lives."

The last two entries in Hodge's journal:

"The riots are growing, they are threatening to come even here."

And:

"Executed today, four o'clock in the afternoon, Captain Leela RT-857."

Joneny turned to the Destroyer's child. "It lived," he said.
The boy nodded. "After I was grown, I could make as many duplicates as we wanted, without going through the whole process."

Joneny suddenly frowned. "And that explains all your antics then. You, like your father, exist a little outside time, and that's why the shimmering and the movement during time stop." Suddenly Joneny frowned. "But the promise, he made her a promise, that you would someday reach the stars and be able to make contact!"

"He didn't say when. Aren't you going to take me back to the University for study?"

"Well, of course, but . . ." Suddenly Joneny began to laugh. "With your mind reading, you *can* make contact with any race. And that coupled with the extra-time facility, why, this might be the biggest discovery in galactic anthropology since . . . since I don't even know!"

The boy nodded. "That's what we were made for. We can take all the information back to my father, and he will digest it for you, and then we'll give it to you. You'll take us to the places where you want to make contact, and that's what we'll do."

Joneny was about to burst. "And that's living up to the promise more than ever, because you'll be making contact for not only half humans, but for them all, the great-grandchildren of completely genetic humans as well. And you'll be sort of a go-between for you and your father. Are you in contact with him all the time, no matter where he is and no matter where you are?"

The boy tilted his head and nodded. "My father and I are one," he said.

Back in his cruiser, Joneny once more reviewed the whole of "The Ballad of Beta-2" and marveled at how clear it seemed now. The story of Leela's attempt to save her people was as immediate to him through those compressed verses as many incidents he had lived through. Who had written the ballad? he wondered. Some last One-Eye? Or perhaps someone from the official sector in whom impotent compassion turned potently to words? He was already planning how to make use of the Destroyer's Children in his research into Creton III, yet through his planning, still the closing verse of the hymn—it was a hymn, in a way—came back:

> Fire and blood, meat, dung, and bone—
> Down on your knees, steel, stone, and wood
> Today are dust, and the City's gone,
> But she came back like she said she would.

New York
August 1964

they fly at çiron

proem

Among the tribes and villages and hamlets and town-
    ships
that ornament the world with their variety, many have
    existed
in mutual support, exchange, and friendship. Many
    others
have stayed to themselves, regarding their neighbors
with unease, hostility, and suspicion. Some have gone
from one state to the other. Some have even gone back.
But when the memory of a village is no older than the
    four
or five generations it takes a grave-scroll record to rot,
there *is* no history—only myth and song. And the truth
    is,
while a minuscule number of these may echo down the
    ages,
only a handful endure more than a season; and the vast
    majority
from such handfuls linger (listen to the songs and myths
    about you!) less than a lifetime.

For

Dennis Rickett

and with thanks to

Sam Debenedetto,

Leonard Gibbs,

& Don Eric Levine

note

In my second-floor flat at the dead end of East Fifth Street in summer of 1962, I first wrote *They Fly at Çiron* as the longest (forty-five pages) of five short stories I'd hoped to cobble together into a novel. From my spiral notebooks I typed the first version on a mechanical typewriter in late spring '62. My editor, Don Wollhiem, did not buy it, however; nor was I really satisfied with the tale. Some time toward 1969 I gave the manuscript of what I felt was the most salvageable section to my friend James Sallis. Jim reworked the opening half-dozen pages. That version appeared as a collaboration under our paired bylines in the June '71 issue of *The Magazine of Fantasy & Science Fiction*. Twenty years later, though, it struck me that the story could still use a pass through the word processor. When I was done, I had a manuscript of 150 pages. For all I've added, two clauses excepted, I've kept none of Jim's inventive amendments. Nevertheless, they formed an invaluable critique, defining lacks I've now addressed otherwise. As none of Jim's language remains, I can no longer reprint *They Fly at Çiron* as a proper collaboration. But neither can I publish it—far truer for this than for the '71 version— without acknowledging that critique as responsible for anything now in it worth the reading. In 1992, equally detailed critiques of the new version came from Randy Byers and Ron Drummond— as did an astute half page of notes from my Amherst collegue and friend Don Eric Levine. In my sunny Amherst study, I responded here and there to all of them as best I could—and the manuscript is now fifty pages longer. In one sense, this is my second novel— but it has taken me thirty years to write.

—S.R.D.

chapter one

They are dogs."

"My prince—"

"They are less than dogs. Look: they inch on their stomachs, like maggots."

"Prince Nactor, they are men—men who fought bravely against us—"

"—and whom we vanquished, Lieutenant Kire." The prince slipped long fingers through the fence's diamond-crossed wires and grasped. "That gives me the right to do anything I want to them." With his free hand, still in its leather gauntlet, he lifted his powergun from its sling. "Anything."

"My prince, yours is also the right to be merciful—!"

"Even this, Kire." Nactor put the barrel end through the wire. "Now watch." The first time he fired, the two who could still scream started in again. Another who could move dragged himself over the dirt, took hold of the fence wire, and tried to pull himself up. His fingers caught. Silently, he opened his mouth, and closed it, and opened it. Nactor glanced back, grinning through his beard. "Smells like barbecue, doesn't it?" Turning again, he thrust the barrel between the wires into the prisoner's eye.

The gun and the fence both jumped at the report.

Charred neck and bloody hands slid to the ground.

He took out the noisiest two last, some forty seconds apart. During those seconds, while the smoke above the fence settled back down, Nactor began to smile. The one huddling into himself opened his eyes, then squeezed them tight—he was making a sound more between a wheeze and a whine than a scream. Nactor's beard changed shape a little as, behind it, his face seemed to grow compassionate. He leaned toward the wire as though at last he saw something human, something alive, something he could recognize.

Without stopping the sound, again the prisoner began to blink.

Nactor lowered the gun.

The man finally let an expression besides terror twitch through the scabs and the mud; he took a breath . . .

Nactor thrust the gun through—and shot.

The fence jumped.

A hand, charred now, slid through the muck. Something no longer a face splatted down.

Nactor reslung his weapon and turned from the corral, releasing the wire. "I find killing these"—the fence vibrated—"easier than those creatures from their cave holdings that we exterminated three attacks ago. These at least were human. But those, with their shaggy pelts and their thickened nails like beast claws—I suppose they reminded me of my dogs at home. There, your requests for clemency, your sour looks and your sulkings, really got on my nerves, Kire. This was worth doing just to keep you quiet." He glanced where Kire's hand jerked, now toward, now away from, the sling at his own hip. "That is, if it doesn't actually cheer you up. Lieutenant?" (Three more jerks, and Kire's arm, in its black sleeve, straightened.) "Is it really necessary to remind you that the purpose of this expedition is conquest—that Myetra must expand His boundaries or He will perish? When the time comes for our final encounter with Calvicon, you will . . . I *trust* you will distinguish yourself in war, in service to Myetra, bringing honor to your superiors, who watch you, and to your men, who trust you." The prince palmed the powergun's handle, moving gauntleted fingers on the sling's silver embossing, worked into Kirke, Myetra's totemic crow. (The silver came from the Lehryard mines; the guns were smithed in the Tradk Mountains. For both guns and silver, Myetra traded wheat taken by force from the veldt villages of Zeneya. Even Kirke, Kire reflected, had come from a distant county he could no longer name, but which Myetra had long ago laid waste to.) "What is our mission now,

Kire? Just so I know you haven't forgotten: To march our troops across this land in a line as straight as . . . as what?"

" 'As straight as a blood drop down a new-plastered wall.' " The lieutenant's voice was low, measured, but with some roughness in it that might have been a social accent, an emotional timbre, or a simple failure in the machinery of tongue, throat, and larynx. "Shoen, Horvarth, Nutting, and fourteen other hamlets lie devastated behind us. Çiron, Hi-Vator, Requior, and seven more villages lie ahead to be crushed, before we reach Calvicon for our final encounter."

The prince raised his gloved hand and with his naked forefinger began to tick off one, two, three . . . "Yes, it *is* seven. I thought it was eight there, for a moment. You might almost think I wanted to prolong the pleasures of this very pleasant journey we've been on almost a year and a half now. But you're right. It's only seven. The best way to spill blood in war, Kire, is to spill it where all can see. You spill it slowly, Kire—slowly, so that the enemy has time to realize our power and our greatness, the greatness of Myetra. Some locales have a genius for work, for labor, for toiling and suffering. And some have a genius for ruling. Myetra!" The prince flung up his gauntleted fist in salute. As he lowered it, however, a smile moved behind his heavy beard that put all seriousness into question. "There really is no other way." With his ungloved knuckles, the prince pushed his rough beard hair to shape, now forward from his ears, now back at his chin. "Those who disagree, those who think there is another way, are Myetra's enemies. You've seen how merciful Myetra is to its enemies, eh, Kire?" Abruptly, Prince Nactor turned and walked toward his tent.

In his black undergarments, black jerkin with black leggings over them, black harness webbing hips and chest, black hood tight around his face (a scimitar of bronze hair had slipped from under the edge), and wearing an officer's night-colored cape that did not rise anywhere as high as you might expect in the steady eastern breeze, the tall lieutenant turned too—after a breath— and walked from the corral.

The troops sat at fires paled to near invisibility by the silvery sun. Some men cleaned their weapons. Others talked of the coming march. One or two still ate. A stack of armor flung a moment's glare in Kire's eyes, brighter than the flames.

In only his brown undershorts, cross-legged and hunched over a roasted rabbit haunch, the little soldier, Mrowky, glanced up to call: "Lieutenant Kire, come eat."

His belly pushing down the waist of his undershorts, the hem of his singlet up, standing by the fire big Uk said: "Hey, lieutenant?"

On the ground, Mrowky lifted freckled shoulders. "Sir, we saved some hare . . ."

But Kire strode on to the horse enclosure, where two guards quickly uncrossed their spears and flung up their fists. (Kire thought: how little these men know what goes on in their own camp.) He stepped between them and inside, reached to pull down a bridle, bent to heft up a saddle. He cut out his mare, threw the leather over her head, put the saddle over her back, and bent beneath her belly for the cinch. A black boot in the iron stirrup, and moments later he galloped out, calling: "I shall be back before we decamp for Çiron."

Passing loudly, wind slapped at his face, but could not fill his cape to even the gentlest curve. Hooves hit up dirt and small stones, crackled in furze. Low foliage snapped by. The land spun back beneath.

Dim and distant, the Çironian mountains lapped the horizon. Kire turned the horse into a leafy copse. A branch raked at him from the right. Twigs with small leaves brushed his left cheek as he pulled—in passing—away. The mare stepped about; behind them brush and branches rushed back into place. At a stream, Kire jabbed his heels into the mare's flanks, shook the reins—

—an instant later, with four near-simultaneous clops, hooves hit the rockier shore. Pebbles spattered back into the water. Kire rode forward, to mount a rise and halt there, bending to run a black glove over the flat neck. He was about to canter down among the trees when a long and inhuman *Screeeeee* made the horse rear. Kire reined hard and tightened his black leggings against her flanks.

Raucous and cutting, the *Screee* came again. The mare danced sideways.

Dismounting, Kire dropped the reins to the ground. Snorting twice, the mare stilled.

Upper leg bending and lower leg out, Kire crabbed the slope, coming down in a sideways slide around a boulder.

Startlingly closer, the *Screeeeeeee* sliced low leaves.

Kire stepped around broken stone, stopped—and breathed in:

A man, a beast—

Yellow claws slashed at a brown shoulder. The shoulder jerked, the head ducked; black hair flung up and forward. Bodies locked. Braced on the ground, a bare foot gouged through pine needles.

Canines snapped toward a wrist that snatched away to lash around behind the puma's neck. This time, as the *Screeeee* whined between black gums and gray, gray teeth, something . . . cracked!

A broad paw clapped the man's side—but the sound failed. The claws had retracted.

Kire let his air out as puma and man, one dead, one exhausted, toppled onto their shadows.

Before Kire got in another breath, another shadow slid across them. On the ground, the man raised himself to one arm and shook back long hair. Kire stepped forward—to see the shadow around them get smaller and darker. He reached for the man's shoulder. At the same time, he looked up.

The flying thing—sun behind it burned on one wing's edge: Kire could see only its size—dropped. Kire's gun barrel cleared the sling. The report ripped the air . . . though the shot went wild.

Above, it averted, wings glinting like chipped quartz, then flapped up to soar away.

At Kire's feet, the naked man rocked on all fours by the beast. "It's gone, now," Kire rasped. "Get up."

The man pushed himself back on his knees, taking in great breaths through lips pulled up from large, yellow teeth. Then he stood.

He was taller than Kire by a hand. A good six years younger too, the lieutenant decided, looking at the wide brown face, the hair sweated in black blades to a cheek and a forehead still wrinkled with gasps from the fight. The eyes were molten amber—wet and hot.

(The lieutenant's eyes were a cool, startling green.)

Pulling up his cape and throwing it over his arm, Kire reslung his gun. "Who are you?"

"Rahm." Still breathing hard, he reached up with wide fingers to brush dirt and puma hair from his heaving chest and rigid belly. "Rahm of Çiron." The lips settled to a smile. "I thank thee for frightening away the Winged One with thy . . ." He motioned toward Kire's black waist cinch.

"This is my powergun." The tall youngster's dialect, Kire noted, was close to Myetra's. "Rahm . . ." The lieutenant snorted; it sounded like a continuation of whatever roughened his voice. "Of Çiron, 'ey?"

The Çironian's smile opened up. "That is a . . . powergun? It's a frightening thing, the . . . powergun." He moved his head: from where it clawed and clutched his shoulder, black hair slid away. "And who art thou, that hast become Rahm's friend?"

"I am Kire." He did not give his origin, though with Kirke on left breast, cloak, and sling, he could not imagine the need.

"Thou art a stranger in these lands," Rahm said. "Whither dost thou travel?"

"Soon to the Çironian mountains. But for now I am merely a wanderer, looking at the land about me, to learn what I can of it."

"So am I—or so I have been. But now I am returning to Çiron." Suddenly the black-haired youth bent, grabbed the puma's yellow foreleg, and tugged. "Here." He thrust one dark foot against pale stomach fur to shove the beast over the pine needles. With its closed eyes, the puma's head rolled aside, as if for the moment it wished to avoid the bright brown gaze of its murderer. "Thou shouldst have the lion for saving me from the Winged One. I had thought to carry it home—it's no more than three hours' walk. But thou hast a horse." He nodded up the slope. "'Tis thine."

Kire felt a smile nudge among his features. "Thank you." A smile was not the expression he'd thought to use with this Çironian youth. So he stepped back, to lean against the boulder. "Rahm?" Kire glanced at the sky, then back. "How is it you travel the land naked and without a weapon?"

Rahm shrugged. "The weather is warm. My arms are strong." Here he frowned. "A weapon?"

"You don't know what a weapon is . . ."

Rahm shook his head.

"Suppose you had not been able to kill the puma with your bare hands?"

"Eventually she would have gotten frightened and fled—once I'd hurt her enough." The youth laughed. "Or she would have killed me. But that could not happen. I am stronger than any animal in this land—except, perhaps, the Winged Ones."

"And what are they?"

"They live in the mountains of Çiron, at Hi-Vator. Their nests are far up the rocks, in the caves among the crags and peaks."

"Çiron," the lieutenant repeated. "And Hi-Vator . . . But Çiron is at the foot of the mountains."

Rahm nodded. Through the remnants of his own smile, Rahm found himself looking into a face not smiling at all.

"Do all Çironians go about so?" Kire asked. "Are you all so peaceful? Perhaps you, boy, are just simpleminded."

"We are peaceful, yes. We have no guns, if that is what thou meanst. Many of us go naked—though not all."

Black cloth hanging close around, the lieutenant chuckled.

And Rahm laughed with him, putting his feet wide and taking a great breath to support his laughter, throwing back black hair—so that he seemed to overflow the space naturally and generously his. "But thou art the first ever to think me simple!"

"Where are you coming from now, Çironian? Who are your parents? How do you live?"

"I come from a week's wandering out in the land. It is our village custom that every person so wander, once every three years. My parents both died of a fever when I was a boy. Old Ienbar the gravedigger took me in, and I work with him—when there is need. At other times, I help in the grain fields."

"Those muscles are all from gravedigging, hoe hefting, and plow pushing?"

"Some, yes." Rahm raised an arm to make an indifferent fist. "I always take a prize at the village games. But much comes from the year I unloaded stones with Brumer and Heben and Gargula and Tenuk, who works with me now in the fields, and the other boys on the rock crew—for our new council-building foundation!"

"And you don't even know what a weapon . . ." From the rock he'd settled against, Kire stood and turned—like a man who suddenly finds the joke empty enough simply to walk away. As he tramped back up the hill, his heavy cape, which no wind made billow or belly, moved only a bit, left and right. The mare raised her head. Kire took up the reins, grasped the saddle horn, and raising one boot to the stirrup, swung up and over.

"Friend Kire!" the Çironian called. "The lion! Wouldst thou go without my gift?"

As the mare reared and turned, Kire called back hoarsely: "I haven't forgotten." He guided the horse down the slope.

Rahm grasped a hind leg with one hand and an opposite forefoot with the other. He hefted the corpse high, its head hanging back.

The mouth was wide.

The teeth were bared.

The horse shied at the dead thing, but Kire bent down to grab a handful of loose fur. He tugged—while Rahm pushed—

the puma across the horse's back. The gift in place, Kire leaned down and, with his black glove, grasped the Çironian's shoulder. "I will not forget it," and he muttered, wheeling, ". . . though someday *you* may want to." But the last was lost in leaf chatter under the horse's hooves and the general roughness of his voice.

Hooves beat the earth—and Rahm leapt back.

Kire of Myetra gained the rise, while his cloak slid no more than from haunch to haunch on his mare's mahogany rump. With a flap of the reins, he was gone—to leave Rahm puzzled at their parting.

_____

chapter two

Naä sings so prettily," said one.

"Naä sings like a bird," said another. "Like a lark."

And between the women Rimgia bent among the rows, which, rising up over her eyes, became a gold jungle webbed with Naä's song. Rimgia wrapped her hands in the stalks and pulled. She'd been working some hours and her side was sore. In another hour the edge of her palms would sting.

But Naä sang.

And the song *was* beautiful.

Did they really work better when the singer sang? From time to time, when one could pay attention to the words, it was certainly more pleasant to work that way. Most of the women *said* they worked better. And all of the men. And it was best, Rimgia knew, not to say too much at odds with what most people said, unless you'd thought about it carefully and long—and selected your words with precision. That last had been added to the village truism by her father, Kern—a man known more for his silence than his volubility.

While Rimgia picked and listened, the squeak-squeak-clunk, squeak-squeak-clunk of the water cart rose out of the breeze and the music. Rimgia stood up, to feel gas rumble in her stomach from hunger. The water cart's arrival was her signal to cease and go home.

Apparently it was Naä's too. At the end of the verse, when the jolly man, so strong and fair, kissed the girl with the raven hair, Naä hefted her harp on its leather strap around behind her back, unhooked her left knee from her right ankle, and pushed herself down from the rock. She shook her brown hair back, hailed stocky Mantice, the water-cart driver. (His name had three syllables, the last with the softest *c*. In that locale it meant a bird, not a bug.)

Receiving the smiles and warm words from the working-women, Rimgia, whose hair was the color of the central length inside a split carrot, got a dipper of water from Mantice at the cart; and laughing at one woman and whispering to another about still another's new boyfriend and giving a quick grin to another who stepped up, full of a story about someone else's four-year-old daughter, she hurried to the path to fall in beside the singer.

When she saw Rimgia coming, Naä lingered for her.

They'd walked together a whole minute when Rimgia asked: "Naä, what dost thou think happens to us when we die?" She asked the question because Naä was a person you could ask such things of and she wouldn't laugh, and she wouldn't go telling other people how strange you were, and you wouldn't hear people talking and whispering about you when you came around the corner or surprised them by the well a day later.

This was more the reason for the question than that Rimgia really wanted to know. Indeed, she rather liked the idea that the wandering singer sometimes found her and her occasional odd thoughts of interest enough to speak about them seriously. So sometimes Rimgia tried to make her own thoughts seem more serious than they were.

"When we die?" Naä pondered. "I suspect it's just a big blank nothing, forever and ever and ever, that you don't even know is there—because there is no knowing anymore. That, I guess, is the safest thing to bet on, at least in terms of living your life the best you can while you're alive." She paused. "But once İ was in a land—oh, three or four years back—that had the strangest ideas about that."

"Yes?" Rimgia asked. "How so?"

"The elders of its villages were convinced that there was only a single great consciousness in all the universe, a consciousness that was free to roam through all space and all time, backward and forward, not only over all of this world but through all the hundreds and millions and hundreds of millions of worlds, from the beginning of time to its very end. You know the little signs Ienbar makes on his bark scrolls about each person he buries, up at the burial field? Even fifty years after someone has died here, Ienbar can go to his scrolls and tell you what his name was, where she lived, who were their children, and what work and what good deeds and bad deeds were once remembered about each person in the village. Well, according to those elders, you and I are not really alive—we're not really living our lives here and now as we walk along the path, pushing the branches aside that grow out of the underbrush." She caught and released a branch; it whooshed back behind them. "What we think and feel and experience as our own consciousness, living through moment after moment, is really the one great consciousness reading over our lives, from our birth to our death, as if each one of us were just an entry in Ienbar's scrolls. At whatever here-and-now moment, what you're experiencing as your present aware-ness is just where that consciousness happens to be—what *it's* aware of as it reads you over. But that one great consciousness is the only consciousness there is, now believing it's Rimgia the grain picker, now believing it's Tenuk the plowman, now believ-ing it's Mantice the water-cart driver, now believing it's Naä the singer. While it reads you, of course, it gets wholly involved in everything that happens, in every little detail—the way you might get involved in some song I sang last evening, in the darkness when the fire's coals were almost out, when the song seems more real than the darkness around. But that one consciousness reads through the full life not only of you and me and every human being—it reads the life of every bug and beetle and gnat, of every worm and ant and newt, the life of every hen whose neck you wring for dinner and every kid whose throat you cut to roast; and of every grass blade and every flower and every tree as well. It reads through every good and friendly and helpful deed and happening. It reads through every painful, harmful, and hurtful thing that has fallen to anyone or any creature either by carelessness or conscious evil."

"But what's all this reading of all of us for?" Rimgia laughed. (Naä's notions could sometimes be odder than the questions that prompted them.) "Is it to learn something? To learn what life is about—the lives of gnats and people and flowers and hens and bugs and goats and trees?"

"That's where the theory gets rather strange," Naä explained. "What that great single consciousness-that-is-the-here-and-now-consciousness-of-all-of-us is trying to learn is what life . . . *isn't*: the greater Life that is its own complete totality. You see, after it's finished reading you, it knows that, however important and interesting and involving the various parts of your life were, that is not *really* what Life is about. But only after it's finished reading through the whole of your life, only after it's actually become you and experienced the length of your years, can it know that for certain. And only after it's finished reading me does it know that my life was not the essence either. And so it goes, with every wise old hermit and every mindless mosquito and every great king who rules a nation. And when it's completely finished with all the things it could possibly read, from the life of every sickly infant dead an hour after birth to every hundred-year-old hag who finally drops into death, from every minnow eaten by a frog to every elk springing from a mountain peak and every eagle soaring above them, to every chick dead in the egg three days before it hatches, only then will it be released from its reading to be its wondrous and glorious self, with the great and universal simplicity that it's learned. That's what those elders thought—and that's what they told their people."

The two young women walked silently.

Then Naä went on: "I must say, though I found it an interesting idea, I'm not sure I believe it. I think I'd rather take the nothing."

"Really?" Rimgia asked, surprised; for as an idea to turn over and consider, like the petals of a black-eyed Susan, it had intrigued her. "Why?"

"Well, when I was a little girl, playing in the yard of my parents' hut in Calvicon, and I'd think about such things—death, I mean—the idea of all that nothing after my little bit of a life used to frighten me—terribly, so that my mouth would dry, my heart would hammer, and I'd sweat like I'd just run a race. From time to time I'd almost collapse with my fear of it; there it waited, at the end of my life, to swallow me into it. Nothing. Nothing for millions of billions of years more than the millions of billions of years that are no part at all of all the years there are. Really, when such thoughts were in my head, I couldn't sing a note! But then a little later, when I heard this other idea, it occurred to me that really, *it* was much more frightening! If I—and you—really are that great consciousness and really are one, that means 'I'—the great consciousness that I am—must go through *everyone's* pain, *everyone's* agonies, *everyone's* dying and death, animal as well as human, bird and fish, beast and plant, and all the unfairness and cruelty and pain in the universe: not only yours and mine, but the pain of every bug anyone ever squashed and every worm that comes out of the ground in the rain to dry up on a rock." Naä chuckled. "Well, it's all I can do to get through my own life. I mean, doesn't it sound *exhausting*?"

They walked in the dust a while. Finally Rimgia said (because this was something she had thought about many times before): "I wish I could change places with thee, Naä—could just put my feet into the prints thy feet leave on the path and from there go where thou goest, see what thou seest. I wish I could become thee! And give up being me."

"Whatever for?" Naä knew how much the youngsters were in awe of her; but whenever it came out in some open way, it still surprised her.

"Once every three years," Rimgia said, "I'll go on a wander for a week—maybe tramp far enough to find a village so much like Çiron that I might as well not have started out. Or I'll sit in the woods and dream. And the most exciting thing that'll actually happen will be that I see a Winged One from Hi-Vator pass overhead. But thou hast been to dozens of lands, Naä. And thou wilt go to dozens more. Thou hast learned the songs of peoples all over the world and thou hast come to sing them here to us— and thou makest us, for the moments of thy song, soar like men and women with wings—while all I do is go home from the fields to cook for my brother and father." She laughed a little, because she was a good girl, who loved her father and brother even as she complained of them. "So now thou knowst why, for a while at any rate, I would be thee!"

"Well," Naä said, "I must cook for myself, and though most days I like it, some days are lonely. Nor is the lean-to I live in all that comfortable." Even saying it, Naä was thinking that she wouldn't change her life with a king's. For the friendly, gregarious, and curious folk of Çiron made real loneliness a difficult state to maintain. "Right now, though, I've got to see Ienbar in his shack at the burial meadow. I told him I would come by today, once the water cart passed. But I shall see you tomorrow— and who knows, maybe make a song about a wonderfully interesting redheaded woman who, while she cooks for her brother and father, takes her questions to . . . the very edge of death and back!"

"Thou'rt the one going to the burial field," Rimgia said, pretending not to be desperately pleased at the prospect of being the subject of a song. "And thou'rt the one who has heard all the strange ideas of the world—not I. Yes, I would change places

with thee if I could, Naä—though if those foreign elders' strange
idea is right, it means that someday I may *have* to live your life,
and you mine—that we might change places yet!"

"Or that we already have," Naä said. "In fact that's one reason, I guess, I have trouble with it. But when I see you tomorrow,
I'll tell you what Ienbar says. That's next best to going to see
him, isn't it?"

"And some time soon thou must come and eat with us. And
sing this new song for Abrid and my father—Father likes thy
singing almost as much as I do."

And, laughing, the two women parted to go their different
ways through the town.

When he reached the first field, Rahm paused to fill his
chest with the scent of grain under hot sun and to listen to the
roar of crickets, to grass spears brushing one another, and to
sparrows and crows and jays, which all, with another breath,
would again become what at any other time he would think of
as silence.

Halfway across the field, Tenuk the plowman looked up,
halted his animal, and waved. Ahead of the plow, the mule was
the hue of cut slate. A distant ear twitched—and waving back,
Rahm imagined the rasping bluebottle worrying at the eyelashes
of that diligent, tractable beast.

With more humor than reproach, Rahm thought: Tenuk's
only three days farther along than when I left. They've missed
me here.

Beets grew to Rahm's right. Kale stretched to his left. He
walked along one field's edge. The earth was soft. Yellowing
grasses brushed and scratched his sweating calves. Moist soil
gave and sprang back to his bare soles. Even as he tried to take
in all that was familiar about his fields, his country, his home,
one new bit of the familiar was wiped away with the next.

He turned onto the path toward town. Moments later, trotting
out under lowering oak branches, he saw the woman at the stone

well halt, clay jug at her hip; she recognized him—and smiled. Rahm grinned back as four children careened from behind the door hanging off the hut across the way, a dog yapping among them. (Three years ago and a head and a half shorter, in her dirty hands the eldest of those children had held that dog up to him as a puppy, and Rahm had said, "Why not call him 'Mouse'? A big mouse—that's what he looks like," and the girl and the others had laughed, because it was such a silly idea—calling a dog a mouse!) They ran toward him, not seeing him. As they broke around him, he caught up the youngest and swung her to his shoulder as she squealed. And suddenly he was among them, the others jumping around him and clapping. The little one grappled his long hair, and her squeal became laughter that, somewhere in it, had his name. And he said all theirs, and their mothers', then theirs again ("Hello, Jallet. Hey there, Wraga . . . How is thy mother, Kenisa? Jallet, dost thy fat old man Mantice still waste his time with the water cart? I did not see thy uncle Gargula in the fields today. Perhaps he's still doing some work for thy mother? But you must not let Veema work him too hard! Tell her I told you so too! Let Gargula get back to the beet fields, where he's needed! Wraga, so long . . ."), and called them all out again in farewell, because it pleased him—almost surprised him—that after a week in the field, those names that he had not thought of over all the adventurous days, names that he might as well have forgotten, came back so quickly to his tongue. A step more, and he set the little girl down. She grabbed hold of his forefinger now, tugging and calling for another ride. But Rahm laughed and freed himself. And they were running on.

Where she'd carried her loom out into her yard, to sit cross-legged on the ground, Hara looked up from her strings and shuttles and separator plank and tamping paddle. A breeze lifted the ends of the leaf-green rag tied around hair through which white flowed like currents in a stream; it moved the hem of her brown skirt back from browner ankles. Her breasts were flat and long, the aureoles wide around dark dugs. Her eyes were black and glittering within their clutch of wrinkles, which deepened when she saw him. "Hello to thee, young Rahm!"

Rahm came over to stand behind her and look down. Crouching now, he frowned at her pattern: blue, orange, green, cut away sharply by the unwoven strings. "What makest thou there?"

"Who knows," Hara said, her smile more full of spaces than teeth. "Perhaps it's something thou mayest wear thyself one day, when they decide in the council house that a bit of youth's foolishness has gone out of thee and more of the world's wisdom has settled between thy ears."

That made Rahm laugh. He patted the weaver's shoulder—and stood, still able to feel where the girl, gone now, had sat on his.

Hara slammed down the treadle. The shuttle ran through quivering threads, drawing gray yarn.

Rahm loped off between stone and thatch buildings. Toward him from an alley end, an ox tugged a creaking cart. The side slats were woven with wide leather strips, the bed piled with rocks.

Its two drivers, man and boy, were gray from cracked, callused toes to bushy beard (on the elder) and hair. The man raised an arm to Rahm even as he frowned—as though the rock dust powdering his face and beard made a fog hard to see through. But the boy, who held a sack on his lap, suddenly pushed it to the bench, stood in his seat, and called out: "Rahm!"

Stopping, Rahm grinned. "Hey, Abrid!"

Washed free of quarry powder, Kern's hair and beard would be the same powder gray. But after a splash from the bucket, Abrid's braids would be as red as his sister's. And because I know that, thought Rahm, that's how I know I'm home!

Kern halted the cart with a grunt. His frown deepened. He nodded to Rahm. But Kern's frown was as welcoming, Rahm knew, as any smile.

Abrid jumped down from the bench and seized Rahm's wrist the way a much younger child might, though the grit on his palms made the boy's hand feel like an old man's. "You will work again with us at the stone pits, Rahm?"

"No, Abrid." Rahm shook his head. "I will stay in the fields."

Inside the house Rimgia had put the dough cakes on the hot stones down at the fire and was tossing handfuls of cut turnips and sliced squash and chopped radishes into the bowl of lettuces she had torn up, when something in the voices outside caught her. She turned from the counter and stepped across the floor mat; she needed more water. As she went, she hooked two fingers in the handle of the jar sitting there, but it was already half full. Holding the jar, she pulled in the door with the other hand and stepped out onto the porch over the high sill (which kept the heavy winter rains from coming up to the door—Abrid had better fix that loose plank soon). She looked out, to call: "Father, Abrid, come in and get your—!"

Her father, Kern, still sitting on the cart seat, and her brother, Abrid, already standing, looked around.

She saw Rahm.

Reaching up to run her hand, still moist from the water in which she'd washed the vegetables, across her forehead and into her hair, Rimgia set the water pitcher on the porch planks and, with a surge of delight, rushed barefoot down the steps. "Rahm! Thou wilt stay to eat with us?" Again a hand to her hair to brush back some from her forehead (yes, Rahm thought, the same red as her brother's beneath his work dust); but her face was full of a smile that wanted to get even bigger, wanted to swallow all the sunlight and breeze around them. She wiped her other hand on her shift's hip. "Come, stay—there's more than enough! And thou canst tell us of all thy adventures in thy wander. Did you get back this morning? Or last night?"

"I only tramped in by the southern fields ten minutes past, and glimpsed Tenuk stalking his mule. I'll come and see thee soon, Rimgia. But I haven't even told Ienbar I'm here."

Abrid jumped down and came around the cart—he almost

bumped the corner, but swung his hip away—to stand near the steps. He lifted the pitcher, frowned into it, then poured some into his hand. He splashed his face, threw another handful against his chest. Water fell to darken the dust on one knee, the toes of one foot. Sitting on the step now, with two fingers together, he wiped his light lashes free of dirt. "Hey, *why* wilt thou not stay, Rahm?"

"I will, but some other time, boy!"

"Well, then." Rimgia went to the cart bench to take down the sack Abrid had left on the seat. (In it, Rahm knew, would be pears and some melons Abrid had gathered from the orchards and fields up near the quarry. Yes, he was home.) As she did so, the scent of the baked dough cakes came from the door. Rahm smiled—and Rimgia wondered if the scent was what he smiled at. (How many dozens of them had she seen Rahm, now sitting on the well wall, now walking across the commons, wolf down in the last year?) "Then thou must come back soon."

Climbing from the wagon beside her, her father turned and clapped Rahm's shoulder. And still frowned, silently—but silence was Kern's way.

Rahm said: "When I've seen Ienbar, I'll return."

"Thou mayest see Naä there," Rimgia said. "Earlier, when I came with her from the fields, she too was off to talk with him." These people here, my brother, my father, and Rahm (Rimgia thought), perhaps we *are* all a single consciousness and only believe ourselves separate, so that we are closest to the truth at a moment like this when we almost forget it. The notion, odd as it was, made her smile even more than the pleasure of her friend's return.

And with all the smiling and nodding and grinning and waving—that seemed the only comfortable thing to do (or frowning, if you were Kern) when you'd been away and come back—Rahm left his friends and their father.

There was another young man in that village, who, though he had lost his parents during the same autumnal fever that had killed Rahm's almost a decade ago, was as different from Rahm as a young man could be—for, though likely he loved it as much, he had a very different view of Çiron.

Qualt hauled a great basket of yellow rinds and chicken feathers and milk slops and eggshells and corn shucks from his wagon, to go, stiff-legged and leaning back against it, over the mossy stones to overturn it, rushing and bouncing down, at the ravine precipice into the soggy and steaming gully. A lithe and wiry youngster of twenty-two, given to bursts of intense conversation, long periods of introspection, and occasional smiles that startled his face but would linger there half a morning, he was the town garbage collector.

And Qualt was in love with red-haired Rimgia.

Qualt stood at the rocky rim, the empty basket in his big hands. (Unlike Rahm, Qualt's hands and feet were the only things you might call big about him; oh, yes, and perhaps his ears, if his hair was tied back—though it wasn't now. Really, he was a rather slight young fellow.) Qualt breathed slowly, not smelling, really, what lay among the rocks below.

A few weeks before, you see, when a number of Çiron's young people, Qualt, Rimgia, Abrid, and Rahm among them, had gone for a full-moon swim at the quarry lake, they'd all sung songs (Rahm the loudest, Qualt the best), most of them learned from Naä, and cooked sweet dough on sticks over the open fire (the way Ienbar had suggested they try) till very late, and finally gone chastely to sleep. Qualt and Rimgia had slept, yes, on the same blanket: Qualt's blanket. Yes, Rimgia and Qualt—head to heel, heel to head—the water a silver sheet beside them. Qualt had woken just at dawn and a bit before the others, to find Rimgia's arm over his calf and her cheek pressed against the calloused ball of his foot and his wide toes. Her eyes had been closed and her breath had made the tiniest whistle he'd almost not heard for the sound of the current, the splash of small fish, and the morning's first birds. But he'd lain staring down over his hip, afraid to move lest she wake, his heart hammering harder and harder, so that it was all he could do to pay attention to the feel of—yes, he could move them without disturbing her—the toes on his right foot in the copper torrent, the cataract, the cool swirl of her hair.

Later he'd decided she was a strange girl. But when, in all the nights between then and today, he'd drifted off to sleep, he kept finding a dark tenderness among his thoughts of her.

Suddenly Qualt smacked the basket bottom, turned it up to peer within its smelly slats, then dragged it behind him, rasping on rock, toward the dozen others that stood around the end of his wagon.

Rahm walked through the village, wondering at how well he knew his home's morning-to-morning and evening-to-evening cycle.

In hours, Rahm thought, the sun will drop behind the trees, and the western houses will unroll shadows over the streets. Then at dawn the sun will push between the eastern dwellings to stripe the dust with copper. He strolled on, hugely content.

Reaching the burial meadow, Rahm glanced over the unmarked graves. (But Ienbar knew the name and location of each man, each woman, and each child laid here time out of memory, and kept all the scrolls about them.) The visiting singer was coming toward the meadow up the road from the fields.

A chamois mantle hung forward over one shoulder but was pushed back from the other. A chain of shells held her short skirt low on her hips. A strap ran down between her breasts, holding something to her back. Its carved wooden head slanted behind her neck. Rahm knew it was her harp. "And hello to thee, Naä."

"Rahm, you're back! Are you going to see Ienbar? I was on my way to visit him, but I stopped at my lean-to to replace three of my harp strings—"

"Yes, Rimgia told me, only moments past," Rahm said. "Kern and Abrid were just home from the stone pits."

"And in your wander, what'd you see?" She fell in beside him. "That's what I want to hear about!"

"Naä"—Rahm looked at the ground, where olive tufts poked from the path dust—"thou makest fun of me."

"What do you mean, make fun?"

"Thou, who hast traveled over all the world, asketh me what I have seen that thou hast not, after a simple week's wander?"

"Oh, Rahm, I wasn't making fun of you. I'm interested!"

"But thou hast come all the way from Calvicon with thy songs and tales. What can I have seen in a week that thou in a dozen years hast not?"

"But that's what I want you to tell me!"

He saw her glance over to catch his expression (he was still pretending interest in the tufted ridge of the path) and saw her surprise that his expression was a smile. "But now thou seest," he said, looking at her again, "*I* am making fun of *thee*!"

"We'll go to Ienbar together, and while we go, you'll tell me!"

"Naä, I saw antelopes come down across hazed-over grasses to drink at yellow watering holes at dawn. I found a village of folk who wove and plowed and quarried as we do, and live in huts and houses that might well have been built on the same plans as ours—though the only words in the whole of their language I could make out, after a day with them, were the words for 'star,' 'ear,' and 'tomato plant.' On the fifth day, as the rituals instruct us, I ate nothing from the time I woke, but drank only water, and stopped three times to purify myself with wise words. And when the sun went down, still fasting, I composed myself for sleep—hoping for a mystic dream."

She grinned. "Did you have one?"

"I dreamt," Rahm said gravely, "that I walked by a great, rushing stream. And as the sun rose and I ambled along beside the current, the water began to sparkle. Then, in the dream, a little branch feeding into the water lay before me, so I decided to wade across to the other side. I stepped in. The water was cold at first, but a few steps on, as the water reached my thighs and finally my waist, it grew warm. Then even warmer. And warmer. I woke"—he chuckled—"to find I had pissed myself, the way I used to when I was a boy in bed, a couple of times a week, even unto my fifteenth year—and my mother would become angry and say I made the shack stink." The chuckle became a laugh. "Then she'd make me go sleep out in the tool cabin. But that, I'm afraid, was all there was of mystic dreaming!"

"Oh, Rahm—well, you'd better not tell Ienbar that." Naä laughed outright. "Then again, maybe you should. He just might find something in it—if he just doesn't find it funny too."

"Then I found a very real, very un-mystic"—Rahm laughed again—"stream and washed myself; and went on my way. And this morning," he finished, "I was attacked by a wild prairie lion and wrestled with her, to break her neck with my arm. Then I came home here."

Naä shook her head. "Rahm, you folk amaze me."

He looked at her as they walked, his amber eyes full of questioning.

"Three months ago, when I first came here, I'd never have believed such people as you existed." Naä paused a moment, as if searching within for her answer. "Sometimes I still don't believe that you do."

"Why, Naä?"

"Rahm, I've traveled to lots of places, through lots of lands. I know songs and stories from even more lands and places than I've visited—more lands and places than you could imagine. But most of the songs and stories I know are about fights and wars, about love that dies, about death and betrayal and revenge. Yet here there is . . ." She raised her shoulders and looked up at the branches, whose early summer green had begun to go smoky after the first bright hue of spring. "But I can't even name it." She let her shoulders fall. "Here I go out and sing to Rimgia and to the other women in the fields. I come and exchange songs and tales with Ienbar, or go sit and talk with Hara over her shuttles. Sometimes I eat with you in the evening or take long walks alone in the foothills of the mountains. If any woman of the village comes around a corner of the path, my heart leaps as happily as if it were my own sister coming to meet me. If any man of the village crosses my path, we smile and call to each other with the same warmth I'd call to my own brother." She glanced at him, then glanced away. "Whenever a group of you get together after work in the evening or before a council meeting, and everyone turns to me and asks me to sing . . . well, I've never sung better!" Naä looked down at the dust. "The only thing any of you say there is to fear in the whole of this land are the flying creatures from Hi-Vator. And no one can even remember why that is, so even that's awfully easy to forget; and since I've been here, I've only once seen what might have been a silhouette of one against some moonshot clouds, anyway.

"Rahm, the last time I was in my own father's hut in Calvicon, when I and my four brothers and my sister were all together, it was when my stepmother, who had been so good to us once my real mother died, was so ill. We sat around with my father beside my stepmother's sickbed, talking together about our childhood. And how joyful and wonderful and loving and free it had been, because of him, because of her. And as we sat there, talking softly and laughing quietly in the firelight, I kept thinking, '*Nobody* has a childhood as wonderful as we're now all saying we did. *I* certainly didn't.' For, like any other parents, however much they loved us, often they had been bored with us, and sometimes they slapped us, and now and again they were sullen and angry that we weren't interested in the things that concerned them—while they were wholly oblivious to what we felt was so important. Yet we all—my brothers, my sister, and me too—went on talking about that time as if the moments of love and concern—my stepmother's smile at a chipmunk my youngest brother caught for a pet, the corn cakes my father baked for a friend of mine's party when I asked him, or the songs the two of them sang together just once, after dark by our bedside—had been, indeed, the whole of it. And while the flames fell back into the embers, it struck me: this isn't a story of some real childhood that we're telling of now. No, this story is a present we're making for my worried old father and my sick, sick stepmother, for having been two very, very fine parents indeed—and who'd certainly given us a childhood fine *enough*. But once I realized what sort of present it was, I was happy to sit there for another hour, completing that present, weaving it together with my brothers and sister. I was happy to make it for them, happy to give it to them; and I went to sleep afterwards content that we'd done it. And three days later, I left on another journey, knowing I would never see that fine old woman again, and that there was a good chance I might not ever see my father again either—but thinking no more about the story we'd given them, those few nights ago, than anyone ever thinks about a present you've given gladly to someone who deserves it." Naä was silent a few steps more. "At least I didn't think about it until after I'd been here, oh, three weeks or a month. Because, you see, Rahm, you've all here given a present to me.

"You've given me—not another childhood; but rather a time like the *story* of childhood we put together that evening to help my parents through their final years. And till now I wouldn't have believed a time or a place like that was possible!" They walked on together over the warm earth. "It's beautiful here, Rahm. So beautiful that if I were anywhere else and tried to sing of this beauty, the notes would stick in my throat, the words would stall on my tongue—and I'd start to cry."

They had reached a stretch of green graves and stopped to gaze at where stone slanted from the smoky grass. "Yes," Rahm said after a moment. "It is beautiful, Naä. Thou art right."

Naä took a long, long breath. "So you brought a puma back with you. Did you leave it down with Kern and Rimgia? I wonder what sort of stew Ienbar will make out of *that*—before he puts the claws on his necklace."

"I didn't bring it back," Rahm said. "I gave it to a friend."

"You gave it to someone in the village before you brought it to show Ienbar?" She laughed. "Now that's the first thing I think you've ever done that's shocked me!"

"Not a friend in the village. This was a man who helped me on my journey. As I fought the cat, a Winged One flew close. This man frightened it away with a powergun."

Naä turned to look at him. "A powergun? In my home, Calvicon, a man came through once with a powergun. He used it to do scary tricks—set a bushel of hay on fire—in the market square. But he told my big brother, who was his friend for a while, that they could be really dangerous, if used improperly. Where was he from?"

Rahm shrugged. "He wore a black cloak. And black gloves. And a black hood. There was a silver crow on his shoulder and on the sling that held his gun. His name was Kire, and I—"

"Myetra . . ." Naä's forehead wrinkled.

"Possibly," Rahm said. "But why dost thou look so strangely at this?"

"Crow, cloak, and hood, in black and silver, are the uniform of officers in the Myetran army. What would such a soldier be doing here—so close you could leave him in the morning and be here by noon?" She walked, considering. "And with a power-gun. Were there others with him?"

"I saw only the one alone. He said he was a wanderer like me, out to see our land."

"With a powergun? It doesn't sound good at all."

"By why, Naä? We do not know them."

"Calvicon knows them," she said. "And what they know isn't good. We'd better tell Ienbar, anyway."

They had reached the center of the field.

"If he is at home." Rahm looked around. He cupped his hands to shout. "Ienbar, I am here! Where art thou?"

On the meadow's far side, a door in a board wall between two trees flew open. A figure lurched out. White hair and white beard jutted in small braids. "Rahm!" the old man shouted and began to rush bandy-legged across the grass. Round his neck jangled half a dozen thongs tied with animal teeth. His long arms were heavy with copper bracelets. At his waist, a leather apron was hemmed with metal pieces worked with symbols and designs. Metal circled his ankle above a skinny foot. Several huge brass hoops hung from his ears, their thickness distending pierced lobe and rim.

Ienbar threw his clinking arms around Rahm, stepped back, then embraced him again. "My son!" he said in a voice cracked and crackling, then stepped back, while Rahm steadied Ienbar's scrawny shoulders in his big hands. "Thou hast come safely from thy wandering." Turning to Naä, the old man seized her wrist. "And thou hast come too, my daughter, to sing and play for me. It is good to see thee this fine day."

"It's always good to see you, Ienbar," Naä said. "Just like it's good to have Rahm back with us."

"Come, the both of you," Ienbar declared. "Well, boy, where hast thou been and what didst thou see?"

In the hut, they sat on mats Rahm tossed across small benches while Ienbar heated his pot. Shelves about them were stacked with bones and parchment scrolls, bits of beautiful uncut stone, lengths of painted wood, dried lizards, stuffed bats, and the mounted skeletons of various ground birds and field creatures. Some of the village children still entered here with fear—but to Rahm it had been his home since the death of his parents when he was fifteen.

"What a dream!" Ienbar chuckled. "What a dream, indeed! Yes, I recall that river, from the first years thou hadst moved in with me here, I do." Ienbar grinned at a reproving look from Rahm. "Well, I do! Sometimes, I think, thy sleeping corner still smells of it—and I've told thee before, I don't mind. I rather like it. A bit of dung, a bit of urine, fresh-turned earth, and new cut grass—those are good smells!" Ienbar broke a small bone and, on the pot's rim, tapped the marrow into the broth. "The smells I don't like, now—charred meat, rotten vegetables, and the stench of clogged water that should be running free." Ienbar turned to serve Naä, then Rahm; for himself, at last, he filled a third bowl. "Well, well, what a dream, what a stream!"

Rahm took one sip; then, bowl between his knees, he began on the rest of his wander. But when he reached the encounter with the Myetran, the old man's face wrinkled.

Ienbar put his soup on the hearth flags by his big-knuckled

toes with their thickened nails, sat back, and moved his tongue about in his mouth without opening his lips.

Questioningly, Rahm lowered black brows. "Why art thou and Naä so concerned about these Myetrans?"

Ienbar sucked his gums. "Oh, sometimes one hears stories—"

Naä interrupted: "I'll tell you a story, Rahm." She looked across her bowl at the old man. "Ienbar, in Calvicon, we hear stories too. And the stories of Myetra were never good. I told you about my brother's friend, Rahm? Well, he said that his powergun was from Myetra. And he told stories of the destruction that went on there—between man and man, between one race and another. You have your flying neighbors at Hi-Vator? Well, Myetra is on the sea, and once there were people who lived and swam in the water, and could breathe under it like fish do in the ponds and the stream in the quarry. But Myetra fought them and made slaves of them and finally killed them. And there are no more waterfolk around the Myetran shore. That's the story my brother's friend told us. Then one day, long after he had told us this, my brother's friend disappeared—and the tale that came back was that he and another man had gotten angry at each other, gotten into a fight, and finally my brother's friend had used the powergun to kill the other man. He disappeared the next day, and we never saw him again."

"To *kill*?" Rahm asked.

"Yes, there have been stories of such things before." Ienbar nodded.

"To frighten a Winged One, yes. But why to kill—and another man? Human beings do not kill each other. Thou killest a goat to roast it, an ox to butcher it. But not a human being."

"If they come by here," Ienbar said, "we must keep out of their way."

"But this did not seem to be a brutal man that I met—not a man who would kill. He frightened away the Winged One. He spoke to me as to a friend."

"That is a good sign, I suppose. Perhaps there's nothing to

fear." Ienbar shrugged, clinking, to pick up his bowl and stare across it at the flames that, because of the open window, were so diminished by the Çironian sun. "Perhaps . . . after all, it is only a single soldier wandering through the country."

"I think that's what he was," Rahm said, and raised his bowl to drink. "Yes," he said between sips. "That is what he was."

"I hope you're right," Naä said less confidently. Then she swung the harp to her lap to pluck a run on the lower strings.

chapter three

Rahm slept deeply, one hand low on his belly. His lids showed white crescents between black lashes. Outside the shack the air cooled. For a while, despite the warmth, it seemed a light rain might come; but at last, without a drop's falling, the moon's curve came out, as thin as what showed of Rahm's eyes.

The clouds moved away, and the night air dried in the new moon's light as if it had been full sun.

Then sound jabbed into sleep.

It grew till it ripped sleep apart—and Rahm sat upright to smash his hands' heels against his head, then again, trying to find his ears to cover them . . . against something he could not, at this moment, distinguish between pain and sound.

Ienbar leaned against the fireplace, shaking, his mouth opening and closing. His arm flailed about, but the clinking of his bracelets was lost in the wailing that filled Rahm's ears with pressure enough to burst them.

Rahm lurched to his feet and staggered to the door, pulling

it open. The sound—because it *was* a sound—came from across the village. As Rahm stepped outside, it became a booming voice:

> SURRENDER, PEOPLE OF ÇIRON!
> SURRENDER TO THE FORCES OF MYETRA!

Then silence.

The absence of sound stung Rahm's ears.

He tried to blink the water out of his eyes.

The wailing began again. Anticipating pain, Rahm stepped back into the doorway as the voice churned through the darkness:

> PEOPLE OF ÇIRON!
> SURRENDER TO THE FORCES OF MYETRA!

Behind him, Ienbar was crying.

Rahm sprinted out onto the path, shaking his head to clear it while he ran, to throw off the pain and the steady high hum, loud as any roaring, that covered all else. Leaves pulled away, and the village lights flickered. As he passed the first houses, he heard distraught voices. Certainly no villager still slept!

To the east, light flared. Then another flare. Another. Three lights fanned the dark, lowering, till they struck—blindingly—among the huts.

Rahm's first panicked thought was that the shacks would burst into fire under the glare. But apparently the lights were for illumination, or for the terror such illumination in the midst of darkness might bring.

Rahm's hearing had almost returned to normal.

Somewhere drums thudded.

Naä dreamed she had stumbled into her harp. Only it was huge. And as she tried to fight through the strings, they began to ring and sing and siren—they were all around her, her arms and head and legs, till the harp itself broke—and she woke, pulling herself out of her sleeping blankets and scrambling from under the lean-to's edge, disoriented at the incredible sound.

Qualt had his own house, but slept outside that night with his back against his wagon's wheel, because the weather was warm and the night was easy.

We won't say that as he lay there, breathing across his large, loose fingers, relaxed before his face, he was actually dreaming of Rimgia. But when, earlier that night, he'd first lain down on this blanket to stretch out beside his garbage wagon, certainly he'd been thinking of her.

For recently sleep had become an entrance into the part of him that was becoming aware that the shape and limit of his tenderness toward her could be learned only from the thought of her hand in his hands, his face against her belly, her lap against his cheek, his mouth against her neck. So when later, the noise came, sirening in the dark, it tore him out of something comforting as a good dream—yet without sound or image or idea to it, as dreams have.

Qualt woke, the sound around his head a solid thing. He rocked back, buttock banging the cartwheel. His hand went off the blanket into grass and gravel. Scrabbling to sit, then to stand, he looked around the darkness. Gauzy light was cut off sharply by the familiar roof of his shack and two trees, rendered wholly strange. He took five steps, stopped—

Then something ahead of him and above darkened the light, the sky—where was it? And how huge was it and what—but before he could ask what it was, it struck him. Hard. And he threw his arms around it, embracing it to keep from falling. And with it, he fell. It was flapping and huge, smelled and moved like a live thing, and was—as he pushed one hand out—surrounded on both sides by a vast, taut membrane, that suddenly ceased to be taut as he struggled in it. Flailing on the ground, in the dark and that single-note scream filling every crevice of the night (but which came neither from him nor from whatever he struggled with), Qualt had two simultaneous impressions. The first was that he'd stumbled into someone else, the two of them had fallen on the ground, and now they were rolling together. The second was that some astonishing beast, with a pelt and an animal scent, was covering him like a puma leaping down at him from a roof or the sky, to fight with him there by his garbage cart—though so far, Qualt realized, he'd been neither bitten nor clawed.

Then the sound stopped—the chattering of twigs and leaves and small stones, because of his ears' ringing, seemed to Qualt to make their own noise now not beneath the two of them, but rather off in some ringing metal pan.

The arms of the thing he fought—for it had arms—suddenly seized him, held him, restrained him. Qualt grasped it back. Distantly he heard breathing, which for a moment he could not tell whether it was his or this other's. Then he felt himself go limp, because suddenly that was easier to do than to keep fighting in the black. Then a voice that was not like any Qualt had ever heard before, because it seemed like a child's, high and breathy, said into his ear, only inches away, at the same time as Qualt scented the breath of a man who had been eating wild onions, so that, if anything, Qualt suddenly felt something familiar in all this strangeness and struggle—because Qualt himself had often walked through the lower mountains, munching the wild onion stalks that grew there:

"Hi-Vator, yes—no! Phew! Çiron, you?"

Rimgia dreamed that somebody, laughing hysterically, thrust a pole into her ear and out the other side of her head, then lifted her by that same pole high into the air, over the glittering stream, and she was afraid she would fall in, only it really hurt to have a pole that deep in your ear.

The pole cracked. She screamed. But before she could fall, she woke in the hut to that incredible sound. Her father, Kern, was already striding about; she saw his shape pass darkly before the hearth embers. Pushing up quickly, a moment later she knelt at Abrid's pallet, shaking him.

"What is it—ow! What?"

"Get up!" she insisted, surprised when she could not hear her own voice for the whining. "Come on!" she shouted, realizing it was a shout only from the feel in her throat. Kern had already opened the door, rushed out—

Rahm neared the common, where men and women had begun to gather. As he sprinted up the side street, someone grabbed his arm, spun him back, hissed: "Rahm!" Then: "Where is Ienbar?"

Bewildered, he stepped back.

"For God's sake, Rahm! Where's Ienbar?"

"Naä? He's . . . at the burial meadow."

"Rahm. We have to leave—all of us. Right now!"

"Leave? But why?"

"The Myetrans are coming! Didn't you hear them? They want you to surrender."

"I heard. Naä, what does this 'surrender' mean?"

"Oh, Rahm!" Then suddenly she was running away into the dark.

Puzzled, Rahm turned back to the gathering in the common.

A few people still dug forefingers in their ears. The drums were louder. From the eastern fields another light struck. Something—a long line of somethings—was moving toward the common. The sweeping beams threw shadows over the beets, the grain, the kale, all bending in the night wind.

Children and mothers and uncles and cousins looked at one another.

"Why do they come across the field? They'll damage the harvest."

"There are so many of them that they couldn't fit on the road."

"Such late visitors, and so many. Will we have food for them all? They walk so strangely . . ."

Grain stalks snapped under the boots in time to the drums. As searchlights swung away, in the inadequate light from the nail paring of a moon, straining to see among the armored figures, Rahm thought to look for his friend from the morning—and thought he saw him there: only a moment later, he saw another tall, cloaked figure. Then another. Among the armed men advancing, a number wore the uniform Kire had worn. Some rode nervous horses; others came on foot. Their capes, despite the wind, hung straight behind them, heavy as night. Above them all, on rolling towers, the searchlights moved forward.

With the others, Rahm waited in the square.

Soon, with their mobile light towers, the soldiers had marched to the common's near edge. The ground was fully lit. Villagers squinted. On a horse stepping about before the visitors, a bearded man in brown leather, wearing a single glove, barked at the short silver rod in his bare hand:

HALT!

Everyone looked up, because the word echoed and reechoed from the black horns high on the moving light towers. The soldiers stopped marching. The drums stilled.

The man with the silver rod rode forward. The villagers fell back. The man spoke again. Again his voice was doubled, like thunder, from the horns:

SURRENDER TO THE FORCES OF MYETRA!

Around Rahm, people looked at one another, puzzled.

Then Kern, the quarryman, who was not really shy—only very quiet—stepped forward.

"Welcome to you," he said uncertainly. Then, which was almost twice as much as Kern ever said, he added: "Welcome, visitors in the night."

"Are you the leader here?" the mounted man demanded.

Kern didn't answer—because, as Rahm knew, Kern wasn't anyone's leader. (He was not even an elder—none of whom, Rahm noticed, seemed to have arrived yet.) Kern frowned back at the villagers behind him.

Someone called out: "No—he's not!"

Which made a dozen people—including Rahm—laugh. Rahm whispered to Mantice, who was standing beside him, "That's Tenuk," though stocky Mantice knew it was plowman Tenuk being funny as much as Rahm did. They both grinned.

"You speak for the people here," the mounted man said, which was funny in itself because Kern probably wouldn't say anything more now. But the man spoke as though he'd heard neither Tenuk's *No* nor the laughter. "You are the leader!" While his horse stepped about, he pushed the silver rod into his shirt, reached down, unfastened his sling, and lifted out his powergun—for a moment it seemed he was going to hand it to Kern as a gift.

Rahm had seen a powergun that morning, but not—really— what it could do.

Flame shot out and smacked Kern just below his shoulder. Kern slammed backward four feet—without either stepping or falling: upright, his feet just slid back across the grass—the left one was even slightly off the ground. Blood fountained a dozen feet forward. The horse's flank was splattered and the animal reared twice, then a third time. Rahm was close enough to hear the meat on Kern's chest bubble and hiss as he fell, twisting to the side. One of Kern's arms was gone.

When it hit the ground, Kern's remaining hand moved in the grass. Kern's heavy fingers opened, then closed, with not even grass blades in them. Kern's face was gone too—and half Kern's head.

The bearded man lowered the powergun from where the retort had jerked the barrel into the air. "Your leader has been killed. So will you all be killed—unless you announce your surrender!"

Rahm felt a vast and puzzling absence inside him. Nothing

in it seemed like any sort of sense he could hold to. Then something began to grow in that senseless absence. It grew slowly. But he felt it growing. At the same time, something—a strange understanding—began to grow in the face of the bearded man on his horse, who raised his gun overhead.

Suddenly the man turned sharply in his saddle and barked back at the troops:

"They refuse to surrender! Attack!"

Though he had learned far back to fight well, like many big men, Uk did not like fighting. Uncountable campaigns ago, he'd also learned that little Mrowky actually gloried in the insult, the attack, the pummeling given and received, the recovery, the reattack. Mrowky could make as much conversational jollity at losing in a melee as he could at winning.

Since men—and sometimes women—so often feel obliged to start fights with big men, Uk had grown grateful for Mrowky's willingness, even eagerness, to jump in when others, to prove themselves, picked quarrels with him in strange towns and taverns. Since people tended not to start fights with runty men like Mrowky (who enjoyed the fight so much), hanging out with broad-shouldered, beer-bellied Uk was a way to guarantee a certain frequency of entertainment—possibly it was the core of their friendship. For both were different enough from each other to preclude close feelings in any situation other than war.

Uk had an expansive, gentle humor he used largely to mask from his fellows a real range of information and some thoughtful speculation, while Mrowky was simply a loud, stupid little man, who'd been called and cursed by just those words enough times by enough people so that, if he did not actually believe they were true, he knew there was *something* to them. Thus the friendship of the big soldier, who was also smart, flattered Mrowky. Both could complain about each other in fiery terms, starred with scatology and muddied with proto-religious blasphemies.

But they were devoted.

Perhaps some of that devotion came from the knowledge both shared, that their time in the Myetran army had taught them: life in the midst of battle was on another plane entirely from that in which relationships could be parsed (a concept Uk would understand) or parceled out (an idea Mrowky might follow), analyzed, or made rational.

With ten other soldiers, Mrowky and Uk had been stationed just along the turnoff at the common's south corner. (Other units of a dozen each had been deployed at seven more points around the green.) When the first villagers hurried by, still unsteady from the grating whine of the high speakers and more or less oblivious to the soldiers (basically because they were just not used to seeing soldiers standing quietly in the shadow), light from an opened door spilled over the flags.

A young redheaded woman passed through it as a young redheaded man—clearly a brother or a cousin—came up beside her. They disappeared, displaced by others rushing to join the villagers gathering on the grass. But Mrowky had given Uk an elbow in the forearm; and in the darkness, his breathing had increased to a tempo Uk knew meant the little man now had the grin that said, "I like that girl—she's hot!"

When the lights had rolled onto the common, Uk and Mrowky had moved up to the edge of the illuminated space, per orders. As, with his microphone, Nactor had ridden out to address the villagers, Uk wondered, as he did so often, just out of sight, whether the populace ever really saw them or not. Just how aware were the stunned and disoriented peasants of the soldiers in their armor, waiting for the word?

In two years, Mrowky and Uk had been through this maneuver seventeen times in seventeen villages. It had taken the first half dozen for Uk to realize that it did not matter whether the villagers surrendered or not; the attack came in either case. Over those half-dozen times, Uk had listened to Nactor's amplified address, watched the elimination of the spokesman (that's how it was referred to: though in half a dozen villages now, the spokesman had been a woman), and awaited the final order with a growing distaste—till, by the seventh time, he'd begun to block out the whole thing.

Over the first ten times (which is how many times it had taken Mrowky to learn what Uk had learned in six), Mrowky had watched the process with hypnotic fascination, awed at its duplicity, its daring, its efficacy. But his attention span would have been strained by any more; so now he too gave no more mind to the details than did the other soldiers.

When the attack sounded, you pulled out your sword, moved forward, and began to swing. You tried not to remember who or what you hit. A lot of blood spurted on your armor and got in the cracks, so that you got sticky at knees and elbows and shoulders; otherwise it was pretty easy. The villagers were naked— most of them—and scared and not expecting it.

Among his first encounters, Uk, out of what he'd thought was humanitarianism, had—with some forethought—not always swung and cut to kill. It seemed fitting to give the pathetic creatures at least a chance to live. Three days later, though, he'd seen what happened to the ones who were just badly wounded: the long loud deaths, the maggoty gashes, the bone-breaking fevers, the cracked lips of the dying. After that, from the same humanitarianism, he'd used his skills to become as deadly as he could with each blade swing at the screaming, clamoring folk—who simply had to be decimated.

That was orders.

Indeed, there was some skill to it—like avoiding the flesh-burning power beams lancing through the mayhem from the mounted officers. Best thing to do (Uk had explained to Mrowky a long time back, when the little guy'd gotten a burn on his right hip) was to glance up from the carnage now and then and keep Kire's horse a little before you, not drifting too far to the left or the right of it—since the mounted lieutenants had the sense (most of them) to avoid powergunning down each other.

You fought.

And you tried not to remember individual slashes and cuts you dealt out to bare shoulders and ribs and necks. (After the diseases and lingering deaths among the wounded in that first campaign, Uk tried for lots of necks.) Sometimes, though, an incident would tear itself free in the web of perception and refuse to sink back into the reds and blacks and chaotic grays and screams and crashes and howls that were the night.

When what happened next stopped happening—

But it was too violent and too painful for Rahm to recall with clarity.

He remembered walking backward, shouting, then—when Tenuk fell against him, like a bubbling roast left too long on the spit and so hot he burned Rahm's arms—screaming. He remembered his feet's uneasy purchase on the flags because of the blood that sluiced them. He remembered a dark-glazed crock smashing under a horse hoof. (With the soldiers, horror spread the village.) He remembered running to the town's edge, to find the gravefield shack aflame.

Ienbar had called, then shouted, then shrieked, trying to get past the fire from the mounted soldiers' muzzles; then Rahm hadn't been able to see Ienbar at all for the glowing smoke, and there'd been the smell of all sorts of things burning: dried thatch, wood, bedding, charred meat. Rahm had run forward toward the fire till the heat, which had already blinded him, made him— the way someone with a whip might make you—back away, turn away, run away, through the town that, as his sight came back under his singed brows, with the chaos and the screams around him, was an infernal parody of his village.

Uk pulled his sword free to turn in the light from one of the towers, parked by an uncharacteristically solid building with a stone foundation. Something was wrong with Uk's knee; it had been throbbing on and off all last week; for three days now it had felt better, but then, only minutes ago, some soldier and some peasant, brawling on the ground in the dark, had rolled into him. Uk had cried out: it was paining him again. Turning to go toward the lit building, he'd raised his sword arm to wipe the sweat from under his helmet rim with his wrist—and smeared blood across his face, sticking his lashes together. But that had happened before. Grimacing at his own stupidity, he'd tried to blink the stuff away.

While he blinked, Uk recognized, between the struts of the light tower, from the diminutive armor and a motion of his shoulder, Mrowky—who was holding somebody. Three steps farther, knee still throbbing, Uk stopped and grinned. The little guy had actually got the redheaded girl—probably snagged her as she'd fled the common's carnage.

You're a lucky lady, Uk thought. Because Mrowky would do his thing with her, maybe punch her up a little afterwards, just to make her scared, then run her off. That was Mrowky's style—even though, when a whole village had nearly gone into a second revolt over the petitions, laments, and finally rebellious preachings of a woman raped by a soldier, Nactor himself had harangued the troops a dozen campaigns back: "I don't care *what* it is—boy, woman, or goat! You put a cock in it, you put your *sword* through it when you *finish* with it! That's an order—I don't *need* to deal with things like this!" But Mrowky wasn't comfortable—nor was Uk—killing someone just because you'd fucked her. And rarely did a woman carry on afterwards like the one who'd raised Nactor to his wrath, especially if you scared her a little. Though others among the soldiers, Uk knew, honestly didn't care.

Really, though, Uk thought, if Mrowky was going to do her now, he'd best take her out from under the light—behind the building; not for propriety, but just because Nactor or one of the officers might ride by. (No, Uk reflected, Mrowky wasn't too swift.) Favoring his right leg, Uk started forward to tell his friend to take it around the corner.

The redhead, Uk saw, over Mrowky's shoulder, had the stunned look of all the villagers. She was almost three inches taller than the little guy. Mrowky had one hand wrapped in her hair so that her mouth was open. As his other hand passed over it, the redhead's arm gave a kind of twitch.

Which is when Uk heard the howl.

From the darkness, black hair whipping back and a body under it like an upright bull's, the big man rushed, naked and screaming. Rush and scream were so wild that, for a moment, Uk thought they had nothing to do with Mrowky and the girl; they would simply take this crazed creature through the light and into the dark again. Then Uk glimpsed the wild eyes, which, as the light lashed across them, seemed explosions in the man's head. The teeth were bared—the image, Uk thought later, of absolute, enraged, and blood-stopping evil. Under his armor, chills reticulated down Uk's shoulders, danced in the small of Uk's back.

The wild peasant was heading right toward Mrowky and the girl.

All Uk had a chance to do was bark Mrowky's name (tasting blood in his mouth as he did so); the careening man collided with them; for a moment he covered—seemed even to absorb—them both. Then he whirled. With a great sweep of one arm, he tore Mrowky's helmet from his head—which meant the leather strap must have cut violently into Mrowky's neck before it broke, if it didn't just tear over his chin and break Mrowky's nose. The big peasant whirled back; and Uk saw that he had Mrowky by the neck, in both of his hands—the guy's hands were huge too! And Mrowky was such a little guy—

With sword up and aching knee, Uk lunged.

The big man bent back (a little taller than Uk, thicker in the chest, in the arms, in the thighs), drew up one bare foot and kicked straight out. The kick caught Uk in the belly. Though he didn't drop it, Uk's sword went flailing. He reeled away, tripped on something, and went down. Blinking and losing it all because of the blood in his eyes, Uk pushed himself up again; but the redhead was gone (doubtless into the dark he'd been about to urge Mrowky into) and the peasant, still howling, was flinging—

yeah, flinging!—Mrowky from one side to the other, backing away. Mrowky's head—well, a head doesn't hang off *anyone's* neck that way! And the peasant was backing into the dark—was gone into it, dragging Mrowky with him!

Uk got out a curse, got to his feet, got started forward—and tripped on another villager who was actually moving. Wildly, he chopped his blade down to still her. (Yeah, in the neck!) Then he started off in the direction they'd gone, but not fast enough, he knew—damn the knee!

O̲n the roof of Hara's hut, Qualt crouched, watching Rimgia, watching Rahm, watching Uk. (But he tried not to watch what Rahm was doing to the little soldier whose helmet Rahm had torn free.) Qualt turned away. Behind him something huge and dark and shadowy spread out from him on both sides, moving slightly in the breeze, like breathing—watching too. When he looked back, Qualt saw Rimgia stagger into the shadows around the council-house corner—and in the shadows, saw Abrid run up to her, seize her by the shoulder, demand if she were all right, and somehow, over the length of his own question, realize that she was not; and slip his other arm around her. Looking right and left, and totally unaware of what had gone on just around the corner (Rimgia's eyes were fixed and wide, as if she were seeing it all again), Abrid helped his sister off along the council-building wall.

Qualt had gripped the edging of twigs and thatch so tightly that even on his hard and calloused palms it left stinging indentations. His hands loosened now, and he moved forward, as if to vault down and pursue them. But the thing behind him—did it reach for his shoulder? No, for it had not quite the hands we do. But a dark wing swept around before him, like a shadow come to life to restrain whoever would bolt loose.

And turning, Qualt whispered, words lurching between heartbeats that still near deafened, halting as the trip from one roof—

over the violence—to another: "This is—what thou seest if . . . thou flyest at Çiron!"

Something had happened to Rahm—not to the part of him staggering through the chaos of villagers and soldiers. Rather, it happened to the part growing inside, the thing that had begun forming when the bearded rider had shot Kern. It had needed a long time to grow: minute after minute after minute of mayhem. But the growing thing finally got large enough to fill up and join with something in Rahm's hands, in Rahm's thighs, in Rahm's gut. It filled him or became him or displaced him— however he might have said it, they all referred to the same. And when from the darkness Rahm had seen Rimgia and the little soldier leaning against the council building, saw him touch her that way in the overhead light, the thing inside, jerking and bloating to its full size, had taken him over, muscle and mouth, foot and finger.

When what happened next finished happening, Rahm had dragged the soldier halfway through the town—till he no longer pulled at Rahm's wrists, till he no longer flailed, struggled, gurgled, till he was limp and still and hung from Rahm's grip, as Rahm stood in darkness—choking out one and another rib-wrenching sob.

Horses' hooves struck around him. Rahm heard a shout beside him. A blade—Rahm saw firelight run up sharpened metal—cut at his shoulder; and a sound that was not a sob but a roar tore up out of him. He'd hurled the little soldier's corpse away (the flung body struck the sword from the soldier's hand, knocked the soldier free of his horse) and fled—till much later Rahm hurled his own body, nearly a corpse, down among the foothills.

He lay in the woods at the mountains' base, his cheek on his wrist; tears ran across the bridge of his nose, slippery over the back of his hand. Breath jerked into his lungs every half minute.

He lay in the leaves, gasping. His eyes boiled in their bone cauldrons. His teeth clenched so tightly, it was surprising the enamel of one or another molar did not crack. His body shook now and again, as if someone struck him hugely on the head, on the foot. What kept going through his mind was mostly names. Names. In the dark woods, he tried to remember all the names he had spoken that day, from the time he'd first reached the field to the time he'd stood in the common. He would start to go through them, get lost, then try doggedly to start again, to remember them all this time. (What were they again? What were they?) Because, he knew, a third of those names—children's, mothers', fathers', friends'—were no longer the names of live people. And they mustn't be forgotten. But his body finally shook a little less. They must *not* . . . Without his mind ever really stilling—

—dawn struck Rahm awake with gold.

He rolled and stood in a motion, blinking to erase unbearable dreams. He was still a long time. Once he turned, looked down the wooded slope, then off into the trees on either side. He began to shake. Then, possibly to stop the shaking, he started to walk—to lurch, rather, for the first few minutes—upward. Possibly he walked because walking was most of what he'd been doing for the past week. And the relief from walking, the feeling of a wander at its end, the astonishing feeling of coming home— something terrible had happened to that feeling.

Rahm walked.

Once in a while, he would halt and shake his head very fast—a kind of shudder. Then he would walk again.

The trees thinned. As Rahm stumbled over the higher stones, bare rock lifted free of vegetation, to jut in crags around him or to crumble under uncertain handholds. Soon he was climbing more than walking. After an hour—or was it two?—he came around a ledge to find himself at a crevice. Fifteen feet high, a cave mouth opened narrowly before him.

chapter four

From inside, a flapping sounded—as of a single wing.

Rahm eased along the ledge. Still numb, he had no sense of danger. His motivation was a less-than-passive curiosity—more the habitual actions of someone often curious in the past.

A fallen branch, split along its length, lay on the rock. Morning light reflected on the clean inner wood, still damp from the breaking. Like metal. Like a polished sword gleaming in firelight.

Rahm grabbed up the stick, as if seizing the reality would halt the memory. He shook it—as if to shake free the image from it. Then, a moment on, the shaking had turned to a hefting. One hand against the stone wall, the other holding the stick, Rahm stepped within the cave mouth, narrowing his eyes. A slant beam from a hole near the ceiling lit something gray—something alive, something shifting, something near the rocky roof. That something moved, moved again, shook itself, and settled back.

Rahm stepped farther inside. Looking up, frowning now, he called out—without a word.

A mew returned.

Rahm took another step. The gray thing made the flapping sound again.

As his eyes adjusted to the shadow, Rahm could make out its kite shape. It hung in a mass of filaments, one wing dangling. A tangle of webbing filled most of the cavity. Ducking under strands, Rahm took another step. Leaves ceased to crumble under his heel. Within, the softer soil was silent. He glanced when his foot struck something: a bone chuckled over rock. Rahm looked up again, raised his branch, brought its end near the trapped creature.

He didn't touch it. Between the branch's end and the leathery wing were at least six inches. But suddenly the mewing rose in pitch, turning into a screech.

Rahm whirled—because something had flung a shadow before him, passing through the light behind.

Suspended nearly four feet from the ground, a bulbous . . . *thing* swayed within the cave entrance, dropped another few inches—much too slowly to be falling—then settled to the ground. It scuttled across the rock, paused, made a scritting noise, then danced about on many too many thin legs. Rahm jabbed his stick toward it.

Mandibles clicked and missed.

It ran up the wall, then leapt forward. Rahm struck at it and felt the stick make contact. The thing landed, spitting, and hopped away, one leg injured and only just brushing the earth. Behind it trailed a gray cord—the thickness, Rahm found himself thinking, of the yarn Hara might use on her loom.

It jumped again. Rahm swung again.

Only it wasn't jumping at him; rather it moved now to one side of the cave, now to the other:

Two more cords strung across the cave's width.

And the cave was not wide.

Backing from it, Rahm felt his leg and buttock push against some of the filaments behind, which gave like softest silk. But as he moved forward again, they held to him—and when one pulled free of his shoulder, it stung, sharply and surprisingly.

This time, when it leaped across the cave, Rahm jumped high and, with his branch, caught it full on its body. It collapsed from the arc of its leap, landing on its back, legs pedaling. Rahm lunged forward to thrust his stave through the crunching belly. Seven legs closed around the stick (the injured one still hung free): it scritted, it spat. Then all eight hairy stalks fell open. One lowered against Rahm's calf, quivered there, stilled, then quivered again. The hairs were bristly.

Blood trickled the stone, wormed between stone and dirt, and as all the legs jerked in a last convulsion—Rahm almost dropped his branch—gushed.

Rahm pulled the stick free of the carapace and stepped back, breathing hard. He looked up at the thing trapped in the webbing above. He looked down at the fallen beast on its back. And above again—where cords, leaves, sunlight, dust motes, and movement were all confused. He raised the stick among the filaments. He did not bring the end near the creature, but tried to pry among the threads in hope of breaking some—possibly even freeing it.

The branch went through them rather easily. The creature shifted above. Its free wing beat a moment.

Then, in a voice like a child's, but with an odd timbre under it not a child's at all, it said distinctly: "Use the blood!"

Rahm pulled his branch back sharply.

"To free me," the voice went on—strained, as though its position was manifestly uncomfortable, "use the blood!"

"Thou speakest!" Rahm said, haltingly, wonderingly.

"Just like you, groundling! Big voice but stuck to the earth! Come on, I tell you . . . use the blood!"

Rahm stepped back again. Then, because his foot went lower down (on that slanted rock) than he expected it to, he looked back sharply so as not to trip.

The cave beast's blood had rolled against one filament's mooring on the stone, and the cord's base was steaming.

Now the filament came free to swing over the cave floor. On a thought, Rahm pushed the stick's bloody end against a clutch of cords beside him. There was a little steam. Half the cords parted. When he felt something warm by his foot, Rahm looked down: blood puddled against his instep. But though it parted the cords, against his flesh it didn't hurt or burn.

Rahm spoke, once more. "Thou wilt not hurt me if I free thee?"

"Free me and you are my friend!" The voice came on, like an exasperated child's. "Quickly now, groundling—"

"Because," Rahm went on, "I have been hurt too much when I thought what would come was friendship."

What came from the trapped creature was the same sound

that Rahm had already thought of as "mewing," though now, since the creature had spoken, the sound suddenly seemed to be articulated with all sorts of subtle feeling, meaning, and response, so that—had it been on a lower pitch—he might have called it a sigh.

Suddenly Rahm threw his stick aside, stepped back across the rock, reached down, and grabbed one of the dead thing's hairy legs, to drag it through the cave. By two legs, he hoisted it onto a higher rock shelf, climbed up beside it, then got it and himself to a shelf even higher. Squatting, he took a breath, frowned deeply—and wiped his hand across the gory wound. Then he grasped first one cord and then another, feeling them tingle within his sticky grip, dissolving.

After popping a dozen, one more and the bound creature fell a foot. The free wing beat. That voice—like a child who has something wrong with its breathing—declared: "You take care!"

The creature mewed again.

Once more Rahm smeared up a handful of blood and began to work.

Later he tried to recall how he put all those aspects that told of an animal together with that childish voice that still somehow spoke of a man. As Rahm tugged cords away from the incredible back muscles, some of the soft hair stuck or pulled loose—and the muscles flinched. But the membrane-bearing limb those muscles moved—what he'd started to think of as an arm—was thicker than his own thigh and more than triple the length of his leg! It was all webbed beneath with leathery folds, folded down and caught between spines that were impossible distortions of fingers—fingers *longer* than arms! The teeth were small in that grimacing mouth. Once, in the midst of the pulling and parting, he saw them and the wedge-shaped face around them laugh at something he himself had missed. But it was still good to see laughter in the face that was not a face, because the nose was broad as three fingers of a big-handed man laid together; the sides of the head were all veined ear; and the eyes had pupils like a cat's—small as a cat's too, which was strange, because, standing at last on the shelf of rock, with one long foot (whose big toe was as long as, and worked like, Rahm's thumb), the creature was a head shorter than Rahm. "Here now, help me get my other foot free?" said this man, this beast, this Winged One with thigh and shoulder muscles as thick as little barrels.

Holding to rock, holding to that astonishing shoulder, Rahm leaned out, bloody-handed, and caught another cord that dissolved in his grip. "Now"—he pulled back, with a quick grunt—"we must find some water to wash off this stinking stuff!" Small twigs and leaves caught up in the webbing fell to the cave floor.

"As a pup"—the Winged One grimaced, flexing—"I used to sneak off with the rough and rude girls who went to collect these threads for our ropes and hunting nets—till my aunt caught me and said it was not fitting for one of my station. Well, don't you know, an hour ago, hanging with the blood a-beat in my ears, I was thinking how ironic that I'd most likely end my life lashed up in the sticky stuff, once the beast, crouching just above the cave entrance there inside, grew hungry!"

They climbed down, Rahm at a loss for what so many of the words (like "rude," "fitting," "station," and "ironic") might mean. "When I was a child," Rahm said, supporting the creature above him, "the elders of my village always taught us to fear thy people—and to stay clear of thee, should one of thee ever alight near our fields!"

"As well you should!" declared the high voice, as the wings, all wrinkled and stretched not a full fifth of their spread, still went wall to wall in that high, narrow cave. "We always tell our little ones, whenever they come near you, to act as frightening as they can—before they fly away! Oh, my friend, we've heard—and seen!—some of the things your kind can do to its own. And that does not portend well for what you might do to our kind or others. Oh, I don't mean your own village in particular—Çiron at the mountain's foot. But we fly far of Hi-Vator, and we fly wide of Çiron; and we listen carefully—and often what we hear is not so good. So our elders have always thought a policy of self-containment, helped on by a bit of mild, if mutual, hostility, was best. I never took it seriously myself—though some I know do nothing else. Certainly I'm glad it's broken through here and now in this direction.

"What's your name, groundling?"

"Rahm. And thine?"

The Winged One tilted his head. "Vortcir."

On the cave floor, Rahm bent, picked up the blood-blackened end of the branch he'd used to kill the cave beast. He looked at it. Blood, dry now, had gone dark all over his fingers and palms and wrists, stuck about with dirt. "And how wert thou trapped by this thing, Vortcir?"

The Winged One cocked his head the other way. The short creature's great shoulders lifted their folded sails—half again as high as Rahm—and brought them in around himself. "I was careless." The expression (on a face that seemed to have so few of them) was embarrassment. "In the night I fled into its cave, unaware that the danger I fumbled into was greater than the one I fled."

"What danger didst thou flee?"

Vortcir's face wrinkled. "In the night a great wailing came to deafen us. It filled us with fear and we scattered from our nests, blundering low among the trees, yowling higher than the crags, till, unable to find our way, I saw many of my people driven mad by that terrible wailing. I could hear the echo from this cave. I flew in here, thinking the sound would be less. But I flew into the web and, by struggling, only entangled myself more. And when I excited the cave-beast enough, it would come over and throw another couple of threads about me. *Uhh!*" Vortcir paused. "But you arrived . . . how is it that you stray so high among the mountains, groundling Rahm?"

Rahm waited while a wind stilled outside in the rocks. "I too fled the great wailing that came last night."

"I hear in your voice many strange things," said Vortcir, frowning. "Will you now go down to your nest?"

"My . . . nest has been destroyed."

"Destroyed? While I hung here, wound in that dreadful web, in this sound-deadening cave? Çiron? How is that?"

Rahm turned suddenly and flung the blackened branch against the cave wall. He pulled his shoulders in. It was as if the thing that had come loose inside him shook, lurching into the body's walls. Rahm felt air on his back. Something on his back was a touch, but it touched so much of him. He looked up.

Vortcir moved his wing away from Rahm's shoulder. The triangular face was puzzled. "You have saved my life," Vortcir said. "By this, we are friends. What, friend Rahm, is this thing that makes your heart roar and the muscles sing on your bones with anger?"

"Thou dost hear the sounds of my heart and bone?"

"And of your tongue's root, a-struggle in your throat for words, as if it would tear itself free of your mouth. My people have keen . . ." followed by a word that probably meant hearing, for the great veined leaves of Vortcir's ears flicked forward, then back.

Rahm looked out at the leaves beyond the cave mouth. "Let us wash this blood from ourselves." His own voice was hoarse. "Is there a stream?"

"You do not hear where the water is, right up there?" Vortcir's wing tip bent down in what first seemed a wholly awkward manner—till Rahm realized he was pointing with it.

Rahm frowned.

"Let us go wash." Vortcir grinned. "And you may tell me what it is that hurts you so deeply."

They left the cave. Rahm moved over the rocks with long strides. Vortcir traveled in short-legged jumps, his wings fanning now and again for balance.

"Vortcir," Rahm said, as they walked, "my people go naked on the ground. Thy . . . people go naked in the air. Both are easy with the land about them. We fight with our hands and our feet, and then only what attacks. We love our own kind and are at peace with what lies about us. But . . . this is not true of all creatures." In a low, quick voice, Rahm began to tell what he had seen happen in the streets of his village last night. As the tale went on, it finally seemed, even to him, simply outrage strung after outrage—so that at last he stopped.

Rahm looked at Vortcir. His amber eyes seemed some substance once molten that had recently set to a shocking hardness.

"But what fills me with terror, Vortcir, is that the evil is now in me too. I am filled with it. Yesterday morning, I killed a lion. This morning I killed the cave creature. And both of them were a kind of sport. But last night, Vortcir, I killed a man—a man like myself, a man as thou. I held his neck in my hands; and I squeezed, and I twisted it till . . ." As they reached the mountain stream, Rahm stopped. He squatted by the water, let one knee go forward into the mud. "I am not who I was, Vortcir." As he began to wash, around his arms water darkened; not all the blood was from the fight in the cave. "Who I have become frightens me. I think perhaps I cannot, or I should not, go back to my village."

Vortcir stepped into the water and squatted in it. One wing unfolded, began to beat against the water and wave about on it. "Why so?"

Rahm turned his face from the spray and spatter of the Winged One's washing—and grinned. The grin was at the splashing, not the thought. Still, it felt good to grin again. Rahm said, "Because if I would go down again, Vortcir, I would do the same to the neck of every blade-wielding soldier, of every black-cloaked officer still in the village of Çiron!" Behind his hard, hard eyes, Rahm was wondering what it meant to say what he said as seriously as he said it and still to grin as he was grinning.

But it felt good—even as it gave him chills.

Vortcir brushed drops from his face with his shoulder. "I hear you well, Rahm. Your people are good folk—we even watch you, time to time." Vortcir gave a quick laugh. "Perhaps yours are a finer people than my own. We strive for peace. But sometimes we do not achieve it. We Winged Ones, as you call us— sometimes we kill each other. We know this is wrong. When one of our number kills another, we catch him and mete out punishment." He shrugged, an immense, sailed shrug. "It does not happen often." Vortcir turned and splashed about with his other wing.

Rahm picked up a handful of wet sand and used it to scrub at his arm, at his shoulder. When blood came away from the cut he'd received last night, it stung. He looked at squat Vortcir—who stood, feet wide in the rushing foam. Both wings opened now, Vortcir raised his head. He began to mew.

Rahm looked up.

Suddenly and excitedly, Vortcir called: "My aunt nears!" Then at once he leapt. Twigs and water drops flew about. Rahm closed his eyes against the rush of leaves and dirt.

When he opened them, Vortcir was clearing the broken cliff, rising before the billowing cloud.

For a moment Rahm lost him. Then a moment later, he saw two Winged Ones, moving together and apart, circling, meeting, one soaring away, the other soaring after—till suddenly both were alighting on the rocks at the stream's far bank.

Vortcir splashed forward, then turned and spoke somewhat breathlessly to the other: "Here is the groundling called Rahm who saved my life!"

The woman Winged One was a breadth larger than Vortcir in every direction: taller, deeper chested, broader sailed. She wore a brass chain around her neck and was clearly the elder. "You are a friend, then, groundling?" While rougher and aged, her voice was as high and as breathy as her nephew's. "You have saved my fine boy; all men and women who fly will be grateful to you and give you honor."

The grin had gone. There was only a smile on Rahm's face now. "All?"

"Vortcir is Handsman of our nest!" she declared as if that explained everything. "Will you now come with us?"

Smiling mirth became smiling wonder: "Where?"

"To our nest in the high rocks—to Hi-Vator!"

"But how could I climb after thee, if—"

"Easily!" Mewing, Vortcir turned to his aunt. "He's tall but scrawny! He can't weigh much. Come, friend Rahm! Climb on my back."

"Canst thou support me?" Rahm stood at the water's edge. He had never thought of himself as light. But, shorter than Rahm by a head, still Vortcir was half again as heavy.

Rahm stepped across the water and behind Vortcir, who turned and bent to take him. Rahm grasped him over the shoulders. The furred back bunched beneath Rahm's chest. On either side of him the leather sails spread and spread and spread! They did not beat but vibrated at first. Without any sense of motion at all—at first—the ground sank away. Then, at once, leaves in the trees above dropped toward them, fell below them. Rahm caught his breath, tightened his grasp. And the wings gathered and beat once more—and yes, they flew!

Looking down over Vortcir's shoulder, Rahm saw far more rock below than green.

"How does it feel to fly, friend Rahm?" Vortcir called back. Then he cried to his aunt: "He's light as a fledgling!" Vortcir's mew rose. Rahm peered over Vortcir's shoulder.

Some bare, some gorse-covered, rocks moved far below them. Wind stroked Rahm's arms, his buttocks, his back. The smell of the fur on Vortcir's neck was like the smell from a casket or cabinet in Ienbar's cabin, long locked and suddenly opened. Sometimes they flew so steeply that Rahm hung against the thick back only by the hook of his arm. More often, they moved horizontally, so that Rahm lay prone on that body, broader than his own, even as his feet stuck free into the air. Sometimes it seemed they just floated, so that the sun warmed Rahm's neck and the trough between his shoulders, and no wind touched him at all. At others, the wind pummeled Rahm's face and arms and chilled his fingers (locked against Vortcir's chest), till he wondered if he could hold much longer. The excitement of flight contracted Rahm's stomach and made his heart hammer. He hugged more tightly to the flexing back.

Others had joined Vortcir and his aunt. As they descended,

pitted cliffs rose. At last Vortcir's feet scraped rock. Rahm caught his balance and stood alone once more, arms and chest tingling, while he looked at the great, windy back-beating maneuvers of the others landing about them—or at Vortcir's own wing-beating, which finally stilled.

Drawing in his sails and breathing quickly (but not deeply; deep breaths seemed reserved for flight itself), Vortcir turned. "At Hi-Vator, here on the world's roof, now you will see how those who fly can live."

Others crowded in then. There was a general cry: "Vortcir! Handsman Vortcir! Vortcir has returned!"

Vortcir's aunt pushed through. "But young Handsman, where is your chain of trust?"

Again Rahm noticed the chain around her own neck.

"I must have lost it when we were set upon by the terrible wailing."

"You cannot very well go without it. As I wear the sign and trust of a Queen, so must our Handsman wear the sign and trust of one ready at any moment to become King."

While this was going on, Rahm looked and blinked and looked again at these furred people, who stood so close to one another—in threes, fives, or sevens, always touching—but who now and then would explode into the air, soaring fifty, seventy-five, a hundred and fifty yards away from any fellows.

Already, in the margins of his takeoff with Vortcir and his aunt, at the rim of their ride together, and at the edge of their landing with the others, Rahm had learned that these were a people among whom the women's furry breasts were scarcely larger than the men's, and that the men's genitals were almost as internal as the women's. The distinction between the sexes was only minimally evident till one paused to urinate, as that male over there was doing, or when one of them was (as he realized at a glance to his left, where several were joking about a young female who evidently was) in a state of sexual excitement.

Carefully, while trying not to be caught staring, Rahm watched them. And in their close, nervous groups, with their small eyes they watched him back. They watched him from ledges above. They watched him from the rope nets strung from staid oak branch to staunch hemlock trunk—apparently the youngsters' favorite place to play. They watched him from other, broader nets strung from the rocks down by the water to the higher ledges, thirty and forty yards overhead—where, it seemed, the elderly gathered to gossip, stretching their wings till they quivered. The watching was particularly strange because, by now Rahm knew, they were doing more listening than looking. What, he wondered, could they hear of him through their constant, mewing intercourse?

Within his first thirty minutes at Hi-Vator, Rahm saw a group of six winged children tease a smaller and younger child unmercifully. The older ones were—as far as he could tell—all boys. The little one was—most probably—a girl. The teasing reached such intensity that twice it became violent: had he been in his own home, Rahm would have stepped in to stop it. But now he could only look about uncomfortably for Vortcir or his aunt, both of whom happened, for the moment, to be somewhere else. Why, he wondered wildly, weren't any other adults paying attention?

Within his first three hours there, Rahm observed a game where you sailed cunningly constructed toys made of twigs and thin leather from ledge to ledge, then took them into the sky to sail them from flier to flier. Also he saw two other children playing with a lemurlike pet. Then he became involved in what he only realized was another game after fifteen minutes of it, as first one then another Winged One politely volunteered to fly him now to this ledge, now to another, now to still one more: and he would grasp the warm, heavy shoulders and be carried here and there around the many ledges of the gorge in which their cave dwellings were sunk, either side of a silvery feather of falling water. Rahm had already noted, upon landing, that it was a lot easier to tell the sex of the Winged One—strong young female or male—who'd just carried him. From the giggling together of those waiting to ferry him about or the others who had just finished, Rahm realized—with sudden humor—that somehow with them this flying and carrying was a sexual game: and some others, he saw now, didn't approve!

For ten minutes later, three older ones marched up and put a rather gruff end to it. The ones who'd been playing with him fluttered off. The older ones apologized to him in a way that, though he smiled and nodded and shrugged a lot, he didn't quite see the point of—since there was no harm in it.

Three hours more, and he'd discovered that while the Winged Ones' word for "star" was the same as his, they had no single word for "ear," but more than ten for its various parts and functions. Also, from repeated inquiry, he finally decided they had no concept at all of the tomato plant.

"What are you thinking, my friend?" Vortcir asked, suddenly at his side, when Rahm, in those first three hours, had once more gone still a moment to stare off at those furry youngsters wrestling together by the falling water's edge, or at the creatures who seemed to be grinding some sort of grain in the great circular stone troughs behind them, or just at the clouds behind them all, in the luminous mid-morning sky.

"I am thinking," Rahm said, slowly and with consideration, "that, with perhaps here and there an exception that perplexes me"—he was recalling the children's particularly violent teasing—"thou art a people, a people very like my own."

And sitting in the sunlight, cross-legged on the blanket beside the wheel of his garbage cart, Qualt broke open a papaya. As its black seeds in their rich juice spilled out over the orange flesh in the morning, Qualt said: "Then, from what thou tellest me—with perhaps here and there something I do not quite understand—thy folk at Hi-Vator are . . . a people too, a people much like mine." And the similarity of what Qualt said to what, miles up the mountain, Rahm was saying (and the vastly differing situations in which each said it) should begin to speak to you of the true differences between Qualt and Rahm.

Qualt tossed half the fruit.

Perched on the wooden frame of some overturned bench that was not used anymore in the village, but which sat here among the detritus lying about in the young garbage collector's yard, it reached out a great wing. The tines at its end caught the fruit and brought it back to the small, dark face. It bit, and juice and seeds ran down the fur at both sides of the mouth. It mewed, resettling itself. "Good! Hey, groundling, my sister was a rude, rough girl who went with the other poor girls to collect the filaments the cave beasts spin, up in the rocks, to make our ropes and hunting nets and webs. But I was only a mischief-maker, too lazy even to help them there. No, my people often thought that I was not a good one. So I took to wandering—flying here, flying there, listening now to these ones, now to those! Even when I was coming back, I saw one of your men fighting with a lion, and dropped to give him my help, but one of those others seared my wing with the kind of flaming evil we saw last night."

"It's a killing evil!" Qualt bit his fruit. "And that's why thou must do as I say. If we keep on, my friend, like we've begun this morning—"

At which point there was jingling from behind the house.

Qualt was on his feet. "Quick now, as I told thee." He sprinted off through the junk strewn about the yard toward the house corner, to step around it, over moist rocks and three piles of old pots—some broken, some nested in one another, hollyhocks grown up between them.

The path up to the garbage collector's shack was narrow, and you couldn't walk without brushing the low branches. Long ago Qualt had strung a rope between those branches, which, if any of them were hit, rang a goat's bell he'd fixed to a post near the front door.

"Hey, there, Qualt," came a familiar voice. Old Hara pushed from the path end. "I wondered if you were home."

Qualt went forward.

"Ah, boy, this is a deadly day!" Yes, it was Hara, with the white in her hair like the froth of the quarry falls, with her skirt the colors of leaves and earth and hides. "Phew!" Her face wrinkled even more as she came barefoot toward the house. "How do you stand the stink?"

"Why dost thou come here, Hara? Why dost thou come here after what happened in the town last night?"

The weaver shook her head. "I go to a council meeting. You know that Ienbar, among so many, was killed—burned to death at his shack by the burial meadow."

"Not Ienbar too? But where are they meeting, Hara? Not in the council building?"

The old woman shook her head. "No, boy, the Myetrans are there now. But it's not a meeting you can linger about the edges and overhear. Not this time." She reached out and pushed the side of Qualt's head playfully with her knuckles. "Oh, maybe when a bit more of youth's foolishness has gone out of thee and some more of wisdom has settled between thy ears—but there's no need for anyone to know where we meet now. The Myetrans are still about all over the town. And they do not want us meeting. No, not after last night."

"Yes," Qualt said. "I see." Hara crossed toward the corner of the house. Qualt hurried after her, just as she stepped around the pots and hollyhocks. But the backyard, with the junk strewn about in it and the garbage cart to the side, was empty.

"It won't be an easy meeting, though, I tell you, boy! There's seven hundred and forty people here at Çiron—oldsters and babes among those. While the Myetrans—well, there are thousands of them, it seems! And we have to figure out a way to—"

"Hara," Qualt said. "Hara, there're *not* thousands of them!"

She stopped and looked at him.

Qualt crumpled the papaya rind and flung it into the bushes. "There're not thousands of them. There're not hundreds of them! There're a hundred eighty-seven. Perhaps I'm off by five or six—up or down. But not by more!"

Hara frowned. "And how dost thou know, little dirty fingers?"

"Because I counted!"

"When didst thou count?"

"Earlier this morning. They get their camp up at sunrise and I . . . I counted. A hundred eighty-seven. A few more than half of them are in the village. Somewhat less than half are at their camp. There's a group of five whom all the others obey. They stay in three tents that are larger than the others, at the back of the encampment; the mounted one with the beard who killed Rimgia's father last night is one of them. Then, among the rest, there are ten who wear the black clothes, with the black cloaks and hoods. These ride horses and tell their men, the ones who have only the swords and their metal and leather plates bound to them, where to go and what to do. The black ones and the five leaders alone have the powerguns, the things they killed Kern and Tenuk and . . . killed so many with. Powerguns are what they call these; someone overheard them speak the word and told me. And there're no more than twenty powerguns among them—and a dozen are resting, at any one time. That's another thing they have to do—after they fire them twenty or thirty times, they have to let them rest a while so the guns regain their fire. Someone . . . I heard them joking about them when they rounded up some forty-three of our people, wounded all, but who could still walk, and herded them into a wire corral where they have them imprisoned."

"Forty-three of us imprisoned?" Hara exclaimed. "Ah, thank the generous earth! For in town, they've started to count the bodies of those who were killed, and there seemed to be more than thirty missing. Do you know who the corralled ones are, Qualt? Do you know which ones are their prisoners? You tell us that, and it would ease a lot of sick hearts, boy."

"I can tell you that and I can tell you more, though I'll have to learn it later. But there are men in black, who, with the five leaders, have the powerguns."

Hara had started walking again.

"But tell the council, Hara! There are five in charge. And only a hundred eighty-seven all together—give or take four or five!"

"You can believe I'll tell them, boy! You can believe it." Hara went on toward the quarry road, making for wherever the village council had decided to hold its meeting.

Qualt stood in the yard, breathing hard—as though the imparting of the information had been a sudden and painful effort.

You see, he was a very different person from Rahm.

Over the edge of Qualt's roof thrust a sharp face with scooped ears. A moment later, a shadow flapped.

Qualt turned as the Winged One moved out onto the air—as if air were water and the Winged One pushed off into it as Qualt might push off from the quarry shore . . . and Qualt himself were looking up at it as a fish might look from the lake bottom.

The Winged One sailed over the yard full of the things that, now and again, curious Qualt had rescued from the irredeemable arc into the ravine, a kind of sculpture garden of furniture, farm equipment, and even more unrecognizable stuff, pieces leaning in odd positions, an occasional rope drawn from one to the other from which some pot or bit of houseware hung.

Flapping wings settled till the Winged One perched on the corner of Qualt's garbage wagon. One sail out for balance, the Winged One moved the other's edge across his mouth, knocking away the little seeds that had stuck to his face fur. "Say, groundling—there! You've told what we learned aloft this morning to one of your elders, like you wanted. Do you think that now you'll let me take you up to Hi-Vator? There it would be fun, and you wouldn't have to hide like you say I have to here! Though there I might still have to hide from a few, because some folk there—some even of my own family—do not like me as much as all that!" The Winged One laughed out shrilly, the mighty sails out full—on which, with the sunlight behind them, Qualt could see scars that spoke of violence and adventure. "Sometimes I think I cannot—or perhaps I should not—go back to Hi-Vator. Oh, there're not many up there who listen for my return. Other times I think maybe I should go visit them, with one of you groundlings on my back to surprise them, as though

I were a Handsman or a noble, who could make and break such laws at will. But if I could make and break such laws, then I would not be the outlaw I am. Oh, I assure you—I'm only a little outlaw. Don't fear me, friend. I never broke any *big* laws. I just forget and do what I want sometimes, and discover it wasn't what someone else wanted me to do. Then I have to fly."

"Yes," Qualt said absently. "This law that thou spokest of earlier. Now what is this law that you are outside of, as thou sayest?"

But the Winged One just laughed. "I know, groundling! Perhaps we can roll around together on the earth the way we did last night—that was fun too, 'ey? Or would you like to try it in the air? That was a good game, no? Even if it came about only by accident from that awful sound, so that I could not tell where I was when I flew into you! You groundlings do it in the dirt. We Winged Ones do it in the—"

But suddenly Qualt turned, vaulted up on the bench of the garbage cart, and stood erect on the seat while the wheels creaked below them both. "No, my friend, there'll be a later time for Hi-Vator." Qualt stepped behind the creature's great sail, like an object rejoining a shadow that had been momentarily lost to it by a mystery beyond naming. "Yes, like last night, we'll fly a bit more at Çiron!"

By his final three hours at Hi-Vator, Rahm had decided that, no, the Winged Ones were a very, *very* different people from his—but that it was precisely those differences that *made* them a people. With each new thought or realization or insight about them, however, there came a moment when Rahm would stand—now for seconds, now for minutes—still as the cliffs rising above him, his mind fallen miles below, turning among memories of the light- and blood-lashed night, trying to hold coherent the idea of a people of his own. When he stood so long like that, some of the Winged Ones watched or listened quietly. Others, better mannered, merely listened and pretended not to watch at all—though more and more mewed about it to one another, out of sight and hearing.

Among the stranger things that had happened to him that afternoon was a conversation he'd had with an old Winged One, whom Vortcir had been eager to have him meet for more than an hour now. The Winged One's fur was more gray than brown. Her eyes were wrinkled closed.

Rahm and the ancient creature hung together on one of the rope webs above the waterfall while the old Winged One explained to Rahm that one of the most important ideas around which all the Winged Ones' lives revolved was something called god—apparently a very hard thing to understand, since it was at once the universal love binding all living things and, at the same time, a force that punished evildoers even as it forgave them. Also it was a tree that grew on the bare peak of the world's highest mountain, a tree older than the world itself, a tree whose roots required neither earth nor water—those roots having secreted the whole of the world under it, including the mountain it perched on. The tree's leaves were of gold and iron. Its fruit conferred invisibility, immortality, and perfect peace. To make things even more complicated, for just a short while—twenty-nine years to be exact, the old Winged One explained—god had not been a tree at all, but rather a quiet, good, and simple woman with one deformed wing, who therefore could not fly and thus limped about the mountains' rocks like a groundling. Various and sundry evil Winged Ones would come across her and attempt to cheat her or rob her or—several times—even kill her, only to be shamed by a power she had, called "holiness," whereupon they repented and often became extremely good, fine, and holy people themselves for the rest of their lives, during which they did nothing but help other Winged Ones.

"There are other peoples," the old Winged One told Rahm as she stretched over the knotted vines, "who represent god as a silver crow, while for others god is a young man strung up to die on a blasted tree . . ." which only confused Rahm further.

Still, something about the old Winged One made her comforting to listen to. Something in her manner recalled . . . Ienbar? The stories of the flightless god were gentle and good and took Rahm's mind off the cataclysmic images just under memory's surface.

Rahm climbed down from the rope net, curious as to why he felt better, but not convinced that this idea/tree/cripple was much more than a story with too many impossibilities to believe, so that while it might have had something he couldn't quite catch to do with the world around him now, he couldn't believe it had much to say of the world he'd left below.

The afternoon sun had lowered enough to gild the western edge of every crag and rock. At the fire, Winged Ones adjusted three mountain goats on wooden roasting spits. Walking up to another ledge, Rahm saw some others pounding nuts on a large rock with small stones held in their prehensile toes. Still others, on the ledge above that, had gathered hip-high heaps of fruit— yellow, purple, and orange—so that when, a few minutes later, Vortcir's aunt came up to him and said: "There's to be a feast tonight!" Rahm was not really surprised.

"In honor of the Handsman's safe return?" Rahm asked.

"In honor of the groundling who saved him!" she declared, shrill and breathy. Then, with wings wide, she turned to drop over the rocky rim at his feet and crawl down a web.

Winged Ones carried a trestle over, piled with fruit and nut bread. "Have some," Vortcir urged him. "Some of us have flown leagues and leagues to bring these to the nest." They brought a chain for Vortcir, who insisted they bring another for Rahm. Vortcir's aunt herself held it on the spurs of her wings and lowered it around Rahm's neck with cooling, windy motions. Several Winged Ones made music on a rack of gongs, while youngsters flapped and scrambled over the rocks, flinging the scarlet, cerise, and leaf-green rinds at each other, now at a furry arm, now at a leg jerked back, from which the peel slid away, falling to the stone as the thrower mewed and the target squealed. Caves pitting the cliffside site echoed with chucklings and chitterings. Across the twelve-foot fire troughs, the spitted carcasses rolled above flame, fat dribbling and bubbling along the bottom of each beast.

"Here, Rahm!" Vortcir led him up to a stone rim. "You must make the first cut." On his spur, Vortcir lifted a great cleaver, long as his thigh. Rahm turned to seize it by a handle carved for a grip wholly different from his own. He planted one foot on the pit stone. Their wings beating up spirals of sparks, the fire tenders swung the first spit out. Rahm raised the blade—

His eyes caught the red light running up the sharpened metal—and as he had done so many times that day, Rahm halted. His chest rose; breath stalled in it.

Some of the Winged Ones fell silent.

One of Vortcir's wings opened to brush and brush at Rahm's back, to smear the sweat that had in moments risen on Rahm's shoulders, his forehead, his belly. "Friend Rahm, this blade is to cut the meat that we will all eat. Use it!"

Rahm swung the cleaver down. Crusted skin split. Juices rilled and bubbled along the metal. And Rahm grinned. The others chittered and laughed and mewed. Some even came up to compliment him on the dexterity with which he carved: "But then, you have so many little fingers. . . ."

Lashed to a wooden fork, a leather sack dripped wine into a stone tub, from which, at one time or another, everyone went to drink. Three times Rahm found himself at the rim beside a female with granite-dark fur, a quick smile, and a sharp way of putting things in an otherwise genial manner. "So," she said, when the wine had made Rahm feel better and they met again a ways from the food, "I overheard you talking to that blind old fool about god," though she spoke the word "fool" with such affection as to make Rahm wonder if it meant the same to her as it did to him. "You know what the real center of our life here is? It isn't god."

"What is it, then?" Rahm asked.

Behind her, her wings . . . breathed, in and out of the indigo, out and into the firelight. "Actually, it's money."

"Money?" he asked. "Money. Now, what is money?"

Apparently it was more complicated than god. It too, she explained, was fundamentally an idea having to do with value—in this case, represented by the hard hulls of certain nuts treated with certain dyes, with certain symbols carved into them. You gave some of these hulls for everything you received or got some back for everything you gave—Rahm was not sure which; "everything" included food, sex, and entertainment, labor, shelter, and having certain rituals performed for you by the Handsman or the Queen.

"I'd like to see some," he said with polite interest, "of this money."

She cackled, in a scrit as shrill as that of the beast he'd slain in the cave. "But that's the whole problem, you understand. Nobody has any anymore!"

He was confused all over.

"We gave it up," she explained, "years ago. When I was a girl—maybe eight or nine. We had a meeting of the whole nest site, and the Old Queen decided we'd be better off without it. So we went back to barter. But no one's really forgotten it—I don't care what the Old One says. Personally, I think it would be better if we had it back again, don't you?"

Around him the Winged Ones caroused through the deepening evening. Now and again Rahm watched five, six, seven, or more rise from jagged rocks, gone black against the blue, in what, for the first moments, was a single fluttering mass, to shrink in the distance and finally flake apart as single fliers. There, among them, was the young woman who'd just been talking to him about this money. How did he recognize her in silhouette like that? (Had she taken part in the afternoon's forbidden game? Of that, he couldn't be sure.) But he did: definitely it was she, among the others, flying away.

With their mysterious and mystic notions—money and god—these folk had again begun to seem wholly foreign. Rahm lifted his hand to finger the chain at his neck that made him, at least honorarily, some sort of personage among these incomprehensible creatures. What, he wondered, would he tell one of the Winged Ones who wanted to know what ideas were most central to his own ground-bound nest site?

Behind him, Vortcir whispered, intensely: "Fly with me, friend Rahm!"

Rahm turned and, with an avidity that surprised him, threw his arms around that powerful neck as Vortcir moved to take him. Rahm bent one arm down across the flexing shoulder. "Watch that thou dost not crash the two of us onto the rocks!" Was Vortcir's head as full of wine as his?

The feeling—he had almost grown used to it by now—was that the Winged One who carried him took a great breath that finally just lifted his feet from the ground, a breath that didn't stop—the air itself taking them higher and higher and higher.

"This is a fine night to fly!" Vortcir called back.

Fires flickered below them. A file of Winged Ones flew just above the flame. Wing after wing reddened, darkened. Loosed from it all and looking down on it over the Handsman's shoulder, Rahm felt the whole nest site and all the flying folk he'd met there, children, adults, and oldsters, to be wondrously and intricately organized—as fine, as rich, and as logical as any folk could be.

"You like the life we lead, don't you?" came the child-voice.

Rahm nodded, his cheek moving against the Handsman's flour scoop of an ear—which twitched against him.

"They are good men and women," Rahm said. They arched away from the cliffside and the water's rush and the jutting trees, all black below them now. "They have all been kind to me."

"And you are happy," Vortcir said. "I can hear it."

Rahm said: "The wine has dulled thy hearing."

"For a moment—for several moments . . ."—Vortcir shook his head in a kind of shiver, though his wings still pumped them steadily across the night—"you were happy. Will you stay with us, friend Rahm?" The only sound was the air, loud in Rahm's ears—though surely much louder in Vortcir's. "I have heard your answer." Beside them, the mountain rose.

Rahm spoke rather to himself than to Vortcir, because he already knew it was not necessary: "I want to go home."

"I have heard," Vortcir repeated.

They descended through the night.

Where are we?" Rahm moved his feet in soil that held small rocks, leaves, and twigs. Neither moon nor stars broke the darkness.

"At the edge of the meadow where you bury your dead." Wide wings beat, not to fly but to enfold him, shaking on him and about him in a manner both affectionate and distressed. "Do not stumble"—the little voice sounded rough and close as the wings parted—"on the corpses."

"Are there many about?"

"They have brought many. No one has buried them yet. Friend Rahm?"

"Yes, Vortcir?"

"I must go back up now to my own people. But I will listen for you always." The high, breathy chuckle. "That's what we say when we leave a friend."

Rahm put his arms around Vortcir's shoulders once more, to grasp the creature to him who, in the dark, was only furred muscle, a high voice, a knee against his, a hot breath against his face and a scent more animal than human. Rahm stepped back. "And I will watch and . . . listen for thee! Vortcir?" Wind struck against him for answer. A little dust blew against his cheeks and got into one eye, making Rahm turn away, rubbing at it with his foreknuckle, so that the beating was at his back. Then it was above, thundering dully. Somewhere, as the sound stilled, a breeze rose over it with its own thunder of leaves and shushing grasses. (It brought with it an unpleasant smell, like rotting vegetables and clogged waters; but Rahm tried not to name it or even pay attention to it.) When it stilled, all sound was gone.

Beneath Rahm's feet, grass gave way to path dust. He walked. Firelight flickered from inside a window. By one shack, he stopped to look in through a crack between two logs under the sill—a crack he realized he'd peeped through many, many nights one winter, years ago, when someone else entirely had lived there.

A woman sat at the table, her head down, her shoulders hunched high. Two grown sisters had lived in this hut for the past half-dozen years. Rahm pulled away sharply when it struck him what it likely meant that only one was there now.

He turned and hurried across the road and ducked into the darkness between two houses. For a moment he wondered if he was lost, but at the glow from another hut's shutter, open perhaps three inches, he realized where he was.

Going up to the dim strip of light, he looked through. On a table a lot more rickety than the one in the last hut, a clay lamp burned with a flame more orange than yellow. Sitting on a bench, back against the wall and staring straight ahead, was a man whose name Rahm didn't know.

But he knew those shoulders and the short, spiky hair and the face. The man, not half a dozen years older than Rahm, worked on one of the quarry crews, sometimes with Abrid and . . . Kern.

Odd, Rahm thought, that there are people in my town whom I really don't know—though I've seen them now and again all my life. I probably know the names and the names of most of the relatives of practically every field worker. But do I know more than a dozen of those who work in the stone pits?

The surprise, of course, was that the man lived *here*. But then, Rahm went on thinking, that is what makes this town mine. It still holds for me perfectly simple things to learn, like what the person's name is or where the house lies of one of its stone workers. . . .

Then the thought interrupted itself: Is he blind? The man's eyes were open. He looked right at the window. Only inches out in the darkness, Rahm could not believe himself unseen. But the man's expression was the complete blank of one who slept with his eyes wide. Standing in the darkness, concentrating to read that blankness, Rahm was equally still, equally blank—

The man started forward.

Rahm started back—but something held him.

The man was up, moving to the window. He looked out at Rahm and gave a grunt—the way quarrymen so often did. "I thank thee," he said softly, roughly—though Rahm had no idea why—and smiled. "But thou hast better go. The patrol comes soon." He pulled the window closed.

Rahm stood in the dark, bewildered by the exchange. What, he found himself wondering, would I have seen had I looked into this same window last night before the wailing? Two other quarry workers sharing the hut with him? Perhaps a woman, perhaps two?

Some children? What absences in the house today did the blankness—or the smile—mean?

The return from his wander the previous day had started Rahm pondering all he knew of his village. But his return tonight, after the violence of the night before and the wonders of the day, had started him pondering all he did *not* know of it.

Rahm crossed the dark path. Nearing the common, he walked by more close-set huts.

Old Hara the Weaver's cottage had never had a shutter—at least not on its back window. But a hanging had been tacked up across it—although, at one edge, it had fallen away so that a little light came through. Within, he could hear the old woman talking—to herself, Rahm realized, as, with his fingertips on the window ledge, he put his eye to the opening between the window edge and the cloth.

"They shall not have it! They shall not! I said it in the council, and I say it now: they shall not have it!" He could see Hara moving about before the fire, a sharp-shouldered figure. Now she put down an armful of cloth—and taking up a cooking blade, she began to slash at one piece and another as she lifted them. "Never for them—they shall not!" With a hard, hard motion, she flung one handful and another of rags into the flames.

Rahm pulled back—even though the pieces did not flare.

He turned from the hut's sagging wall, to start away, when, from around the corner—

—lights, horses, hooves!

"There, Çironian! What are you doing out?"

Rahm whirled, hands up over his eyes against the light.

"You know the ordinance, Çironian. No windows or doors are to be open after dark! No man, woman, or child is to be on the street! You're under arrest! Come with us."

"With you?" Rahm began, squinting between his fingers as he pulled them from his eyes.

"Anyone the patrol catches out past sundown is under arrest, Çironian. Do not make further trouble for yourself."

A rope dropped over his shoulders to be yanked tight. Another soldier was down off his horse to grasp Rahm's hands and pull them behind him. "We'll take him with us on the rest of the patrol around the common before we deliver him to the holding cell." Another rope went round his wrists.

As the horse in front started away, Rahm was tugged forward so that he stumbled, nearly falling.

He kept his feet, though. The feeling was a kind of numbness. (The other Myetran soldier was back on his horse now. Horses clopped on the street at both sides of him.) But within the numbness there was something else: it was a feeling hard for Rahm to describe. It was as if the thing that had, the night before, grown to fill him, that had almost become him, had now, at the horse's first tug, torn loose from him. It was as if his flesh had parted and the thing that had filled him had remained standing, unmoving on the street—so that only the rind of him was dragged away, a limp thing collapsing through the light-lashed dark.

Not that the thing left behind stayed still.

It followed. It came steadily, easily after them, even as Rahm stumbled on. It moved firmly, watched impassively. (For moments Rahm was convinced that if he glanced back, he would see it, coming after them, lowering in the dark.) It observed them, impartial, now like something circling them, now like something walking with them. That impartiality, that impassivity, that sheer chill, was more unsettling than the indifference of the soldiers in front of him and beside him, taking him through the streets about the common—because Rahm's stumbling was, anyway (most of it), feigned. When his wrists had yanked from the soldier's hands, the knot hadn't been pulled tight yet: it would have been nothing to bunch his fingers and, though the hemp might burn, wrench a hand free. The rope around his arms and chest was only, he was sure, one great shrug away from coming loose. These Myetrans, Rahm thought, were used to dealing with terrified men and women.

But Rahm realized, as he stumbled and blinked in their passing lights, trying to look terrified and cringing, the thing that went with them—the thing that was really he—was *not* frightened. (Did they, Rahm wondered, find the sight of a frightened man or woman somehow beautiful? But they did not even look at him. Were they, perhaps, like the Winged Ones, listening? He did not think so.) It was not frightened at all.

chapter five

From the corner of Hara's hut, Naä watched the soldiers ride off with Rahm. She had seen him at the first house, followed him to the second—recognizing him only in the light from the open shutter before it closed (till now, she'd assumed him killed in the first night's massacre)—and come behind him quietly at the third. She'd followed him through the breezy night, excitement growing, anticipating what he might say to her, his surprise at seeing her, his pleasure at knowing she was alive and free as he was, when finally she would overtake him with a word—

Really, she'd been *about* to speak when the patrol had come up, and in a moment's cowardice she cursed herself for, she'd ducked back out of the light and stood, still and stiff as she could stand, one fist tight against her belly, her back against the shack wall's shaggy bark.

The whole capture quivered before her, leaving her with the anger, the frustration, the outrage you might have at a child or lover snatched from your arms. She watched them ride off with Rahm—and by starts, hesitations, and sprints, at a safe distance, one street away from the common, she followed them.

Since she had first left Calvicon, Naä had pretty much done as she wanted—within the constraints necessity placed about a wandering singer's song. She was a woman of strong feeling and quiet demeanor. Last night she'd watched what had happened in the Çironian village, but from the ends of alleys, crouching behind fences, up through the chink in a grain-cellar door, while soldiers and villagers had rattled the boards above her, till one arm broke through to flail, bloody, about her in the dark, hitting her on the ear and shoulders, while she knelt in the three-foot space below, trying not to make a sound while others screamed above her.

Before sunup, Naä had climbed quietly out, stumbled over the bodies, and—like Rahm—started from the town.

She had not, however, gone as far.

She walked an hour in the dark, till the salmon-streaked promise of sunrise hemmed the night. She stopped beneath a maple grove, looked down among dark roots squirming at her feet, put her hands to the sides of her head, and, breathing deeply, stood awhile, now with eyes opened, now with them closed. A few times, she gave an audible gasp.

Once she shook her head.

Then she took her hands down slowly to let them fall finally against her thighs.

A minute later, she whispered, *"No!"*

Then she turned and began to walk briskly back. At the edge of the burial meadow, she crouched in a clump of brush, while one and another wagon pulled up to the field all through the morning, each accompanied by three or four soldiers, to dump its corpses.

To the sound of creaking cart beds and thumping bodies, she fell asleep—and woke, hours later, in the hot sun, with a nauseous smell in her nose and a bad taste in her mouth. Looking carefully through the brush, she saw that no attempt had been made to cover the bodies on the grass.

One cart had been left near.

But no one was about.

Keeping to the woods, she went around to the charred ruins of Ienbar's shack. Again, she waited for moments. Then she pulled her harp around before her, dropped to her knees, tugged aside a half-burned log, and gutted out a hole for the instrument. With some cloth, burned along one side, she wrapped it. A large rock went over the opening. Then she scattered dirt and cinders on it. Fifteen minutes later, as she kicked away knee prints, footprints, then stepped back onto the grass, she was sure no one would know her harp was entombed there. Walking along the burned foundation, she paused to look back, then beat at the charcoal on her knees and hands, now and again wiping at her smudged face. Just inside, on a log gone gray and black over its burned-away side, the blade discolored near the bone handle with burn marks but the point sharp and the edge bright, one of Ienbar's well-sharpened cooking knives lay. She stepped in, picked it up, looked at it on both sides, then pushed it under the sash at her belt.

Very soon she'd hunted up the site of the Myetran camp.

Hidden in the brush and low trees on a slight rise, Naä watched awhile. She thought hard. When she had decided what she might do, she turned back—

And caught her breath.

She let it out again, with one hand at her throat; then, as she recovered herself, touched the tree beside her. "Qualt, I didn't realize you were . . ."

When he dropped from the low branch on which he'd been sitting, she caught her breath again, because he was so loud in the leaves around them. "Naä," he said, though obviously he'd been watching her for minutes, "what dost thou here?"

"The same thing I bet you are. Look." She turned back to the camp below them. "Those open carts there—can you believe it, they've brought their water in them, over from the quarry. Someone goes to get a dipper of water from them perhaps every five or ten minutes. It would be easy to get behind them and . . . What could you put in them, Qualt, to foul the supply and make the drinker gut-sick? And—"

The youth settled on one hip, grinning. "Yes?"

"Right over there is the back of their enclosure, where they've put their horses. It's very close to the woods. If I could get some tinder and start some dry weeds burning, I could heave them inside—I know horses, Qualt. They don't like fire. And if they bolted, those railings wouldn't hold five minutes. Now if there was only something we could do about the prisoners. I think that's the corral where they've got them, way across there. But I don't believe I could get that far without being spotted. There was all this activity there, just about twenty minutes back—"

The young garbage collector nodded, dappled light behind one ear making it luminously red—Qualt had tied his long hair back. "They took many of them back into town to put them in the council building."

"In the council building?" Naä asked.

"It looked to me as if they took everyone between fifteen and fifty years old and decided to put them in the cellar of the strong building. Only the Old Ones and the little children are left out there, in the hot sun."

"You saw them?" she said. "I was here twenty minutes ago, and I couldn't . . . But you saw them—take the prisoners from here all the way into town and put them in the council building?"

Qualt pursed his lips a moment, blinking. Then he said, "Come. Thou knowest where my hut is, by the dump?"

"I've never been there. But Rimgia once pointed out the path to it."

Qualt snuffled, grinning; she realized it was a joke when he said, "There—thy nose will tell thee where it is if thou comest anywhere close. Go on and meet me there."

He turned, grabbed a branch of the tree he'd been perched in, and started to climb.

"Won't you come with me, Qualt?" she asked, surprised.

"Go on." He looked back over his shoulder. "Go there. And I'll meet thee." He vaulted up to the next branch. A moment later his outsize feet pulled up among the leaves. "Go on. Don't worry. I'll be there!"

It wasn't a time for questioning. And besides, she couldn't see him any longer, even when she squinted—though she could still hear the leaves and the branches gnashing against one another. Naä started through the trees again.

She couldn't imagine she'd taken much time. When, not half an hour later, she came around the corner of his house, she was as surprised to see him standing in the yard, among his odd and leaning collection of junk, as she had been when she'd turned to see him in the woods.

"Here," he said, with no explanation as to how he'd gotten from one place to the other so much ahead of her. "This is for their water." He picked up the old basket sitting on the moss by his foot. On both the basket edge and the handle, bits of wicker had come loose.

"What is—" Then she wrinkled her face. In the general stink from the proximity of the dump, this stench cut through with distressing putrescence. Leaves lined the wicker. In among them nested something odorous and black—no, a wet green so dark it might as *well* be black.

"Where in the world did you *get* that?" she asked.

Qualt nodded to the side. "Down in the ravine. There's lots of stuff I know about in there. Likely thou mayest get this on thy hands. Thou must wash them well with both soap and salt, before thou touchest thy face or mouth—otherwise, thy guts shall soon run loose as the Myetrans' when this stuff goes in their drink." Qualt handed her the foul basket. "Under the leaves are iron and flint for fire. The cattail fluff that you can get down this side of the quarry lake will give thee lots and lots of smoke—if smoke is what thou wishest."

Behind Qualt stood a much larger basket, brim full, that Naä glanced down at now: millet cobs, some half-eaten yams, a chicken head—

"And any of the dried stuffs from the side of the hill beside the big rocks near their camp will flame up nicely."

"All right," she said. "This should do, I think—at least I hope it will."

There were no thanks. But both grinned at each other. Then, the little basket at her thigh, she was moving off through the woods, making again for the Myetran camp.

Naä was astonished how easily the carrying out of the plan went. Behind one wagon, a handful of slop, up and over the edge—splash; then on behind the next—splash again; and behind the next. Back under the cover of the trees, she tried out the flint and metal on a bit of the bale of dried brush she'd gathered, repeating to herself as she crouched in the shadow, "It's the idea and not the doing—and having the stuff to do the doing with!"

At the horse enclosure, she thrust five big bales of dried kindling one after the other through the back fence. With spears crossed, way on the far side the two guards looked resolutely in the opposite direction.

She was back in the woods, starting to bring down another bale, when an officer rode up to return a horse to the enclosure—so she waited. Minutes later, she was down on her knees, behind the last bale, beating and beating the iron against the stone till the oiled rag suddenly caught. A moment later, there was a rush of heat, of crackling, of orange flame—and she was running off again, into the woods. She turned back once, as two horses trotted over to examine the fire, then suddenly reared, whinnied, and galloped away—and do you know, the spear guards *still* had not looked!

She ran faster up the forested hill. Only twenty steps later, when more horses began to whinny behind her, did she hear the first man shout.

A moment later, she was again on her knees, laughing.

She laughed again, about an hour on, when, as she walked among the houses nearer the common, chubby Jallet, Mantice's boy with the cast in his right eye, stopped to tell her what had happened to the soldiers, returning to camp under the trees behind the council building:

"When those bad men went under the stand of trees that are so thick in their branches that they make noon look near night, an old cabbage hit one of them on the shoulder; then eggs and goat offal and chicken heads and other nasty things began to pelt them from up in the leaves—from someone who could aim too. For one got a splat of shit in his visor and another with his helmet off got cut on the face with a broken pot!"

Still laughing, Naä managed to say: "But it must have been—" Then she caught herself. "It must have been quite a little rain of slop and garbage!"

"It wasn't Qualt," Jallet said.

Naä was surprised that the child's thoughts had gone like hers to the dump. But then, what else would a town person have thought?

"It wasn't anybody at all," Jallet explained, "because the Myetrans got real angry and began to climb the trees and look about, and there wasn't anybody in them. Nobody had gone up them. And nobody—except the Myetrans—ever came down!"

"I see," Naä said. "So it just . . . happened!"

Jallet nodded, with his unsettling glance that, because of the cast, you never knew where it was fixed. But while Naä laughed, she wondered.

Later that evening, though, when she was passing through the common, she saw four Çironians bound before a group of bewildered villagers. As she stopped to watch, the bored officer in his black hood and immobile cloak announced their crime was "mischief against Myetra! For the crime of which, ten lashes each!" Their hands thonged together before them, their clothes torn from their backs, the woman and the three men shuffled from side to side, blinked, and looked frightened. Were they, she wondered suddenly, being lashed for her misdoings? Or Qualt's? It was the first moment of circumspection she'd had in the heady rush of her mischief. When the first lash fell, little Kenisa, standing next to her and looking very serious, reached up quietly to take Naä's hand—Naä flinched a moment, so that Kenisa glanced up at her. But then, Naä had already gotten the soap and salt and done the obligatory hand washing earlier at Hara's house.

Several times and very loudly, the sunset curfew ordinance was read out at all corners of the common.

And finally, in full darkness, Naä was still slipping between the houses and along the back paths behind them, contemplating what more she might do to cause the soldiers inconvenience, when she saw Rahm.

For the first minutes behind the horses, Rahm had stumbled and crouched at the end of the rope. Then he just walked, head low and half bent over. Finally he'd come on behind them, the tall, muscular youth Naä knew as Ienbar's helper and her friend—almost as if, bit by bit, he'd put aside some mime of weakness he'd been performing for his captors that they had not even bothered to notice. It's amazing, Naä thought, hurrying on beside, they really haven't looked at him once.

I could run out, take my knife, slash the rope, and the two of us could be free and off in the dark in seconds! She grasped the knife at her belt, finally pulled it loose. But whenever she squeezed the handle, picturing herself sprinting forward, she felt a glittering web of terror, a web flung up between her and the figures moving through the dark streets.

If I surprised him and he *really* stumbled or cried out . . .

If just one of them *chose* to look back, by chance . . .

If he or I made some *accidental* sound . . .

This bravery of the body in sight of bodies was very different, she realized, from the sort she'd managed earlier, with a camp half asleep under the hottest of the day's sun.

But still, across the little span of night, not one of the soldiers had actually *looked* at him, so smug were they in their superiority! Naä was still thinking this when the soldiers, Rahm bound behind them, returned to the common's edge and started across for the council house. Qualt had been right: the strongest building in the town was now being used as a Myetran prison. She stepped out, then stopped as though the stone wall were only feet in front of her instead of cattycorner across the square. Naä stepped back into the last doorway, to watch the soldiers and her friend mount the ten stone steps and enter the plank door. Torchlight flickered within. She cursed, cursed again. But there was no way to breach those well-set rocks. She turned among the houses and began to hurry down a back street.

Half an hour later, Naä was again among the dark trees, the Myetran camp before her—though, save a cook fire off over there or a line of light under the edge of a tent to the right, it was all but invisible. She crossed between the underbrush and a back wall of canvas, that, bellying with the night's breeze, gave a snap, then sagged. Moving closer, she heard a voice within:

"Lieutenant Kire, this will stop! I ordered them executed. You had them flogged."

A softer voice, with a roughness to it almost menacing: "Nactor, my prince—"

"I want no explanations! You, Kire, have been given a great opportunity, an opportunity allowed to few—to lead a brigade of Myetra. Is this how you use your officer's privilege? This is how you'd have Myetra known? Were you not so good a soldier with different family connections, things would go badly for you now—very badly. It is only your skill at arms that saves you from my anger." There was a pause. "It's dangerous to cross me, Kire. You know that, don't you?"

"My prince, truly I thought—"

"What *did* you think, Kire? At this point I would like to know if you were thinking at all. Personally, I thought you'd lost your mind. Did you think perhaps it was an accident when a fire started in the horse yard? Did you think perhaps it was happenstance when most of three platoons came down with dysentery in the same hour?"

"My prince"—the man's breath came stiffly, hoarsely, uncomfortably in his throat—"all we know is that it was not the villagers I had flogged who did it. What I thought, my prince, I thought we might . . . learn something from them—who is responsible for the fire, the water."

"We could take any one of them from the street and beat that knowledge from him."

"You've tried that, my prince." He drew a loud frustrated breath. "Sire, these are a peaceful people. They don't even have a word for weapons. The tactics we are using here are inappropriate—more than inappropriate: wasteful of our time and energy."

"Peaceful, are they? If they have no word for them, that just means they will be that much cleverer in coming up with weapons you or I would never think to name as such. There have already been attempts at sabotage—"

"But let me at least try a method that seems to me right for this situation. Let me pick out someone, gain his confidence, then send him among them so that we can learn and direct both. Let me select a man who—"

"Choose a woman." Nactor's voice was hard, almost shrill. "A girl, rather. I am not interested in confidences, Kire. I'm interested in terror, fear, and domination. And she must be terrified of you, Kire—she must know that if she displeases you in the slightest thing, then . . . you will kill her!" (Near Naä's cheek the canvas snapped once more. She pulled sharply back, though more at the indifferent cruelty than the surprise. Again she moved forward.) "Peaceful! If they seem peaceful, it is because we have given them no opportunity to be otherwise. Peaceful? Ha! Get this woman. Yes—there are three things you must do to her: bed her, beat her, and let her know her life hangs by no more than your whim, a hair . . . a hair that can break any moment you decide. Then . . . well then, use her as you will." (In the pause, Naä tried to picture the lieutenant's and the prince's expressions.) "You understand, Kire: this is an order. Break her, violate her. Then, when you've done that, you may use her as you wish for whatever spying—or instruction—you can. And when we depart here, you will kill her—like any other soldier finished with an enemy whore. You've disobeyed me once, Kire. If you do it again . . ."

Naä heard the sounds of boots over matting and hard-packed earth. Canvas scratched against canvas as the flap was pushed back. Kire spoke to a guard: "Go into town, Uk. Take horses and two more men; requisition a portable light from Power Supplies. And bring back some woman of Çiron—"

The prince laughed: "Go into town and find a young and pretty one. I really think this should be rather fun; I'm going back to my tent."

"Obey your prince." Kire spoke to the big soldier.

Naä realized she was gripping the edge of the canvas in her fist. Stupid! she thought, and released it, hoping no one within had seen. She moved back into the darkness.

There—the guard was going toward Supplies.

Naä backed up half a dozen steps, turned, and sprinted into the trees alongside the drop that in the autumn became a stream, but was now no more than a marshy strip of leaves at the bottom of the night.

There'd not been much pleasure that day for Uk. In the morning he'd stuck his head out from the warmth of his sleeping bag into mist cut through with birch trees. Squatting by him the tall soldier on cleanup detail, who'd shaken him by the shoulder, said: "Your friend's over there in the wagon." Uk had been confused enough to believe for a moment the man was telling him

Mrowky'd come back. "If you want to see him, before we put him under."

Then, understanding, Uk pushed himself out of the bag to stand in the inverted evening that was dawn. In his brown military underwear, occasionally scratching his stomach, he walked the quarter mile to the casualty wagon.

The men had already finished the grave pit. The wagon detail had found only three Myetran dead around the village—the perfect average for this operation.

"You want his armor?" one asked.

Uk glanced over the wagon's edge, where—with the two other corpses—Mrowky sprawled, hair plastered to his head with mud, mud dried over one side of his face, neck swollen, purple and black, bulging over the rim of his breastplate. Uk started to say he'd take the armor till he realized he'd have to take it from the corpse himself. "Naw. Naw, you bury him in it. He was a good soldier. He was a good—" Uk turned from the cart abruptly, to start back, thinking: Mrowky was a stupid, lecherous pest who'd talked too loud and too much.

Was Mrowky a bad man? he let himself wonder. Then, thirty meters from the wagon, Uk said out loud: "Mrowky was the best!" because a friend seemed somehow such a rare and valuable and important thing in the hazed-over dawn by the trees at the edge of this ragged village who knew where. He thought (and knew it was true, thinking it): Mrowky would have killed for me. I would have killed for him. . . . There in the wet road, the fact stopped him, struck his eyes to tears, then, moments on, dried them. He took a loud, ragged breath and walked back among the morning cook fires.

Some hours later, on a patrol through town, when the dozen of them were a street away from the market common, just across from the well, Uk glanced aside to see the redheaded girl, being hurried by her equally redheaded brother up some low steps and through a shack door. And that's the woman Mrowky died for, Uk thought. No, it wasn't fair.

And what about the crazed peasant who'd murdered Mrowky? Would I even recognize him, Uk had pondered, his face once more returned to normal, after that murderous frenzy?

Later, cross-legged on the ground, while he was eating his dinner, Uk was called for guard duty at Lieutenant Kire's tent. And the lieutenant himself, on going out, stopped in a swag of black, his cloak a dark tongue thrust straight down behind, to ask in the evening's slant-light: "How's it going for you there, Uk?"

Clearly the lieutenant had heard the others speak of the big soldier's loss. "I'm all right, sir," Uk answered, and wondered why even that absurdly small bit of concern made him feel better. Perhaps, he reflected, as, in the east, indigo darkened the village roofs, it's because any and all concern in this landscape—by anyone or for anyone—was so rare.

Only a bit of light lit a few western clouds as Prince Nactor had marched up to Kire's tent flap; when, outside, Uk heard the altercation within, he did not exactly listen to their conversation. (That's what Mrowky would have done—then been back to whisper about it half the night . . .) Not that it kept their words from him. But while they'd talked, voices rising and lowering, he tried to move his mind years and miles away, to fix on a stream in his own village, with its dark and muddy bank rich in frogs and dragonflies.

Then light fell in his eyes, and Kire was saying: "Go into town, Uk. Take horses and two more men—requisition a portable light from Power Supplies. And bring back some woman of Çiron."

Behind Kire, the prince laughed: "Go into town and find a young and pretty one. I really think this should be rather fun. I'm going back to my tent."

Kire said: "Obey your prince."

Surprised, the big soldier threw up his fist in salute.

Minutes later, with two other soldiers, their mounts stepping carefully in the dark, Uk rode off between the last of the cook fires, red and wobbling against a black so intense it was blue. One of the riders, the box holding the illuminating filament slung around his neck, reached down now and clicked it on. A beam of white fanned to the left of his horse. (In the bushes to the right, with twigs pricking her thighs and wrists, Naä pulled back in loud leaves—and stopped breathing.) Clucking at his stallion, while some animal thrashed to his right in the brush, Uk glanced over at the beam. "Douse that. We don't need it."

The light died.

What had been in Uk's mind was that the moon's sliver from the previous night should have grown a bit by this evening. But either the world had moved from crescent moon to moon's dark, or overcast hid all illumination. Probably they could have used a light, Uk decided, as the horses left the smell of burning for the town's dark streets. But that only resolved him, out of whatever stubbornness, not to have it on at all.

Really, he thought, later, it was not so much a conscious decision. Rather, as Uk led the other two soldiers through the night village, at a certain point he simply realized where he was going, what he had already started to do, and let himself go on to do it. The lieutenant had told him to bring back a village woman. What other woman should he bring? He knew where this one lived. If he started looking in houses at random, it could take forever. Between the dark shacks of the village, he let his horse take him out of the market square. "Break her, violate her!" the prince had ordered. Well, he thought, reining to the left, it was only what had already started to happen to her.

In the light from one window, he made out the well and turned toward where the door to the house should be—yes; there were the steps. He gave the order to dismount, dropped to the ground himself, stepped up on the porch, and with his fist hammered on the door.

Then he hammered again.

When he struck the door a third time, a voice within, like a child's, asked: "Yes? Who—" so that, when light rose up along the crack in the door, he expected the figure standing behind it to be her.

But it was the boy, his hair coppery in the firelight inside, one braid falling in front of his strong little shoulders, one behind.

Uk pushed the door in. "Where's the girl, Çironian?"

Stepping back, the boy said, "Sir?"

"Where's the girl who lives here . . . your sister?" Certainly in a village like this, she must be his sister.

"What wouldst thou—?"

Surprised at his own impatience, with the heel of his hand Uk hit the boy's naked shoulder. "Call her!"

A girl's voice came, somewhere from within: "Abrid?"

The boy's fearful face looking up at Uk seemed wholly absurd. Behind, one of the other soldiers moved closer.

The frightened boy called over his shoulder: "Rimgia?"

In the part of the room that, outside the firelight's immediate range, was shadow, a hanging moved. The girl stepped hesitantly in. The first thing Uk thought was how ridiculously young they both were! Surely this afternoon, when he'd glimpsed them in the glaring street, they'd been older than this?

Her bright hair, unbraided, was tousled; her eyes looked sleepy—swollen with tiredness? Or was it something else? She came forward, her face full of questioning.

Uk stepped, reached out, and grabbed Rimgia's arm. Her eyes came immediately awake, as he said, "Come on! You're wanted at Lieutenant Kire's tent."

Abrid said, "Touch her gently or not at all!"

While the girl said, "Please, let me get my—"

Where the rage came from, Uk didn't know. Really, they were only kids. But he released the girl, turned, and gave the boy the back of his hand, against his cheek and neck. Abrid went stumbling back and sat down hard, his head cracking against the wall—sat blinking, terrified. "I have no patience with a silly boy's playing at being a man!" Uk growled.

Rimgia, who had grabbed a shawl from some peg on the wall, froze where she had started to wrap it around herself.

"Go on!" Uk barked. "Cover yourself, you dirty hussy! If you'd done that last night—" The hand with which he had struck the boy was shaking. What he'd started to say was that the little guy might be alive now! But that was stupid. They'd never known his friend—even the girl. "Come on!"

The cloth went over her head, wrapped down tight on her shoulders. Her blinking eyes were suddenly shadowed by the indifferent print covering her hair.

Uk took her by the arm and pulled her outside, while she kept trying to look back over her shoulder at her brother within still sitting on the floor. "Rimgia?" That was the boy.

She called out once: "Abrid!"

Which made one of the other soldiers with them grab her and push her farther into the dark: "Come on, now!" which, Uk realized a moment later, might have been to keep him from hitting her; for at her cry, Uk had raised his shaking hand again.

Why could he not control this absurd anger at these silly, frightened children?

One of the other soldiers gave him the rope when he asked for it. He and the one with the light over his shoulder bound her clumsily in the dark; then the soldier who'd pushed her said, "Come, behind the horse—and don't dawdle. If you're thinking about running, forget it. We'll just come back and kill your brother—before we catch you again!"

And a moment later, they were riding through the town, while, now and again, Uk heard—or felt—the girl at the tether's end stumble or, once, cry out.

She'd winced with each of big Uk's barks. She'd bitten down hard as he'd struck Abrid. Now, from doorway to doorway, Naä hurried on beside the three mounted soldiers, with Rimgia going, bound, behind. And Naä thought, as she had thought before: They really *don't* look back.

And then: *Suppose* I did it?

Fool, she thought. This isn't some ballad or folktale about some bit of birdbrained bravery! This is my *life* . . . But, she thought, it's *her* life too.

Then she thought: this time I *am* going to do it.

And as she thought it, she realized she was, rather, going to do something else!

The web was bound wholly around her now, glittering against her back, her cheeks, her calves, her forehead, her thighs. (Let it, she thought, be an energy flowing into me, not a draining!)

Naä thought: If I do what I know I'm about to, I am going to be killed. If I do what I know I'm about to, I'm going to be . . . I'm going to be killed. She repeated it in the darkness until it meant nothing to her. And dashed for the next doorway. But I have a knife—and so I will kill one or three or, who knows, even more of them. Maybe I'll get away. And Rimgia will get free. That's what's important. That's—

Then, in a movement that was beyond thought, she sprinted out to Rimgia, reached the stumbling girl, put one arm firmly around Rimgia's shoulder and her other hand over Rimgia's mouth, and kept her pace moving forward. *"It's Naä!"* she whispered—less than whispered: mouthed rather, with just the faintest trace of breath, her lips touching Rimgia's ear; and she was still sure the girl didn't hear.

With her free hand, Naä tugged at the rope, loosening it, pulling it up to Rimgia's shoulders. In the faintest light from some passing shutter, Naä saw Rimgia staring at her (their faces were only inches from each other's) in terror; yet her head shook a moment, with some recognition of what was happening. As Naä got the rope free, she glanced toward the horses before her, where none of the men had as yet looked back. *"I'm changing places with you!"* she whispered suddenly to Rimgia.

There was a convulsive movement from the girl beneath Naä's arm, which, though it was wholly without sound, might as easily have been a laugh as a quiver of fear.

"Go!" Naä went on. *"Get Abrid. Take him somewhere out of the village, into the hills, the both of you!"* She had gotten the rope over her own shoulder when from Rimgia, still against her, clinging to Naä even though she was no longer bound, there was abrupt movement—for a moment Naä was confused and fright-

ened and sure that, in a moment, the whole thing would end. But Rimgia was pushing her shawl over Naä's head, pulling it forward, tucking it down under the rope, now here, now there, all the time half running along beside her in the dark. *"All right!"* Naä whispered again, in that whisper less than sound.

Now, at once, Rimgia pulled away—or perhaps Naä pulled from Rimgia. Naä stumbled for real, but did not fall. Ahead, the horse to whom she was bound made a corresponding adjustment in his step. And the big soldier astride him—once again—did not turn around to look! Beneath Rimgia's shawl, Naä felt the length of blade at her belt; it seemed small and silly and the idea of killing somebody with it even sillier. Her mouth had gone dry. Her heart was thudding loud enough to make her stagger in her tracks. At least the children might actually get away—

I will be killed, Naä thought once more. But, blessedly, it was still without meaning.

They crossed a stretch that, from the smell and the stubble underfoot, was a burnt field. Fires were burning in the distance. Then other fires were closer. The black-cut gray of birches leaned off into the dark. In front of a tent, the soldiers stopped the horses, dismounted—and, believe it or not, *still* did not bother to look at her!

The big soldier whose horse she was tied to pushed back the flap and, leaning within, said, "I've got your girl for you, lieutenant."

The voice she'd heard before, the one called Kire, said: "Bring her in and leave us, Uk."

Naä clamped her jaw, clutched the shawl tight over her hair, her other hand on the knife hilt under the long cloth, under the rope. Strike, she thought. Who? Which one? Would it be the brutal, vicious soldier who'd struck Abrid and bound Rimgia? Or the lieutenant? Or maybe the prince, if he was still there? If things had gone this well so far, perhaps it was not so foolish to expect success after all? But she mustn't get cocky. Bravery, daring, courage, yes—but don't abandon common care and sense—though, she wondered, was there anything of sense about this?

Remember, she thought, men who do what these men have done are not human, are without feelings, are dogs, are maggots, are worms.

Who will it be first? she thought. Will it be the lieutenant or one of his hulking, beer-gutted guards?

The big guard, Uk—what a name!—came back and took her arm. As he pulled her into the wedge of lamplight that was the tent opening, she started to look away so that he might not recognize her. Then something made her stare straight at him.

His heavy-featured face was looking directly ahead, neither to the right nor left. A soldier, she realized, following orders— doing nothing more, nothing less. For all his brutality to Rimgia and Abrid, that's all he was. A pig, a dog, a worm; and yet as much without will, she thought, as without sensitivity. He really doesn't see me at all, Naä reflected. Do any of them—

"Thank you, Uk. Dismiss the others and return to duty."

And the big soldier, with a fist flung high, backed through the flap.

The lieutenant stood by the desk against the tent's striped wall. There was a smell in the tent that made her recall both the smell in Qualt's yard and the stronger smell in the malodorous basket from the afternoon—without its being exactly like either. Was it the mildewed canvas itself? But no, it was a spoiled scent far closer to animal than vegetable.

Like a black-draped statue, the lieutenant turned in the light of the lamps, one of which—a shallow tripod brazier on a low table by the cot, where a puma skin, the skull still in it, had been thrown across the dark wool blanket (was that what smelled? she wondered)—had a yellow hue: the lamp hanging from the tent's center by its several brass chains and the lamp on the desk's corner both burned with the harshest white fire.

Outside the tent, Uk stepped to the left of the entrance, breathed deeply in the darkness, spread his legs, put his hands behind his back, taking the at-ease guard position, and thought: There, that's done, however little it was. What am I? A man following orders, nothing more, nothing less. I'm a soldier. Forget this sensitivity. It doesn't become me. Though the night had grown chill around him, there was almost a warmth in the realization, so that, for the first time that day, it seemed he could let his mind drift, let his eyes fix on a bit of light from the tent flaps that fell on a grass tuft and a flat stone while he remembered a stream somewhere, with broken mud, dragonflies, frogs . . .

When the lieutenant looked at Naä, she lowered her eyes, to let the edge of Rimgia's shawl fall as low across her face as it could, even as she thought: but *he* doesn't know what I'm supposed to look like at all!

The lieutenant walked over to her and pulled at the rope. It was tied so loosely that its two coils dropped down around her feet even as he tugged them once. (There had been three coils when Rimgia had first been tied . . . .) Naä held the shawl closed at her neck. But he did not seem to think it particularly odd. The feeling that none of them, none of them at all, actually saw her became for a moment a dazzling conviction. I could be anyone here, and it would make no difference—

The lieutenant stepped toward the desk again and turned, his black-gloved fingers on some parchments there. A day's beard peppered his cheek.

"Thou lookest to be hard worked," she said shortly, assuming the Çironian idiolect. Her own voice sounded breathless and faint to her. But the words would not stop. "Has doing injury worn thee down?"

He glanced up at her with a smile, which, she realized, looked simply tired. In the brazier's light, his eyes were a smoky hue, as if the irises were circles cut from the undersides of oak leaves, around black pupils.

He said, "I haven't slept much—or well, recently." The oddly hoarse voice, with the carrion odor all around, made her feel as if she'd entered some place more primitive, primordial, and basically lawless than any she recalled from her travels.

"Bad dreams?" Bitterness whetted her voice to a greater sharpness than she'd intended.

Kire walked across the rug, reaching up to push a black pom through a black loop. His hood slipped from bronze hair. It and his cloak dropped to the ground to make a motionless puddle of night, frozen in the moment of its fall. Turning to sit on the cot's edge, absently he felt the prairie lion's skull with black-gloved fingers. Kire's green eyes strayed back to Naä's.

She pulled the shawl tighter and felt her body tingling with impatience for him to make the move, say a word, give her one reason to lunge with the knife—at his neck. Yes, certainly in the neck. Could she slip beneath the back of the tent? And the stabbing itself—could she do it so quickly, so deftly, that there would be no noise? Should she wait for him to turn from her? Or should she move closer now—

"You're not a very tall woman," he said, looking up at her. "See over there?" He nodded toward the back of the tent. "One of the ground cords"—and she had the momentarily uncanny feeling that he had heard her thoughts—"at the rear wall has come untied. You can easily slip under the canvas there if you like—yes, you can go. I have no reason to frighten you any more than you've already been frightened." He gestured to the tent wall. "Go on."

"You want me to *go*?" she said, dropping the Çironian inflection, but realizing that she had only when he glanced back with raised eyebrow. "Suppose I don't want to. Suppose I want to stay and find out what kind of man you are."

"You're not of Çiron," he said after a moment. "Who are you?"

"You're called Kire," she said. "My name is . . . Naä. I'm a wanderer, a singer; I'm someone who's come very much to love this place, over which you wreak fire, slaughter, and misery."

What he did next rather surprised her. He lifted the puma pelt from the bed and swung it over his back. She caught a glimpse of its underside, where bits of red and things rolled into black fibers and filaments, only just dried, still clung to the uncured hide. With the motion came a heightened smell—it *was* the source of the stench! The catch under one set of claws, sewn there clumsily with a thong, he hooked to a fastening on the other side of the pelt. Affixed to the Myetran that way, the puma head leered from his shoulder, beside his own.

"Why do you wear that?" she asked.

"This?" He spoke as though the dropping of the cloak and the donning of the hide had been the most unconscious and happenstance of acts. "It was a gift. From a friend. I like it. Cloaks are supposed to blow and ride out behind you on the wind, but ours are too heavy. It takes the glory out of soldiering. This, at least, looks like what it is." With a black glove, he caressed the face beside his own, with its sealed lids, its bared fangs. "And it will remind you, no matter how pleasant I seem really, I have teeth." (That he might call this odd and smelly space pleasant almost drew a surprised comment from her. But she held it in.) "Come—if you're going to stay, sit here, in the chair"—he indicated the seat at his desk—"where we can talk more easily. Won't you take off your shawl?"

She only held it tighter. But being closer to him would be good. Yes, get closer. She sat in the chair, her knees inches from his.

Yellow fires ran round within the copper rim of the small brazier by his elbow. "You know these people well," Kire said. "Tell me, are they really as gentle as they appear?"

"Yes," she said, unable to keep the challenge out of her voice. "They are."

He smiled. "Couldn't you tell me something small-minded, mean, and nasty you've found among them; or maybe even some overt and active evil: a crippled child teased and made fun of? An old woman's milk stolen from her goat so that she must go hungry, once again? Something that might ease my dreams just a little? Certainly the ordinary pettiness, jealousies, the envy and ire that hold any little town together, beneath the polite greetings and pleasantries in the market square about last week's rain and today's fine weather, must be as common here as they are in any other village. You're a well-traveled woman. You've seen none of the provincial nastiness here that makes the children of such places so frequently loathe their home and yearn to flee somewhere with breathing room, intelligent conversation, and fine music?"

"They've been happy with the music I've brought," Naä said. "And I've been happy with their conversation. I haven't looked for more. And what sort of fool are you"—she looked at him as sharply as she spoke—"that you think the things you speak of could possibly balance the death, the misery, the evil you inflicted here within the hour of your coming?"

He looked back at her directly. The lion beside him, for the instant, seemed a creature who'd closed its eyes to keep from hearing. A muscle moved in the lieutenant's unshaven jaw. Then he said: "Do you know anything about Myetra, singer? If you visited us, you might be surprised at how pleasantly our farmers and their daughters can dance in a spring evening to the great log drums their wives make in the mountains; or how colorful and cunning the representation of sea creatures and sea plants on the tiles decorating the facades of the waterfront warehouses. It's a pleasant place, but there are too many people in it. There is not enough food—and above all not enough land for our people. It's very simple, singer, what we've chosen to do. It's a plan as clean and as imperative as . . . as a blood drop rolling down a new-plastered wall. You see us now taking lives, breaking apart cultures and traditions, here at Çiron, next at Hi-Vator, after that at Requior, then Del Gaizo, and eventually at Mallili—finally even at Calvicon. But soon what you will see, in a band from water to water, is the growth of a rich, intelligent, and wonderfully hardworking and resourceful people, taking land, making food, imparting their ways and wonders on these myriad backward folk who have no notion of their own histories for more than five or six generations into the past—the length of time a burial scroll will last before it simply rots away. It's a fine plan, singer. And it inspires the officers above me as well as the simple soldiers below me."

"And does this plan give you the right to do anything, anything at all—at any level of cruelty and destruction to anyone in your way?"

The lieutenant mused. "There are some among us who think that it does." At every third sentence, the roughness to his voice made her wonder if he weren't drunk.

"And you? What do you think?"

"There are some, both above me and below me, who probably say that I think too much."

In the stench of the uncured hide, within hearing of the burry tones that, really, sounded more animal than human, Naä wondered how anything that anyone might call thinking at all could go on here.

But he moved his forearm, with the black glove on his hand, along the edge of the desk by the yellow-burning lamp. "Tell me, singer, what would you do if we were in each other's place? What would you do if you wore a stiff black cloak and, despite your love of your home, a sense of injustice—if not of justice itself. But yes, the truth is: I'm troubled at justice's absence, and that trouble stays as close to me as this lion's face is to my own. Would you try to leave, feign sickness, resign your post to another? Or would you stay, mitigating the crimes those around you commit—changing a death sentence to a prison term, making an execution a flogging, reducing a flogging of twenty lashes to ten? Tell me, singer?"

Naä frowned. Then stopped frowning and thought: this is perhaps the moment to do it. But the words came from somewhere: "I would get very little sleep." And because these words came too, she said: "If you love your own home, can't you love the idea of home that other people have? That's what a sense of justice is, isn't it? And the plan you talk of, it's not a just one at all. I've looked your men in the face. I've heard your superiors talking. Your men have forgotten all plans and are only faithful to following orders. And all your superiors are after is the power and privilege the plan has most accidentally ceded them! So without justice behind it or real commitment to support it, what is your plan after that?" The words came, she found herself thinking, like the words to a new song. "Why not turn openly against it? Why not fight it and them until they strip skin and muscle from you, till no muscle moves, till there is no blood left in you to move them—"

"Now—" And she was thinking, Will actions come as fast and as easily as those words? when he said, "I should probably smash you across the face with my fist for daring even to suggest resistance to Myetra." He raised his hand, and the gloved fingers curled slowly in. "And show you why, through sheer force, that is such an absurd notion. But I don't think I shall . . . this time." He looked at her seriously.

Again she felt her whole body begin to tingle. "You mitigate," she said. "You turn twenty lashes to ten. And when you are told to rape, break, and violate, you turn it into talk—"

He raised a bronze eyebrow. "Who told you that?"

"Your guard," she said quickly, "when he was bringing me back from town. Those were Prince Nactor's . . . orders, yes?"

"Uk?" The lieutenant looked honestly puzzled. Then he barked a syllable of laughter. "You're a liar—or a fool! That sort of loose tongue is not Uk's style. Believe me, I know my men. No, we had a guard here once who might have said that. But he's . . . not with us now. And what I said to Nactor, I left with Nactor, young lady. Right now I hate Prince Nactor as he hates me. No . . . I think perhaps I will walk you back to the village. We will go together: this way you will have no problems with obstreperous or loose-tongued guards." He rose.

And amidst the tingling, she thought, Somewhere on the burnt field, somewhere in an alley of the town, yes, when the two of us are alone together, *that's* where I'll do it. Certainly that would be better—

He stood and reached down for her shoulder. But suppose he binds me again? she thought as she rose in his grip. Wasn't it better to do it now and have done? (His black-gloved fingers on her shoulder were strong.) Or was hers simply the endlessly rationalized delay of someone blatantly terrified of killing?

"I think," she said softly, "you are a good and thoughtful man."

What she thought was: you are an evil pig a-wallow in a rotten sty. . . .

He didn't pick up the rope as, holding her arm, he walked her by the brazier, the chair, the desk, across the matting toward the tent flap.

Still supporting her, with his other black glove he took the canvas and pulled it back.

Standing just outside, the prince ran his gauntleted hand down one side of his beard, then the other, and said: "Kire, you *are* a fool! '*Hate* Prince Nactor'? *Guards!*" Naä pulled back as Kire released her arm. A dozen shadowy soldiers waited in ordered formation behind the bearded prince "Arrest Lieutenant Kire—for incompetence, insubordination, and treason! And also the woman—"

The hesitation that had plagued her moments ago vanished before the immediate. Naä dodged behind the lieutenant, lunged for the table, thrust her hand under the brazier, and hurled fire—in a sheet that astonished her, even as it hung a moment in the air and flickered and threw up coiling smoke tendrils, a curtain of blue and yellow effulgence, of falling, flaming oil, dropping to the matting, arching toward the striped wall opposite. That same moment she hurled herself to the floor and rolled against the tent's back canvas. Guards shouted. Were any of them dodging around the back? But yes, and she was under, up in the dark and the cool night, running. Mercifully no tree or water barrel stood before her, or she would have smashed into it and knocked herself unconscious.

Naä ran.

Branches raked at her, bushes snatched at and scraped her. Rimgia's shawl caught and tore. Naä paused to jerk it (swallowing the impulse to scream); she pulled free, snatched it after her, and ran again in a chatter of brush and leaves till she tripped and went sprawling. What she'd tripped on was large and rolled a little, loudly.

Flies in the dark make an unholy sound—and hundreds of them scritted, disturbed now, from whatever she'd fallen over. She caught the stench—like the puma pelt and the basket and the ravine itself, intensified to gagging, eye-watering level—and pulled herself away.

(She would forever recall it as some villager's corpse, slain and left to lie. Actually, though, it was a prairie lion carcass: the evening just before the attack, Mrowky and Uk had been ordered to dump it in the forest three hundred paces off. But Mrowky couldn't stand the thing and had insisted on leaving it here: *right* now, we've taken it far enough, nobody'll find—no, I *mean* it! I'm leaving it! I don't care what you do. Put the damned thing *down,* I said—now!)

Turning, gasping, Naä saw flames behind her; between the sounds of her breaths, back in the camp she heard soldiers shouting.

Another sound: the splat of water tossed on canvas (with the sound of the last flies setting)—how close she still was! How little ground she'd covered! And there were soldiers beating loudly in the brush behind the burning tent. Naä pushed herself up and ran again. For a long time.

Qualt's and his companion's mischief had also continued on, as you surely inferred. At various places about the town and the camp there'd been four more rains of garbage from the trees. The one Qualt felt most satisfied after was when, during the distraction that the last shower of fish heads, peach pits, and old bird's nests provided, his flying friend, still unseen, had been able to drop two skins of water into the diamond-wired corral where more than a dozen oldsters and infants were sitting or standing, more or less bewildered, in the burning sun.

But now, with the Winged One, in the darkness, Qualt was

once more crouched among the trees beside the Myetran camp, listening—rather the Winged One was listening and reporting to Qualt what he heard, for they were too far away from the tent for Qualt to hear directly. Heads bent together in the dark, ear touching ear, the Winged One related: "He asks if you folk are as gentle as you appear. . . . She says yes, you are. . . . Now he wants to know what town secrets, what petty jealousies, envy, and ire she can tell him of; while she . . . she says you like her music, and she likes what you have to say. . . . He tells her what a pleasant place his own home, Myetra, is, and how, after they have crushed Çiron, they will go on to destroy Hi-Vator, Requior, Del Gaizo—"

Somewhat to Qualt's surprise, it was at the mention of Hi-Vator that the Winged One suddenly went a-quiver in the dark. The wind of his sails set the leaves about them shaking and shushing. And one membrane brushed and brushed Qualt's back.

"We must go to Hi-Vator—now, we must go! Don't you think so, groundling? And you can hide there as I have hidden here—and maybe we can even play some tricks as we have played here? But I will tell them of their danger! Though perhaps, after we get there, it would be best if I hid and *you* went up to implore the Queen and her Handsman to save themselves; for there are few in Hi-Vator who ever paid much attention to me—and then, most of them, only to curse me. Of course we could go together . . . and no one who knew the true import of the message I bring could really think evil of me anymore—do you think?"

"Dost *thou* think," Qualt demanded, his hand on the hard, furry shoulder beside him, which flexed and flexed in darkness, "that the Winged Ones there might help us here?"

"Help you?" The beating paused a puzzled moment. "I daresay they could if they wanted. But help you? After all the help I've given you today, carrying you here, getting you there, lifting you out of this danger and away from that one, don't you think it's time, given the gravity of this turn, for *you* to think about helping *me*?"

"Then we must go to thy nest at Hi-Vator! Here, let me mount thee . . ." and, rising in the darkness from his squat, steadying himself on the shoulder below him, Qualt stepped over and around to the soft dirt behind. The warm back rose against his belly, his chest.

"Hold tight—we have not gone this far before! But you know now how it's done!"

In the black, Qualt clutched the Winged One's neck. Great vibrations started either side of him. Twigs and soft soil dropped away beneath his bare feet. Swinging free, his legs brushed their calves by the Winged One's tough heels.

"But what of the singer?" Qualt thought to call.

"Oh"—and the head strained back beside his—"she has already escaped them—and is off running in the woods! There, look, their tent's on fire. And all is confusion with them." And they rose above the trees, Qualt looking down over the furred shoulder to see flames lapping at the striped wall flare now, then retreat under the slap of water, then surge still again. Beside him, wings gathered up, beat hugely down—

How, Qualt wondered, could such flight be carried on in the dark—even as the first moonlight cleared. Then he forgot the paring of light above and simply clung, sometimes with his eyes closed, sometimes merely squinting against the wind.

They rose before the mountains.

And rose.

And rose—till, beside the rush of water over the rocks, at last Qualt stepped away from his flying companion, arms tingling, oddly light-headed.

"See there, the fire up on that ledge?" the Winged One said while Qualt tried to catch his breath. "Climb for it, groundling!"

"Climb?"

"Up the webbing there. See the guylines running from under those rocks?"

There was no talk now—and Qualt was glad of it—of either of them continuing alone or either of them hiding.

They climbed the sagging net.

As Qualt passed one ledge, a Winged One, very fat, waddled

quickly to the edge and, with lips pulled back from little teeth and little lids squeezed closed, followed them with her face from below to above.

They walked along a stone cliff, Qualt picking his way carefully, lagging farther and farther behind his companion, who, wings wide, bounded ahead, till three youngsters half ran, half soared from the cave mouth beside him to freeze, ears cocked and gawking. At a sudden mew within, they retreated. But now his companion waited for Qualt to catch up, making some disgusted comment about the children Qualt didn't wholly follow.

Steps had been carved into the mountain that they had to climb. Some of the edges were stone. Some were roots, with earth packed behind them. Qualt moved his hands along the stone walls on either side and wondered why his companion, behind him now on the stairs, didn't fly this last length of the ascent— which was apparently not the last length after all, because now they had to climb up another fifty feet of webbing, with the rush and rumble of falling water invisible below among dark rocks.

Finally they gained a ledge where a dozen Winged Ones waited. Qualt was very confused for a while, since no one seemed to want to speak to them.

Fires burned in several stone tubs. The cave entrances flickered and resounded with wings going in and out, with mewing retreating and emerging. Finally Qualt heard someone say beside him, in that high, childish voice they all spoke with: "But you can see, that is *not* the groundling who was here earlier; that is *not* the one who saved my life. I took him home. He has not returned. They look alike, yes, but not that much alike. Don't you see how much smaller he is?

"And you—" This was addressed to Qualt's companion, who, on reaching the ledge, had suddenly seemed to become indifferent to the whole enterprise and was now sitting on the rocky rim, hanging his heels in space, with his sails drawn in about him and feigning great interest in the night breezes and the night clouds and anything that was not the confused converse behind him. "Well," continued the standing Winged One, who wore some

sort of flattened chain around his neck (the only dress or ornament Qualt had seen among them so far), "we certainly didn't
expect to see *you* here, just now—"

"Please," Qualt said, suddenly stepping forward, "please,
thou must understand. But we *heard* something!"

At which, with a sudden straightening of his hips, his companion pushed himself off the cliff, dropped into the black, like
a feetfirst dive into ink, then a moment later rose out of it, into
the firelight, soaring now beside them, sailing now above them—
with a triumphant hoot that Qualt had *never* heard before!

After that, Qualt and his companion both were given lots of
attention.

Naä ran—well beyond the camp now . . . still waiting for
the sound of footsteps behind her, wondering at the fact that
somehow she was still alive, to flee, to run, to escape—from her
own absurd and dangerous plan. She took long breaths with her
mouth wide, to make as little sound as possible. Ienbar's knife
was still in her belt. She still held Rimgia's shawl at her neck.
Only an hour later, in the woods at the other side of the village,
did she realize that she had gone beyond the town as well. She
was going up a slope: this way, she realized, would take her
toward the quarry where the stone workers went to hew in the
day.

Leave this village, she thought. I am a singer! (In the dark,
she clutched the knife hilt till it hurt her hand, till it bruised
the undersides of her knuckles, till it stung with the salt on her
palm.) I am no woman for this sort of thing, whatever this sort
of thing was—killing on the sly, making brainlessly heroic res-
cues. A bit wildly she thought: I could make a ballad out of what
I've already done today and tonight and have the satisfaction of
knowing no one will ever believe it! You may have lost Rahm.
But you saved Rimgia. Reasonably, you can't do more. So go!
Go on!

Which is when her foot went into the ditch—and with the shooting pain, she turned, she fell. I've probably twisted my ankle, she thought. She got herself free, stepped gingerly on it— it didn't hurt that much. But in ten minutes, or when next she got off it, certainly then the throbbing that precluded walking would begin.

From somewhere, the moon (that, earlier, Uk had expected to light his way into town) rose with its crescent of illumination to light Naä's way through the woods. The underbrush tried to slow her, but she hurried on. Then, at the height of another slope, brush gave way to grasses and trees—one of the pear orchards above the village. She started out across it, still cursing her fool-hardiness and shivering when she thought of the mad luck that had let her get this far.

She shivered again, though the night had grown warmer— and was of the sort that, any other evening, would have been pleasant.

Between moonlit trees, in a small space a few yards to her left, Naä saw dark forms stretched on the grass. More corpses, was her first thought. Even up here . . . ?

Nothing particularly happened to change her mind; but she decided to go closer. Would it be villagers she knew? When she was a yard away, it occurred to her that they might be sleep-ing soldiers the Myetrans had stationed—which was when one propped himself up on an arm and whispered, "Who art thou?" in a voice that, even as it started chills on her back, she recognized.

"Abrid?" she asked the shadowed figure.

"Who art thou?" he repeated.

She told him, "It's Naä!"

The moon had leached all red from his braids, leaving them near the gray they were after his workday in the quarry, so that one could see his father in his face . . .

"Rimgia!" she heard the boy whisper, leaning toward the other sleeping figure. "It's Naä!"

A moment on, Naä crouched between the two youngsters, demanding: "But what are you *doing* here?"

"Thou saidst I should get Abrid," Rimgia whispered sleepily. "I did. We came here to hide."

"But they'll find you if they look for you!"

Rimgia sat cross-legged now, rocking backward and forward a little, clearly exhausted. "Why didst thou come up here?"

"To bring you your shawl," Naä said shortly. She tugged the printed cloth from her shoulder. It had gotten torn several more times. Naä's legs and arms were scratched, and she was still waiting for the ghost of the pain to reassert itself from when she had gone into the muddy ditch. But that was long enough back so that, if it hadn't started to pain her yet, then maybe she hadn't really twisted her ankle at all. She laughed at the thought that luck could go with you as easily as against (the escape seemed beyond luck, like the luck of being born at all) and tossed the cloth toward the girl; who simply looked at it, where it landed in the grass, tented in three places on stiff stalks.

Naä said, "It got a bit messed up, I think." Then she laughed. "I'm so glad to see you, girl; I'm so glad to see you both!"

Abrid was squatting now. He said, "Naä, nobody will find us up here!"

"*I* found you," Naä said. "And I wasn't even looking! You've got to go much farther. And really hide this time. But the two of you together!"

Rimgia lifted both hands to her neck, rubbing. "Naä, how did you get away? What happened? Why did you come here? Where are you going?"

"Get away? It was dumb luck. What happened? I'll tell you the next time we see each other. Where am I going? I—" and she stopped because she couldn't bring herself to say: I'm terrified and I'm running away. . . .

Then Abrid asked: "Where is thy harp?"

Naä looked down at the knife in her hand, its blade black as water. For the first time in many minutes she relaxed her fingers;

the pain bloomed like a hot glow around her fist as her fingers loosened on the handle. "I . . . I put my harp away for a while. It's not a time for singing. Look, you two must keep going— you must get miles from the village. As if you're on a wander together. And then you must hide, not anywhere you've ever hidden before. But somewhere new." Slowly the glow went out. "And so must I."

"You'll go with us?" Rimgia demanded, leaning forward now, her eyes, for a moment, bright in the moon.

"I don't know whether I—"

But then Rimgia's eyes turned away, up toward the sky. Abrid was looking too.

Like a vast and strangely shaped leaf, a figure crossed the moon. Then another. And then another—going in the other direction. A cloud's tendril touched the crescent. Another flying form swooped below it.

"They scare me," Abrid said, dropping back on his buttocks, his crossed feet coming down loudly in the grass. He hugged his knees in tightly, looking up. Half a dozen of the creatures moved in the sky. He spoke in a whisper. "Everyone's always been afraid of them. . . ."

"Dost thou think they can see us?" Rimgia asked. "There're so many frightening things around. I've heard of creatures that can weave a man into a web and suffocate him; and lions that roam the level lands; and the Winged Ones—"

"I wish thou wouldst sing a song for us now," Abrid said.

"I don't have my harp," Naä said shortly. "And the Myetrans, I'm afraid, have stolen my voice for a while."

Again she looked at the knife. Again she looked at the sky. "You two," she said, "at least get out of the orchard here and back somewhere in the woods. And hide! I have to go—"

"Where art thou going?" Rimgia asked, now on her knees, now rocking back to get her feet under her. She stood.

"I think," Naä said, "I'm going back to town—to Çiron. Again."

"Naä?"

For the singer had abruptly turned.

She turned back again. "Yes?"

Rimgia bent to pick up the shawl. "Thank you!"

"For going back?"

"For trading places with me!"

Naä laughed. Then she started again through the trees. If they've stolen my voice from me, she thought as she entered the woods to descend the slope, I must steal something from them in return. But what can it be that they'll sorely, sorely miss?

Qualt was in love with Rimgia.

We've written it; it was true.

Thus it would be silly to believe that in the course of all Qualt's enterprises, she was never once in his mind. But it would be equally simplistic to think she formed some sort of focus for him—that somehow all his acts were envisioned, performed, and evaluated with her image bright before him; that they were done *for* her. Rather, the sort of social catastrophe that Çiron had undergone takes selves already shattered by the simple exigencies of the everyday and drives the fragments even farther apart, so that the separate selves of love and bravery, misery and despair, run on apace, influencing one another certainly, but not in any way one.

As such catastrophes occasionally evoke extraordinary acts of selflessness or bravery, they sometimes evoke extraordinary efforts to make one part of what is too easily called the self confront another part.

Naä had found Rimgia doubtless because she was not, in that final dash through the woods, looking for her. But once he had conveyed the gravity of what his winged companion had overheard to the Handsman and—a few minutes later—to the Queen at Hi-Vator, Qualt decided with the same force of will that had impelled him for the whole of the day, even to this height, that he must now find Rimgia and speak to her.

Perhaps Qualt's failure—his only failure, really, among all he'd attempted since the Myetrans came—was because he was so certain he knew where to find her.

The scrabblings on the roof were the footsteps of one Winged One, or three, or perhaps more. On the ground beside the hut, light from the crescent moon was lapped and loosed by a score of beating, crossing, conflicting wings.

Someone, unthinking, mewed.

Someone else went *"Shhush!"*

Then Qualt lowered himself down from the roof's edge, feeling for the window, the toes of his right foot catching on the shutter's planks, while the night air, which minutes before had been a torrent around him, was just a breeze at his back. When he swung his other foot against the shutter, the catch gave and it swung in. Stepping about and finding purchase on the sill, he caught the fingertips of his right hand over the upper lintel and let himself down till he was sitting in the window, holding on to the beam above with one hand and the window's side with the other, his head—along with both legs—thrust into the darkened hut.

Recalling the motion with which his companion had pushed himself off the upper ledge into the night, Qualt jumped forward and landed in a squat that dropped him low enough to scrape the knuckles on his right hand painfully on the floor. His left hand flailed out because the floor was closer than he'd thought.

Regaining his balance, he whispered, "Rimgia? Abrid?" He stood. "Rimgia . . . it's me, Qualt!"

The darkness across the room to his left he recognized as the fireplace, its embers dead. There, next to it, that must have been Kern's pick. And that was probably Kern's—or Rimgia's—fishing pole against the wall.

"Rimgia?" He took another step across the kitchen, feeling suddenly the emptiness of the house as the noises on the roof caused him to lift his eyes but brought forth no sound within.

Didn't Rimgia sleep in the back, over there?

He pushed the hanging away and stepped inside. From a half-open shutter, light from the moon lay over a pallet, with a wrinkled throw across the matting—not unlike the one he so rarely slept on these summer nights in his cottage down by the dump. "Rimgia?" And Abrid's sleeping space just beyond the wall . . . "Abrid?" He said that out full voice three times. Then he said again more softly: "Rimgia?" He stood there; and while the hanging swung behind him, he pulled his lower lip into his mouth to press it with his front teeth—till, at sudden pain, he let it free and put his tongue up over his upper lip now. He rubbed both forearms against his ribs and swallowed and coughed and swallowed again. The chill aloft on the night had been refreshing, but the memory of it made him want to hug himself in his desire for warmth. A vision he'd had, during the whole of the flight down, was of coming in (through the window, more or less as he'd done) to kneel on one knee by her bed, to reach out and touch her shoulder as she slept; then, when his touch startled her awake, so that she lifted her head, pulling copper hair over the pillow (the moonlight was supposed to be full silver, not just this gauze of half shadow), he would say . . . Qualt took another breath, stepped forward, dropped to a squat, knees winging up beside him, and reached for the bed. He only rested his wide fingers on the wrinkled throw, however, while he tried to take in the fact that she was *really* not here.

Still, if she was absent, it was *her* absence. And everything hers was, it seemed, extraordinarily important at this moment.

"Rimgia," he said, "I like thee—like thee a lot! Dost thou like me? I mean . . . *really* like me?"

Then, because of the scrabbling above, Qualt was up, into the other room (to flee the vacant house that had just held his bravest act that day), to vault onto the sill and twist about, reach up for the lintel, his broad feet—a moment later—disappearing above it.

chapter six

What's going to happen to him, do you think? They're gonna kill him?"

Uk said, "Executed at dawn—that's the prince's order."

There was a grunt in the darkness. "Pretty rough on the lieutenant."

Uk said, "About as rough as it gets." He chuckled. It was a dry, dreary, unfeeling chuckle—one he'd started coming out with to make himself seem less feeling than he was. Now, he noted, he did not indeed feel much.

"He was a good officer, Lieutenant Kire," another voice said from the dark on the other side. (No one else had laughed.) "He was always fair."

And another: "He was the best."

"He was a damned good officer," Uk said. "It's too bad—but I guess I understand it. I don't like it. But I understand it."

"Sabotage? Incompetence, treason? You think the charges are fair?"

"I don't know," Uk said. "I don't know if anything in this war is fair or unfair. But I was standing right out there with the prince when the lieutenant was in there talking to her. He's in there telling her how he's been disobeying orders, trying to make things easier on the villagers, making a flogging of ten lashes into two, things like that. She's supposed to be a prisoner, and he told her right out she could leave if she wanted. I heard him."

"Well, he was good to us too—and he tried to be good to them, where it wouldn't hurt. It doesn't sit right with me, executing a man 'cause he's fair-minded."

"Naw," Uk said, "it don't work like that."

"How is it supposed to work, then? What do you mean, it don't work that way?"

"That's how I thought it worked too, when I first got here," Uk said. "We'd come into one of these places, hacking up the locals—and I'd think, just like you: it's like swatting at flies with a swatter. Everyone you hit goes down—dead! This isn't fair. So one time I started pulling my sword swings, aiming for the arms and legs, rather than the neck or the gut. But then I saw what it looked like later—the ones who didn't die right off. And that was awful—the time it took and the pain it took for them to die anyway. I was walking around, looking at all these people, not dead—but half dead. Half dead's a *lot* worse than dead, when you know you're gonna die in another three, six days no matter what anyone does. No, if the lieutenant wanted this war business over, the way to end it is to go in there, fight as best you can, as hard as you can, and get it over as fast as you can. That's how it works. Holding things back, holding things up, slowing things down—that doesn't do any good for anyone. Not for the villagers—and certainly not for you and me. He was just making it longer and harder for us, and the longer and harder it is for you and me, the more chance you and me got of getting killed. No, I liked the lieutenant. He never did anything to me personally; I'm sorry it worked out this way for him. But if I can understand it, he should've been able to figure it out too. He's an officer."

"Now that's common sense speaking there, Uk," a soldier said from the dark.

"Sometimes I think Uk is the only one in this outfit with any common sense at all," another said.

"That means I'm talking too much," Uk said. "Go to sleep now. We have to get up early."

"You mean we got to go see it, like that other time? Aw— good *night*!"

"The lieutenant's really going to be executed?" asked still another, younger, troubled voice.

"That was the order, boy." Grunts and shushings came as a soldier slid farther down into his bag. "Now go to sleep."

Rahm sat in the corner, looking over the dark figures who slept, crowded together on the council-cellar floor. A dozen feet away, Gargula was breathing loudly and irregularly; he'd worked on this foundation with Rahm. Old Brumer leaned his shoulders against the wall, head nestled down in his near bushel of a beard: he'd been their foreman. Now all of us, Rahm thought, are prisoners here. At the tiny window, just beneath the ceiling, gray had nudged away a corner of black, enough to silhouette the stems outside. Small leaves shook with a breeze.

Then the door creaked.

Someone looked up. Two turned over without looking. Between two black-caped officers, with a regular soldier behind them, a bearded man stepped in. One officer carried a light box that now he flipped on. A harsh filament glowed white. A fan of light put harsh blacks on the far side of the two dozen sleepers about the floor.

"Well, we have some men in here," said the bearded Myetran. He wore one brown leather gauntlet. His other hand was bare. From some time that seemed at once impossibly immediate yet long ago, Rahm recognized the man who had ridden his horse on the common, who'd spoken into the silver rod—who had burned down Kern. "For a moment, I thought this was the women's holding cell. Lord, it stinks in here!" (A depression in the far corner was full of urine and feces; but it had long since overflowed, to wet almost half the floor.) The man took a few steps over some sleeping figures. "I have a job for one of you. For a good and lively dog. A strong dog. You perhaps, or you?

"A bunch of dogs, you are?" The man ran a hand down his beard, to pull it back from morning wildness. "Dogs are vicious; they fight one another, tear at one another over the leavings. What I see here is a bunch of simpering monkeys, crawling mag-

gots without the strength to get up off their bellies. Is there someone here that can do a job that needs a man?" He reached aside
for the light box hanging around the black-cloaked officer's neck
to turn its beam toward the floor. "Have you ever killed?"

Eyes squinted; a hand rose to block the glare.

"Why did I waste the question on such a child!" The beam
moved on. "Have you, old man, ever taken another's life?"

The old man, coughing twice, seemed bewildered.

"What about you—you look like a strapping fellow. Have
you ever killed?"

In the beam, Rahm did not even lower his eyes.

"Come—give us a yes or a no."

Rahm breathed out—dropped his head and raised it.

"Well, have you, now? I wouldn't have thought so, from your
eyes. Or then perhaps I would . . . Get up! Come with me."

Rahm's hips ached; Rahm's knees hurt; his back was stiff—he
pushed himself up, one palm behind him on the rough rock—
from sitting the night long, almost without movement.

"Come, this way. To the door."

Rahm came slowly, lumbering really, feet seeking bits of bare
stone between the bodies. Once he stepped on the hand of someone who woke, grunted, and jerked away. Toward the ground,
Rahm mouthed syllables without sound that, had they had it,
would have been an apology.

"That's right, Çironian. Over here."

When they were outside in the basement hall, Rahm realized
how strong the stench was within, as the door closed behind him.
Fresher air struck, hard enough to make him, for a moment, reel.

"I am Prince Nactor. I do not want to know your name, at
least not until you have done what it is I need you for. Then when
it is time to reward you for doing your work well—I *trust* you
will do it well—then I'll ask you. And we can celebrate who you
are." Tucking his beard back under his chin, the prince turned to
the steps. Starting up, he glanced over his shoulder. "You understand, if you do *not* do it well, you will be killed. And there will

be no need for anyone to know your name ever again. Tell me, Çironian, can you handle an ax?"

Surrounded by soldiers, Rahm followed. "I can swing a quarryman's pick."

The prince glanced back again. "Likely that will do."

In the building's ground-floor hall, again holding his beard back, the prince stopped to lean close to Rahm. "Aren't you curious about what this work will be?"

"Thou wilt tell me in thy time."

Nactor chuckled. "And the time is now." Faint orange lay along the windowsill, left of the door. "I need an executioner. I wish to show a treasonous man—and I wish to make it the *last* thing I show him, the last thing that he will ever see—just how gentle and peace-loving you Çironians are."

Against the far wall sat two women prisoners, one of whom, Rahm realized with a quiet start, was the woman with whom he'd first pursued his earliest, happiest, most single-minded sexual explorations. The other was a woman who, during that same summer, had hated him roundly, loudly, adamantly; for she kept a small set of beautifully tended fruit trees beside her house, which he had taken to pillaging, more for the pleasure of her stuttering outrage than for the fruit. (That, he'd simply handed out among his friends.) It had been only Ienbar's threat of a switching that had finally moved him on to other mischief. Indeed, for a while he'd wondered why his relation to either of the women—one was asleep now; one looked dully across the room and did not seem to see him—had not netted him more, the start of a family in one case or, in the other, the reputation as a troublemaker that, had it gone far enough and the elders' council in these very halls received enough complaints, could have gotten him, after a short public trial, turned out of town—at least that was the rumor. In his own memory, he'd never known it to happen. . . .

Of the two soldiers standing near the women—guarding them apparently—one was shaking his head and grinning over something the other had just said.

On the other side of the hall, in a black cloak that in knife-edged folds hung to the flagstones, an officer crossed quickly toward the door and, with the heavy plank complaining behind, left.

"I also want to show you something," the prince was saying. "I want you to see—and to tell all around you, once you've seen it—how strict we are with our own. Thus, you'll likely maintain a more realistic picture of how little in the line of mercy you can expect for yourselves. Come this way now."

A soldier reached over to tug open the door for them—creaking, as Rahm had heard it creak a hundred fifty, five hundred fifty times, three years ago, coming in and out as a workman. Now the sound was alien. Rahm stepped out and looked up among the few branches, where, near summer's end, brown leaf-clutches were scattered through the darker green.

Here and there, set irregularly toward the common's corners, stood some five of the spidery structures that were the Myetrans' movable light towers: a great illuminated lamp on one, as Rahm looked at it, went dark, like the rest.

Above it in the sky's lavender-layered gray, something moved.

Rahm frowned.

Four, six, ten of the Winged Ones passed above in a pattern that dissolved and re-formed farther away and dissolved again—a pattern that was no pattern.

"Bring the block and the ax!" the prince called. Then his voice returned to conversational level. "You are going to cut off a man's head. That shouldn't be too hard for you—and since he's one of ours, who knows: you might enjoy it."

Still squinting from his sweep of the sky, Rahm looked at the bearded prince beside him. Rahm's nod was not intended to mean agreement, only to register he had heard. But from the smart move the man gave—signaling to someone halfway across the grass—Rahm realized, without particularly marking it, agreement was how the prince had taken it.

Across the common, soldiers stood—at attention, in three rows.

"You can bring the prisoner out," the prince said to one of

the several soldiers accompanying them, who turned and hurried across the common. The grass, with the few trees here and there on it, seemed to Rahm as oddly unfamiliar as the creaking door to the council house.

They started down the ten stone steps and across the gravel toward where grass took up again. The common at evening was a familiar place. But the common at dawn—when was the last time he'd been here at this hour? Certainly it was more than three years ago. Maybe four or five. If only because all the shadows were pointing in the wrong direction, it might have been a public square in a wholly alien town.

In the back row, two or three soldiers glanced at the sky, then brought their eyes back to the field.

More than a dozen of the Winged Ones turned and turned, infinitely high, infinitely small, infinitely distant.

By two poles, four soldiers carried a large block onto the grass. It looked black and old, at least down to its base; there it was a little lighter. Another man was coming toward Rahm and the prince, carrying an ax by its handle, the double blade hanging before his knees; his small steps, high chin, and pursed lips attested to its considerable weight.

Rahm took it in one hand.

The soldier who'd carried it did *not* take a heaving breath; but when Nactor dismissed him, he threw up his fist, turned, and walked heavily back across the field.

The ax *was* heavy. Rahm brought it slowly before him, lowered the blade to the ground, and put his second hand on the haft.

The four soldiers had lowered the block.

"Bring out the prisoner," Nactor said.

Beside them one of the soldiers halloed across the common: "Bring out the prisoner!"

A beat later, some of the Winged Ones swooped, swooped, and swooped again—without, as a group, getting any lower. Then they went back to their lazy flight.

"You will have no trouble with this ax, Çironian. That I can see. At my command, you will cut off the prisoner's head. Do it cleanly, with a single cut. We do not need unnecessary mess, cruelty, or pain. I am very fond of this man. But since he has to die, I want him to die swiftly. You understand me?"

Rahm nodded. He did not see which of the houses on the common the prisoner was led from, for at that moment, with the prince's signal, another soldier stepped up beside him. The world blinked out, then reappeared through eye slits in the black cloth hood dropped over his head.

Rahm looked about.

The cloth tickled his collarbone.

The prince touched Rahm's shoulder, nodded ahead.

Six soldiers walked now with the tall man among them toward the block. Rahm blinked to realize the man—who wore black—was not bound. Only a black cloth was tied around his eyes, though this one was without eye slits.

Rahm leaned to ask the prince softly: "Why is he not tied?"

"When we execute common soldiers, we bind them," Nactor said as softly to Rahm as Rahm had spoken to him. "It's Myetran custom to let our officers die like men. Come."

Across the prisoner's chest, two puma claws were fastened one atop the other, from the pelt he wore around his back.

Inside the hood, Rahm frowned and hefted up the ax. With the prince and the several others, he started across the grass toward the block. Even without his officer's hood, Rahm recognized him. Rahm's stomach went cold and heavy with that recognition—as if all at once he'd eaten to bloatedness.

When the prisoner raised his hand to adjust his blindfold or scratch his chin or whatever, a guard struck Kire's hand down viciously; and three more guards seized both his arms, even as no one in the group broke step.

Rahm's hand tightened on the haft. Inside the cloth, his breath whispered.

As they reached the block, a soldier near Kire suddenly kicked him behind his knees, so that he went down. Immediately two others grabbed him, kneeling beside him on one knee so that

they could hold him. Two others held his legs. Still two others
steadied his shoulders. Kire's head, mouth, and jaw, cut off from
bronze-colored hair by the black blindfold, lay left cheek down
on the scarred block.

Beside Rahm, the prince sighed.

Rahm looked down at the puma's pelt across Kire's back. The
beast's skull had been pulled aside, as if in some scuffle, so that
it hung askew.

Inside his hood, without sound, Rahm mouthed, *"Friend
Kire,"* lips brushing cloth.

Beside Rahm, the prince said: "Lieutenant, you will now see
just how gentle and peace-loving your Çironians are." He bent
down, reached down, thrust a finger beneath the blindfold, and
pulled—not gently. With the tug, Kire's head slid inches across
stained wood. As the cloth slipped free, the lieutenant grunted.
"Look here, now, a nice, gentle Çironian is going to cut your
head off." The prince stood up.

From the block, the lieutenant glanced up, green eyes gone
near gray with dawn and fear.

There was no recognition in them. But why would there be?
Rahm thought, inside his hood.

The prince turned to Rahm. "Kill him now, Çironian."

Rahm took a step to the side, spread his legs, slid one hand
forward on the haft, and hefted the blade over his head. A breeze
flattened the cloth to his face, so that any of the guards, looking up, might have seen, under the black, the form of his lips,
strained apart with effort.

On the block, Kire pulled his shoulders in. His own lips parted
while his eyes squeezed tight, as if by not seeing it he might delay
the stroke. His bronze hair was stringy.

The breeze moved it.

Then Kire blinked rapidly three or four times, as if eager for
a sight of the morning, the grass, the men around him, even the
stained wood obscuring the vision in his lower eye.

The breeze ran in puma fur, parting the hairs to show their
lighter roots.

And Rahm brought the ax—not down, but in a diagonal that became even more acute with a twist of his body.

Prince Nactor did not scream but rather looked down and staggered at the ax blade sunk inches into his chest. Rahm yanked the handle now one way, now the other, as his hands, his shoulders, and the cloth on his face wet with what spurted. As the prince fell, Rahm jerked the ax loose and swung it back around, the blade's side crashing against two of the heads of the guards holding Kire. The swing took it all the way so that it struck another man and sent him sprawling. Then up, then down: honed metal cut into and severed the arm of the officer standing with them, who alone had had the presence to reach down and unsnap his powergun sling—the first man to scream!

Rahm turned again with the ax; one of the soldiers was going backward on his knees, lots of blood on him that wasn't his. Rahm's next chop took off most of a hand—not Kire's—on the block edge. There *were* shouts now. Rahm dropped one hand long enough to rip off the hood and fling it from him over the grass: "Hey, friend Kire, do you know me now? Do we show them now?"

Again with both hands on the handle, Rahm pulled the ax free, leaving a gouge on the blood-splattered hardwood.

The heart-hammering paralysis for Kire ended with the Çironian's voice. The soldiers had all released him. One was running, turning, pulling out his sword as he danced backward; now he began to feint forward.

And Kire crawled, scrambled, clambered around the block and under the swinging blade. A moment later he came up with, first, Nactor's powergun and, a moment after that, in his other hand, the other officer's.

There was still a desperate string of seconds when the lieutenant seemed uncertain if he should fire on his own men—who'd been about to kill him—or obliterate this Çironian madman who was now wreaking mayhem and death among men who, till a day ago, had been his own guards. Finally, when another soldier started toward them, sword drawn, Kire, still on the ground, turned and fired, destroying most of the man save one leg, in a swirl of black smoke and red flame. But it was only then that Kire, glancing up, realized who the marvelous madman was.

Afterthought would have certainly made Kire's decision self-evident. But to some of the soldiers watching, especially from the second and third rows, it seemed—for those moments—as moot and, for the moments after it, as illogical as anything else that had happened in what was still no more than a dozen seconds.

That illogic held them—Uk was one—fixed.

Someone in an officer's cloak had started to run—not toward the mayhem around the block, but toward the soldiers, whose ranks, with each blow and hack and thrust before them, became looser and looser, as some (around Uk) stepped forward and others (in front of him, knocking against him) stepped back.

Crawling on his knees at the end of a swath of bloody grass, doubled over in a kind of moving knot, the officer with the severed arm was *still* screaming. The flap at the crawling man's waist bobbed above his empty sling. His scream seemed at last to move—though very slowly—people about the common's edge.

As, with the powergun in his right hand, Kire dispatched another Myetran and, with the one in his left hand, fired wildly, Rahm paused a moment with his ax, drew a great breath, turned his face to the sky, and shouted, *"Vortcir!"*

He did not shout for help. The young Çironian meant by it only: I am here. See this now and behold me . . . before I die! (For such actions as his—just as much as Naä's—cannot be undertaken other than in the certainty of death.) As such, it was a far more desperate cry than any call for aid. Probably no one about the common's rim understood its meaning: but a chilling combination of triumph and desperation rang through it.

His own powergun drawn, the officer who'd run up to the observing soldiers shouted: "Get in there and stop that—take them down! Go on! Stop it! Forward! Now!"

Perhaps a third of the soldiers began to run forward, some pulling their swords loose from their scabbards as they sprinted across the grass. Looking for a clear spot between them for some sort of shot, the officer, shaking his head, trotted behind them.

At the center of the fray, which had turned both Kire and Rahm by this time toward the council building, Rahm's ax sank into another shoulder; and as he lugged the blade back, he gasped: "You see, friend Kire? You see how peaceful I am!" And swung the ax again.

RAHM! KIRE—TURN AROUND!

The thunderous voice crashed against the air itself. The sound staggered all about them. Every man on the field halted a moment—except Kire and Rahm.

Turning, Rahm saw the light tower beside the council house. Halfway up its ladder of beams and girders, a woman—it was Naä—crouched in an angle of metal, clutching a small silver rod.

LEFT, RAHM—DUCK!

Rahm threw himself to the left and to the ground as smoke and flame burned through the air above him. Someone who had not ducked screamed—very briefly.

BEHIND YOU, *KIRE*!

From the ground, as he pulled his ax to him, Rahm saw Kire whirl and fire—obliterating two soldiers and causing half a dozen more to scatter.

Because he was on the ground, Rahm looked up—and saw suddenly the great forms dropping from the sky. Near the edge of the common, he realized, half a dozen Winged Ones fought with half a dozen Myetrans!

Rahm scrambled to his feet and swung up the ax with one hand so that the blade rose over his head, gleaming red and silver.

For Uk, all this—execution, rebellion, the voice from the tower—had played out like a fatigued dream. At the point the officer shouted, "Forward!" he was actually running the thought through his mind: in the morning, I must get up, march to the common, and with the others, observe the lieutenant's execution. So this is surely some wild night vision that will end in a moment with a breath of cold air through the opening of my sleeping bag and the smell of morning gruel.

But in the real world, such thoughts do not linger. And when, at the "Forward!" order, other soldiers started toward the fray, Uk unsheathed his sword and started too. He'd gone two dozen steps, cutting the distance between him and the wildly fighting figures by a third, by two thirds, when he saw the berserk executioner swing his ax high—Uk had not even seen the hood thrown free. But that was not black cloth wrapped about his head. It was hair, swinging. And the naked face—

Between them, Uk saw Nactor on his side, one hand above his head, the blindfold still looped on three fingers, one eye wide, one closed, and drooling blood. Uk looked up again and recognition hit. It chilled him, turning all possibility of dream into the nightmare whose specific horror was that it took place in one's own bed, in one's own room, in one's own house, in a world that was indeed supposed to be precisely his. If, in fact, he had dreamed some beast had, howsoever, been thrust with him into his sleeping bag, and he'd waked to find it clawing and biting at his unarmored belly and unhelmeted face to get free, it would have been exactly as frightening as the realization that this incarnation of evil, who had wildly and insanely murdered Mrowky, was now wreaking death and murder (an arc of blood followed the Çironian's ax blade through the air) among the dozen men around him!

Uk was terrified; but he was also a brave soldier; moreover, he was an intelligent one, which meant he'd already had several occasions to learn that terror in battle—a different thing from ordinary rational fear—had best be moved into and through so that you came out the other side as quickly as possible—if it were at all possible. That, indeed, is what bravery, military or otherwise, was. Uk took a great wet breath, with a lot of noise in it—much like a sob, had anyone heard it among the shouts and shrieks. (The damned traitor of a lieutenant was on one knee, firing to the right. Would Kire's beam be what cut Uk down? No matter. This other one had to be stopped—had to be!) Uk crouched, his sword back for the thrust, and ran forward, hammering the ground with his boots, gasping air, one fist pumping at his side, the other, holding his sword, awkwardly poised, his whole body aimed for the space between the backs of two soldiers who were already feinting at the ax wielder with their blades.

RAHM! THE ONE COMING UP
ON THE RIGHT OF—!

Rahm swung his ax, and one of the feinters dove aside and rolled away. The other danced back. And Rahm saw the big soldier, crouched low, coming at him—for an instant.

It was a very long instant, though.

Beneath the helmet's rim, the soldier's eyes, as gray as stone, seemed only a moment away from magma red. The effort that twisted the face (the soldier's teeth were bared) seemed to Rahm an image of absolute, blood-stopping evil.

Recognizing it, Rahm felt himself lose purchase with his right foot on the grass and earth that had grown so black and slippery. The part of him that knew how his own blows were timed saw, as clearly as if it had been written out on one of Ienbar's scrolls, that the only backswing he could get in would not connect with any vital part—maybe knock aside the running man's forward arm, if that. This mad creature—who had started to holler now—would collide with him, surely cut him, and likely stab him and stab him and stab again. . . .

Then something fell between them—ropes? But they were moving, Rahm saw, backward, away from him. Rahm glanced left and right. The ropes—tied together in some sort of net—had taken several others of the soldiers too.

If a big man runs head-on into a rope net, the net should give some—two feet, three feet, maybe even twice that. The berserk soldier was no more than five feet from Rahm when the net caught him and started sweeping back.

The big soldier hit those ropes as though they were solid. His free hand grasped a cord near his head. His sword arm went directly through, between thick strands. If you were a wall and someone ran smack against you, that's the only other way you'd ever see that expression on a man's face: the jaw-jarring jerk—when his chest hit—shook Uk's whole body. The sword flew forward from his hand—Rahm winced to the side, slipping more.

But the blade went clear of Rahm's right hip, by a palm's width—before it slid, spinning, back from grass onto gravel. Rahm reeled again but kept his balance.

Winged Ones—fifteen, twenty of them, or more—pulled the vine web back across the common. Soldiers stumbled back behind it. At the sides Winged Ones ran with it. At the top others flew with it. Some cords in the web were of a lighter color than the rest; and from the way some soldiers within were struggling to pull one loose from a face or an arm or a leg, Rahm realized in a strangely attenuated knowledge that *those* lines were cave-creature filaments! The Winged Ones at the net's top now descended, making the web a cage. Within were at least twenty-five Myetran soldiers. And the Winged Ones had their own, strangely gripped blades—

"Friend Rahm!" It was not Kire's voice, but a familiar mew.

Gasping, Rahm turned to see, like a huge and moving shadow beside him, wings spreading, beating in dawnlight—

"Vortcir?"

"Jump on, friend Rahm!"

While the wings turned before him, Rahm dropped the ax and staggered forward. He threw himself at the furry shoulders, caught himself. As they lifted, he called out, sliding, holding his breath, then letting it all out: "Vortcir! I cannot hold thee!"

"Of course you can!" declared the Handsman. And he banked, so that they moved in a far gentler rise; and Rahm, pulling himself forward on his friend's back, sucking in exhausted gasps, looked over Vortcir's shoulder. They sailed left, swooped around, then sailed right, then left again, gaining only a dozen feet each sweep. Wings labored either side of Rahm as Vortcir circled and circled the common.

On the ground, with their long blades, Winged Ones were not being kind to the soldiers under the net. But Rahm's eyes fixed on the lieutenant.

Kire stood, head hanging and powergun pointed straight into the air. He looked as exhausted as Rahm felt. Slowly Kire's arm went down and his head rose so that the gun was pointed at the Winged Ones fighting around the netted Myetrans. There were far more Winged Ones about than Myetrans!

KIRE, NO!

(Vortcir's translucent ears jerked. Beneath Rahm, the jerk went through all of Vortcir's body, as if it were a moment's pain.) Kire's arm dropped to his side. Then his gloved hand with the gun started to rise again.

KIRE!

(Vortcir's ears flicked.) The gun dropped again.

And over Vortcir's shoulder, Rahm saw Naä reach the ground at the light tower's base and run toward Kire, to take his arm. He saw Kire try to shake her off once—saw her take his shoulder again . . .

Vortcir soared higher, and beyond the trees and hut roofs, Rahm could see the Myetrans' tents. Moving among them and occasionally taking off from among them were not Myetrans, but Winged Ones! Not twenty or thirty, but what seemed hundreds!

"Look there, beside us!" Vortcir called in the wind.

Rahm looked out to his left. By some kind of rope, two Winged Ones pulled something through the air—a kind of glider. It was a larger version of the wood and leather toys Rahm had seen skimming between the fliers in the mountains. Much larger, though—larger than one of the Winged Ones! Piled on the upper side of this one—and there were more of them, many more of them in the air—was a bundle of net. On another was a rack of long-handled knives. On still others, were bound-up balls with spikes jutting from them, whose use Rahm could not even imagine.

"You smell of blood," Vortcir remarked. "But that's better than your skinny friend who stinks of garbage. And"—because, on Vortcir's back, Rahm had started to shake and could now see only shimmering and shifting cloud and light—"you are crying." Though—certainly anyone could hear—they were the grinning sobs of relief.

What's going to happen to us? Hey, Uk—what's going to happen? I'm bleeding bad! I'm bleeding bad now. What's going to happen!"

"Shut up, boy!"

"Shut your mouth—and be quiet!"

"What's going to happen to us? What's going to happen?"

There was a grunt in the darkness. "You want to know what's going to happen? You're going to have a red hot fever by tonight. And in three days that gash in your leg is going to be filled with little white worms. And you're going to have flies crawling all over you. And your mouth's gonna dry up, and you're going to cry for water, only if somebody brings it to you, you won't be able to drink it; and if somebody pours it in your mouth it isn't going to make no difference, and you're gonna hang around like that for seven, eight, nine days, with your tongue cracking and bleeding, turned all black. Then you're going to die. That's what's going to happen. An' I just hope I'm dead already when it does—probably will be. 'Cause what I got's a lot worse than what you do."

"Don't tell him *that*, Uk. You don't have to tell him—"

"Hey, Uk? That's not what's going to happen, is it, Uk? That's not what's gonna happen? Oh, no, don't tell me that!"

"The boy don't need to know that kind of thing."

"Then why'd he ask, if he didn't want to know? They pulled their damned blades when they had us under that net, hacking at us. They didn't cut to kill—you can't fight a war like that! You can't do it like that! That's not the way to do it!"

"They're not going to let that happen to us, are they? You don't think that's what they're going to do? Oh, don't tell me that!"

"You can't pull back when you're fighting like that. If I had my blade, boy, I'd kill you now. Put you out of your misery—and if you don't shut up in here, I may just try it anyway with my bare hands. Only I'm too weak—too bad for you. But keep quiet, I say!"

On the council building's cellar floor, at first making figures like red feathers, blood leaked out to mix with the urine still there from the village prisoners released that morning.

"Oh, don't say that—I'm bleeding, Uk. I'm bleeding so bad!"

"Will you shut up, boy? Are you a man or are you a howling dog? There're men dying in here. And there're going to be more men dying. So will you have some respect and shut up?"

But after minutes, all form to the red shapes spreading the wet floor was gone.

---

chapter seven

From high in the mountains a stream drops in feathery falls to bubble along beside the grassy fold through the quarry at Çiron.

When Rahm threw a last handful of sand and grit back to pock the water and, elbows high and winging, waded up the bank, his hair was a black sheet bright on his back and his dripping skin was raw—but both were free of blood.

Vortcir perched on a log jutting above the rocks, wings waving like a great moth's.

A leg still in the foamy rush, Rahm looked down to finger the chain around his neck.

"They were planning to come through the mountains to Hi-Vator. Hi-Vator was right in their line." Vortcir cocked his head to the side, above his own Handsman's chain. "We heard what they'd done to you and your village. Certainly we couldn't let that happen to us. No sense of weapons, god, or money—you're not far enough along toward civilization for anyone to take you seriously. Still, I did not like these Myetrans—and my aunt said attack. Then, my friend, I heard your name through their accursed speakers—and after that, your own call. Well, these are all things to put out of your mind. You are free. Your village is free. A third of the Myetran soldiers run wildly even now, away in the woods. My scouts say most are heading southeast, in the direction of Myetra Himself. More than a third are dead, and the few captured are penned in the basement of your council building. It could be a lot worse."

Along the path to the bank, dappled light spilling bits of even brighter copper down his braids, Abrid ran half a dozen steps, stopped; and, copper spilling hers even faster, Rimgia overtook him. Behind, wings waving in their own rose dapple, the female Winged One who'd once told Rahm about money came after them. "These are the ones you wanted, the two with the red hair—yes, Handsman Rahm? These are the ones, no? Certainly they must be!" Her voice was between a piping and a whine.

"Rahm!" Rimgia declared, Abrid right behind. "The Winged Ones—they drove off the soldiers!" and she excitedly began to tell him many things he already knew; and while Abrid looked excited and kept silent, they started back to the village.

The path crossed the bristle of a burnt field. Halfway over, Rahm halted. "I'll see thee back in town in a little, Rimgia, at the common," and he turned across the stubble toward the remains of the shack.

As he came around where half a wall still stood, he stopped.

On her knees, Naä looked up from where she had been pulling earth from under a charred log. "Rahm?" She smiled up at him, then dug some more.

Three double handfuls of black, cinder-filled dirt, and she leaned to reach in under with one arm. Sitting back, she lifted free the harp and unwrapped the charred cloth. Two dead leaves were caught in its strings. Fingering them loose, she pulled the base back into her lap, laid her hand against the strings, but did not pluck.

Rather, she reached down to her hip and loosed the knife from her sash. "This is . . . this was Ienbar's." Clearly unsure what to do with it, she held it out to him. "Rahm?"

He didn't take it; so she put it on the log.

"The children." Rahm nodded across the field. "Rimgia and Abrid. They're all right. A Winged One found them."

"Oh!" Suddenly she stood. "They found them!" She smiled at him, looked across the field, at Rahm again—then called: "Rimgia, Abrid!" Pushing her arm through the strap, shrugging the instrument to her back, with Rahm following, Naä began to run across the charred grass.

Elbows forward on his knees and gazing at nothing, Lieutenant Kire sat on the blackened block, where he'd been sitting, silent on the common, forty minutes now. The villagers moving about sometimes glanced at him, then—a few and a few more— moved about him without looking at all.

On foot or in air, passing Winged Ones ignored him.

Mantice was chattering away at Rahm as they came across the grass: "Four of them we bandaged up and sent south on their way—though, phew!—they'd only been down there six hours, and already it was halfway between a cesspit and a shambles. One of them, a young fellow, was cut bad in the leg and already down with a fever. But Hara took him into her hut and says she can nurse him back to his feet—although, I allow, he'll limp the rest of his life. But that woman's as wise with medicinal weeds as she is at weaving. If anyone can save him, it'll be she. Three, now, I'm sorry to say it, were too far gone. Two of those were already dead when we went in there. And one died even as we were carrying him up the steps and out into the clear air. Thou wouldst have thought the ones alive and turned loose would have had some gratitude—or at least a smile for the favor. But all of them were sullen fellows. Well, they'd been through it too, I suppose. I had them put the dead ones back over in my water wagon."

Here the lieutenant looked around, got to his feet heavily, and turned. "Rahm, he says there are more dead about. Myetran dead. In his wagon. May I see them? I . . ." His rough voice snagged on itself. "I've been trying to get an idea whom we lost—among the men I knew, I mean."

"Of course," Rahm said, though, from report, the lieutenant

had not done much of anything in the past hour. "Mantice, canst thou take me and friend Kire to see?"

"But only come thou along," said the stocky water-cart driver. "My cart is this way."

Five minutes later, off on a side street, with one hand on the wagon's edge, the lieutenant peered within. The puma's head beside his, save for its sealed eyes, might have been peering too. Standing at Kire's shoulder, Rahm looked in. The lieutenant's next breath was a little louder than the one before it. But the one after was quiet again.

On his back at the cart's far side by three other bodies, the big soldier had a gaping slash along his flank, through which, beneath a carapace of flies, you could see both meat and bone. Rahm recognized him more from his size. The full features, unshaven, held a slight grimace in death.

"Friend Kire?"

"Yes?" The lieutenant looked over across the lion's muzzle.

"That one there," Rahm said. "Didst thou know him? Was he a bad man?" though, even as he asked it, the idea of this dead soldier with his annoyed expression, as the evil figure he remembered, seemed ludicrous.

"A bad man?" The lieutenant gave a kind of snort. "Uk there? Uk was the best—he was a *very* good man. Or at least a good soldier."

"Ah," Rahm said. "I see."

The lieutenant took another, louder breath, dropped his hand, and turned from the cart. "Rahm, I want to thank you, for . . . for my life. Though I guess there's no proper way to give such thanks formally now, is there?"

Rahm grinned. Then he said: "Friend Kire . . ." but nothing else.

So finally Kire said, "I must go and look about among the other men, to see whom I can recognize."

"Certainly."

As the two men turned again toward the common, a young

man with his hair tied back hurried up toward them. "Art thou the one they call Lieutenant Kire?" He was a lean-flanked youth, with big ears and big hands. (Rahm grinned at Qualt.) "I was just back at Hara's and Jallet told me—thy prince, he wishes to see thee. Then Hara asked me if I would . . ." While Kire looked uncomfortable, Qualt glanced at Rahm.

"Yes, of course."

"Thou knowest the house—it's the one they kept thee in, earlier?"

"Of course," the lieutenant repeated in his unnaturally rough voice, then started back along the street.

When the lieutenant was gone, Qualt resumed his quiet smile. "Hey, Rahm, I heard about him and thee, what thou didst together at the common this morning!"

"And what are we supposed to have done that anyone wouldn't do who had to save himself and a friend?"

"Oh, *I* heard!" Qualt nodded. "It was a terrifying battle—so says everyone who saw it; and so do a good many more who've only heard of it. Thou gavest the Myetrans a show and a fight, 'ey?"

And Rahm, who had heard nothing at all of what Qualt had done (for even the Winged Ones he'd talked to had not mentioned Qualt by name), put his tree trunk of an arm about Qualt's lean shoulders and, leaning toward the garbage collector, said: "Well, if thou wouldst talk about it to gossipy old men and women from the back of thy cart when thou makest thy next dawn rounds, let me tell thee a little of what it was *really* like. Here's how it was, for mayhap thou dost not know; but I have even been to Hi-Vator!" and the two youths, Rahm leaning his head down to Qualt's, with Qualt listening and Rahm explicating and gesturing, walked back toward the common.

Minutes later on the same side street, Rimgia and Naä passed Mantice's wagon. Rimgia stood on tiptoes, looked in, then turned away with a sour face. "Guess who's in *that* one." But there was a quick grin, impossible to squelch at the sourness's end. After all, it was not another villager.

"Who?" Naä asked. She looked too. "Oh . . . *him!* Well, good riddance, I suppose."

"Naä?" Rimgia walked forward once more as again Naä fell in beside her. "Isn't it odd? Yesterday, the idea of what happens when we die seemed just the most fascinating thing in the world to think about. And now, with so many dead about us—our people, theirs—it just seems silly. What today dost *thou* think?"

Naä shrugged. "Well, I've always thought thinking about how to live was more important than thinking about after we die. One likes to assume death will take care of itself. It's just a bit disconcerting to see so many other people putting so much energy into taking care of it for you. Life has always been such a surprise; death, I expect—even if it's nothing—will be one too."

Which, to Rimgia, sounded very wise. The two women walked on through the late afternoon, looking up in the air again and again.

The shack was dark and hot. At one side of the room, blinking about sullenly, a young soldier lay, his leg in a wad of bloody bandage. At the fire, the old weaver glanced up, then went back to stirring her pot over crackling flames. The smell of wintergreen and something vinegary escaped in the steam whipping from the rim.

Some rural remedy, that—however bitter on the tongue, however turgid in the belly—would return the moribund to life?

Or perhaps a country potion that if one was lucky did nothing, or if one was not, hastened the end?

The pallet on the near side was *much* bloodier; and when, from where he lay, the prince began to speak, the young soldier turned away, in a lack of interest or exhaustion.

"Ah, you've come—it is you, isn't it? I can't see very well. How odd . . . excuse me; this terrible lack of breath, panting—

it's all I can do. How odd it is that we have come so near to changing places, you and I. What a very little time ago it was when here in this shack in which we were keeping you, you knew that you'd be dead in hours . . . then in minutes . . . then when you were led across the grass, in moments—and I looked down on it all. Now I'm the one who knows I have only hours left, perhaps not even that. And there you stand, watching, with not much to say. Come here . . . come closer. We share a mission, you and I. Ah, when that boy's blade went into my chest, I could actually feel—beyond the pain as I fell, not quite unconscious—I could *feel* the metal inside, against my heart, feel my heart beating against the ax blade, pushing against the edge that actually touched it with each pulse, doubtless cutting itself to ribbons, even as he wrested it free of my ribs . . . If only I could get in a real breath! This panting, like a woman in labor, just to bring forth my death! But I wonder if you'll ever know how cursedly annoying it is to *feel* the inside of your body. It's quite the strangest thing there is. That poor, mad Çironian with his ax—I liked him, you know? Is it so strange to say? He rather reminded me of myself—myself a long, long time ago. I wouldn't be surprised if, years from now, *he* doesn't begin to remind a few people of *me*! Give me your hand there—no, take mine. Take it . . . did you take it? By Kirke, I can't even feel it! Really, it's probably him I should be talking to, not you. Though in all likelihood he can make the transition . . . I *trust* he can make the transition without my help. I can't see him staying on here in this town much longer—any more than I can see it for you! They will be happy to have him certainly—for a day, a week, a month even. But he will not be able to stay here long. Soon he will have to go—of his own accord, if the town is lucky. Else they will have to drive him out or kill him: an outlaw in this grotty village with no laws to speak of. For soon they will realize they are harboring that most dangerous creature, a young man who has defied the highest, most rigorous, most rigid law, defied it with mayhem and destruction and most wanton murders—ten, eleven, twelve murders I have heard; thirteen, when I die—and gotten away scot-free! No, he must go—even if it takes him a month, a year, five years to be on his way. Really, I would like to be around to observe what happens. . . . Come closer, closer. We must be closer, you and I. I can't even see the color of your eyes. Please, you must come closer. . . . Excuse me for whispering. But I have to conserve my strength—though for what, I cannot guess. But still—I still feel something separates us, like . . . like what? Like a blood drop run down a . . . Oh, I cannot *tell* you how the notion of eternity bores me—not to mention all the silly stories we're always making up to render the idea palatable! A universe where one has to die is so uninteresting; you can understand how we're always flirting with the idea of letting in a bit more evil, then just a bit more—to liven things up. No, come closer. No, this place, in its stinking particularity, doesn't have much of the eternal about it. We're probably in one of those benighted little cultures where every three, five, or seven years, the locals go off on a journey in the wilds, in hopes of becoming a little less local after all. Well, I think that's what *you* probably need, just about now. You were *not* a good officer. But you might still make a good man. I think you would like to be a certain *sort* of man— even, yes, I dare to say it, a good one. But no, you aren't now. At least not yet. Just ask that boy staring at the thatch across the room. Or any one of them down in the council-house cellar. Still, to be the man you want to be, you have merely to pursue yourself—passionately, brutally, blindly, looking for no thanks! It means yes, doing what you feel is right—I have always tried to do what was right. But long ago I learned that being right was a brutal, cruel, and thankless position. Ah, I wish I could see you more clearly! If you pursue yourself in that manner, your friends will criticize you for it, call you a fool—as I have called you. But then, with only a few unhappy moments, I've always considered myself your friend. The things that made you hate me, I did only to shock you, to wake you up, to make you become yourself . . . and you are chuckling bitterly now, saying: *Yes, that's why he condemned me to death!* Well, what we criticize in you, cultivate. That's you. And promise me—promise me, that you will indeed . . . you will go on to pursue the person you are so close to becoming yet are so far away from. It isn't a very big promise; but I want that promise to fall, like a severing blade, between you and your ever taking the notion for granted that finally you have achieved it. For then, my friend, you *will* be in my position—I promise you. So we have promises to exchange, you and I. Oh, I would love to be able to promise you more than that—more than what is simply inevitable. Come closer, please . . . hold my hand tighter. Don't let anything hold us apart—not now. Let me do this. Let me . . . I can't feel you at all. Tighter! A little tighter? Oh!" The prince made a sudden attempt to pull air into his ruined ribs, which would not respond. And another. Then he whispered, "It's going to *happen*! It's going to—" For choking moments behind the beard, his face took on a look of pained surprise that slowly subsided till the head dropped to the side. Bubbles in the red froth at his mouth's corner burst against beard hair. Breath was gone.

At the fire, the weaver tapped her long-handled spoon on the cauldron's rim and looked up. A naked back, with its small, sharp vertebrae curved toward the room—the young soldier sighed, but did not even glance around.

Across the commons a dog pranced and, its head back, yipped, till, loping past, Rahm turned and called jocularly: "Come on, there—cut it out now, Mouse!"

A child standing near turned to declare: "His name isn't Mouse, and you *know* it, Rahm!"

Then both laughed: the girl's, a brief, high sound, like a single note of the dog's yipping; and Rahm's, a broad-chested, doubled-over, head-shaking, arm-waving, hand-clapping, loud-then-high-then-low-again laugh that took him three, four, five steps along, going on and on and *on*—so that for uncomfortable moments he looked like a man with a creature clutching his shoulders whom he was trying to shake free.

Again seated on the edge of the blackened wood, Kire looked at his hysterical savior, as if Kire himself were hundreds of feet above and Rahm, dog, and child were on the ground. His miraculous rescue that dawn had catapulted Kire to some altitude from which, like a man afraid of heights, he could appreciate none of the view for the vertigo. Kire was *still* trying to recall the names of his units' dead—unhappily aware that he could now really remember only one: Nactor, off in the shack. Then of course, there was his big guard in the wagon. And what had been the name of his little friend, the one with the freckled shoulders—a soldier whom Kire knew had died early in the operation, but for his life he could not remember a name or a face for the man. Somehow what had happened to Kire had so immersed him in life that little of death would stay with him—which made him feel awkward, uncomfortable, and inadequate.

His big body still lost in its laugh, again Rahm glanced at the seated Myetran. Kire looked out with green, distant eyes. Somehow the dark clothing, with the puma skin around them, had come all askew. I call him friend, Rahm thought. We have now each helped the other, yet I don't know him—at all. And Rahm was glad the laugh's remains kept the thought's discomfort from his face.

The day of the Winged Ones' coming and their routing of the Myetrans was a day of wonder—wonder that spread from the town dump, where Qualt finally drew up his own wagon full of baskets of yellow rinds and chicken feathers and milk slops and eggshells and corn shucks, to go once more, stiff-legged and leaning back against them, over the gravel to dump them from the ravine precipice into the soggy and steaming gully; wonder that spread over the common at the village center, where the grassy expanse was worn away down the middle by the daily setup of the barter market's stalls just before the council house, where most of the women and many of the men mentioned in these chapters came to walk, judge, and trade; wonder that spread to the outlying grain fields and cane fields and cornfields and kale fields, in one of which Gargula stood, calf deep in greens, beside his plow, rubbing his nose and not quite ready to work, because he'd taken Tenuk's mule from its shed under the thatched-out roof that day, fed it, watered it, and brought it to the field without asking anyone—because there'd been no one to ask; and the whole silent operation had left him with a tongue too heavy to speak.

The wonder and the mystery, as the village children would remember it, was that over all, now on the ground and more and more frequently in the air, the great shapes, like flitting shadows, moved, awkwardly on the earth and gracefully through the sky, translucent ears cocked left or right to hear, it seemed, every-thing, their little eyes fixed (it seemed) on little for very long. Thus, as had Naä and Rimgia, one walked about the streets—or the common or the refuse pit or the fields—with eyes continually lifting.

Back at the ravine, Qualt smacked the bottom of his last bas-ket, turned it up to peer within its smelly slats, then dragged it behind him, rasping on rock, toward the dozen others, and looked up—as Rimgia came out into the clearing that held his hut as well as his yard full of odd, awkward, and broken things.

She walked thoughtfully, glanced up casually: a dozen Winged Ones circled above the ravine.

Have we mentioned that Qualt, even before the coming of the Myetrans, had for a while now been the most respected young man in town? In such a village, the garbageman knows more about what goes on (and goes out) than anyone else. As garbage-man, Qualt was expected not just to know this but to study it and to record anything about it of interest, which he did two or three evenings a week, on parchment scrolls, with great diligence. It was Qualt, rather than Rahm, who as a child had pestered Old Ienbar to teach him his writing system. In the course of learning it years ago, Qualt had copied out, several times over, almost the whole of the death scrolls on store in Ienbar's shack (he still had those early exercises in trunks piled beneath his grandmothers' marriage blankets in his back storage room), and it was he to whom would soon fall the task of reconstructing them. Hara's joking with Rahm about a possible seat on the council of elders was a gesture simply to make the big youth feel better. Hara's jokes with Qualt, though they took the same form, were signs of a foregone conclusion of the whole Çiron council, that the lean youth would get the next seat—and would be the youngest "elder" ever to sit with them.

Over the next weeks, as his various accomplishments during the Myetran siege (from his gathering of information, to his help to Naä, to the water for the prisoners, to the multiple garbage peltings, and finally to his own night journey to Hi-Vator) would come to general awareness, they would make this modest young man into a true town hero—and the already high respect and regard in which he was held would become something quite stellar. What Rahm and Naä had done was the stuff of song. But what Qualt had done was finally the stuff of myth.

At this moment, however, neither Qualt nor Rimgia knew the reputation for heroism that was to accrue. Right now Qualt was moody, because an hour back he'd had to take his garbage wagon, along with ten other carts (along with Mantice and Brumer and some others), full of corpses, piled so high one or two regularly fell off—soldiers and villagers both—down some two hundred yards, to dump them into a part of the ravine his predecessor at the dump years ago had told him about: the safest place to put corpses when, through man-made or natural catastrophe, the death toll exceeded what the burial meadow might reasonably hold.

The fact and the location were always with him, but this was the first he'd ever had to use it.

Rimgia wandered toward Qualt. Three days ago, she had wanted to make her questions interesting for Naä, but she'd wanted to take the most interesting of their answers to Qualt. Now, however, as she'd explained to Naä only a bit before, those answers in the aftermath of the violence seemed somehow irrelevant, so she'd come here feeling oddly empty—yet had come just the same.

Between her fingers, she turned the stem of a black-eyed flower with yellow petals she'd thought to show him; but then, because even that seemed so childish, she threw it to the gravel. And Qualt, because he had seen her father burned down on the common the night before last and had wondered at her mourning, looked at her seriously and said: "Wouldst thou come in? I have some broth heating. I've knocked the marrow from half a dozen pork bones into it."

She stepped within the curve of the lean arm he held out, and they walked between the piles of junk about his yard. From the Winged Ones flying above, shadows passed and pulled away from them, till at the door hanging she turned and looked up, shifting her shoulders under his grip—which he loosened, but did not release. "Qualt, isn't it odd?" she said. "The Winged Ones saved us—saved our whole village. They turned out to be brave and wonderful and generous. Yet we've always been taught to fear them; and now it seems there was no reason to fear. All this time, perhaps we could have been friends with them, learning from them, enjoying their ways and wonders while they benefited from ours. Doesn't that make us seem like a *very* small-minded little village?"

"Perhaps," said thoughtful Qualt. He squeezed her shoulder with his hard, large hand, near permanent in its glove of dirt.

"Dost thou *not* think so?" she asked, looking up—at him and at three (then three more) Winged Ones passing through the luminous space between his long curly hair and the roof's edge.

"Perhaps," he said. "But there still might be reason to fear."

"To fear? The Winged Ones who saved us? But why?"

Qualt took in a breath, squeezed her shoulder again, and looked slowly at the flying figures around them. "Maybe it's only a little thing—but when it happened, it made me afraid. There was a Winged One who was with me, and whom I thought my friend. And when the Winged Ones came down at our request and were triumphant, and the soldiers had all surrendered, he was with us when we penned some of the Myetrans up in the corral of crossed wires they'd imprisoned some of our people in before. I'd put in both soldiers and officers. And my winged friend now called through the wires to one of the officers standing just inside, all in black, still in his hood, with that straight, straight cloak they wear lapping smack to the earth. The only thing that let you know he was a prisoner, really, was that his powergun sling was empty; I'd taken it away from him and smashed it. *Well,* the Winged One wanted to know, *how do you like being a prisoner? Wouldn't it be better to be free? And wouldn't you like to fly, loosed from this cage, free of the fetters of the earth itself?* He kept on teasing him, in his little scrap of a voice. Then, with three flaps to take off, he was up and inside. *Wouldn't the officer like to climb on my back, just put an arm around my neck and hold to my shoulder?* I stood outside, grinning as broadly as a child, watching and wishing I'd been offered the ride—that I could change places with him. Myself, I think the officer was afraid at first; and the other soldiers inside the enclosure only looked at the ground. But finally, perhaps because he was also afraid not to, the officer stepped up and put his arms around the Winged One's neck; and with a few beats of those great wings, making the leaves both inside and outside the fence spin up into the air, they were up among those leaves, then above them, then above the corral itself, moving into the sky, higher and higher toward the sun. In less than a minute, they were small as a bird, flying now this way, now that way, against the sky's burning white. Because of the scale, it was hard to tell what was happening; but I remember, as I watched them, it seemed that the backward and forward turnings of that Winged One were awfully quick—dazzlingly fast, faster than I'd seen any of the others fly: a moth about a fire, darting back and about before the sun. Then I realized the speed was real—for the officer's cape spread and billowed and fluttered and flapped, for all the world like a third wing! Had the officer tried to choke the Winged One in his flight? For the Winged One, I realized, was trying to dislodge the man and throw him loose! He flew sideways, he dove headfirst, then whirled about and rose, now flew upside down, now back again! One thought the officer's cape had gone mad! In no more than thirty seconds, I saw the man tear loose—and fall!

"For the first moments of his plummet, I wondered if my friend might swoop down below him and catch him. But he only flew away. Then I wondered if the falling man might spread that cloak and use it somehow to fly with, but no. It closed in the air above him, straight over his head. He arrowed down, landing among the trees, some hundred yards off.

"When my companion returned, I was still sure there'd be some explanation—that something had happened on the flight; but no, back on the ground the big fellow was laughing and strutting and boasting to us and all his fellows what a joke it had been; it seemed a joke—to some of them, and to some of them not.

"*But why? I asked him at last. Why did you do it?*

"He cocked his head at me and said: *He was wearing a cape, like the one who seared my wing with his accursed powergun!*

"*But it probably wasn't him, I told him. All the officers wear capes. You can't just replace one person for another like that!*

"But he shrugged his huge shoulders. *Well, I wasn't ready to be a ground-bound female, limping along with only one wing and holiness to help me. Why not replace one with the other? Didn't they flog four at random for the mischief of you and me? Oh, I see, he went on. I can hear it in your voice. Like all the others among my people: You're no longer my friend. You don't like me anymore. You disapprove. You are afraid. Well, there was no reason to think you'd be otherwise. I'll find someone else to play with.* Then he spread his great wings, with all their scars, and shook them in the sun and beat them and flew away.

"But that's when I was afraid."

Rimgia shuddered. "That's terrible!" And after she shuddered, she watched his face and thought what a sensitive and intelligent young man he was, to have such wonderful feet and hands. "If you wanted to do something like that, it would be better to take one of their dreadful guns and just shoot them through the fence!"

"Mmmm," Qualt said. But it was uncertain if he meant he agreed with her or merely that he'd heard her. "Later"—shadows around them became smaller and darker, larger and paler—"I and some of the others went to look at the Myetran who'd fallen among the trees. He'd taken down a lot of branches, and we put his body in a wagon." Always the shadows moved. "As soon as I came back, I ordered the corral to be opened; and I told the soldiers inside to go—it was the corral I was in charge of; I mean, what were we going to do with them? And sullenly they went."

"Mmmm," Rimgia said now, though it was as hard to tell what she meant as it had been when Qualt had said it. Then she said, because it was really why she'd come looking for him in his yard anyway: "Qualt, I like thee—I like thee very much. Dost thou like me?"

"Yes, I . . . Yes . . . yes!" he blurted, stepping away from her to look at her wonderingly, then moving back to hold her tightly in his one arm—even while his other suddenly felt astonishingly empty.

Rimgia looked up at the flying creatures, who crossed and parted and reversed and lowered and rose. "Maybe they're not like us," she said. "Maybe they're different."

Qualt said very carefully: "They are brave and wonderful and generous. They saved our village. . . . He did so many things for me—for us. He was my friend—he's *still* my friend. But because they do things that make me so afraid of their difference from us, that perhaps is why we might still be afraid of them a little. But come inside now, Rimgia." He turned with her and pushed back his door hanging. "There's something I must say to thee, must ask thee."

"Whatever is it?" and she stepped within.

Gargula stayed on in the field. Several times, sensing the hour, Tenuk's mule had turned to start back; but Gargula pulled him steady, sometimes with a jerk, staying late for much the reason he had started late.

The first night on the common where Rimgia had lost her father, Gargula had seen an older sister whom he loathed burned till, screaming, she'd fallen dead among so many others screaming—and watched an aunt whom he'd loved far more than his mother trampled by her own friends. Like Rahm, Gargula had spent the night in the fetid and fouled cellar of the council house that, as a boy, he had helped build. On his release he'd brought dead Tenuk's mule to the field, a man—the only man to go to the fields that day—looking for something. But because the monotonous furrows would not yield it up, he might well have gone on plowing into darkness unto dawn.

What halted him, however, was—well, it was music. But it was also thunder. A house-sized hammer struck among metal mountains might have produced those notes. Then a voice joined them, but a voice like the sky itself opening up and starting to sing—or *was* it singing?

The mule, then Gargula, stopped.

Before the phrase ended, incomprehensible within its own roar, it collapsed into a laugh—but a laugh as if the whole earth had become woman and was laughing. Finally, there was a voice, with words actually recognizable:

OH, DEAR! NO, I SOUND *AWFUL*, RAHM!
I'M AFRAID THAT WASN'T A GOOD IDEA AT ALL!

JUST WAIT A MINUTE, WILL YOU?
LET ME SWITCH THIS THING—

Gargula stood, the field ahum about him.

Then, for whatever reason (not like a man who'd been given what he needed, but like one whom a certain shock had informed that what he needed was not to be found where he was looking), he unhooked the plow and, as the mule twitched a slate-colored ear, turned with the animal toward town.

To the west the sky was a wall of indigo, behind mountains whose peaks were crumpled foils, silver and copper. To the east above the tree's back fringe, salmons were layered with purples, separated by streaks the cold color of flame—before which burned and billowed golden clouds. Above in the vault, coming together in yellowish haze, insect tiny, Winged Ones turned, one after the other, to fly toward the rocks.

Gargula walked Tenuk's mule to the path.

As they came out under oak leaves, he heard the visiting singer's voice, harmonizing with her harp notes. A group had gathered at the well—a number of the village young people who were friends. Rimgia and Abrid and Qualt were there. Though he could not see her, certainly Naä sat at their center, on the well wall, singing, playing.

As he looked among the listeners, Gargula saw that Rahm's black hair was now braided down his back—the way you were *supposed* to wear it after you'd come in from a wander. Things, Gargula reflected, were finally settling into the ordinary.

And a bit of the weight at the back of his tongue, that had made it too heavy for speech all day, he finally and surprisingly swallowed. (Across the common a line of elders, in their woven robes, walked toward the council building's plank door for that evening's special meeting.) Gargula blinked in the road at the branches leaning from the underbrush—so that only when the Myetran officer was three steps away, sling buttoned down over his gun hilt at his leggings' black waist and puma pelt fastened around black shoulders, did Gargula see him.

Without a nod, the lieutenant walked by man and mule, to the southeast, the sun's last fire falling slantways on the puma's lids and side teeth, on the bronze hair and brown cheek, making him squint—so that Gargula, who turned to watch Kire as he passed, did not even catch the color of his eyes.

—New York/Amherst
June 1962/June 1992

ruins

Lightning cracked a whip on the dark, scarring it with light.

Clikit ran for the opening, ducked, fell, and landed in dust. Outside, rain began with heavy drops, fast and full. He shook his head, kneeled back, and brushed pale hair from his forehead. Taut, poised, he tried to sense odors and breezes the way he fancied an animal might.

There was the smell of wet dirt.

The air was hot and still.

Blinking, he rubbed rough hands over his cheeks, pulling them away when the pain in his upper jaw above that cracked back tooth shot through his head. A faint light came around corners. Clikit kneaded one ragged shoulder. Dimly he could see a broken column and smashed plaster.

Behind him, the summer torrent roared.

He stood, trying to shake off fear, and walked forward. Over the roar came a clap like breaking stone. He crouched, tendons pulling at the backs of his knees. Stone kept crumbling. Beneath the ball of his foot he could feel sand and tiny pebbles—he had lost one sandal hours ago. He stepped again and felt the flooring beneath his bare foot become tile. The strap on his other sandal was almost worn through. He knew he would not have it long—unless he stopped to break the leather at the weak spot and retie it. Clikit reached the wall and peered around cautiously for light.

In a broken frame above, a blue window let in Tyrian radiance. The luminous panes were held with strips of lead that outlined a screaming crow.

Clikit tensed. But over the fear he smiled. So, he had taken refuge in one of the ruined temples of Kirke, eastern god of Myetra.

Well, at least he was traveling in the right direction. It was Myetra he had set out for, uncountable days, if not weeks, ago.

In a corner the ceiling had fallen. Water filmed the wall, with lime streaks at the edge. A puddle spread the tile, building up, spilling a handsbreadth, building again, inching through blue light. As he looked down at the expanding reflection of the ruined ceiling, he pondered the light's origin, for—save the lightning—it was black outside.

He walked to the wall's broken end and looked behind for the source—and sucked in his breath.

Centered on white sand a bronze brazier burned with unflickering flame. Heaped about its ornate feet were rubies, gold chains, damascened blades set with emeralds, silver proof, crowns clotted with sapphires and amethysts. Every muscle in Clikit's body began to shake. Each atom of his feral soul quivered against its neighbor. He would have run forward, scooped up handfuls of the gems, and fled into the wild wet night, but he saw the figure in the far door.

It was a woman.

Through white veils he could see the ruby points of her breasts, then the lift of her hip as she walked out onto the sand, leaving fine footprints.

Her hair was black. Her eyes were blue. "Who are you, stranger?" And her face . . .

"I'm Clikit . . . and I'm a thief, Lady! Yes, I steal for a living. I admit it! But I'm not a very *good* thief. I mean a very bad one." Something in the expression that hugged her high cheekbones that balanced over her lightly cleft chin made him want to tell her everything about himself. "But you don't have to be afraid of me, Lady. No, really! Who are—"

"I am a priestess of Kirke. What do you wish here, Clikit?"

"I was . . ." Dusty and ragged, Clikit drew himself up to his full four feet eleven inches. "I was admiring your jewels there."

She laughed. And the laugh made Clikit marvel at how a mouth could shape itself to such a delicate sound. A smile broke on his own stubbled face, which was all wonder and confusion and unknowing imitation. She said, "Those jewels are nothing to the real treasure of this temple." She gestured toward them with a slim hand, the nails so carefully filed and polished they made Clikit want to hide his own broad, blunt fingers back under his filthy cloak.

Clikit's eyes darted about between the fortune piled before him (and beside him! and behind him!) and the woman who spoke so slightingly of it. Her ebon hair, though the light from the brazier was steady, danced with inner blues.

"Where are you from?" she asked. "Where are you going? And would you like to see the real treasure of the temple?"

"I am only a poor thief, Lady. But I haven't stolen anything for days, I haven't! I live out of the pockets of the rich who stroll the markets of Voydrir, or from what I can find not tied down on the docks of Lehryard, or from what is left out in the gardens of the affluent suburbs in Jawahlo. But recently, though, I've heard of the wealth of Myetra. I only thought I would journey to see for myself."

"You are very near Myetra, little thief." Absently she raised one hand, thumb and forefinger just touching, as if she held something as fine as the translucent stuffs that clothed her.

And dirty Clikit thought: it is my life she holds, my happiness, my future—all I ever wanted or all I could ever want.

"You must be tired," she went on, dropping her hand. "You have come a long way. I will give you food, rest; moreover, I shall display for you our real treasure. Would you like that?"

Clikit's back teeth almost always pained him, and he had noticed just that morning that another of his front ones (next to the space left from the one that had fallen out by itself a month ago) was loose enough to move with his tongue. He set his jaw hard, swallowed, and opened his mouth again. "That's . . . kind of you," he said, laying two fingers against his knotted jaw muscle, eyes tearing with the pain. "I hope I have the talents to appreciate it."

"Then follow." She turned away with a smile he desperately wanted to see again—to see whether it was taunting him or shining at him. What he remembered of it, as he trotted after her, had lain in the maddeningly ambiguous between.

Then he glanced down at her footprints. Fear shivered in him. Alabaster toe and pink heel had peeked at him from under her shift. But the prints on the white sand were not of a fleshed foot. He stared at the drawn lines—was it some great bird's claw? No, it was bone! A skeleton's print!

Stooping over the clawlike impression, Clikit thought quickly and futilely. If he went to search along the walls for pebbles and stones and fallen chunks of plaster, she would surely see. At once he swept up one, another, and a third handful of sand into his cloak; then he stood, gathering the edges together, twisting the cloak into a club—which he thrust behind him. At another arch the woman turned, motioning him to follow: he was shaking so much he didn't see if she smiled or not. Clikit hurried forward, hands at his back, clutching the sandy weight.

As he crossed the high threshold, he wondered what good such a bludgeon would do if she were really a ghost or a witch.

Another brazier lit the hall they entered with blue flame. He went on quickly, deciding that at least he must try. But as he reached her, without stopping she looked over her shoulder. "The real treasure of this temple is not its jewels. They are as worthless as the sands that strew the tile. Before the true prize hidden in these halls, you will hardly think of them." Her expression had no smile in it at all. Rather, it was intense entreaty. The blue light made her eyes luminous. "Tell me, Clikit—tell me, little thief—what would you like more than all the jewels in the world?" At a turn in the passage, the light took on a reddish cast. "What would you like more than money, good food, fine clothes, a castle with slaves?"

Clikit managed a gappy grin. "There's very little I prefer over good food, Lady!"—one of his most frequent prevarications. There were few foods he could chew without commencing minutes of agony, and it had been that way so long that the whole notion of eating was for him now irritating, inevitable, and awful.

A hint of that smile. "Are you really so hungry, Clikit?"

True. With the coming of his fear, his appetite, always unwel-come, had gone. "I'm hungry enough to eat a bear," he lied, clutching the sand-filled cloak. She looked away. . . .

He was about to swing, but she turned through another arch, looking back.

Clikit stumbled after. His knees felt as though the joints had come strangely loose. In this odd yellow light her face looked older. The lines of character were more like lines of age.

"The treasure—the real treasure—of this temple is something eternal, deadly, and deathless, something that many have sought, that few have ever found."

"Eh . . . what is it?"

"Love," she said, and the smile, a moment before he could decide its motivation, crumbled on her face into laughter. Again she turned from him. Again he remembered he ought to bring his bundle of sand up over his own balding head and down on the back of hers—but she was descending narrow steps. "Follow me down."

And she was again just too far ahead.

Tripods on the landings flared green, then red, then white—all with that unmoving glow. The descent, long and turning and long again, was hypnotic.

She moved out into an amber-lit hall. "This way."

"What do you mean—love?" Clikit thought to call after her.

When she looked back, Clikit wondered: was it this light, or did her skin simply keep its yellowish hue from the light they had passed through above?

"I mean something that few signify by the word, though it hides behind all that men seek when they pursue it. I mean a state that is eternal, unchangeable, imperturbable even by death . . ." Her last word did not really end. Its suspiration, rather, became one with the sound of rain hissing through a broken roof in some upper corridor.

Now! thought Clikit. Now! Or I shall never find my way out! But she turned through another arch, and again his resolve fled. She was near him. She was away from him. She was facing him. She faced away. Clikit stumbled through a narrow tunnel low of ceiling and almost lightless. Then there was green somewhere. . . .

A flood of green light . . .

Again she turned. "What would you do with such a treasure? Think of it, all around you, within you, without you, like a touch that at first seemed so painful you thought it would sear the flesh from your bones but that soon, you realized, after years and years of it, was the first you had ever known of an existence without pain."

The green light made her look . . . older, much older. The smile had become a caricature. Where before her lips had parted faintly, now they shriveled from her teeth.

"Imagine"—and her voice made him think of sand ground in old cloth—"a union with a woman so all-knowing she can make your mind sink toward perfect fulfillment, perfect peace. Imagine drifting together down the halls of night, toward the shadowy heart of time, where pure fire will cradle you in its dark arms, where life is a memory of evil at once not even a memory." She turned away, her hair over her gaunt shoulders like black threads over stone. "She will lead you down halls of sorrow, where there is no human hunger, no human hurt, only the endless desolation of a single cry, without source or cessation. She will be your beginning and your end; and you will share an intimacy more perfect than the mind or body can endure. . . ."

Clikit remembered the burden clutched behind him. Was it lighter? He felt lighter. His brain floated in his skull, now and again bumping against the portals of perception at eye or ear. And they were turning. She was turning.

". . . leading toward perfect comprehension in the heart of chaos, a woman so old she need never consider pain or concision or life. . . ."

The word pierced him like a mouse fang.

Clikit pulled his cloak from behind him and swung it up over his shoulder with cramped forearms. But at that instant she turned to face him. Face? No face! In the blue light, black sockets gaped from bald bone. Tattered veils dropped from empty ribs. She reached for him, gently taking an edge of his rags between small bone and bone. Empty?

His waving cloak was empty! The sand had all trickled through some hole in the cloth.

Struggling to the surface of his senses, Clikit whirled, pulled away, and fled along the hall. Laughter skittered after him, glancing from the damp rock about him.

"Come back, my little thief. You will never escape. I have almost wrapped my fingers around your heart. You have come too far . . . too far into the center." Turning a corner, Clikit staggered into a tripod that overturned, clattering. The steady light began to flicker. "You will come back to me." He threw himself against the wall, and because for some reason his legs would not move the way he wanted, he pulled himself along the rocks with his hands. And there was rain or laughter.

And the flickering dimmed.

A tall old woman found him huddled beside her shack door next day at dawn.

Wet and shivering, he sat, clutching his bare toes with thick, grubby fingers, now and again muttering about his sandal strap—it had broken somewhere along a stone corridor. From under a dirty, thinning tangle like corn silk, his gray gaze moved slowly to the tall woman.

First she told him to go away, sharply, several times. Then she bit her lower lip and just looked down at him awhile. Finally she went back into the shack and came out, minutes later, with a red crock bowl of broth. After he drank it, his talk grew more coherent. Once when he stopped suddenly, after a whole dozen sentences that had actually made a sort of sense to her, she ventured:

"The ruins of Kirke's temple are an evil place. There are sto-

ries of lascivious priestesses walled up within the basement cat-
acombs as punishment for their lusts. But that was hundreds of
years ago. Nothing's there now but mice and spiders."

Clikit gazed down into the bowl between his thumbs.

"The old temple has been in ruin for over a century," the
woman went on. "This far out of the city, there's no one to keep
it up. Really, we tell the children to stay away from there. But
every year or so some youngster falls through some unseen hole
or weak spot into some crypt, to break an arm or leg." Then she
asked: "If you really wandered so far in, how did you find your
way out?"

"The sand . . ." Clikit turned the crock, searching among
the bits of barley and kale still on its bottom. "As I was stumbling through those corridors, I saw the trail of sand that had
dribbled through my cloak. I made my way along the sandy
line—sometimes I fell, sometimes I thought I had lost it—until I
staggered into the room where I had first seen the . . ." His pale
eyes lifted. ". . . the jewels!"

For the first time the old woman actually laughed. "Well, it's
too bad you didn't stop and pick up some of that 'worthless
treasure' on your way. But I suppose you were too happy just to
have reached open air."

"But I did!" The little man tugged his ragged cloak around
into his lap, pulling and prodding at the knots in it. "I did gather
some. . . ." One knot came loose. "See!" He pulled loose another.

"See what?" The tall woman bent closer as Clikit poked in
the folds.

In the creases was much fine sand. "But I—" Clikit pulled
the cloth apart over his lap. More sand broke out and crumbled
away as he ran his fingers over it. "I stopped long enough to
put a handful of the smaller stones in. Of course, I could take
nothing large. Nothing large at all. But there were diamonds,
sapphires, and four or five gold lockets set with pearls. One of
them had a great black one, right in"—he looked up again—"the
middle."

"No, it's not a good place, those ruins." Frowning, the woman bent closer. "Not a good place at all. I'd never go there, not by myself on a stormy summer night."

"But I *did* have them," Clikit repeated. "How did they . . . Where did they . . . ?"

The woman started to stand but stopped because of a twinge along her back; she grimaced. "Perhaps your jewels trickled through the same hole by which you lost your sand."

The man suddenly grasped her wrist with short, thick fingers. "Please take me into your house, Lady! You've given me food. If you could just give me a place to sleep for a while as well? I'm wet. And dirty. Let me stay with you long enough to dry. Let me sleep a bit, by your stove. Maybe some more soup? Perhaps you or one of your neighbors has an old cloak. One without so many holes? Please, Lady, let me come inside—"

"No." The woman pulled her hand away smartly, stood slowly. "No. I've given you what I can. It's time for you to be off."

Inside the tall old woman's shack, on a clean cloth over a hardwood table, lay small sharp knives for cutting away inflamed gums, picks for cracking away the deposits that built up on teeth around the roots, and tiny files—some flat, some circular—for cleaning out the rotten spots that sometimes pitted the enamel, for the woman's position in that hamlet was akin to a dentist's, an art at which, given the primitive times, she was very skilled. But her knives and picks and files were valuable, and she had already decided this strange little man was probably a wandering thief fallen on hard times—if not an outright bandit.

A kind woman she was, yes, but not a fool. "You go on now," she said. "I don't want you to come in. Just go."

"If you let me stay with you a bit, I could go back. To the temple. I'd get the jewels. And I'd give you some. Lots of them. I would!"

"I've given you something to eat." She folded her arms. "Now go on, I said. Did you hear me?"

Clikit pushed himself to his feet and started away—not like someone who'd been refused a request, the woman noted, but like someone who'd never made one.

She watched the barefooted little man hobble unsteadily over a stretch of path made mud by rain. As a girl, the old woman had been teased unmercifully by the other children for her height, and she wondered now if anyone had ever teased him for his short-ness. A wretch like that, a bandit? she thought. Him? "You'll be in Myetra in half a day if you stay on the main road," she called. "And keep away from those ruins. They're not a good place at all." She started to call something else. But then, if only from his smile and the smell when she'd bent over his cloak, those teeth, she knew, were beyond even *her* art.

She watched him a minute longer. He did not turn back. In the trees behind her shack a crow cawed three times, then flapped up and off through the branches. She picked up the red bowl, overturned on the wet grass, and stepped across the sand, drying in the sun, to go back inside and wait for whichever of the townsfolk would be the first of the day's clients.

New York
1962

return to çiron

When he was an old man and the Calvicon historian sought him out in his hut outside the fishing village, with the sea below gnawing at the stones, one evening after they'd gone over yet again the organization and exploits of the Myetran army, he began to speak of something unmentioned in their previous conversations.

When I left him there, my prince and leader, dead in the old peasant woman's shack, I had the strangest feeling—as though I . . . were not I at all. Ah, I wish I could find some trace of the *I* I was then. You understand, there are moments when it seems it would solve so many problems today. But that old self has been all but squeezed out of existence, between my total absence of self at the time and my own voice and consciousness exploring the ashy detritus of that time now—I don't know: *can* you put yourself in my place? Not my place today, the place I occupied then. I had seen my executioner revealed as my savior and, only a breath of time on, had watched my mentor—who had been, of course, my *real* executioner—die. Well, as I left him in the stifling, peasant's hovel, to step into the light and air, I thought again that I must return to our camp and make one more try to get an idea of the damages, if only in terms of names.

But the last time I'd been taken from the camp to the execution site, I'd been bound, it had been dark; nor had my mind really been on the route we followed. Thus the village was for me a wholly unknown landscape. At one point I turned from an alley to step through some trees I thought must put me out at the Myetran camp after only thirty or forty paces—and after eighty or a hundred, about convinced I was lost, came out at the edge of a field, covered with charred patches, like ashy lakes, several of them joined to one another. On the far side, I saw a scattering of what had to be, from the carrion birds swirling above them, corpses: at this distance, they were the size of flies. A wagon stood among them. To one side, between some trees, were the burnt ruins of a shack.

Near me, on the grass, where I'd emerged, the first thing I saw was a vine web—like the one that had saved us on the town common. This one was staked out at one edge along the ground. Then it slanted upward toward a branch of gnarled oak. Bales of that vine webbing lay about, higher than my waist. Against another tree, one of their gliders leaned. Two others sat on the ground.

On the branch where the net went, a Winged One perched. Another squatted on the ground, wings sloping out across the green and ashy stubble. As I stood, a third flew down into the web, caught the vines, pulled in those great sails, and turned back to stare at me—then laughed, with the most shrill and astonishing *Screeee!*

I had no idea if they'd attack or let me pass. But the one on the ground suddenly looked up and cried: "Play a game with us, groundling! Play a game!"

The one on the branch mewed distractedly, glancing at the sky: "We are here to play with the hero!"

"But the hero is away, playing a hero's games, with the prisoners and the victorious villagers!" declared the one who'd arrived at the net. "Perhaps you will let us play with you?"

"What do you mean?" I asked. "What . . . sort of game?"

"A game of desire," said the one clinging.

Knowingly, the one perched looked down. "A *sexual* game."

The one squatting said, "Climb on my back! Let me fly with you just a little ways—just a short flight . . . just enough!"

I'd seen my friend take off and land, on the back of Handsman Vortcir. Who, so seeing, could not covet such flight!

Also, I suppose, I was afraid not to. For they were so strong—
they'd just vanquished the whole of a Myetran brigade!

These particular three, you understand—well, I was not even
sure if they were females; though now I assume so. But it was
hard to tell. Certainly they were younger members of their tribe.
And clearly they brought an enthusiasm, if not an avidity, to
their play.

I bent to take the back of the one who squatted.

The wings pulled in, rose, opened, and fell—and I was borne
up, grabbing at the great shoulders.

And what was the game?

Now—now, in the air, I was to transfer to the back of one of
the others! But how in the world—

Just do it!

First, one came close. I threw my arms around the neck of
one flying so near their four wings beat each other's. And I was
pulled away to hang till, at a certain maneuver, we flew upside
down—and I lay with my carrier, belly to belly, looking at that
strange smile, just under mine!

Then again, when I was not really holding, I was rolled loose
and actually fell, my heart blocking my throat with its beats,
as if my head were back on the block, to land on the back of
the third—and I scrambled over to grasp and hold the shoulders
while we sagged down with my added weight and recovered,
while the others, flying just above, mewed caressive reassur-
ances. Now I was urged to leap from the one I rode to one who
flew just under us, and rather than be thrown again, in a perfect
panic I leaped and was caught between those billowing leathers.
They passed me among them, while, between the wings of one
and the wings of another, the village lay hundreds of feet below.
Next time I looked, the stubbled field passing back beneath was
so near—not a full two feet under us, every daisy and grass
blade and burnt twig speeding clearly—I was sure we'd wreck
ourselves on the smallest rise. We lifted again. Somehow I was
tossed again for a last time—and caught in the net, on my back.

They swarmed over me!

One pulled loose my waist cinch, another the fastenings on my jerkin. They mewed into my ears such things as: "We play the game of desire, along the chain of desire, serving the Winged Ones' Queen! We serve the beloved of the Queen, who is the Handsman. We serve the beloved of the Handsman, who is the brave groundling. We serve the beloved of the brave groundling, who is the groundling's black-clad friend. . . . We tangle the chain in our play!" One piece and another, my clothes came away, till all that was under my naked back was the harsh uncured skin—and folded over it, the wondrously soft fur—of the puma.

The three of them at me, there, shook me and pleasured me, bit at me—yes, in several places, my shoulder, my inner thigh, they sipped blood—while I rebounded in the web.

Do you understand? Moments before, I had been by a dying man, with whom I'd constantly felt I was not present to his words—a man who had urged me to exchange promises with him, as if we'd been a pair of lovers, yet to whose urgings, my own perceptions had been so blighted I could not tell if he knew or not I was unable to respond, for he might as well have been addressing the lion skull, already dead, by mine.

But now, with these three lovers upon me, my bodily perceptions were cajoled, caressed, excited to a pitch, an altitude, where language could not follow, so that promises themselves were impossible. As I floated and flowed and soared above words, listening to their mewings and scrittings, I let a sound that was wholly animal, as inhuman as if the beast's skull beside me had for a moment returned to life.

I finally slid down the web. On the burned earth, when at last I could stand, I looked about for my clothes, pulled on my leggings, my boots, my gloves.

The three Winged Ones all perched on the branch, as indifferent to my fumblings below with belt hooks, bootlaces, and button fastenings as lords of the air might be.

I threw the puma skin over my back and, fastening it, stumbled off into the trees—unable to look back, bereft of all my initial desire: to survey the damages among my troops.

I remembered it only when I was again walking between the shacks in some narrow alley. Reaching the end, I saw I was back at the common—with no progress at all in my project.

But perhaps you can understand why this is not an event I often tell. Really, I can't think how it concerns your own researches. It might, if you have any sense of delicacy, be better left unmentioned. As I said, put yourself in my place. . . .

In evening light, the Calvicon historian listened to the little stones the waves raked away, then, returning, flung up the shingle. He sipped from his drink and nodded (for the historian was tired, and as they'd sat in the small yard, his host had refilled both their glasses several times), not certain just what he'd been asked.

Amherst
September 1991

Afterword

I.

Something happens when a writer's readership grows substantially larger than the dozen odd members of a university workshop or even a full auditorium of listeners at a college or a library reading. Approximately every seven or eight years, with each book of fiction and nonfiction I've written (though not every essay collection), I've cycled through the experiences I'm about to discuss.

I will meet a new person, sometimes a young woman who has just published her first book and with whom I'm giving a reading, or an editor who has recently joined a publishing house to whom my own editor is introducing me in an office hallway, or a stranger who has recognized me a moment after I have stepped from the door of Barnes & Noble onto Union Square North. Over fifty years these people have been male, female, black, white, Asian, Native American, Dominican, Inuit, African, southern or northern European, Haitian, Jamaican, Martinican, half a dozen sorts of Latino and Latina; they have been gay; they have been straight; they have been transgendered or cisgendered; they come from New York or San Francisco, Boston or L.A., from Peoria or Salt Lake City, and many places between; they have been Jewish, Baptist, Episcopalian, Catholic, Mormon, Muslim, Buddhist, atheist, disabled, or temporarily abled. Sometimes it's a teacher at a university or a high school where I'm giving a talk, sometimes it's a student—though once, as I was walking down Eighty-second Street, leaning on my cane, a city sanitation worker in a green T-shirt, who, recognizing me from a picture in a recent *Entertainment Weekly* article, leaped from the back of his groaning truck, ran up and gripped my shoulder with an oily orange rubber glove, to tell me what I will tell in its time, and, six months ago, when I was returning to New York from a guest professorship at the University of Chicago, it was the uniformed fellow at the curbside baggage stand outside the United Airlines terminal at O'Hare, who, after I'd gone inside to wait for a wheelchair (arthritis makes getting around airports on my own all but impossible these days), ran in after me, stood in front of me, and declared: "Samuel R. Delany . . . ? The writer guy? I'm right, aren't I? Hey, my absolutely *favorite* book of yours is . . ."

That's what so many of them want to tell me.

This one or that one will name *Through the Valley of the Nest of Spiders*, my most recent novel, or my very first, which you have in this book, or my tenth, or my fifth, or my fifteenth, or my book of science fiction and fantasy stories, *Aye, and Gomorrah*, or my book of naturalistic novellas, *Atlantis, Three Tales*, or one of my contemporary novels, *Dark Reflections*, or *The Mad Man*, or a science-fiction novel like *Nova* or *Trouble on Triton*. It can be a nonfiction work. The book named can be an award winner or a one-time bestseller or something published by an independent publisher that not two thousand people have read. It can be my twentieth, from a press out of Normal, Illinois, and Tallahassee, Florida, specializing in avant-garde fiction. It can be my 1,200-plus-page fantasy series in four volumes, Return to Nevèrÿon, or a ninety-page novella once sold as a stand-alone paperback, such as *Empire Star*.

And it can be—and has been, repeatedly, over fifty years as well as at least once over the last seven or eight—each of the novels here.

It pleases me to think there might be a connection between that experience and the way I write. Do I know there is? No, I can't know. No writer can. (So we decide—or hope—it's because we're quite smart . . . as we take a wrong turn, lose a laptop, drop and step on our reading glasses, or inadvertently call a business acquaintance the name of someone she or he despises, who, the moment we met, came to mind—or something else stupid.) Because such indications of popularity, however poorly they correlate with quality, hinge on reception rather than creation, they suggest—even if it's never a sure thing—a reason to gamble on reprinting.

The forty-five-odd experiences over the more than fifty years from which I've culled these instances might seem a lot, because I've crammed more than half of them into not a page and a half, with a number doing double, even triple, duty—the woman outside of Barnes & Noble, the most recent one to mention *The Jewels of Aptor*, was a Mormon here in the city with her brother (who'd never heard of me); the last young man who liked *The Ballad of Beta-2* was a student and an African Muslim (in a motorized wheelchair). Sometimes three or four such encounters have happened in a year. Some years have gone by, though, with no such encounters at all. Were you waiting for the next one, you'd be more frustrated than not.

Here's something that better suggests how little public attention that is: only three times in fifty years have I seen someone reading a book of mine in public. Once, while I was sitting on an IRT subway car in 1964 or '65, I saw a woman across from me reading the second volume of my Fall of the Towers trilogy. Once, when Marilyn and I were returning from London a week before Christmas in 1974, coming through Kennedy Airport we saw a book rack full of just-released *Dhalgren*s and, minutes later, a sailor in unseasonal whites relaxing at his flight gate reading a copy. (With his knees wide in a tubular chair that they used in airports back then—he must have been flying back to somewhere in the Caribbean or Central or South America—as we walked by with our daughter in a stroller.) Finally, on a Philadelphia bus, three years ago, I saw someone, certainly a student at Temple where I teach, reading a trade paperback of *Atlan-*

tis, Three Tales, a week after the publishers had released a new printing.

Three times in fifty years.

It doesn't seem so many now, does it?

II.

Not just *Aptor* and *Beta-2*, but all three books here had a run of almost two decades in bookstores—and that was in a book environment where the average life of a new volume on the store shelf was under three weeks. That interests editors and marketing folk, trying to anticipate how this book will do. I'm interested in that peripherally, of course—but not centrally. "No man but a blockhead," said Dr. Samuel Johnson, the poet, scholar, and writer who put together the first comprehensive English language dictionary, "ever wrote, except for money." A surprising number of writers since Dr. Johnson who have pursued the life of writing, however, have been blockheads—many of them good writers too. You have to think about too many other things while you're writing that drive such considerations from the mind, so that dwelling on money is distracting, intimidating, and generally counterproductive. Also, the number of people who, if they were not calling me, personally, a blockhead for wanting to write at all, thought I was nuts, strange, or patently out of my mind for doing it (and it was never a munificent living) seemed at the time innumerable—starting with my dad. When I won a prize in high school or a scholarship, he was proud. And when his best friend, our downstairs neighbor, who wrote and published children's books for black kids like myself but made his living editing immense economics textbooks he called "doorstoppers," read some of the work I'd written at sixteen or seventeen and told my father I would probably be in print before I was voting age (back when that was twenty-one and the drinking age was eighteen; since then, they've reversed). Dad even paid the sixty-seven dollars to have my third novel—the one that got me the

Bread Loaf Writers' Conference scholarship I mentioned in my foreword—retyped by a professional typist in Queens.

It never appeared.

Mom had a more liberal attitude. She wanted me to do whatever would make me happy, and from childhood on she encouraged me in all my enthusiasms. Clearly, though, she shared Dad's misgivings. Except for intermittent lapses in which he tolerated my career choices—which were most appreciated and probably the only reason Dad and I had any positive relationship at all—generally my father argued and raged about those enthusiasms. My mother mulled over them and looked glum. They had lived through the Great Depression. Like many parents in the 1950s, they were concerned about security and their children's livelihood. They had seen many disasters themselves. We, who were too young to remember those disasters firsthand, however, felt the manifestations of their fears were the harshest parental oppression. I wish I could say eventually I learned they were right, as they kept telling me I would. ("Just wait. You'll see . . .") In truth, however, they weren't. Some things were much worse. Some things were far better. Many were different. The world had changed—including the speed of its changing.

Novel writers, short-story writers, science-fiction writers, and many writers from the "unmarked" category, which bears the genre mark "literary," have told me they cannot read their past or early work. When they try, many say, they feel something akin to pain.

That's not me, however.

Possibly it has to do with how I write—though I can't be sure.

I'm dyslexic—severely so. Therefore, to put together a manuscript that's readable, much less printable (by my own standards), I must read it and correct it and reread it and correct it again and reread it again; not three or four times, but twenty-five, thirty-five . . . some sections I must read forty-five times or more. (Now you know one reason so many people—not just my parents, but teachers and friends—thought I was nuts for wanting to write at all. Clearly I was so bad at the basics and everyone around me was better.) It's the first five or so readings, however, I find painful. Between them, someone who is not dyslexic has to read it too and mark those places, usually with underlining, where the words are out of order and often incomprehensible or even missing, where I've spelled words so badly you can't tell what they are, or where I've dropped other words and phrases that must be there for the sentences to make sense.

I'm a grammar fanatic. I have been since I was in the sixth grade—probably to compensate for the other things I did and still do so poorly. Mistakes slip through even now; now and again other readers catch them, for which I am always grateful. (You may find some among these pages.) I couldn't—and I still can't—spell some simple words correctly three times in a row. But I was the best in my fifth-, sixth-, and seventh-grade English classes at diagramming sentences on the blackboard (in those days when blackboards were black, not green) or on tests. ("If you can do that, I don't understand why you can never remember how to spell 'orange.' It doesn't make sense," my seventh-grade English teacher would say. It didn't make sense to me, either. But her sincerity, concern, and honesty made me love her at the same time that it made me feel I was profoundly and irrevocably flawed.) Still, it's why today I'm comfortable using both formal grammar and informal grammar at all colloquial levels. Point out the errors you find, and I can usually tell you why they're errors and often the formal names these errors have or once had and how to correct or improve them. But these are what my dyslexia initially prevents me from seeing. (Today we know it's neurological. Back then we didn't.) In the course of my rereadings, however, phrases, words, or sections that to me are painful—for stylistic and content reasons that become one as the hand falls from the keyboard, from the page, and the ear and the eye take over to judge or to approve or, more frequently, to find fault with what I've put down—I excise or clarify so that, over time, the manuscript moves closer and closer to something I can enjoy. That's how I wrote my earliest books, the ones here; that's how I write them today. That's how I build a text I'd like to read: by way of retardations, excisions, expansions, compressions, simplifications, and rewordings, along with numberless additions and plain corrections. Each layer is the trace of a different "self" as much mine as the self who tries to impose the effect of a controlled voice by suppressing one or enhancing another—to form a text I hope will fall within sight of my notion of the way a "good writer" writes, even though I am not one "naturally."

The only way I can get a text to feel (to me) that it is one my true thoughts might inhabit is through layers of revision.* If I try

---

* The larger point: I am as much the person who makes the mistake as I am the one who corrects it. I am as much the person who gets to the place in a sentence or a paragraph where I realize I am ignorant of a date or the name of a city where some historical event occurred as I am the person who, twenty minutes later, returns from the encyclopedia on the lower library shelf or turns from the computer screen after a ten-minute Google hunt to fill it in. Writing above a certain level requires, however, that you gain some understanding of both, not only within your "self" but out in the world. Perhaps this is what has given me a career-long fascination with people who cannot speak or write at all, as well as an equal fascination with poets (which etymologically means "makers" and more recently "makers of things from language"), though the "self" I present the world is neither one nor the other, thanks to the Other that is always there in me, the "I" that "I" am always struggling to overcome. This is the only way I can resolve the *aporia* (the contradiction; and *aporia* was Plato's word after all) as to why Plato, who was such a fine writer in the Greek of his time, in his hypothetical and optative society so famously excluded the poets from his Republic. Plato wanted the poets who were there to be better than they were, that is, to choose the option to be more faithful to the idea of truth—which, when talking about an imagined world, is not quite the same as actually banishing them from the actual. I am not in the least suggesting, as some folks have, that Plato wrote science fictions. But *I* do. That helps me read him—as, doubtless, having written one novel himself (*Marius the Epicurean, His Sensations and Ideas* [1885], a favorite of both Virginia Woolf and James Joyce) and started another (*Gaston de la tour*), helped Walter Pater, seven years later, in his wonderful *Plato and Platonism* (1893), have the insights about the philosopher that he did. (Far closer to our day than to Plato's, Pater noted that, had he been writing in ours, Plato could have been a great novelist.) The ten-volume set of Walter Pater's complete works—which her father had not allowed in their library when he was alive—was among the first books Woolf bought with her inheritance on her father's death. And, a favorite of all the young readers of the Oxford Aesthetic Movement of the

to express anything directly that I believe deeply and intensely without a fair amount of thought beforehand and during a many-layered process afterwards, what comes out is banal, over-wrought, and riddled with errors in which clichés and imprecisions mock anything one might call intention.

Another way of saying the same thing is that the unexamined "I" in an unexamined "world" is boring.

I'm much too much like everyone else—because, presumably, the world has made me so: more venal than I would like to appear or admit, shy, deluded by clichés and commonplaces, eager to be liked, and for accomplishments, intellectual or social, that most of the time I feel I do not possess.

Possibly this is also why, ten or fifteen years after a book of mine has appeared, when I pick it up and again start reading, I find sentences that strike me as pleasant, scenes that seem well-orchestrated, passages that appear to project their ideas with clarity, or an observation on the world that registers as true for its time and that goes some way toward delineating, if not re-creating, my feelings, or other passages whose grammar and logic convince me they are the utterances of a single mind rather than the dozen deeply flawed selves I had to be shattered into by the world to live in it, much less to write about it. (Is it the layers of correction or the illusion of unity that does the pleasing? I can hope. But I can never know. They are the same thing seen from different sides: an effect and what creates it.) If they please, they please to the extent I have forgotten how the disjunctive cataclysm that I am wrote them—though also I know that so much rereading can, as easily as it might produce excellence, fix the mistakes in a text in our mind so deeply that when we come back

previous twenty years (and one of the great forbidden books of its age), *Marius* is among the first books directly alluded to (by Buck Mulligan, on page eight of the Vintage International edition of *Ulysses*), through its subtitle. Usually such allusions are literary love—though they can also, sometimes, be literary hate. The unconscious, Freud suggested, uses no negatives. Strong emotion is strong emotion. To me, however, this one has the feel of an enthusiasm.

to it years on, we skim errors in expression and thought without seeing them because unconsciously they are so familiar.

Neither the writer's pleasure *nor* pain justifies returning a work to print, however; nor is either a reason for letting a text languish. (Sometimes a work is about something no longer of current or compelling interest, but that's another tale.) All language is habit, as I remind my writing students regularly, speaking or writing. You learn to write badly, to overwrite, or to write dull, banal stories much the way you learn to write well—as well as a given epoch sees it. (Lacking a National Academy, of the sort France, Italy, and Spain have had for centuries, America finds the surface criteria changing radically every twenty or thirty years.*) I do believe, however, that the amount and quality of mentation that go into the fictions I find interesting are different from the amount and quality that go into the ones I find thin. Only hard-won habits can fix the difference within us—if we're lucky. And no one can be sure it has—ever. As well, I believe the writer must look at the minute places where her or his relationship to the world is different from most, for me personally to find that relationship of interest. (Often I've wished I had broader tastes.) To find what deeply engages us, within a field of our apparent differences we must interrogate, our similarities for the sake of potential and possibilities, either good or bad. That can mean, for the same ends, the writer is trying to dramatize a feeling of difference within that field of similarities, so that often the writer has a sense of having undertaken a more difficult analytical dance than anticipated. The writer sig-

---

* Modernist experimental French writers in the twentieth century, such as Louis-Ferdinand Céline and Jean Genet, used largely the not quite four-thousand word vocabulary—with bits of added slang—that the seventeenth-century writers Jean Racine and Pierre Corneille used, three hundred years before. This is not the case with, say, American modernists such as Hemingway and Faulkner on the one hand and our seventeenth-century English writers John Donne and John Milton on the other. The difference between the two traditions, French and English, is an effect of the French National Academy in the one and the lack of the same in England, America, and Australia.

nals both differences and similarities by additions to the text, by organization of the textual elements, or by absences in the text, vis-à-vis the average productions of that day or era—and, as much as they are frowned on today, by direct statements of emotions, most effective when they are used indirectly. How to distinguish between which texts are better and which texts are worse is, ultimately and finally, anyone's guess, and the shifts in criteria, decade after decade, century after century, even place to place in what we always assume is a more unified culture than it ever is or could possibly be, and the general attitudes toward following the various paths of least resistance that mark out the cliché, the cluttered, or the thin, *don't* make it easier. Those shifts in criteria, however, all indicate traces of a struggle with those problems, though not necessarily in a manner that either you or I might feel was successful. That's why it's worth it for us to accustom ourselves to the way things were written a generation or two, a century or two, a millennium or two before us, in India or Italy, in China or Czechoslovakia, in Timbuktu or Teheran, Portugal or Japan, Leningrad or Moscow, Brazil, New Orleans, Mexico City, Argentina, or Chicago—which is to say, the ways of reading that the texts were written for, in various places at various times—for the pleasure of the game, if only because of what, here and there, we can learn about how they made the game pleasurable and use it for our own profit, if it still works today. It's the concert of all these that justify republication, a decision from which, for the reasons outlined here (mostly in dependent qualifying clauses, or even parentheses) the author, if still living, is always excluded. Only someone else who has managed to educate him- or herself to read the texts of the past, even from only forty or fifty years ago, and is sensitive to the problems and concerns of the present, can make the call—and finally for pretty personal reasons—as to whether or not a text merits republishing. We all hope—readers and writers both—we will be lucky enough to have such editors.

III.

When *The Jewels of Aptor* came back from copyediting, Don Wollheim asked me to cut 720 lines—about 10 percent of the book.

Standing at the far side of his desk, I must have looked surprised.

"Huh?" I asked. "Yeah, sure. But why? Was there some particular place you thought it was too . . . loose?"

"Oh, no," Don said. "But it has to fit into a hundred forty-six pages. It casts off at seven hundred twenty lines too long." He would do it for me, if I wanted—

"Oh, *no*!" I said. "No. . . . That's all right. I'll do it!" I reached across the desk for the manuscript in its red rubber band.

Completed when I was nineteen, contracted for not quite a month after my twentieth birthday (since the copyright laws changed in 1976, the phrase has become "in contract"), and cut down by fifteen pages a few weeks later, the first edition of *The Jewels of Aptor* was published that winter—where I pick up the story:

In 1966, an editor a few years older than I, Terry Carr, joined the staff at Ace Books, the U.S. publisher of all the books I had written up till then except *Nova*. I have written before, as have many before me, that the history of post–World War I science fiction is the history of its editors: Hugo Gernsback, F. Olin Tremaine, Raymond Palmer, J. Francis McComas and Anthony Boucher, Howard Browne, Ian and Betty Ballantine, John W. Campbell, H. L. Gold, on through Avram Davidson, Cele Goldsmith, Don Wollheim, Harlan Ellison, Frederik Pohl, Damon Knight, Michael Moorcock, Larry Ashmead, David Hartwell, Judy Lynn and Lester Del Ray, Betsey Wollheim, Beth Meacham, Patrick Nielsen-Hayden, Betsy Mitchell, L. Timmel Duchamp, Steve Berman, Kelly Link, and Warren Lapine. (In this incomplete list, many were writers as well—Campbell, Davidson, Pohl, Knight, Moorcock, Ellison, Duchamp, and Link are *significant* writers, whose fiction remains influential for any real understanding of our genre's development—though their editorial force and direction is central to their careers.) Carr is among those editors. He edited the first novels of William Gibson, Joanna Russ, and Kim Stanley Robinson, as well as Ursula K. Le Guin's *The Left Hand of Darkness* and a dozen other memorable titles for his Ace Science Fiction Specials series.

In 1967 Carr did for me one of the most generous things an editor can do. "Chip, I was just rereading your first novel, *The Jewels of Aptor*. I enjoyed it. Don told me we cut it for length, though. I was thinking of doing a new edition. Do you have an uncut copy? I'd like to take a look."

"Actually," I said, "I do . . ."

In the top drawer of a file cabinet in the kitchen of the fourth-floor apartment where we had lived for a couple of years on Seventh Street, I'd left an uncut carbon copy. The apartment had been more or less inherited by a woman I'd known in Athens during my first, six-month European jaunt. Later I'd brought it up to my mother's Morningside Heights (aka Harlem Heights) apartment, where it stayed in an orange crate full of manuscripts and journals in a back closet—and left all the other papers, manuscripts, contracts, and correspondence in the Seventh Street kitchen filing cabinet.

I came up to get it.

As Mom and I walked down the hall to what had been my bedroom when I'd lived there, and was now my grandmother's room, my mother asked: "When are you going to take the whole thing?" Over the years I'd transferred the most important papers and my growing stack of journal notebooks to my mother's bedroom closet.

"Soon," I told her. "I'll take it soon."

"Well, please do."

And I carried the uncut *Jewels of Aptor* back on the subway down to where I now lived, farther along Sixth Street. At home I read it through: I crossed out the odd word or phrase and moved a few more subjects up against their verbs. (Full disclosure: and I have done similar reading once more, here, for the same end.) My personal sense is that this was no sort of rewrite. There was no revising of incident, characters, setting, or structure. Pages went by without an emendation. I wouldn't call it "editing," so much as "copyediting." As I remember, no more than six pages were corrected so heavily (more than five corrections on a sheet) that I put them through the typewriter once more. (This was before there were copy centers or home computers or word processors; even Xerox machines were rare.) The rest were done by hand on that "onionskin" copy, typed with carbon paper. I finished the final work two days later and took it in to Terry Carr that afternoon.

Some time on, I was able to oblige Mom: a letter came from the Curator of Special Collections at Boston University's Mugar Memorial Library, Dr. Howard Gotlieb. He asked if I would let his library house my papers. "Thank you," I told him when I phoned back. "I'd be happy to." Dr. Gotlieb and his staff sent a station wagon from Boston to get them from the places around Harlem and Alphabet City where they'd been stored (such as my mother's bedroom closet).

Mom and I stood back while two graduate students in slacks and sports jackets carried the very full crate—yes, made of wooden slats in which oranges had been shipped from Florida, with a dark blue, white, and orange paper label pasted onto each end—to the apartment door and out into the echoing co-op hallway with its florescent lights, to take it down to the car parked on Amsterdam Avenue.

While getting ready for sending things up to Boston, I'd learned that the conscientious super's wife had had the wooden file cabinet, with its four drawers still stuffed with papers, manuscripts, and letters, moved to the building's cellar only days after I'd removed *The Jewels of Aptor* carbon. A few months later, the building had been demolished. Everything in the basement had been buried beneath brick, glass, shattered beams, and plaster, to be steam-shoveled into dumpsters and hauled to a landfill, while a new building went up in its place on the north side of Seventh Street. The paper trail of my life till then—contracts, correspondence, completed manuscripts of both novels and stories, along with countless false starts on countless stories and other projects—today is ripped, scattered, soaked, and soiled beneath the mud of the Jersey flats.

Certainly I felt *Aptor* read better with the text intact. But I had been prepared for Terry to say he thought the cut version more commercial and that he'd stick with it. When he called me into the office, and I asked him what his verdict was, however, he told me, "It certainly makes more sense, now. And it doesn't lurch quite the way the cut version did a few times. Yes, we're going to do it."

That is the version Ace republished in 1968, which has generally been in print since. Regardless of what it says on the back of whatever paper or hardcover edition, it has not been "expanded," except to restore the missing pages and paragraphs, nor has it been "completely revised" or "updated," other than to return to the initial version, along with one more read-through to make sure it was as close as I could get it to what I'd first wanted. Those mass-market claims on the paperback are Ace's concession to what, at the time, Wollheim felt fans would like to hear, however misleading. But even the actual changes I inserted are no more than any conscientious copy editor might have suggested, the majority of which—the vast majority—were spelling and typing corrections that had slipped through because of my dyslexia.

It's what appears here.

Over the years, Dr. Gotlieb and I exchanged notes between the Mugar and New York, between the Mugar and San Francisco, between the Mugar and New York again. Regularly Boston University's Special Collections Archive sent me birthday cards, Christmas cards, update announcements on its other holdings from other writers—and every year or two I would FedEx cartons of my journals and manuscripts and hand-corrected galleys to Boston. Since Elizabethan days publishers have called these "foul papers" or "foul matter" and were happy to be shut of them. In any publishers' storage spaces it accumulates faster than clothes-hangers breed in clothes closets.

I didn't meet Dr. Gotlieb or see the collection in person, however, until a 1982 visit. Elderly, genial, and eccentric, he was a white-haired library science scholar, at home in his office and among the extraordinary things he had gathered about him over the years for Special Collections (today the Howard Gotlieb Memorial Archive) at Boston University. While I was there, I broke down and asked him why, fourteen years before, he had decided to collect me. He said, "I used to pick your books up from the newsstands, read them, and I liked them—as well, I had a dream of making the collection here a portrait of the twentieth century for future scholars: you were part of the second half of the twentieth century. So why not?" That's how my papers joined the papers of Samuel Beckett, L. Sprague de Camp, Martin Luther King, Jr., Dan Rather, Philip Roth (Roth's mailbox from one country house or another sat on a side shelf in Dr. Gotlieb's office), Isaac Asimov, and Bette Davis—whom Dr. Gotlieb also liked.

Talk about luck.

IV.

During 1999 and 2000, I taught at the Poetics Program at SUNY Buffalo. Henry Morrison had been my agent since I was twenty-three, and by then was also a film producer. At a New York lunch he told me: "As far as I can see, Chip, this is the worst time to be a writer—a regularly selling writer with a market—in the history of the United States. And I mean back to Charles Brockden Brown. I don't see how you guys do it anymore."

To which the answer is, most of us don't. That's why, today, so many of us teach. I would like to be able to say to the young, "You think you have it rough? Well, when *I* was your age . . ." But I can't. Today's young folks, especially in the arts, have a much harder time than those of us—who now have some sort of track record and, possibly, tenure—did fifty years ago when we started. I wish it were otherwise. It would be healthier for the entire country.

V.

From January 1969 through '70 and again in 1972 and part of '73, I lived in San Francisco. By late '70 I was staying on Oak Street, in something of a commune. The building was a medium-sized Victorian, painted gray on the outside. To the right of the building was an alley less than three feet wide, half-way down which sat a baby stroller missing a wheel. You had to climb over it or really squeeze by to get to the back. From the broad kitchen windows, out over a green board fence, you could see behind us the yard and rear balconies of the San Francisco Buddhist Center. A counterculture artist who'd owned the place ten years earlier had painted the inside walls and ceilings along the halls and in the major bedrooms with pastoral murals.

But not in mine.

Mine was just over the size of the small downstairs bathroom and at the very front of the house. Probably at one time it had been used for storage or as a maid's quarters.

In that year's foggy West Coast winter, the Modern Language Association was holding its sprawling annual academic meeting in the Bay Area. One Professor Thomas Clareson had invited me to address the Continuing Symposium on Science Fiction that year—the second oldest of the two continuing symposia in the organization. (Once I'd asked Professor Clareson what the oldest continuing symposium in the MLA was. He'd said, "Oh, it's something like *Shifts in the Umlaut through Two Hundred Fifty Years of Upper High German* . . . or some such." I assumed he was joking.) The night before I had been out drinking with a handful of science-fiction scholars, including Clareson, who was to moderate the next day's panel on which I was to give my talk.

It was my second MLA appearance in three years, though at the time I was neither a teacher nor a member. (You could do that then, but you haven't been able to for the last decade or so.) Apparently he had been keeping track of what I was drinking—I hadn't—and he had driven me home afterwards. He'd figured, correctly, that I might need some . . . support getting to my event by one o'clock the next day.

At ten I had opened an eye, squinted at the sun coming through the curtain, and thought, "Oh, Christ . . . *no*, I'm going to blow this off. Can't do, can't do, can't do . . ." and I'd rolled over and gone back to sleep. Stuck in my notebook, on the desk wedged beside the head of my army-style cot, was the typescript of my talk.*

In about an hour, though, the doorbell rasped. Loud knocks, now. The bell rasped again. Someone else in the house answered and, soon, called through my closed door: "Chip! Someone's here to see you . . . !"

I had no idea who it might be. But in that haze where you are too wiped not to respond, I sat up, pulled on some jeans, stepped to my room door and opened it.

Looking fresh in a gray suit, a pale blue tie, and a paler blue

---

* "Critical Methods/Speculative Fiction": initially I had written it in the Autumn of '69 and delivered it to a group of enthusiastic science-fiction fans who met in a house in the beautiful Berkeley Hills. That meeting was hosted by a member of the family who made Tanqueray Gin—surely a resonance with what I will shortly write. At that year's MLA, I read a version cut by half. The complete text was published in *Quark/1* (Paperback Library, NYC, 1970), edited by Marilyn Hacker and myself. Today you can find it in *The Jewel-Hinged Jaw*, a revised edition of which is available from Wesleyan University Press (Middletown, 2010). For the record, that '69 talk is among the last times I used the term "speculative fiction" before returning to the phrase, adequate for any critical use I have found myself in need of since: "science fiction." As far as I can see, the basic meaning of "speculative fiction" is: "whatever science fiction I, the speaker, happen to approve of at ten o'clock Wednesday morning or at whatever moment I use the term," which makes it a very slippery shifter and too vague to sustain a useful critical life in any analytical discussion. I have not used it, except more or less ironically, and then rarely, for forty-five years, though even today I run across people claiming it's my "preferred term." It's not.

shirt, Professor Clareson—far more experienced in such matters than I—said, "Morning, Chip. Into the shower with you. Come on, get your clothes on. We'll pour some coffee into you. You'll feel a *whole* lot better!"

I said, "*Unnnnnnn* . . ." and then, "Tom, hey . . . thanks. But I don't think I can do this, today—"

"Yes, you can," he said from behind silver-rimmed granny glasses. "It's eleven. You don't have to talk till one. Hot shower, then cold, then warm again . . ." White hair receded from the front of his skull. (I thought of Death . . .) "Come on," he repeated.

I took a breath, looked around, and grasped a fistful of clothing. Tom walked with me along the hall's gray runner while, on the walls, oversized shepherdesses loped among blue and pink sheep and, with halos neon bright around their naked bodies, male angels did not look down at me. Clouds and eagles—and one angel who was also a skeleton, refugee from some *Dia de Los Muertos* celebration—drifted over the ceiling. Tom pulled a wicker-backed chair in front of some large shepherd's knee and settled on it, slowly, glancing down at both sides. I think he was wondering if it would hold. "I'll wait. . . ." It did. "If you really feel sick, give a yell. I'll help, if you need me." He smiled up at me. "You'll be okay."

"Okay . . . ?" I repeated, queasy, between questioning, confirmation, and the entire conceptual impossibility. I went inside— white tile to the waist, a few pieces cracked or missing, dark blue walls for the rest—and pulled the door closed. A cat box sat under the sink. Kitty litter scattered the linoleum, and a blue plastic toy lay on the shower's zinc floor.

There five weeks, it belonged to the kid who belonged to the stroller in the alley. But the people whose kid it was weren't there that month.

I dropped my jeans, tried to kick them off—one pants leg wouldn't come away from my foot till I sat on the loose commode ring (it had no cover), leaned forward and pulled my cuff down over my heel. Standing again, I stepped into the stall, moved the plastic curtain forward along its rod (it had torn free from two of the odd-shaped metal wires), and—stepping toward the back—reached forward and turned the knobs that looked more as if they were for two outside garden hoses than for an inside shower stall. Between my forearms, water fell.

When it reached reasonable warmth, I moved forward and, for a minute or so, turned one way and another, under the heated flush. A soap bar lay in a metal dish edged with rust and bolted to the blue. I slid the bar free—soft at one side—and soaped chest, underarms, groin, and butt, while warm water beat away the foam. Then, a knob in each hand, with a quick twist I made the water cold—

"Oh, *Christ* . . . !" shouted a committed atheist. (In foxholes and in cold showers . . .)

Outside, Tom chuckled.

Taking a breath, I held it and made myself stand there for a count of three, four, five—then sharply turned up the hot and turned down the cold. It took three long seconds for the warm water to creep up the pipe and spew from the showerhead.

Again I began to breathe.

Out in the bathroom once more, I turned for my towel, among four others filling the rack. My glance crossed the mirror, and, remembering I had a beard, I was glad again I didn't have to shave. But I wondered—for the first time in years—if I'd look foolish speaking in public with bushy black whiskers.

When I was again sitting on the commode and my legs were dry, I pulled on my dress slacks. Outside the closed door, Professor Clareson went on, "You know, Chip, I was thinking this morning. My favorite book of yours has always been *The Ballad of Beta-2*. I must have read it four, even five times since it came out—but I keep returning to it. The reason, it occurs to me, is because it's about learning."

Inside, I thought: I *hope* I've learned not to do *this* again. . . .

I stood once more, stepped over and got the blue toy from the stall, turned, and put it on the bathroom shelf where I noticed my aerosol deodorant. I'd thought I'd left it in my room and would have to go back for it—

"You've told me about your dyslexia. I wonder if that has anything to do with it. Though there's nothing about that in the book. Still, it's about learning—yes. But I mean a particular *kind* of learning, one I have so much trouble as a teacher getting my students to do: getting them to understand texts that don't make a lot of sense unless they also acquire some historical knowledge that clarifies what was really going on, why it was important, even to the point of what actual phrases mean—in Charles Reade, in Spenser, in Milton, and in Melville. Your book deals with a problem very close to me. And it deals with it interestingly—at least each time I reread it, I find it so. And each time in a new way."

While I finished drying, I told myself I'd take the toy to the kitchen and put it in the parents' mail cubby next time I went in, then started for the door to get my deodorant from my room—with my hand on the knob, I remembered it was on the bathroom shelf, turned back, got it.

And knocked the toy—it was a blue airplane—onto the floor. I sighed, left it, took the aerosol can and sprayed under one arm and the other. (The antiaerosol campaign to help preserve the ozone layer and retard the greenhouse effect was a few years off.) It was cool—cold even, but not as cold as the cold water. I put the deodorant can back on the shelf. At least that stayed there.

After pulling my T-shirt down over my head, I shrugged into the dress shirt I'd carried in, buttoned it—incorrectly, I realized—unbuttoned it, breathed three times, sat again and rebuttoned it. Looking around, I realized I had left my socks in my room.

Standing, opening the door, jeans hanging from one fist, I stepped out barefoot into the hall.

Still in his wicker-back, Tom smiled.

I said, "Well, thank you—for telling me." It was at least three minutes since he had stopped talking, and I felt foolish.

The full version is, *Oh, why thank you so much for taking the time to tell me. That's very nice of you.* Before (and since) I've used it in such situations. That morning, however, I hadn't made it all the way through, and had waited too long—and was wondering if the hungover version had only been confusing. Or if I'd sounded *very* foolish. In that state, though, every other thing you do is infected with foolishness, and you spend a lot of time wondering how and why *nothing* you say or do feels right.

Feeling foolish, I walked to my room, glancing at smiling Tom—who got up and followed. Inside, putting my jeans over a chair back and sitting on the iron stead's mattress edge, I got my socks, shoes, and sport jacket on, reached over, and picked up my notebook and my talk.

We went out and down the steps to the door. I felt foolish because I went out first then realized I hadn't let the older Tom step from the house before me. I mistook the car he indicated and felt foolish as I walked on to the one, in a moment, I realized was his. Tom drove us to breakfast, and I sat—foolishly—on the front seat beside him, fixated on the fact that my attempt to thank him for his compliment had been so inept.

I was quiet, but my mind kept running on, obsessively, unstoppably, uncomfortably: nobody had suggested I say it, you understand. Rather, after several encounters with people who had complimented me without warning—with the result that I'd felt awkward and clearly they'd felt awkward too—I'd sat down, a few years back, and decided, since probably I'd be in the situation from time to time, that I'd better put together a response that let people know I hadn't been annoyed and that acknowledged their good intentions. "Why, thank you so much for taking the time . . ." is what I'd come up with; if I responded with that, both of us would feel a little better and neither of us would leave the encounter feeling . . . well, like a fool. I sat beside Tom, mumbling it over and over without moving my lips and wondered if I should say it out loud again, properly this time—but I was sure, if I did, it would sound . . . foolish. (The next time it happened, months later, it worked perfectly well.) At that point, however, the most foolish thing since I'd waked seemed Tom's preference for *Beta-2*. (Was I becoming a writer who couldn't bear his previous work . . . ?) I hadn't felt this way yesterday.

Could all this be chemical . . . ?

Then we were walking into a San Francisco breakfast place, with loud construction for the new BART line outside, and aluminum doors and mirrored walls inside, on the way to the MLA convention hotel, to join Tom's wife, Alice. She had dark hair and sat smiling in one of the booths.

I ate some toast and bacon (I wasn't up to eggs) and drank some black coffee—and was surprised I could.

We got to the MLA hotel twenty minutes before my talk.

Among the anecdotes above, whether someone is talking about a book in detail or just running up and saying, "Hey, I really liked . . ." and running off again, I have *not* been recounting all this to speak about either popularity or quality.

Because I'm not talking about popularity, that's why, except in one case—to come—I give only one example per person. (That's also why I'm not giving numbers, of people or of books.) Of course it happens with some books more than with others. Those mentioned more often are ones that have been better advertised—though not always—by whatever method—or have simply been more available; and we all know what a meaningless indicator advertising or hearsay is for quality.

Well, then, what *am* I talking about?

A lesson comes with someone running up to you, taking the time and putting out the energy to cross the natural barrier that exists between strangers (and though I'd known Clareson a couple of years, I'd only met him in person four times), telling you she or he liked something you wrote. The lesson is not entirely about politeness—or kindness, either. The lesson occurs, yes, when someone tells you why he or she likes a particular work, and—through the fog of your own current concerns (we always have them even if we're not hungover)—it even makes a kind of sense. It also occurs when you encounter a full-fledged academic paper that seems preternaturally astute (or completely wrongheaded).

It occurred fourteen years later too on an afternoon when I

was at a theater in New York City for the matinee of a musical. I was stouter. My beard was bushier—and largely gray.

And I had a ten-year-old daughter, whom I'd brought with me. (With a music teacher at Columbia and a Chase bank vice president, I'd helped found a gay father's group, which met monthly and now had more than forty members—though, at this point, it has little to do with the tale, in parentheses it will play it part. Marilyn and I had separated for good nine years earlier, though we'd arranged for joint custody.) Just that week a well-known rock musician had taken over the lead in the show, and at that matinee the rest of his band had come to sit in the front orchestra seats to see their lead singer's first performance that afternoon. During intermission, a third of the audience had moved to the balcony rail to gaze down at them, and, once we stood up, from our own seats in the balcony's rear, both my daughter and I could see that downstairs, another third in the theater's orchestra had moved to the front to crowd around the young men, who were being friendly and behaving as if they were old hands at this; but there was no leaving the theater for them to get a breath of air outside, as my daughter and I were getting ready to do.

My daughter attended a school where, if there were not a lot of celebrities, there were a few celebrities' children. As she looked down, she commented: "They're not even letting them leave. That doesn't seem very nice."

"Probably," I said, "they're tourists, and they haven't seen a lot of famous people before."

My supremely cool New York ten-year-old turned away, and we went to the orange stairway and down to street level, to stretch and get a breath before the bell rang, the lights under the marquee blinked (a custom discontinued in Broadway theaters how many years ago?), and we returned to our balcony seats for the second act.

Occasionally I've written about how rarely our lives actually conform to the structure of stories that writers have been using for hundreds, if not thousands, of years. But, sometimes, they do. A reason I remember that day is because, through coincidence and propinquity, things approached one.

After the show, while we were standing out on Eighth Avenue at the bus stop, the bus pulled up, the door folded back, and two teenage boys got off as I was getting ready to guide my ten-year-old on, to take her home. (My sister had given us the tickets; back at the apartment, my partner—and Iva's co-dad since she was three—had said he'd make spaghetti, Iva's favorite, that evening.)

One of the young men frowned at me:

"You're Samuel Delany, aren't you? You wrote that book I really liked. What was it, again . . . ?" The young man's friend had read it too and supplied the title.

"Yes, I am. Why, thank you for taking the time to tell me. That's very nice of you." I smiled.

They smiled—and walked off.

My daughter and I got on. We went to the rear of the bus and sat as it started. Then my daughter pushed her ponytail back from her shoulder. "Dad, are you famous?"

I smiled. "Fortunately, no. The band at the theater today is famous. But things like people recognizing me in the street who've read something of mine only happens once, maybe twice a year—*occasionally* two or three times in a week, the way it did right after I was on the *Charlie Rose Show*, or when that newspaper article came out in the *Times*. Now, though, it's right where I can enjoy it. Too much more, however, and it would get *really* annoying."

"Oh," she said.

And that's the single time in my life—and my daughter's—where I was able to make such a point, with comparative examples coming within an hour.

Forty-four years after Tom Clareson helped me through a hangover, and thirty years after I took my daughter to the theater matinee, the point is still true.

The lesson, then, is this: there exists a *possibility* of something happening when someone reads a book that is important enough for the person to respond to the writer who wrote it in that manner. And it doesn't happen because of direct communication from person to person any more than sunrise occurred this morning because the sun lifted itself from behind the horizon into the dawn sky.

A possibility. Not a certainty. (There are too many other reasons for running up to speak when you see someone you recognize in public.) The lesson is about possibility and potentiality, not about a probability for communication to have gotten through. It is no more—but no less—than that.

In no way is it any confirmation about communication, even when in practical terms you'd be willing to bet on it. That's because we know that communication *doesn't* actually "get through," any more than the sun actually "rises" in the morning or the moon actually "sets" in the nighttime (or daytime): that's simply how it feels, not how it works. Sunrise, moon-down, and language-as-direct-communication—*all* are effects of something more complex: a spinning planet among other spinning planets in their elliptical orbits about a stellar bole of violently fusioning hydrogen millions of miles away that is releasing immense energy and light—which is drenched in information about what created it as well as everything it deflects from in passing. That light spews its information through the multiverse at 186,200 miles per second to tell of the workings of other planets, other stars and their planets, the workings of other galaxies of stars or the workings of other minds a few years, decades, centuries, a few thousand miles behind the pages of a book, behind a Nook or a Kindle or an iPad screen, till it passes too close to a gravitational force too large for it to escape and falls into it—while its stellar source millions of light-years away goes on creating the heavier elements—and singing about them in its light waves. As we career through the great spaces along our own galaxy's swirling edge, our own sun takes its planets and their satellites, its belt of asteroids, its Oort Cloud, and its comets along with it (which is why so much of the turning moves more or less in the same direction), while our galaxy itself moves along the gravitational currents flung out by billions of galaxies in a veritable net throughout the multiverse,* much of whose material is dark matter that light (I use the term loosely for all electromagnetic waves) doesn't seem to tell us about directly, but only by its absences.

Then why *don't* meanings move from me to you by means of the words that I say and that you hear—or that you read? Why do I say that's just an effect too like the rising and setting of the sun, moon, and stars?

They don't, for the same reason we need a lens—the one in your eye, the one in your camera, the water drop on a spider web—to retrieve the information from the light—something to focus the data and repress the noise, which may or may not be another sort of data that to us isn't as useful or (such as heat when it grows too great) is harmful to organic systems that are

---

* With some eight thousand-plus others, our own turning galaxy arcs toward the Great Attractor in our supercluster of the galactic net, a cluster containing the Virgo galaxy cluster at the end of one peninsula of galaxies off the parent cluster, while ours is at the end of another, next to it. Till recently, we thought we were part of Virgo. But we're not. Both our galaxy—the Milky Way—and the Virgo cluster are on short chains of galaxies that feed into the major supercluster (more like an unraveled ball of string than a swarm of bees), which is about a hundred times larger than astronomers thought even a few decades ago. Only this year have they started calling that larger structure Laniakea—Hawaiian for "Immeasurable Heaven." Now it's been measured and is currently among the biggest structures the descendants of our million-times great-grandmother (or great-aunt) "Lucy" and her many-times-grandson (or great-nephew), "Red Clay Man" (the meaning of the Hebrew name "Adam"; which tells not only what they thought he looked like but what they thought he was made of) have individuated, mapped, and named—though Lucy and Adam both probably saw fragments of it when they looked up at the naked night, as we can today. It's about a hundred million light-years across. But, about that size, many more link to it, to make the gravity-enchained galactic net. Google Laniakea or Perseus-Pisces or the Great Attractor or the Shapley Supercluster; or the Axis of Evil or the Bright Spot—all galaxy markers in our expanding map of the multiverse. All are impressive.

For all it doesn't tell us about dark matter and dark energy, light carries an awesome amount of information throughout the multiverse, whether from the edges of the visible or from the leaf by my shoe sole at a puddle's edge, information that links through evolution to why and how so many creatures—including most humans—have eyes.

largely liquid and ultimately destructive to all systems composed of solids.*

Think about the electrical signals in the brain that are your thoughts and the electrical signals that make your tongue move and your larynx stretch or contract to utter sounds when you push air out over them, and the physical vibrations that go through the air and strike your own and others' eardrums and the electrical signals that the minuscule hammer bone attached to the eardrum's back that shakes as the eardrum vibrates, the tiny anvil bone and tiny stirrup bone transferring those shakings that, in turn shake the little hairs within the spiral of the cochlea, which transform those vibrations into the electromagnetic pulses that travel to the brain where other electrical impulses are created as sound (already a vast oversimplification) and are associated with the meanings of words, phrases, and much larger patterns of language *already lodged in the mind/brain* of the hearer, the reader—patterns that must already be there, or else we would say that the hearer does not know the language yet or understand it. (In the late 1920s and early '30s, a Russian psychologist, Lev Vygotsky [1896–1934], observed that children tend to learn first to talk and only then to internalize their own speech as thinking, though it's a continuous developmental process.) And because everyone learns his or her language under different circumstances, those patterns simply *cannot* be identical for any two of us. That they can adjust thoughts as far toward similarity as they do in many different brains is a result of the amazing intricacy of the learning materials and the stabilizing discursive structures that they are capable of forming.

Rarely do we get a new meaning from the rearrangement of old ones, helped on by language and the part of language (the signified) we call experience. Still, perceived experience is one of three ways we can "experience" linguistic signifieds; another is through memory and imagination—sexual and secular, practical

---

* They burn up, melt, or both, and finally, with enough heat, defuse as plasma, and under increased radiation even their atoms may eventually shatter.

and preposterous—and generally conscious thought; a third is through dreaming. (And all three relate. And all three are different. And none of this should be taken to contravene Derrida's notion that the world is what language cuts it up into.) But the meanings understood by an other are *always* her or his own meanings, learned however she or he learned them, and never the speaker's or the writer's, though the effect is usually that they are the same—because we are mostly unaware of the stabilizing discursive circuits that we know so very little about, though we also learn those and learn them differently in different cultures.*

---

* Those discursive structures stabilize our metaphysical assumptions that, as Derrida remarked, we are never outside of and are most deeply enmeshed in precisely when we are critiquing someone else's.

There is a story, possibly apocryphal, about the philosopher Ludwig Wittgenstein, who was wandering one day over the lawns of Cambridge and looking at the sky, when one of his students saw him. "Professor Wittgenstein, are you all right? What are you doing . . . ?"

The philosopher looked down and saw the student. (The novelist in me at this point always assumes Wittgenstein blinked.) "I'm trying to understand," said the perplexed philosopher, "why, when the earth is turning and the sun is—relatively—in one place in the sky, it feels and looks as if the earth is still and the sun is moving around it."

"Well . . ." said the student, perplexed now by the philosopher's perplexity, "it's because, I suppose, it just feels and looks that way when the earth is moving and the sun is standing still."

"But if that's the case," replied the philosopher, "what would it look and feel like if the earth were actually still and the sun was actually moving." And on that question, Wittgenstein turned, looked up again, and wandered off across the grass, leaving a very perplexed young man, now looking after him, now squinting toward the sun. Your words and mine evoke—rather than carry—approximate meaning, already there at their destination, meanings that the order of words alone will rearrange and that must be interpreted further by probabilistic approximation to mean anything at all. It is only the effect that feels as if they carry actual meanings from speaker or writer to hearer or reader. But if that's the case, what *would* be the effect if they felt as if they only evoked meanings already there by probabilistic approximation . . . ?

Life is made up of lots of "experience puns," with an "obvious explanation" and several "not so obvious ones." Enlarging on this property was the basis for much of the work of the surrealist artists, such as Pavel Tchelichew, Max Ernst, and M. C. Escher.

Our metaphysics arises from assuming perceived resonances are causal even though we have no evidence for it, but without doing so we would be left

Unconscious thought, Freud was convinced by a lot of research and study, is a mode of thinking we *don't* experience directly as such. I am pretty sure he was right. (Whatever that level of brain activity is, I suspect it controls the discursive levels of language.) But without unconscious thought, we literally would not know what other people are talking about, even though we recognize the words whose meanings we have already internalized.

And, remember, every dolphin and whale and octopus and dog has some version of this problem and neurological solution; every pig, porpoise, penguin, or porcupine; every bird or four-legged animal or six-legged cricket that "receives" communication with its ears or an earlike structure, or emits communication by rubbing its legs together or whistling songs or clicking or crooning underwater or meowing or purring or barking or growling—that is to say every creature who has to negotiate sexual reproduction and/or attraction; every creature who, at a food source or a watering place, needs to communicate "move over" to a fellow with a push or a shove.* Without something akin to

with solipsism—itself a limit-case metaphysical assumption, but an assumption nevertheless. In short, we can either assume that stuff is there—or that it isn't. (Maybe it's something else, energy, idea, or pure God . . .) We have no logical proof for any of them. What we have is effects that seem to make us comfortable or uncomfortable, but comfort and discomfort, remember, are also effects. (We can work directly with the brain to change them, both temporarily or permanently.) We seem to be most comfortable assuming the very complex world we live in is there, and that all the complex things that have developed in it over the last five billion years to deal with are, in fact, the case—and many of us feel even more comfortable when we can untangle contradictions in what appears obvious by means of other patterns we have been able to see in other places, with the aid of other techniques. (It's called science.) Explore it, play, have fun, and try to learn and understand, even adjust—but is it really worth fighting with it to make yourself miserable about the way other folks want to explore, play, and learn? And most of us seem to feel better when we can help people who are suffering—because we all suffer.

* Because the situations are so different—situations which always entail a worldscape with conditions unique to it—that individuals, pairs, smaller or larger communities of living creatures, find ourselves moving through or settling down in, it is not particularly efficient to wire in one set of responses to all

discourse, they (and we) wouldn't be able to tell if the other was attacking or wooing or warning, or if they should hold it till the morning walk or until they reach a public john or do it in the litter box, or if they want their offspring to suckle them or their owners to stroke them—whether it's time to play or to eat or to get off the couch. (The great mid-twentieth-century actor couple Alfred Lunt and Lynn Fontane were famous for owning a pair of dogs named "Get-Off-the-Couch," and "You-Too.") In humans, discourse learning and management are probably among the main tasks of the unconscious mind. But that's speculation.

In short, it's not just humans who communicate indirectly. It's all dogs, cats, bats, birds, and buffalos, as well as every creature that makes and hears sounds and sees movements that are meaningful; every creature that feels a touch or a lick or a bite from another.

With the sound-making/sound-gathering system we commu-

---

situations. But it has been efficient since before the advent of language to wire in the ability to learn to adjust to different conditions, both by establishing habits and habit-systems and through more thoughtful responses; both always involve actions and inactions. To the extent these are always patterns, they are what rhetoric cuts the world up into and discourses stabilize, but have had very little to do—at least up until recently (say, since the development of writing)—with our understanding how the "process" works. Today, in the context of our hugely expanded world population, even over the last five hundred years—as the plurality of our cultures increasingly becomes the condition within which we must negotiate—our survival would appear to hinge more and more on understanding the process. Pollution is rampant. The climate has changed and not for the better. Because, as part of our cultures, we have already made such changes, along with our population expansion, in our so-varied worldscapes—the atmosphere, the ocean, the mined hills and fishable rivers, the arable lands and the slashed-back rain forests—it is imperative we do something about it or as a species we will suffer far worse consequences than we have already started to. Types of bees, certain species of starfish, as well as tigers and wolves—and dozens of fish, birds, and butterflies—have become endangered species over the last three decades. Our own human population numbers are out of hand and the inequities among us controlled by stupidity or mistaken for reason are only going to do us and the planet in. We need to bring the population down, slowly, over generations, and with consent, though genocides, direct and indirect—both of which seed our own destruction—become more and more prevalent.

nicate within our species. With it we communicate between species. With it we "receive communication" from plants—think of
all the information different sounds, such as wind in the leaves,
can bring us under different conditions (i.e., evokes in us)—as
well as from the entire inanimate world: falling rocks, breaking
waves, thunder, and trees cracking and crashing to the forest
floor. But in all cases, the meanings of those sounds and their
attendant contexts must be built up *in the mind of the hearer* (or
wired in by evolution: some of us animals are *wired* to wire ourselves that way upon the encounter with certain "experiences"
or "linguistic signifieds," such as learning to walk upright or
learning to speak) through experiences for any subsequent interpretation to take place, whether curiosity or fear, recognition,
prediction, or negotiation ("I don't want to get wet. Let's go
inside. Listen to that . . ." "I *am* listening. Hey, we can make
it to Margaret's before it really comes down . . .") is the function. But mammals in general and primates in particular—as
well as whales, dolphins, and octopods—seem to have a knack
for learning.* Because, until recently, there has been no pressing need to understand the complex mechanics behind some of
evolution's effects, that's why many of us don't—though we are
capable of learning and, with the help of writing, remembering.
There is also an educational, stabilizing superstructure, however,
where intervention can reasonably occur, and where it is possible to stabilize necessary discourses with the help of beneficent
technologies—if you allow cultures to learn in their own way.
But this must be both an active and a passive process. This is not
cultural relativism (which always moves toward an initially pas-

* The evolutionary journey from blindness to the ability to visually recognize individuals and places is as amazing as the journey from deafness and
 muteness to spoken language, if not more so. (And neither journey has been
 completed. Consider the importance of the overlap in the past five thousand
 years.) But it couldn't have happened if we—and I include all of humankind's
 forerunners—hadn't first developed our ability to recognize groups of us and
 individuals among them by smell, and all of which was innately entailed in the
 sexual imagination and—if people will let it be—still is.

sive approach that ignores learning and eventually tends toward a dominant destructive approach to behavior, which is sometimes confused *with* learning), but is rather cultural respect (which acknowledges that learning/teaching is always an intervention in the elements that comprise culture, during which both sides must learn if there is to be beneficent change). There is a difference between dialogue-and-respect and imposition-and-domination. And if many more of us don't start to understand those process-effects and their imperfections as well as their successes, soon, directly or indirectly, we'll kill each other and ourselves off. It's that simple.*) The fact that so many creatures—from mice (who squeak) to mastodons (who trumpeted), bats to beavers, giraffes (who mostly listen but sometimes mew) to gerbils (who chitter), pigeons (who coo) to primates (who grunt, growl, or talk)—share an auditory form of data emission and reception (i.e., hearing and making more or less informative noises; though we all do different things with them) attests to its efficacy for multiple tasks at every level of development as well as to our genetic connectedness over the last 250 million years since the early Triassic and before, and the incredibly intricate road to language that a purely synchronic linguistics system is inadequate to untangle without a great deal more extension into semiotics, animal and human, and their evolutionary history, much of which is lost.

---

* The indirect nature of communication, which we so easily mistake for direct exchange (because it is all we know), especially at the indistinct and misunderstood level of discourse, is the seat from which cultural misunderstandings rise up to rage and shake our fists against an uncomprehending Other. The understandings required are best gained by exposure and participation in the conditions of life (now covered—though clumsily—by the notion of social construction), rather than through observations and explanations of them. Lacking that, the best textual aid is description of the conditions in the form the anthropologist Clifford Geertz called "thick description," where the scribe endeavors to avoid imposing her or his own notions of what's important and what's not. But even this hurls us into the realm of chance. Experience is still all important. But language must organize experience before experience can reorganize language. If that was not the case, there would be nothing or little to reorganize.

Given that we have separate brains, that we can "communicate" as well as we can is quite amazing—but don't let your amazement make you forget that "communication" begins as a metaphor for an effect (a door that opens directly from one room to another, a hall that leads from one place in a building to another) but is thus neither a complete nor an accurate description of many things that occur with sound-making and sound-gathering. The fact that so many different creatures have eyes, ears, and kinesthetic reception systems speaks of the efficacy of these effects as well as the genetic relationships among us since before they and their precursors—from gills, extraneous jaw bones, and light sensitive spots on algae and the forerunners of nerves themselves—evolved over millions of generations. That is an index of their usefulness in this landscape. Bear that in mind, and you may start to perceive how complex the process is and why language is *only* the effect that something has passed from person to person, creature to creature, from landscape to creature, whether from speech or in writing or by touch or through any sound—or perceptible signs.*

---

* Even communication of affection and the acknowledgment of the existence of others through touches and nuzzlings and lickings and caresses work the same way. Smell and taste are only slightly more direct, because they start out by depending on the shape of molecules that actually originate with the other, instead of wave functions that are not as material but more process, such as sound or light. But only slightly more so. And once within the thinking-experiencing-interpreting-feeling part of any creature (the brain), all are wave functions again. Smell is still our most intense memory prod. We fight it more and more; we use, it less and less. But before you die, watch it save your—and maybe someone else's—life at least three times, i.e., it gives the group a survival edge, which is only one piece of evidence for its usefulness and efficiency. To have evolved, it has to have others. Brain structures have built up to take care of "meanings" at the level of the word, of the phrase, of the sentence, of the topic, and any kind of physical pressure in general for every other stage of interpretation. Primates—not to mention mammals in toto—learn them mostly by exposure and some evolutionary pre-wiring. But learning must precede the "reception" of communication of what has been learned, and in all individuals the associational patterns that comprise learning occur at slightly different times and at different positions in the world and thus the learning process itself is different for each one of us, particularly today among

It was Ralph Waldo Emerson who said, "We must treat other people as if they exist, because perhaps they do"—though we've gotten a lot more biological and neurological evidence *that* they do.* Because of this, the force behind that "perhaps"

us humans; which is to say, communication by sound is primarily a vibratory stimulation of something already there, not a material (or ideal) passage of something that is not.

This both *is* and *is why* information cannot pass directly between living creatures of any biological complexity. Information is the indirect evocation/creation of congruence, of pattern.

This is what discourse is and controls.

From one side, language can only be explained communally. From another, it can only be experienced individually. That's because "community" and "individual" are abstractions that have been extremely efficient for negotiating lots of problems since writing came along. (Before that, we have no way to know for sure.) But as our population has grown so much bigger in (arbitrarily) the last two hundred fifty years, it's begun to look more and more efficient to expand "community" from something tribal to something far more nuanced and ecologically inclusive. Some people see this as a return to tribalism. But it's just as much a turn to science. As for "individual," I can even entertain an argument that holds that "logos/discourse" was initially a metaphor put forward by philosophers such as Heraclitus and the Mesopotamian rabbis (which means "teachers") to help stabilize the notion that language is never "our own," but was always from another, at a time when there was not the technological or sociological support for a model that was, nevertheless, in its overall form, accessible to anyone who had ever learned to speak a language other than the one she or he grew up with, and/or watched a child learn its "own." Most of a century later, Plato called all this prelearning "remembrance" and speculated it came through reincarnation. I don't believe that was a step in the right direction, other than to nudge thinkers to pay attention to history. But little or nothing that creatures who have evolved do or think has only one use. That's another thing evolution assures. That's what we mean when we say an adaptation is efficient.

* The German philosopher Arthur Schopenhauer first made a large portion of the reading public for philosophy aware of the mediated (that is, indirect) structure of sensory perception for humans. But the fact is, this is true for all creatures who have senses as well as for plants that seemed to be slowly developing something akin to them. Remember that the next time you take a walk in the woods. Yes, 95 percent of our genes are identical with chimpanzees. But 50 percent of them are identical with oak trees. We share genes with lizards, chickens, pond scum, mushrooms, and spiders, not to mention gnats, lichens, elephants, viruses, bacteria, nematodes, and the rest of life's teeming species. That's why we eat each other in so many directions; and it's why a number of species, such as poisonous snakes and poisonous plants, have developed

has strengthened to a strong "probably," though in theory we haven't gotten much further. The similarities and differences from which—neurologically speaking—we learn to interpret the world, unto birth and death, comfort and discomfort, safety and danger, pleasure and pain, and the existence of other people and other creatures and other minds and—whatever ours is—other sexualities and orientations and the worldscapes we share, are all still effects, even as they form our only access to the life, the world, the multiverse they create for us. But they would appear to be extremely useful effects for keeping us alive and functioning in our nanosection of a nanosection of that multiverse—that is, if what many of us take to be failures of tolerance among the general deployments and our own employments of these effects of difference don't lead to our destruction.

VI.

Now that we've had a romp through space and time, and a general ecological agape, which—since Poe obliged an audience of sixty with a talk taken from his then unpublished

---

defenses to keep from being eaten. The fact that we share as many genes with everything that lives is one, but by no means the only, bit of evidence for our direct connections. And that creatures with ears and eyes and tactile feelings look, sound, and move as if they are alive in the world and care about being so—that is, they exist as subjects—is another; but, again, by no means the only or determining one. We live in a world constructed of a vast number of suggestions—and a relatively few explanations (relatively few because we only have the ones, however, we've been able so far to figure out, in which there are bound to be inaccuracies and incompletenesses). Many of the explanations contravene the suggestions. The French psychiatrist Jacques Lacan called these two very human orders the Imaginary and the Symbolic. Different cultures have different Imaginaries and different Symbolics. What science says as a larger philosophy, at least to me, is that this multiplicity is a negotiable condition of the world, accessible to language and its potential behaviors, not an ontological bedrock of the universe: an effect, an illusion if you like that can be explained. I would only add: however you want to talk about it, it damned well better be. If not, we've had it.

Eureka, A Prose Poem*—we still expect certain sorts of imaginative writers to indulge in from time to time, I can tell the following without, I hope, its taking on more critical weight than it can bear: an anecdote that pleases me and makes me smile. For—largely—that's what it is. (The indirect gesturing toward metaphysics is done with for the nonce. And, no, we can't say anything about it directly, which is probably why it takes so long to suggest anything about it at all; and, no, we are still never outside it . . .)

All three books of my Fall of the Towers trilogy sold.

Every once in a while, even today, someone writes about them: "Hey, these are interesting—certainly better than I ever thought they would be. . . ."

I don't make too much of it.

Still, the trilogy was the favorite of a young man who wrote subtle and involving avant-garde fiction, published by a very respectable press, and also of a sharp young woman who wrote crafted and exciting science fiction—and, in his green T-shirt and his orange rubber glove, my neighborhood New York sanitation worker.

Before he let go of my shoulder, though, he held me long enough to say that *They Fly at Çiron*—which had just come out

---

* At the New York Library Society on February 3, 1848, Poe had hoped for hundreds to support his new magazine, *The Stylus*. It was the same month in the same year in which France would erupt in a revolution that, for a few brief months, would result in universal male suffrage and the hope for even more reforms, and which, in the weeks following it, America would celebrate that victory almost as joyfully as Paris, with fireworks from Washington, D.C., to Pittsfield, Massachusetts, and where, at his Pittsfield home, The Arrowhead, Melville was rushing through *Mardi* and *Redburn* so he could get started on *Moby-Dick*. Initially he'd planned to have a happy ending, say some critics, but all too shortly, within the year, the advances of the Revolution of 1848 had been rescinded—and *Moby-Dick* (1851) was rewritten with the tragic conclusion we know today, possibly on some level a response to the great historical disappointment, suggests the critic C. L. R James (in his brilliant reading of the novel *Mariners, Renegades, and Castaways, Herman Melville and the World We Live In* [1952; reprint 1978]), written while James himself was "detained"—like Cervantes, like Thomas Paine, like Thoreau, like Gramsci—in James's case on Ellis Island, in the first years of the 1950s.

in paperback—was his *second* favorite work of mine: a possibility for a similarity, or even for a partial congruence having arisen from his encounter with the text in his mind and from the very different encounter with it in mine, but no certainty, no identity.

I smiled. "Why, thank you for taking the time to tell me— about both. That's very nice of you."

Glancing at the glove, he dropped his hand back to his side. "Oh, sure. Any time, I guess. You're welcome. I'm glad it's okay . . ." He told me about the magazine in which, two weeks before, he'd seen my picture and read its few paragraphs about me. He was a black American man like myself, which meant we'd shared many experiences and much cultural history. He was a black American man like myself, which meant his world and his upbringing were unique, as were mine. (For all our human species' similarities, if we look carefully enough, uniqueness— fingerprints, retinal patterns, the synaptic links in our three billion brain cells, genetic variations in both essential and nonessential genetic material that reflect the different specificity each of us inhabits and our ancestors inhabited [i.e., it didn't kill us in that particular landscape before we could pass it on], even if we live in houses next to one another, or in the same house in the same family—is our most widely shared trait.*) Did that have anything to do with his stopping me? Possibly. In the twenty-five seconds we spoke, the next thing he let me know was how much he liked Octavia Butler's work. "*Kindred* . . . ? Those stories in *Blood Child*?" he asked. "*Patternmaster* . . . ?"

I nodded, smiling.

"Did you ever meet her?"

---

* That sharing is one of discourse's functions, though it has not caught up to the expansion of population, cultures, and cultural encounters that has so increased in our last few thousand years. The dissemination of the unique— through an incredibly complex set of filters that the illusion of intelligence, not to mention intelligence itself, are what we and the world are—is among evolution's most powerful tools as well as its fuel, as long as those filters can receive and utilize energy.

"She was a student of mine, many years ago," I told him.

"Oh, wow," he declared. "That's amazing! She was?"

"That's right. She was discovered by a white Jewish writer, Harlan Ellison, who was running a special program in Los Angeles, and encouraged her to come to the place where I and a number of other SF writers were teaching."

"I didn't know that."

"Well—" I laughed—"now you do."

For a moment he frowned. "Hey, I like his work too." Then his frown relaxed into a smile.

"So do I." I didn't mention how many other SF writers I'd taught over the years—or had Harlan or any of the other writers and editors who had taught at Clarion, including Butler herself several times.

The article had mentioned that I was black—and gay. It hadn't mentioned that my wife and I, though divorced, had raised a daughter. (Or that, for several important years, not only my partner but my mother, my ex-wife and her partner, and forty other gay men and their children had been a part of that raising.) I was wondering if he had a family—when he added, "Great meeting you. Hey, I gotta get back to work."

I called, "Thanks again. So long . . . !" while he loped off past the blue plastic recycling tubs that had already been emptied, to follow the once-white Isuzu refuse collection truck up the street, on which, above and outside the hopper, someone had wired a big, stuffed, grubby bear.

If you enjoyed *Çiron* too I am happy. My apologies, if you didn't. But maybe the extension of this anecdote—here—will suggest a further explanation for the sanitation worker's reaction, not so different from why Professor Clareson enjoyed *Beta-2*.

VII.

Initially, at the conclusion of this afterword, I'd planned to revert to our A, B, Cs, and to discuss how what started, after all, as a random collection of signs for sounds, developed into such a powerful ordering tool, beginning with the fact that, at our opening, we *didn't* alphabetize the titles of the books, but only the first letter of the final proper noun in each.

Older alphabets, such as Hebrew and Greek, begin, in effect, "A, B, G: *aleph, beth, gamil . . . alpha, beta, gamma . . .*"; which suggest a great deal about the history of written language, because so many of those alphabets from that relatively small arc of the world share so many sequences with one another, which means contact between the cultures: the Arabic *abjad* has several orders, two of which begin a, b, d, (*abjad, hawwaz, ḥuṭṭī*) and two of which begin a, b, t. (We would have neither algebra—which is a Arabic word—nor the use of the Hindu zero, nor the names of so many of our stars, without the Arabic language and its cultural flowering through the centuries, in poetry, science, medicine, mathematics, and astronomy.) Other writing systems, which developed in different places—China and India, Korea and Malaysia, Central and South America— are as rich and as creative as any of the "classic six" (up through much of the nineteenth century, these included Latin, Greek, Hebrew, and Arabic, along with Sanskrit and Aramaic), but work differently, sometimes at very fundamental levels. My first idea was to go on with what an alphabetic ordering could accomplish and what it couldn't.* As I began drafting it, how- ever, I got caught up in still another meditation on "social" evolution, an idea I distrust as much as I believe in what we call Darwinian evolution, a distrust for which the huge collapse of the time frame in "social" evolution is only one bit of the evi- dence against it—that is to say, reduces it to a misleading and highly abusable metaphor instead of an efficient explanation of another effect, another illusion, which often contravenes what biological evolution itself so overwhelmingly suggests. But that

* Readers of my Return to Nevèrÿon series may recognize this as relating to the "Naming, Listing, and Counting Theory" that occasionally crystallizes in one or another of its appendices.

seemed a bit off topic for where I wanted this consideration to go.

I decided, therefore, to go back instead to some advice I'd encountered by the time, in Amherst, I settled down to do the work—the rewriting—on *They Fly at Çiron*. (I'd dedicated *Çiron* to my current life-partner, Dennis, and, after twenty-five years together, I include him in the dedication to this omnibus as well.) The advice was helpful—to me; very helpful. But, like any writerly advice, it didn't *replace* the work. If I'd only applied it to the textural surface rather than to the fundamental narrative logic, it would have resulted in more confusion (and perhaps it did), whether I was writing fiction or nonfiction. It had to be a guide for where—and the way—to do the work, which, throughout, habit demanded I do as nonhabitually as I could. It also suggests why, today, this version of *Çiron* is three times as long as the text I salvaged from the old manuscript I'd carried with me from New York to Amherst, and why it has six characters who weren't in the first version at all.

The 1925 Nobel Prize–winning Irish (though he lived much of his life in England) playwright and critic George Bernard Shaw was a great favorite of an astonishing American writer, Joanna Russ, whom I was privileged to have as a friend from the middle sixties until her death in 2011. (Though we met only six or seven times, our letters back and forth starting in 1967 fill cartons.) She was an enthusiast both of Shaw's plays and of his criticism, musical and dramatic. From adolescence on I'd enjoyed Shaw's theater, but Russ was the first to remind me of his other pieces,* some of which I had been lucky enough to have read before on my own, so that I could reread them in the twin illuminations of her knowledge and enthusiasm.

After she started writing, Russ enrolled as a student at the Yale

---

* George Bernard Shaw's "The Quintessence of Ibsenism" (1891), "The Perfect Wagnerite" (1898), *The Intelligent Woman's Guide to Socialism and Capitalism* (1928), and *The Black Girl in Search of God* (1932) are all still entertaining as well as informative, as is reading the plays themselves and their extraordinary prefaces.

School of Drama. Among the things Shaw had written, in a letter to a younger friend, which Russ once passed on to me: when actors are told that they are taking too much time to say their lines, and because the play is too long they should speed up or even cut the lines, often the better advice is to slow things down even more. Frequently, what makes parts of it seem muddy, slow, or unnecessary is that the development is too compressed for the audience to follow. Expand it and make the articulations of that development sharper and clearer to the listeners. Then the play will give the effect of running *more* quickly and smoothly and what before were "slow" sections will now no longer drag.

That can apply not only to reading texts but to writing the texts themselves. (Not to mention prefaces, afterwords, and footnotes—or simply reading.)

In a world where cutting is seen as so much easier and the audience is far too overvalued—and simultaneously underestimated (the audience is, before all else, ourselves)—this is important advice. One of the things that make it important is how rarely you will hear it or anything like it these days—which is why I've ended with it. It's one way—but only one—to guide the work I must always return to.

A good question with which to begin that kind of revision is: if I set aside, at least momentarily, what I hoped I was writing about when I first put all this down, what is this text in front of me actually about that interests *me*? How can I make that clearer, more comprehensible, and more dramatic to myself? Can I dramatize or clarify it without betraying it?

(And suppose I can't . . . ?)

In revising even this sketchy guide through what is finally a maze of mirrors, several times that's been my question here.

If, like me, you are someone who reads the foreword and afterword before you tackle the texts between—and often I do, then go on to chuckle over how little they relate to what falls before or after, the world, the text—now, however abruptly, I will stop to let you go on to read the text, the world that contains them and of which for better or for worse, however briefly, they are a part. Who knows if there might or might not be something between these covers that, later, you'll want to read again. Again, I cannot know. But I can hope. We can even think about how my or your hope inspires you, if we will also talk about why it guarantees nothing, either to the young or to the old, either to me or to you. But that's one of the things books are for. That's why they have margins—which, in a sense, is where forewords and afterwords (and footnotes) are written.

And when you encounter the flaws in the texts here (and you will), you can decide whether or not Shaw's advice applies, or if they need more—or simply different—work.

August 2014
New York

DHALGREN

In *Dhalgren*, perhaps one of the most profound and best-selling science fiction novels of all time, Samuel R. Delany has produced a novel "to stand with the best American fiction of the 1970s" (Jonathan Lethem). Bellona is a city at the dead center of the United States. Something has happened there. . . . The population has fled. Madmen and criminals wander the streets. Strange portents appear in the cloud-covered sky. And into this disaster zone comes a young man—poet, lover, and adventurer—known only as the Kid. Tackling questions of race, gender, and sexuality, *Dhalgren* is a literary marvel and groundbreaking work of American magical realism.

Science Fiction

NOVA

Given that the suns of Draco stretch almost sixteen light years from end to end, it stands to reason that the cost of transportation is the most important factor of the thirty-second century. And since Illyrion is the element most needed for space travel, Lorq von Ray is plenty willing to fly through the core of a recently imploded sun to obtain it. The potential for profit is so great that Lorq has little difficulty cobbling together a crew that includes a gypsy musician and a moon-obsessed scholar interested in the ancient art of writing a novel. What the crew doesn't know, though, is that Lorq's quest is fueled by a private revenge so consuming that he'll stop at nothing to achieve it. In the grandest manner of speculative fiction, *Nova* is a wise and witty classic that casts a new light on some of humanity's oldest truths and enduring myths.

Science Fiction

AYE, AND GOMORRAH
And Other Stories

A father must come to terms with his son's death in the war. An architecture student commits a crime of passion. A white southern airport loader tries to do a favor for a black northern child. The ordinary stuff of ordinary fiction—but with a difference! These tales take place twenty-five, fifty, a hundred-fifty years from now, when men and women have been given gills to labor under the sea. Huge repair stations patrol the cables carrying power to the ends of the earth. Telepathic and precocious children so passionately yearn to visit distant galaxies that they'll kill to go. Brilliantly crafted, beautifully written, these are Samuel Delany's award-winning stories, like no others before or since.

Science Fiction

BABEL-17/EMPIRE STAR

Babel-17, winner of the Nebula Award for best novel of the year, is a fascinating tale of a famous poet bent on deciphering a secret language that is the key to the enemy's deadly force, a task that requires she travel with a splendidly improbable crew to the site of the next attack. For the first time, *Babel-17* is published as the author intended with the short novel *Empire Star*, the tale of Comet Jo, a simple-minded teen thrust into a complex galaxy when he's entrusted to carry a vital message to a distant world. Spellbinding and smart, both novels are testimony to Delany's vast and singular talent.

Science Fiction

ALSO AVAILABLE
The Fall of the Towers

VINTAGE BOOKS
Available wherever books are sold.
www.vintagebooks.com